and she was

By Alison Gaylin

AND SHE WAS
HEARTLESS
TRASHED
HIDE YOUR EYES
YOU KILL ME

ALISON GAYLIN

and she was

A NOVEL OF SUSPENSE

HARPER

An Imprint of HarperCollinsPublishers

This is a work of fiction. Names, characters, places, and incidents are products of the author's imagination or are used fictitiously and are not to be construed as real. Any resemblance to actual events, locales, organizations, or persons, living or dead, is entirely coincidental.

HARPER

An Imprint of HarperCollins*Publishers*
10 East 53rd Street
New York, New York 10022-5299

Copyright © 2012 by Alison Gaylin
Untitled excerpt copyright © 2013 by Alison Gaylin
ISBN 978-1-61793-873-3

Printed in the United States of America

*For my beloved dad Bob Sloane
and favorite aunt Myrna Lebov,
alive forever in my heart—and memory.*

Acknowledgments

Many thanks to my wonderful agent Deborah Schneider, as well as everyone at HarperCollins—especially the great Lyssa Keusch and Wendy Lee.

For their law enforcement/investigation expertise—and patience with stupid questions—Lee Lofland, Gisele Fraseur, City Island expert Marcelle Harrison, Joel Ludlow, Carol Gray, and Sergeant Josh Moulin, Commander of the Southern Oregon High Tech Crimes Task Force.

For their support, writing advice, and all-around awesomeness throughout all phases of this book—Abigail Thomas, Karen E. Olson, Jeff Shelby, Lori Armstrong, Megan Abbott, Jason Starr, Paul Leone, Claudette Covey, Bar Scott, Rik Fairlie, Ann Patty, Austin Metz, James Conrad, artist/manga expert Hali Barthel . . . plus anyone not mentioned who should be. You know who you are. This is the one and only time I wish I had Brenna's memory.

Finally, thanks goes out to my dear mom Beverly Sloane, first-rate in-laws Sheldon and Marilyn Gaylin—and, most of all, Marissa and Mike. I love you guys.

and she was

Prologue

September 20, 2009

Carol Wentz's life now had a "before" and an "after." She'd never thought of it that way, but the passage of time brings perspective, and ten years later, Carol could see it—the moment before she made the Neff girl disappear and the moment after.

A clear, clean mark.

For forty-one years, Carol's life had moved from day to day with no real marks at all—no children, a marriage that Carol had eased into gradually, with a whimper of a city hall wedding that took place on a Wednesday at lunch hour and for health insurance reasons, after she and Nelson had been living together for almost a decade. She supposed she could track time before and after Nelson—her single years versus her conjoined ones—but the truth was, before Nelson wasn't really all that different from after Nelson, each day stretching out and ending with Carol still the same old Carol—the Carol she'd been in grade school, reedy and knock-kneed and mostly alone.

But then Labor Day, 1998, happened and everything was different. Carol was different. Well, she supposed she'd always been different—she'd just never known it before. How would she have described herself in book club? *An unlikable character. Too weak and petty. I don't believe her motivations. The girl was only six, after all . . .*

Carol didn't like to think about it, the actual day. But there was a long list of things that Carol didn't like to do—cooking the turkey for her church's Thanksgiving dinner, feeding her neighbors' cats when they were out of town, jump-starting their cars or picking their kids up from school on a moment's notice—yet she did all those things anyway, and without complaint. Carol didn't used to be like that. Before she made the Neff girl go, she did her part for others by staying out of their way. But now she was a helper, a *go-to gal*, and everyone on her block—even Nelson—treated her as if this was nothing new. As if it had always been a defining quality of Carol's, when really, it was just part of her penance. A symptom of "after."

The day, the important part of it, began with the Neff girl approaching Carol at Theresa and Mark Koppelson's barbecue. Carol had been alone. The last she'd seen of Nelson, he'd been speaking to the girl's mother, Lydia, who was helping out with the cooking. "You look incredible," he had said. *Incredible*, as if Nelson hadn't seen Lydia Neff in years and she was wearing something other than jeans and an apron smeared with barbecue sauce.

Nelson and Lydia hadn't noticed Carol, and so she'd been able to step away and feign searching for the bathroom—another one of those times when she felt so intensely awkward, as if someone were holding a giant magnifying glass to her body, amplifying every gesture.

Carol had just pushed through the kitchen door when she felt the tap on her leg. She stopped, and saw Lydia Neff's daughter, whose first name was Iris, staring up at her with those eyes, her mother's black eyes, slick and hard and knowing. Carol's jaw tensed up. Her scalp tingled. She thought of that word again. *Incredible.*

"What do you want, Iris?"

"Juice box." No "please," but she hadn't been rude. Actually, Iris Neff had said it meekly, if Carol's memory was to be trusted. And so Carol had made for the red ice chest that Theresa Koppelson had placed next to her refrigerator. The sign on it read "Drinks for Kids." Carol had lifted the lid and gazed at the bright little boxes littering the cans of Sprite and orange soda like confetti, all of them bearing pictures of happy cartoon fruit. Carol wasn't familiar with the brand. Of course, she wasn't a mother and hardly ever entertained memories of her own childhood, and so they all confused her, these youth-aimed products. Why did children need to drink juice from a box, anyway? What was the appeal of fruit with eyes?

She'd yanked one of the boxes out of the cooler—green, with a smiling, bucktoothed apple on the label.

"Here you go," she said, handing it to Iris.

The girl scrunched up her face.

"What?"

"This is apple juice," Iris said. "I like orange pineapple."

Carol's gaze moved from the girl's face to the kitchen door, the small window affording a view of Lydia Neff's shiny black hair and Nelson, leaning in close, as if to hear her better . . .

"Orange pineapple," Iris said again.

"I am not your *mother*. Get it *yourself*."

The black eyes widened.

Carol's skin heated up. Her voice hung in the air like an odor. *What am I?* she thought. *What am I turning into?* For some reason, this made her angry with Iris, which, in turn, shamed her even more. "I'm . . . I . . . I'll get the juice for you."

But by the time she'd gone back to the ice chest and pulled out a new juice box—this one with a winking pineapple in a baseball cap and a doll-faced female orange—the little girl was gone.

Carol stared at the stack of papers in her hand—another symptom of "after," but this one more painful. Carol had built a fire—her first fire of the fall—and she nearly threw the papers in, just for the pleasure of watching them turn to black dust. It would have been better than reading them, that was for sure. *Why read nothing?* In five years of searching for a girl that wouldn't be found, she'd at least learned that much.

Carol could never burn the papers, though. And so she moved over to the closet near the bookshelves—Carol's crafts closet as far as Nelson was concerned—and slid out the small black trunk she kept under her knitting bags. She threw back the lid and removed the layer of bright fabric scraps and squares sewn together in festive clusters, removed the spools of thread and pattern books and the wooden needle box (all remnants of the quilting phase she'd gone through fifteen years ago). Then she removed the piece of cardboard she'd cut to fit the floor of the box, and she placed the stack of papers in. Placed it in without reading it, on top of all the other stacks of papers she never should have read, repositioned the cardboard, and arranged everything back on top until it was her quilting supply box again.

These new papers had come from Mr. Klavel—a ferrety man with a basement office in neighboring Mount Temple, a large, sweaty forehead, and breath so foul that it almost felt intentional. Mr. Klavel, latest in a line of cheap private investigators Carol had hired in secret, and possibly the least sensitive man she'd ever met. *The fruits of my search*, he had said as he handed Carol the ten-year-old police files, the photocopy of Iris's first grade class picture, and phone call transcripts and addresses of known pedophiles living within a twenty-mile radius of Carol's home in Tarry Ridge, New York, a decade ago. *All rotten.* Carol still couldn't believe he'd said that.

After Carol had gotten the trunk closed and everything back in the closet, she stood staring at the door, Mr. Klavel's words still ringing in her head.

"You built a fire?" Nelson said.

Carol jumped. Nelson had a way of sneaking up on her. It wasn't that he had any interest in spying on his wife. Nelson rarely even asked her questions and when he did, it seemed more out of habit than curiosity. It was simply the way Nelson moved—as if he didn't want to disturb the carpet by putting too much weight on it.

Still, Carol felt a tinge of worry. *How long have you been here?* she almost asked. *What did you see?* But then she noticed the look on his face, that same bland acceptance he always wore, and it was enough to calm her. "I was cold." Carol put her back to her husband and moved toward the window . . .

After the Koppelsons' barbecue, the setting sun had poured through this window, made it glow gold like something out of a dream. If she concentrated, Carol could still feel that otherworldly glow from eleven years ago, she could still hear Nelson's feet hurrying up the stairs, fleeing for his computer as he always did, as he still did to this day whenever they came home, rushing to stare into a screen.

Incredible. Had Nelson called Carol that, ever, once? In the before or in the after?

If Carol closed her eyes tight, she could travel back to the before—to the very last moments of it, with the setting, glowing sun and the breeze through the open living room window and herself, moving to close it. She could look through that window and she could see the two little girls crossing the street, walking hand in hand. *Two children alone at sunset, the taller one's hair shining black like her mother's . . .*

Carol squeezed her eyes shut. "Go away," she told the memory.

"What?" Nelson said.

She swallowed hard. Her mouth was very dry. "Nothing."

For days, weeks, months after Iris's disappearance, Carol had waited, her heart dropping whenever the phone rang.

But no call came, and Carol was able to keep her secret, keep it for months and then years as the search parties thinned and Lydia Neff grew quiet and heavy, the fire dimming in her black eyes, her hair graying until she was a faded copy of herself, until she aroused nothing but pity and even Nelson couldn't look her in the eye. Two years ago—three years after the police had officially closed the case—Lydia had left town. For where, nobody knew.

You got what you wanted, said the mean little voice in Carol's head. *No Iris. No Lydia. You made it happen, and you will never be able to set it right.*

"I'm going up to bed," Nelson said.

Carol squeezed her eyes tight. "Okay. I think I'll read for a little while."

No answer. Nelson was already upstairs. Carol picked up the book she'd been reading for her group—a memoir called *Safekeeping*. She opened it to the page she'd marked and let her eyes run over the words as she listened to the rush of water in the upstairs bathroom, the groan of the pipes, the hum of Nelson's electric toothbrush . . . As adept as she'd grown at keeping secrets, Carol was still a terrible liar and somehow, going through the motions of what she claimed to be doing made it feel closer to the truth.

Finally, the bathroom noises stopped. Carol heard the

light squeak of the floor in the upstairs hallway, the bedroom door brushing the carpet, and finally the creak of the bed as Nelson slipped in. Carol closed the book. She crept up the stairs and paused there, waiting for Nelson's breathing to slow, waiting for sleep. Only then did she walk into Nelson's office, turn on the computer he thought she didn't know how to work; only then did she go online and call up her chat room and sign on. Families of the Missing, New York State, the chat room was called and now, just two months after she'd found it, they felt like Carol's family, her only family. There were eight of them in the room tonight, and when Carol typed in her greeting, it was as if they'd all been waiting for her. *Welcome*, they typed, and Carol imagined them shouting it in unison. *Welcome, Lydia!*

Carol fell asleep in front of the computer. Only for about ten minutes, but it scared her. What if it had been more than ten minutes? What if the sun had risen and Nelson's alarm had gone off and he'd woken up in an empty bed and walked across the hall to find his wife at *his* computer, asleep at the keyboard he never knew she could *use,* remnants from last night's chat scrolling up the screen?

> *Don't give up the fight, Lydia. We're here for you.*
> *Lydia, you're the strongest person I know.*
> *Lydia, I found my daughter after twelve years.*
> *You can find your daughter, too.*

How would she ever explain that?

Carol shuddered. She said a quick *Night* to her friends and signed off, standing up before she could drift again.

AlbanyMarie had mentioned the name of a private investigator specializing in missing persons cases—Brenna Spector, who had an office in New York City. Marie's husband had been missing for five years, presumed dead in a small plane crash, and Brenna Spector had just found him. *In Vegas of all places*, Marie had typed. *If all goes as planned, I'll see him in a few days!*

Without thinking, Carol had typed, *Are you happy about that?*

After LIMatt61 had typed, *Wouldn't you be happy, Lydia, if your husband was found alive?* Carol had sat there for what had to be a full minute, her fingers hovering over the keys. Finally, she'd come up with this:

Brenna Spector. That name sounds familiar.

Carol winced. Had that sounded strange? Cold? *Oh well. Can't take it back.* She shut down Nelson's computer and switched off the lights.

Gazing into the bathroom mirror as she applied moisturizer to her face, Carol realized that she did, in fact, know the name Brenna Spector. She wasn't sure from where, but she did.

In the middle of the night it came to Carol, jolting her out of a dream in which she was chasing a tiny, scared puppy through a computer screen, the two of them running wildly between lanes of typed words . . .

Brenna Spector. It was from one of her book club books, a nonfiction account by a psychiatrist (Lieberman? Leopold?) about children with special mental abilities. The case studies had all been from the seventies and eighties and one was a teenage girl named Brenna Spector. *Could it have been the same . . .*

Carol heard an electronic trill, and she realized it wasn't the name recognition that had woken her up at all, but the ringing phone at her bedside. She looked at the clock: 3 A.M.

Carol's breath caught. Nelson was sound asleep as she picked up the phone, and she was aware of the contrast. Her husband's deep, easy breathing and her own pounding heart. "Hello?"

She heard nothing, just static. A cell phone maybe. "Hello? Is anyone—"

The reply was barely audible—a push of air with no voice behind it. Words she couldn't distinguish, one with an "el" sound. It could have been "hello" or "hell" or "cell" . . . It could have been "help."

Carol's chest tightened. "Who is this?"

Beneath the static, more whispered words—still all breath, but clearer now. Carol could hear what was being said.

There was a click on the other end of the line, and for several seconds after the phone disconnected, she sat there frozen, the receiver in her hand, unable to hang it up or stop the tingling in her skin or the rush of blood to her ears.

"You're not my mom," the caller had said. "You're not my mom, Carol."

1

"Are you ready, Brenna?" Dr. Lieberman says.

"Yeah."

Dr. Lieberman presses play and record on the tape recorder that sits on the far left edge of his desk. Lots of tape recorders in this office, Brenna thinks. It's June 29, 1985. This is her forty-sixth trip to this psychiatrist, and each time she comes here, the tape recorders seem to multiply.

There are three small, battery-operated ones in his top desk drawer, and then there's the reel-to-reel on the wall behind the desk, next to the black-and-white photo of Bob Dylan in a cowboy hat—an original Elliott Landy, according to Brenna's mother (whoever Elliott Landy is supposed to be. And then there is the plug-in on the desk with the big silver microphone attached that Dr. Lieberman uses to record all of Brenna's sessions. Such a weird feeling that recorder gives her. Like Lieberman is Friday from Dragnet, and she's some hippie he's interrogating. (Brenna likes reruns.)

"Your name," says Dr. Lieberman.

Brenna shifts in her chair. The air-conditioner is up full blast, but it's a hot day outside, and she's wearing her aqua

Dolphin shorts. When she moves, the leather sticks to the back of her bare legs and then releases, making an embarrassing snapping sound. She's sweating. Who wouldn't be, when he's about to . . . Well, Mom calls it "important research," but Brenna prefers "screwing with my brain."

"Name."

"Brenna Nicole Spector."

"Age?"

"Fourteen and seven-eighths."

Dr. Lieberman gives her a smile. "Well aren't we specific today?" He's wearing a bright red tie with dogs and fire hydrants all over it. Dr. Lieberman has a million of these ties, which Brenna's mother calls "whimsical," but Brenna calls dorky—each one exponentially dorkier than the next. She wonders if Dr. Lieberman wears these idiotic ties because he actually likes them, or if he thinks they put his young patients at ease. She hopes it's the former because on her they have the opposite effect and she's about to tell him exactly this when Dr. Lieberman says, "March 13, 1982," and Brenna gets knocked back three years and three months, just like that.

She was eleven and a half, and it was her third visit to this office. Instead of Bob Dylan, there was a print on the wall, with a picture of a stained glass window—flowering branches over a blue lake and the words "New American Wing. Metropolitan Museum" underneath.

On March 13, 1982, the office smelled like Brenna's kitchen did when her mom forgot to clean out the coffeepot. Dr. Lieberman was wearing a brown tie with a giant Superman S at the center and when he smiled, Brenna noticed a poppy seed stuck between his two front teeth. She still wasn't sure she liked him. It was very hot in the office, and her head hurt a little. Brenna wanted to ask for an aspirin

*but she didn't feel she knew him well enough for that, and
so she just sat there, hurting, as he pushed play and record
on the big tape recorder.*

*"Alrighty, Brenna, I'm going to put some blocks out," Dr.
Lieberman said. Then his phone rang . . .*

*"On March 13, 1982, I took some blocks out of a box and
set them in a line on my desk," Dr. Lieberman says now.
"Do you remember the order?"*

"How is your dog?"

"Excuse me?"

*"Your dog, Shelly? She had pythiosis. Your wife, Gwen,
said the doctor prescribed Natamycin?"*

*Dr. Lieberman stares at her. His mouth is tight, and
Brenna can see his throat moving under the collar of his blue
and yellow striped shirt. Slowly up, slowly down. He removes
one of the tape recorders from his top drawer, as well as a
cassette with a piece of masking tape on it marked "MARCH
13, 1982." He puts it in the recorder and presses play, and
Brenna hears his voice—exactly the same as she'd heard it in
her head, the same cracks and cadences. "Alrighty, Brenna,
I'm going to put some blocks out—" The voice is interrupted
by a ringing phone. "Sorry, Brenna. Just one moment. Hello?
Gwen? I'm with a patien—Oh, how's Shelly? What? That's
pythiosis, Gwen, not pathosis . . . Yeah, I'm familiar with—
No, no, no. Natamycin is perfectly safe for a dog—"*

He clicks the tape recorder off. "Amazing," he whispers.

*Brenna says, "Can I be blunt with you? It's about your
tie."*

Brenna Spector felt something purr against the top of her
thigh. It took her several seconds to identify it as her cell
phone, to get that this was September 29, 2009, rather than
June 29, 1985, that she wasn't in Dr. Lieberman's office at

250 West Fifty-seventh Street in New York, but . . . God. She was working.

Brenna was in Las Vegas, at an off-the-strip casino named Nero's Playground that Caesars Palace needed to sue for both copyright infringement and defamation of character.

Nero's Playground smelled a little better than the public restrooms at Nassau Coliseum, but that was only because it was less crowded. It was also a hotel, which terrified Brenna a little, as did the name of the lobby bar she was standing in right now: Orgi. With an I. Which somehow made it worse.

Honest to God, this whole place could benefit from a good, long liquid nitrogen bath.

Brenna was leaning against a papier-mâché Corinthian column (painted gold, to match the waitress's mini togas and gladiator sandals) holding the world's largest glass of cheap white wine—the Emperor's Goblet, the shivering waitress had called it—and she was standing face-to-face with her missing person—Larry Shelby aka Rod Clement, John Thomson, Julio Vargas, and no doubt several other identities she'd yet to unearth. Because Larry had supposedly perished in a single-engine plane crash in the Berkshires five years ago, Brenna and her assistant Trent had been referring to him as the Dead Guy, which was ironic considering all the living he seemed to have done since then.

"You checkin' out on me, babe?" the Dead Guy asked.

"I'm . . . getting a call."

"At five-thirty in the morning?"

Brenna shrugged. "Eight-thirty my time." She slipped her vibrating phone out of her pocket and glanced at the screen. Trent. He could wait. "Telemarketer. Once they get hold of your cell number, they're relentless."

"They haven't found me yet."

Why am I not surprised? "Lucky."

"You've got a real sweet smile, you know that?"

"Thanks." Brenna normally didn't talk to her subjects—it was best if they didn't see her at all—and here she was, drinking with one of them in Orgi at dawn. But her job was, by nature, unpredictable, and the best thing to do in a situation like this was to act naturally, ignore the prostitute in hot pants at the end of the bar who kept glaring at her like she was competition, and to not, under any circumstances, lapse back into another memory.

Brenna called one of the waitresses over—a fluffy blonde with eyes so big and green and utterly bored that, with all the kohl liner she was wearing, she resembled an angry tabby cat. "Yeah?"

"Can I get a glass of water, please?"

"You want a *twist* with that?"

Brenna was pretty sure she was being sarcastic, and so she said, "No, but if you have one of those sweet little umbrellas . . ."

Tabby rolled her eyes and walked away.

"Somebody's on the rag," the Dead Guy said.

"Really." Brenna hoped she was sounding natural, but she was still rattled from that scene with Dr. Lieberman. How could she have let her mind go there, and for so long? She'd suffered from this disorder—or "special gift," as her mother used to say—since she was eleven. It was called hyperthymestic syndrome and it meant she recalled every day since then perfectly, down to the date and with all five senses—every emotion involved as if she was reliving it.

Hyperthymestic syndrome was "ridiculously rare," a neurologist had once told her. It affected a handful of people with "differently shaped brains" and could be triggered by any major life change—a move to a new home, the birth of a sibling . . . The change didn't need to be very traumatic. Though, in Brenna's case, it had been.

At any rate, the syndrome was huge—a great big gift she'd never asked for, like a trampoline or a polo pony. Brenna had needed to rearrange her whole life in order to make it fit, yet still it poked into everything—her work, her relationships, all that she cared about. There's a reason why most memories dull with time, Brenna now knew. There's a reason why we see the past in softer and softer focus until it's forgotten down to snippets, sensations. Few people understood what a luxury that was, the ability to forget. But Brenna did. She understood completely.

Over the years, Brenna had developed tricks to keep her memories at bay—reciting the Gettysburg Address, digging toothpicks into her palms, biting her lip so hard, she sometimes drew blood . . . Not pleasurable, but they kept her in the present. It had been a very long time since she'd had a memory on the job that lasted as long as this one had. She didn't want to think about that too hard, though, for fear she'd slip back to the last time it had happened (February 27, 2003), and then the Dead Guy might really start to wonder.

"So, that was really your husband, wasn't it?" he said.

"Huh?"

"The telemarketer. The one who called you." He sighed. "Oh never mind. It was a joke. Kind of." Brenna's gaze slipped from the Dead Guy's face to the beer he was holding, and she realized what had triggered the memory. His tie. No dogs and fire hydrants, but it did have cats and canaries all over it, which was close enough. "You like the tie?" he asked.

"Can I be blunt?"

"First things first. You chained?"

"Chained?"

"You got a husband? It's okay, baby. What happens in Vegas stays in—"

"I'm divorced." This was the first true statement Brenna

had made all night. It was a good thing the Dead Guy was so drunk, because she'd let loose some awful whoppers this evening, starting from when he first approached her, asking why she was taking his picture.

Brenna had slipped the new HRC–20HEX she'd borrowed from Trent back into her bag and smiled up at him. He was a big man—taller and broader than he'd seemed in the family pictures she'd seen, but the curly mullet (now dyed jet black), the swollen-looking eyes, the jaw so square it seemed to have been drawn with a protractor—they were all unmistakable. "You mean," she had said, "you're *not* George Clooney?"

The Dead Guy had told her he was a lawyer named Paul, and Brenna had told him she was a Web site architect named Sandy, in Vegas for an IT conference. "You're a tall drink of water, Sandy," he'd said. "I like that." Then, he'd bought her the Emperor's Goblet, which she'd nursed while watching him polish off two Jameson/rocks, and a Jack straight up before moving, very quickly to his latest, a Heineken.

This is one guy, she'd thought, *who really wants to escape*. Then she'd glanced at his tie and sailed back to Dr. Lieberman's office.

"I'm not married, either," he said now. This was a lie. His wife, Annette Shelby, had retained Brenna on April 23. *I know he's alive*, Annette had said in the office Brenna kept in her New York apartment, her eyes trained on those spread-out family photos, glistening . . . *I can feel him.*

Brenna asked him, "Ever wish you were?"

"What?"

"Married."

"No. You?"

"Yes." Another truth. "But then again, Paul, I wish for lots of things."

"Like . . ."

She reached for the goblet and took a gulp. "Being . . . loved, I guess. Having someone care enough about me to really miss me." *Is this sinking in?* Brenna watched his gaze travel from her face to her cleavage to the cleavage of a nearby waitress to the ass of the glaring prostitute at the end of the bar.

"You know," Brenna said, "sometimes I feel like if I just left town, no one would care, no one would—"

"Shit."

"Huh?"

"My wife."

He was staring over her shoulder. Slowly, Brenna turned around and saw a woman heading toward them—busty and redheaded and not Annette at all. "Gregory! What the—"

"Vivica, I can explain," he said, which Brenna used as her cue to get away from the couple, as fast as possible. On her way out the door, she plucked Trent's spy camera from her bag and got a few shots of Vivica. *Poor Annette . . .* Too many times, it was a mistake to find the missing—especially guys like this, who worked so much better as memories than as living, breathing men.

"Sorry, no umbrellas."

Brenna turned and saw the tabby-faced waitress. Here by the door, the air wasn't as close, and she was standing near enough so that Brenna could smell her perfume.

Brenna breathed, "Shalimar?"

The waitress squinted at her.

"My sister . . . she wore Shalimar." Brenna dug her fingernails into her palms, but still her mind took her back to the room she had at eleven, to the coolness of the Marimekko sheets and her grandmother's handmade quilt weighing heavy on her chest. To her sister's T-shirt. Clea's T-shirt. Extra large, pale gray, with the tag cut out of the collar. The Led Zeppelin ZOSO logo printed small and black on the front and on the back—in huge, gothic red letters—"THE SONG REMAINS THE SAME." Clea had stolen it from one of her boyfriends and used to sleep in it all the time . . .

Brenna sleeps in it now. It's been washed so many times that the cotton is thin as Kleenex, but if Brenna stretches the collar over her nose and breathes very deep, she can still smell Shalimar. Shalimar and cigarettes and . . .

September 30, 1981. One month after the syndrome had kicked in. A month and nine days after Brenna's big sister, Clea, had gotten into that blue car, and the car had driven away.

"Please come back," Brenna whispers to the glow-in-the-dark stars on her bedroom ceiling. "Please, please God let Clea come back . . ." She squeezes her eyes shut. Tears seep out the corners. They feel hot enough to leave marks.

Brenna's phone vibrated again.

"Are you okay?" the waitress asked.

"Yeah, I'm . . ."

"Because you look like you're—"

"I'm *fine*." Brenna yanked her pulsing phone out of her pocket and looked at the screen. She expected Trent again, but this time she read a number instead of a name. It had a 914 area code. Westchester County.

Brenna hit send and said her name into the phone. And when a Brooklyn-accented voice asked if this was Brenna Spector, she remembered the voice, remembered it the way she always remembered voices—the same cracks and cadences. She remembered where she was when she'd first heard the voice, and started to feel the way she did back then, too . . . *October 16, 1998*. Brenna bit her lip. Stayed in the present. Yet when the caller told her his name, she couldn't stop herself from saying it along with him. "Detective Nick Morasco from the Tarry Ridge Police Department."

Morasco drew in a sharp breath. "I'm sorry," he said. "Have we ever met?"

Brenna wanted to explain—but tiredness, combined with that swelling memory, had done away with her filter, and again, the words on her mind flew out of her mouth: "Is this about Iris Neff?"

Morasco said nothing for a very long time.

2

Brenna was exhausted—not a bad thing, as it kept her from thinking. Immediately after she ended her conversation with Morasco, she headed back to the Mirage, ate a huge plate of pancakes at the lobby café, rode the elevator up to her room, and passed out until midnight, when she showered, dressed, packed, checked out, and caught a cab to the airport to make the red-eye back to LaGuardia. All this, without a single, memorable thought.

She continued on that way at check-in, then as she moved past the slot machines lined up along the center of Las Vegas Airport, one dinging softly as a sad-looking old woman fed it a twenty (*Think of the odds*, Brenna wanted to shake her and yell. *Would you please just think of the odds?*) And then still as she waited dully at the gate, listening to Iggy Pop's *Lust for Life* album on her MP3 in order to drown out the CNN feed—something about a fire at a group home in upstate New York—that kept looping, over and over again, through the two overhead TVs on either side of the gate, the screens glowing like devil eyes with footage of the blaze. (Why was cable news so pyromaniacal?)

It wasn't until Brenna was in her seat and the plane had taken off and the pilot had announced they'd reached cruising altitude that she allowed herself to recall the truncated phone conversation she'd had with Morasco, twenty-four hours earlier.

"Why did you ask about Iris Neff?"

"Sorry. I'm a blurter."

"Mrs. Spector—"

"Brenna. Mrs. Spector is my mom."

"Your assistant here tells me—"

"My assistant here?"

"He says—"

"You're with Trent right now?"

"He says you're out of town."

"Yes."

"I'd like to meet with you as soon as you get back."

"Could you please tell me what this is regarding?"

"I think we're better off discussing it in person."

"Discussing *what*?" Brenna said out loud.

The woman next to her—a nervous flyer who had been fingering a rosary right up until the pilot's announcement— looked at Brenna as if she'd just sprouted another nose and the nose was about to detonate.

"Sorry," Brenna said. "I was just . . . remembering something."

"Oh," said the woman, whom Brenna never would have pegged as the rosary type. She had spiky pink and white hair, rhinestone-edged librarian glasses, and a filmy, black vintage dress, a rose tattoo snaking up the length of her thin, pale arm. She was about Brenna's age, and back in New York City, where she no doubt lived, she was probably the coolest teacher at the Center for Design. But here she wasn't much, was she, other than scared? She asked, "Have a daughter?"

"Odd question, but . . . yes, actually," Brenna said. "Maya. She's thirteen. How about you?"

"What?"

"Do you have a daughter?"

Yesterday, at 3:28 P.M., Brenna had gotten a rare text from Maya: *Dad says you're picking me up a day late.*

Brenna, who viewed texting as a form of torture, had poked out a few sentences on her most-basic-of-nonsmart-phones, explaining how her hotel source had told her Larry Shelby was coming in from Los Angeles a day later than he'd initially planned, how Brenna was so sorry but there was nothing she could do, how she missed Maya and loved Maya and would make it up to Maya for sure . . .

No response. Of course. Ever since she was a first grader, Maya had chosen to express her deepest anger by saying nothing at all.

"I was asking for water," said the hipster design instructor.

"Huh?"

"Water. Not daughter. I was trying to get the flight attendant, but she didn't hear. Nice you have a daughter, though. I'm going to sleep now."

Edging away from Brenna, she squeezed about as much of herself as she could into the space between her chair and the window, and then she closed her eyes. *Disappearing.* That was fine. Brenna shut her eyes, too, disappeared in her own way . . .

October 16, 1998. The first and last time Brenna had ever spoken to Detective Nick Morasco of the Tarry Ridge Police Department, but that hadn't happened until after Jim had come up behind Brenna in the kitchen while she was in her tank top and pajama pants, scrubbing the remains of last night's salmon out of the Calphalon pot. It wasn't until after she'd felt the gentle pressure of Jim's palm on her bare stomach, shirt buttons against her back, his lips at her ear . . . *"I should be home by six."*

The kiss, soft and distracted, hits her collarbone. Brenna turns and puts her hand on Jim's just-shaved face and kisses him on the mouth.

His lips, soft on hers, his hand tangled in her hair . . .

The TV chirps, "Elmo's been thinking about trains!"

From the living room, Maya calls out, "Daddy! Bring me home a surprise!" And Jim pulls away and smiles. Brenna looks into his eyes. Like somebody lit a match behind them.

She whispers, "Bring me a surprise, too."

The plane bucked. "Oh God," the design prof said. "Oh God. Oh God."

Brenna looked at her. "It's okay. Just rough air," she started to say. But the woman's eyes narrowed and Brenna realized she was a little teary. She forced a smile. "Allergies."

The plane dipped again, and the seat belt light flashed on. "You need to fasten your seat belt," Brenna's seatmate said—weirdly insistent, as if universally fastened seat belts were the only thing that could possibly keep the plane in the air.

Brenna complied.

"Thank you, I . . . I just really hate flying."

"Never would have guessed." She put out her hand. "I'm Brenna, by the way."

"Sylvia." She didn't take Brenna's hand, though, because she was too busy working the rosary. Brenna sighed. Trent was a nervous flyer, too—ever since his plane got struck by lightning en route to the MTV Beach Party in Fort Lauderdale—but he was nowhere near as bad as this. Those times when she was forced into flying with her assistant, Brenna could usually calm him with a gin and tonic and/or a lie about the flight attendant wanting him.

"Please, please, please . . ." Sylvia was whispering.

Brenna didn't get it, the fear of flying. Sitting in an airplane was so safe, compared to what could happen to you on the ground.

The plane hit an air pocket and bounced sharply. Sylvia let out a yelp that sounded oddly like three-year-old Maya, and Brenna was back in October 16, 1998, only thirty minutes later . . .

"Mommy! Can I have some apple juice?"

"Sure, honey." Brenna pulls the bottle out of the fridge, pours it into a purple sippy cup with a spotted cartoon dog on the side.

"Mommy! Radio!"

Brenna sighs. She hurries into the master bedroom, handing Maya her juice as she passes. Jim bought a new clock radio five weeks ago, and they've both read the manual and still, neither one of them can figure out how to keep it from randomly going off several times a morning.

The only thing that seems to work is unplugging the clock, then plugging it back in and resetting it. The digital face reads 9:23 A.M. Brenna has the cord in her hand when she hears the radio announcer say, "Possible break in the Iris Neff case."

She stops.

Brenna knows the Iris Neff case—everybody does. Six-year-old girl, goes to a Labor Day barbecue, just forty minutes out of the city in peaceful, suburban Tarry Ridge. The party winds down, her mother leaves for home, and Iris stays on for a playdate with the hosts' children—perfectly normal, until Iris wanders off when the hosts' backs are turned.

No one ever sees her again.

The announcer says, "An unnamed witness saw the child in front of her own house, getting into a blue car with a dent in the right rear fender."

Brenna's eyes widen. It couldn't be the same car. That was seventeen years ago.

But still. Still.

Maya calls out, "Mommy! More juice?"

"Just a minute, sweetie!" Brenna grabs the bedroom phone. She calls information. She asks to be connected to the Tarry Ridge Police Department and then for the detective in charge of the Iris Neff case.

"That would be Detective Nick Morasco," the desk sergeant tells her.

On hold now, Brenna tries to picture the blue car that took her sister—the make, the sound of the engine running, the feeling that must have been welling within her as she pressed her face against the screen of her bedroom window at dawn, watching Clea lean into the passenger's side window and say, "I'm ready," watching Clea open the door and get inside . . . And then hearing that voice—his voice—the voice of the shadow behind the wheel. She can't. The event that triggered her perfect memory is hazy in her mind, dim as the childhood that came before it.

"This is Detective Morasco. What can I do for you?"

"I . . . I heard something on the news about a blue car."

"Who is this?"

"My name is Brenna Spector. I'm a former private investigator."

"Okay, well listen. That never should have been leaked to the press."

"No, I'm glad it was leaked because—"

"It was a bad lead."

"A bad lead?"

"It was false."

"So . . . you're saying that she didn't get into a blue car."

"We aren't looking for a blue car. Thank you for calling." Click.

That was cold, *Brenna thinks.*

"I'm sorry," Sylvia said now. "Were you talking to me?"

Brenna blinked. "Huh?"

"Never mind."

The engine roared as the plane settled into a new altitude, and soon the bumps smoothed out, the seat belt light switched off, and Sylvia removed her glittery specs and drifted into a deep, post-traumatic sleep. Brenna plucked her iPod out of her purse and jammed the buds in her ears and put *Lust for Life* back on. She listened to Iggy's yawn of a baritone, begging for some weird sin—not just any sin but a *weird* one. Brenna loved that—loved it ever since she first heard the song—February 21, 1988, her second and final year at Columbia, while sitting cross-legged on the unmade bed of Dan Price—green-eyed, scrawny, agonizingly attractive.

But Brenna didn't go back to that night. And she didn't go back to the morning of October 16, 1998, either. She didn't remember the week that followed her conversation with Morasco or all that time she spent in Tarry Ridge, searching for Iris Neff . . . She didn't allow herself to recall the people she met, the questions she asked, that awful, crawling suspicion. Nor did she let herself remember the way her heart had beat all the way up into her throat as, finally, she picked up the kitchen phone and tapped in the number she'd promised never to call again . . .

Brenna didn't let herself remember any of that week. But she knew that once she spoke to Morasco, once she finally met him face-to-face and heard that voice again, once he asked her what he needed to ask, whatever that could be, Brenna would remember Tarry Ridge. She would remember Iris Neff. She would remember that week—the week her marriage ended—whether she wanted to or not.

3

Five hours later, Brenna was back in the city, climbing the stairs to her apartment on Twelfth and Sixth, Trent calling out to her as she opened the door. "About time you got back! I've got something to show you—and it is *so cash*."

"I have no idea what that means."

Trent LaSalle had been working for Brenna for nearly six years, yet his presence in her apartment still made her cringe a little. Technically, it was only the front part of her apartment—an unusually spacious rent-subsidized two-bedroom she'd found eight years ago, shortly after her divorce. The bedrooms—one for Brenna, one for Maya during the three days a week she spent here—were located in the rear of the floor-through space and strictly off-limits to Brenna's assistant, who'd set up his desk at the start of it, in the far corner of her otherwise tasteful office/living room.

Aesthetically speaking, Trent's desk was a form of assault. Neatness wasn't the issue; Trent was very tidy. It was the Megan-Fox-in-a-bikini screensaver, the World's Best Booty trophy he'd received from an ex-girlfriend, the Mardi Gras beads and lacy garters strung over the back of the chair. Most of all, though, it was the bulletin board tacked with pictures of Trent—flexing his pecs on the beach, using a bottle of Grey Goose as a microphone, at various clubs, making kissy lips and/or gangsta rap–style hand gestures next to a series of beautiful young babes he'd managed to rope into photo ops, the discomfort on their faces obvious to everyone but Trent himself.

Trent was twelve years younger than Brenna—and as far as she was concerned, the worst type of twenty-seven-year-old male. He could've benefited from an old-fashioned with-holding father—coddled as he was into thinking he was a superstar in the making, a sparkling wit, every inch of him spectacular. He also had that weird macho/effeminate thing that a lot of young guys had today. He wolf-whistled women and bragged to his friends about how much *quality ass* he was *tappin'*, but waxed his chest, plucked his eyebrows, sprayed himself a glowing, orangey tan. In short, Trent was a douchebag. But he was surprisingly sharp and organized, and a genius on the computer. Over the past few years, he had created and perfected an aging program for missing children's photos that rivaled the one used by the FBI. And outside of the one time Brenna overheard him on the phone referring to her as a "grade A MILF," he was respectful of her, too.

Still, he was not the type of guy she relished having in her apartment. And when Trent said, "I've got something to show you," it wasn't always a thing you wanted to see.

"I hope you're talking about something related to our case files," Brenna said, after she'd opened the door and dropped her suitcase on the couch and acclimated herself to her assistant's cologne.

Trent grinned. "Not even close." Before Brenna could turn away, he whipped up his tight, lime green AX T-shirt, revealing two silver nipple rings. "Pierced 'em yesterday during lunch hour. You likey?"

Brenna winced. "You are aware of my condition, right?"
He nodded.

"So you know it means that every time I hear, feel, or *see* something, it's burned into my mind forever?"

"Yeah, duh, of course I know that."

"So in other words, if you ever show me anything remotely like what you just showed me again . . ."

"Whoa, sheesh, here's a dollar, buy a sense of humor. I was just trying to make you smile before—"

Brenna held up a finger. "One sec." She pulled her cell phone out of her pocket, tapped in Maya's number.

"Mom?"

"Hi honey. For once my flight wasn't delayed, so I could come pick you up now, so long as you're . . ."

Out of the corner of her eye, Brenna saw Trent gesturing at her, his hands flying out in front of him as if he was trying to guide a small plane to safety. She turned away. "You're back from school, right? You all ready, or do you have other plans first?"

Several seconds of thick silence. Maya's phone skills had long left something to be desired. Laconic to begin with, she went even quieter when talking was the only thing required of her. Still, Brenna could tell there was more to it this time . . . "Maya," she started to say. *I'm so sorry I'm a day late in getting you . . .* But Maya spoke before she could get any of the words out. "I'm spending the night at Larissa's tonight. I told Trent."

"Oh . . ."

"We're going to study for the science test together. Dad and Faith said it was okay."

"Wait. Larissa?" Brenna said, a memory flashing through her mind. "Her mother left you two alone in her apartment. You were just eight years old."

"I don't know what you're talking about."

"Come on, Maya. Remember? May 4, 2001. You came home all proud. You said, Larissa and I got to babysit each other!"

Maya sighed heavily. "Mom, she just went downstairs to get the mail. Like for *three minutes*."

"A child can disappear in less than three minutes, Maya. Her mother should have known that. She should have—"

"You're breaking up, Mom," said Maya, though Brenna knew the line was clear. "See you tomorrow. Try not to be late."

Brenna put the phone down.

Trent shrugged. "Kids."

Brenna said nothing. Just stared down at her quiet phone, the way it sat on her desk, so smug in its stillness. She wanted to throw it across the room.

"You wouldn't have been able to get Maya right away anyway," Trent said. "Military's due here at 0-fourteen hundred."

"Huh?"

He deepened his voice. "Detective Nick Morasco, Tarry Ridge PD."

Brenna sighed. "What the hell does he want?"

"No idea, but he is a serious piece of work. So freakin' *intense*."

"What did he say?"

"He wanted to know when you'd be here. I told him around four, and it's what . . . four-fifteen now so—"

The bleat of the front door buzzer cut into his words, and when Trent answered it, there was that deep voice again, that Brooklyn accent. "Detective Morasco. Is Mrs. Spector back?"

Trent looked at Brenna. "What'd I tell you?" he said as he buzzed Morasco in. "*Intense*."

* * *

At first glance, Morasco was neither military nor intense, but he was a lot of other things, all of which bothered Brenna.

What irked her most was his age. Barring plastic surgery, the detective was forty, tops. It would have put him at less than thirty eleven years ago—a contemporary of Brenna's, which, to her mind, gave him no right to be so patronizing and dismissive over the phone. *We aren't looking for a blue car.* Like he was chastising a child. *Thank you for calling.* Please.

Also setting off Brenna's annoyance meter was the bookish look he was working. Morasco was at Brenna's desk now, lanky and bespectacled and in a tweed jacket for chrissakes, hair like Orlando Bloom in a pirate movie. He really was the farthest possible thing from any police detective Brenna had ever seen, and she'd seen plenty. "Nice to meet you Mrs.—"

"Brenna."

"Brenna." Morasco was rooting through a beat-up canvas bag that seemed to be serving as his briefcase—one of those earth-friendly shopping totes from a big, guilty supermarket chain, "Go Green" printed on the side in look-at-me letters—and he didn't glance up when he said her name. In fact, he'd yet to look her in the eye, having made straight for her desk after telling Trent sure, he'd like a cup of coffee, black with sugar (the request directed not at Trent's face, but at some spot on the wall behind him). Call her demanding, but when law enforcement was in your living space and it wasn't there to arrest you, eye contact was the least you deserved.

Brenna thought of her ex-husband with his thinning crew cut, his big build, his tweed-free wardrobe and well-honed people skills . . . It hit her that Jim Rappaport, a reporter turned op-ed page editor, more closely resembled a cop than this supposed detective—and then Morasco finally found what he was looking for in the bag and dropped it on her desk.

It was a library book. Lieberman's book.

"This is you, right?" Morasco said as he cracked it open. "Chapter five?"

Trent returned carrying Morasco's cup of coffee and read the chapter title out loud: "The Girl with the Tape-Recorder Mind."

"Yeah," Brenna said. "That's me—Well . . . me when I was a kid, anyway." The book, *Extraordinary Children*, had first come out in 1990, with Brenna referred to simply as B. But after she was outed in the Science section of the *New York Times* on April 14, 1995, the book's editor called and got permission to use her full name in subsequent editions.

"I didn't know you were in a book," Trent said.

"It was a long time ago." Brenna's gaze ran down the page. She saw that she was called B. in this library copy—a first edition—and her own signed first edition clicked into her mind, the one that Lieberman had sent her right after it was published, the one she couldn't bring herself to read, but used to keep by her bed because she intended to read it, someday.

She could see the book on the green wicker nightstand of her first New York apartment on 112th and Amsterdam, her white metal reading lamp trained on the cover . . .

"Yo!" barked Trent.

Brenna cleared her throat, focused on Morasco, who was watching her intently behind his wire-framed specs—making up for lost time with the eye contact, as it were. His eyes, she noticed now, were quite dark, with a disarming softness. Brenna suspected that the quality was a result not of inherent compassion, but of myopia—the glasses were very thick. But it probably helped Morasco a lot when questioning witnesses.

He said, "You were remembering something, weren't you?"

"Huh?"

"The book—looking at it triggered something in your mind."

Brenna nodded. "It's just the way this . . . condition works, so . . ."

"I have to show you something."

Unfortunately, the way he said "show you" triggered the image of Trent and his nipple rings—she could have killed him for that—but Brenna blinked hard and squeezed the thought away.

Morasco was back at the bag again, rifling through it. "You asked about Iris Neff over the phone. Did you know Iris Neff?"

"Huh? Oh . . . No, I—"

"How about me?"

"You?"

"How did you know who I was before I told you?"

"I talked to you on the phone once."

"Once."

"October 16, 1998," she said, "9:23 A.M."

He stopped rooting through the bag and looked up at her. "Must have been some conversation."

"I happened to be looking at a clock."

Morasco went back to the bag. "What was the conversation about?"

"I called the station to ask a question. You blew me off. Lasted about thirty seconds."

Trent said, "Dude, she remembers the exact date when they aired that master-of-my-domain episode on *Seinfeld*. You know, where they all make the bet about who can go the longest without—"

"So the conversation she had with me is in good company."

Trent nodded. "She also can tell you when Shirley MacLaine called David Letterman an asshole, the date *Star Wars: Phantom Menace* opened at the Ziegfeld, and . . . oh, and the one day last year when Hostess Cupcakes were half-price at Gristedes."

"Trent," Brenna said. "Can you contact Annette Shelby and arrange time for me to meet with her about her husband?"

"Already did. I told you it's tonight at seven-thirty."

"Well can you call her *to confirm*?" Brenna gave him a meaningful glare. "Then you can check the traffic on our Web site? Maybe call your mother?"

"Oookay. Got the hint."

As Trent left them for his workspace, Morasco slipped a manila folder out of his canvas grocery bag and placed it on the desk. "Cupcakes, huh?" he said. "I'm a Twinkie man myself." He looked up at her, and Brenna knew he wasn't a Twinkie man. He probably hadn't touched a Hostess product since he was eight. *Nothing like being patronized by a guy in tweed.*

Morasco opened the folder. Inside was a series of photographs, all of the same woman—in a cream-colored suit and stiff white blouse holding a bouquet of flowers, in a red apron, carving a turkey at a church soup kitchen, on the beach, in a modest black bathing suit. "Do you remember her?" Morasco asked.

Brenna peered at the bouquet shot—a photo from a very low-rent wedding. "No," she said. In the picture, the woman appeared to be standing in front of an office cubicle, literally fading into the background with her cream suit and her lank sandy hair and her pale lips and skin . . . Everything about this person more or less off-white—save her eyes, which were large and silvery—not so much haunting as *haunted*. Brenna couldn't stop staring at them. "Who is she?"

She could feel Morasco's gaze on her, and when she turned to him his eyes were narrowed, sharp. Now she understood what Trent meant by intense. "You don't know the woman in these photos."

"I've never seen her before."

"You're sure."

"Yes."

The irises were jet-hard now, the pupils like drill bits—amazing interrogation tools, those eyes of his. Good cop and bad cop, rolled into one. "Have you spoken to her on the phone? Received any e-mails from her?"

"I don't even know her name."

"Carol Wentz." He leaned on the name, aiming it at her.

"I don't know anyone named Carol Wentz."

"She's fifty-one years old," Morasco said. "Married, no kids. Happy, more or less. In good health. She went missing five days ago. Her husband says before that, she hardly ever left Tarry Ridge, even. Last night we found her wallet."

"Detective," said Brenna. "Why are you telling me this?"

"In the wallet, we found a piece of paper with a name and phone number printed on it."

"Why are you telling me this?"

Morasco watched her face for a drawn-out moment, as if he was trying to see through it to her brain. "The name and phone number on the paper," he said. "They were yours."

Brenna's eyes widened. "Maybe she'd looked me up," she said. "Maybe she was planning on hiring me."

"The wallet was found by a Realtor. You know where?"

She looked at him. "I told you I don't know Carol Wentz. How would I know—"

"2921 Muriel Court."

Brenna swallowed hard. She felt some of the color drain from her face.

Morasco exhaled and took a step back, and Brenna knew she'd given him what he wanted. "You know the address," he said. "You remember it."

She nodded.

"Why do you know it?"

Brenna didn't want to answer that question, not with so many other questions running through her mind. So she turned away, cast her gaze across the room at the back of Trent's head as he talked on the phone, oblivious. And then she said aloud what she and Morasco both knew. "That house," she said. "The house where her wallet was found. It was Iris Neff's house."

4

1. I remember the name of the dog I had when I was in kindergarten.
2. I remember what I ate for lunch on my first day of junior high school.
3. I remember my father's favorite brand of Scotch.

Nelson Wentz stopped typing and stared at the screen. The assignment for his online memoir-writing course was to write four things you remember, four things you don't—but was this really enough information? Should he have typed, say, that his father liked Glenfiddich? Should Nelson have said that his dog's name was Coco and he wasn't allowed to keep her because his mother was allergic, or that he remembered what he'd eaten for lunch that day because it had been an egg salad sandwich and the children at his new school had teased him, telling him his locker smelled like feet? He didn't see why some writing instructor three thousand miles away would care about these things—Nelson barely did himself. But then again, he knew that when writing memoir, all sorts of details were important—just as they were in police investigations.

4. I remember what Carol was wearing on the day I
   met her.

Nelson wasn't sure why he'd signed up for this course. At
this point, he really wasn't sure why he'd done anything he'd
done prior to five days ago, when he'd woken up in bed to
find Carol gone—not in the kitchen, not in the bathroom or
the living room or anywhere. When he checked the garage
and saw that her car was still in it, Nelson had thought, *Visiting a neighbor.* An odd thing to do at 7:30 A.M., but not so
very odd for Carol, who'd rush to neighbors' houses on a
moment's notice when they called her for help with so much
as a sticky jar. ("You're the Wonder Woman of the suburbs,"
Nelson had once joked. Carol hadn't found it funny.)

So that morning, which had been a Friday, Nelson had
showered and gotten dressed like it was any other Friday
morning. He had taken the train into the city and worked
eight hours at the reference service Facts of Note, just as he
had done for the past thirty-two years. When he got home
at five-thirty and saw her car still in the garage, Nelson had
fully expected Carol to be in the kitchen starting dinner. But
she was not.

The day I met her, Carol was wearing a dress
with red and blue sailboats on it and the type
of flat-brimmed straw hat you see in Impressionist paintings. I am now head of research
at Facts of Note, but at the time, I had just
started there as a junior copy editor. It was
our company picnic, and I saw Carol from a
distance, talking to a group of people I still
hadn't met. I learned she was the cousin of one
of the women from accounts payable. She didn't
look like someone's cousin, not in that hat.
She looked as if she'd been beamed into Shep-

herd's Field via time machine. I had an urge to pick flowers for her.

Nelson started to read what he'd just typed, but he couldn't get through it. He kept picturing that police detective—Nick Morasco—standing over his shoulder and reading the screen. *Why are you doing a writing assignment when your wife is missing?* the detective said in Nelson's mind.

Detective Nick Morasco, while nice enough, had repeatedly referred to Carol as "your wife" this afternoon—the possessive, lest Nelson forget she legally belonged to him, and here he'd gone and lost her. *Has your wife been acting strangely lately? Would your wife have had any reason to visit 2921 Muriel Drive? Before her disappearance, would you have described your wife as happy?*

"Define happy." Nelson said it out loud, even though he hadn't intended to. He didn't like the sound of his voice—quavering in the empty room. *Manic.* Was this the beginning of insanity? Had Carol's presence in this house all these years been the only thing keeping Nelson from losing his mind? *I'm just trying to help you, Mr. Wentz. You wanted to talk to me about your wife.*

"Her name is Carol!" Nelson fairly shouted it. *Don't think about him anymore.*

He started to read his paragraph again—just for the sake of doing something normal. He'd gone to work today for the same reason. Why take another personal day? He would rather be in his office than in this empty house, thinking about Carol. He'd rather be top-editing pages at Facts of Note than hearing, "Nothing new," from that snide female desk sergeant every single time he called.

He hadn't been on his computer since Carol had gone away, but somehow it felt better to be in this room than in any of the others—the room Carol never ventured into, on the computer she'd never learned to use.

A hat from an Impressionist painting . . . I wonder if Carol still has it. If she does then maybe someday we could visit Provence together and I could take pictures of her in that hat among the haystacks. Surprising we've never been to Provence . . . Carol loves French cooking. In fact, Provence would be the perfect place for us to retire to. Why didn't I ever think of that before? Why didn't I ever tell Carol, "We could retire to Provence"? If I had brought up the idea, we'd both have something to look forward to. Today we might be in the city, taking French classes at the Lycée. Afterward, we'd be drinking wine at some little bistro on the Upper East Side, practicing our French together, laughing at how bad we both were, but knowing we'd be better in time.

When Nelson had first gone to the police station, the desk sergeant had asked, "What was Mrs. Wentz wearing when you last saw her?"

"Excuse me?"

"Last night."

"Yes."

"When you went to bed, your wife was still wearing her street clothes?"

"Yes, yes she was."

"Describe the clothes."

"Well . . . I . . . I don't really . . ."

"Is there one item of clothing you remember enough to describe? A sweater? A piece of jewelry?"

"Jewelry?"

"Mr. Wentz."

Nelson had felt as if he was flunking a test. He'd closed his eyes and opened them again, and after what seemed like an eternity, he was able to picture Carol on the couch Thursday night, reading a book. But he couldn't remember the book's title, or what she'd been wearing while reading it. "Her wedding ring," he had told the desk sergeant, finally.

"What did the ring look like?"

Nelson pointed to his own. "Like this."

"Plain gold band?"

"Yes."

"Okay. What is the inscription?"

"No inscription."

"No inscription?"

"We didn't . . . We . . . No. Just blank."

If Nelson and Carol were to retire to Provence, they wouldn't need a sprawling chateau. There were only two of them, after all, and they had simple tastes. All they really needed was a cottage—a one-bedroom, with a nice garden and a big, beautiful kitchen for Carol to cook in.

We'd be better in time.

Carol's wallet had been found inside the old Neff house. "The wallet contained your wife's driver's license and one hundred dollars in cash," Detective Morasco had said over the phone today. "No credit cards."

"She only has one credit card, and she keeps it in the kitchen drawer," Nelson had said. "She is very frugal."

Frugal. Nelson's voice had cracked on the word—though on the positive side his instinct had told him to use "is" to describe Carol, not "was." She was still an "is" in his mind. That was something, wasn't it?

At first, Nelson had believed that Carol had left him voluntarily. He'd imagined her calling one of the neighbors—perhaps Gayle Chandler from her book club. He'd pictured Carol picking up the phone late Sunday night and asking Gayle in a whisper to drive her to the bus station in White Plains. He'd pictured his wife of fourteen years buying a one-way ticket for some distant town she'd never been to before—Phoenix or Cleveland or Memphis or Des Moines—his practical-minded wife, thrown off her head by the mother of all mid-life crises, leaving home with nothing but her wallet and the clothes on her back and some dream about starting a new life, and it infuriated him. Made him angrier than he'd ever thought he could feel, angrier than he'd ever admit to feeling.

Driving to the police station that first evening, it had been more an act of spite than concern. *This will show her*, he had thought. *She'll come back to a full-blown police investigation and won't she be embarrassed?* Making it even worse, the police seemed to agree that Carol had left of her own volition—their "full-blown investigation" amounting to that desk sergeant limply filling out a report.

Nelson had driven home hating the world. Parking in his driveway, he had glared at the garage that held Carol's car. A one-car garage, and all these years he'd let Carol have it—let her keep her Volvo in there, protected from the elements, while his Volkswagen Golf camped out in the driveway at night and in the train station parking lot every weekday, his car a second-class citizen—a worker-drone.

He'd glared at that Volvo through the narrow window at the side of the garage, Carol's garage, the closed door like a giant closed mouth, smirking at him. He'd walked straight up to that door and kicked it so hard his foot bled.

Waking up alone again the next morning, though, and again the next and the next, Nelson's anger had quieted to loneliness, only to be replaced by gnawing dread. Carol hadn't left him of her own accord. She would never do that, and Nelson knew her, knew her better than anyone. He had known her for twenty-five years.

Carol's wallet. Left at the Neff house. That had sealed it.

No one had lived in the Neff house for two years. It was nicely kept up by Realtors, and Nelson had just heard that a developer had finally bought the property—the same one who built those expensive Waterside Condominiums at the eastern edge of town, which was good news, he supposed, for Lydia Neff, wherever she was . . . But for all intents and purposes, the house was abandoned. And Carol's wallet found in an abandoned house—the abandoned house of a woman Carol had never liked in the first place. Carol's wallet dropped in a house she'd never go to voluntarily. That couldn't mean good news.

I don't remember the last time I kissed Carol.

Nelson felt a tear slip down his cheek. He exited out of his assignment, then clicked on the file and dragged it into the trash folder. Only after he did it, though, did he realize that the images he described—Carol, talking to her friends at the Facts of Note picnic, Carol's old hat with the pink satin bow—they were, for now, all he had left of her.

He clicked on the trash icon, opened it up. The memoir file was easy to find—Nelson emptied his trash with relative frequency, so there weren't many others. He undeleted it, amazed at how relieved that simple action made him feel. Then he shut down the computer.

As he was getting up from his chair, though, it struck Nelson that there had been another file in trash. An unfamiliar file . . .

Nelson booted the computer back up. The process took longer than he would have liked—he needed to do something about the spyware on his PC once and for all—but finally the computer booted up and the desktop loaded. He clicked on the trash icon again, three quarters convinced he'd hallucinated the file.

But he hadn't. There it was—a download, from Thursday at 10:30 P.M. Nelson knew he had been asleep by then—he always tried to get to bed before ten on work nights—and when he clicked on it, the empty feeling in his chest loosened. Carol had downloaded the file. Suddenly, the present tense fit Nelson's wife. *Carol does know how to use the computer. She does, she does.*

The file had been downloaded from the DMV Web site. Its name was "Replacing Your Missing Driver's License."

Nelson wanted to laugh, but laughing while alone was for crazy people, and Nelson Wentz was not going crazy. Not anymore. *Carol downloaded the file, and she did it here, at home,* after *losing the wallet.* He opened up the DMV file and stared at it for several minutes—as if he expected it to tell him something else. Then he went online, clicked on recent history . . . and learned exactly how, as he slept, his wife had been using her computer knowledge.

When he "died," Larry Shelby had left his wife, Annette, more than twenty million dollars, furthering Brenna's belief that he was far more attractive as a memory than as a man.

Annette Shelby, however, felt otherwise. As soon as she'd heard from Brenna that he was alive, Annette had flown down to the city from her home in Great Barrington and spent a significant amount of that inheritance on a deluxe suite at the St. Regis. "It will be the perfect spot for our reunion," she had explained over the phone.

Brenna had tried to talk her out of it. Odds were, a man with six new identities wouldn't be ripe for a reunion, no matter how classy the hotel. But Annette wasn't having it. And Brenna, who'd been going through a hell of an ordeal booking a last-minute flight to Las Vegas with a beyond-bitchy airline rep, couldn't find the energy to argue with her.

So now the two of them—investigator and client—were stuck in this gorgeous room with its Central Park view and its sculpted, chandeliered ceiling and its king-sized bed with the tulle canopy pouring down on it like something out of a Cocteau movie—the whole scene romantic to the point of mockery, not to mention the mix CD that Annette had brought—"Larry's Favorite Songs"—inexplicably, sadistically playing out over the room's stereo system. And they were *doing business.*

On the plus side, it took Brenna's mind off what Morasco had told her three hours earlier—a missing woman's wallet, her name and number in it, found at Iris Neff's old house. It took her mind off Morasco's questions, too.

But the fact remained that, for anyone with a shred of empathy, the business being done here was achingly unpleasant. Brenna had already showed Annette copies of her husband's various IDs and now she'd gotten out the photos she'd taken at Nero's Playground of Larry aka Gregory getting screamed at by his latest spouse, Vivica. "You don't have to look at these, Annette," she tried.

"Oh yes, I do." Annette had just polished off her fourth airplane-sized Johnnie Walker Black and was now washing it down with a handful of chocolate-covered cashews. That was one thing that could be said for this room—it had an excellent minibar.

Brenna slid the folder across the desk as the next of Larry's favorite songs kicked in—Elvis's "Are You Lonesome Tonight," of all things. Brenna managed a sip from the bottle of seltzer that Annette had insisted she take and watched her slide open the folder, wincing at its contents. She had never felt quite this uncomfortable in her life. "Should I . . . Do you want me to turn off the stereo?"

Annette shook her head. "Larry's gained weight."

The sad truth was that physically speaking, Vivica seemed a better match for Larry. Annette was willowy and waspy-elegant, with golden hair and sculpted cheekbones and tiny, implacable pores. Upset as she clearly was now, she still looked as if she couldn't break a sweat if she tried, whereas Larry and Vivica seemed to be cut from the same earthy cloth. But that was neither here nor there, was it? *Looking* as if you belonged together? If you were going to judge on looks—*real* looks—Annette looked right now as if someone had stuck her with something huge and sharp and drained all the hope out of her. "Can I ask you something, Brenna?"

"Sure."

"How did you find him?"

Brenna cleared her throat. "Well, the first credit card he applied for . . ."

"I know—you told me that, but Larry got rid of that card fast. How did you pick him up after that? He went from New York City to Wyoming to—"

"Montana, not Wyoming."

"How did you keep finding him, Brenna? How, when he obviously . . . didn't want to be found?"

Brenna looked into her eyes—a pure, pale blue, fogged slightly from alcohol. She nipped the bud of a memory— Larry calling her a tall drink of water—then realized that within two days, she'd watched both Shelbys get drunk. "We found Larry the same way we find most adults. Interests."

"Interests?"

She nodded. "You can change your name, your hair color, you can get plastic surgery. But it's a lot harder to change what you like, and no one really thinks they have to. Some- body likes guns, for instance, they're going to apply for a license, maybe join the local NRA. Or say they're into golf- ing, they'll join a country club."

"What was it with Larry?"

"Sorry?"

"What interest couldn't Larry give up?"

Annette asked the question in a way that made it clear she knew the answer, but still Brenna was careful with the response. "Expensive restaurant reservations," she said.

"Private club memberships, purchases at high-end jewelry stores . . ."

"Women."

Brenna opened her mouth to speak, but no sound came out. What could she say? "Would it help if I told you you're best off without him?"

"Not really."

The Elvis song ended, and then Brenna recognized the opening notes to "Wishing on a Star" by Rose Royce. Larry had some goddamn heartbreaking taste in music, that was for sure. Annette closed her foggy eyes, the singer's voice like clear water, wishing and wondering what a dream means . . . Brenna tried not to think about the fact that "Wishing on a Star" had been Clea's favorite song—the one she said "told the truth about love, real love." Brenna tried not to feel the pink shag rug beneath her bare legs as she sat in Clea's vacant room at 11 P.M. on June 2, 1983. She tried not to remember listening to "Wishing on a Star" with her eyes closed, her head resting on Clea's quilted futon, searching the song for clues. She tried not to feel her eyes squeezing tight, tears hot in the corners. *The song is empty. Empty as this room . . .*

"You look a million miles away," Annette said. "What are you thinking?"

Brenna swallowed hard. "Nothing. Larry wasn't the right guy for you."

"I know," Annette said. "But who the hell wants the *right guy*?" She slipped an envelope out of her Prada bag and handed it to Brenna. "Your check," she said. "You'll see I included a little extra for that yummy assistant of yours."

"Yummy? *Trent?*"

"Come on. Don't play dumb. Those pecs!" Annette cracked open another Johnnie Walker Black, downed it in one gulp. "God, he's a delicacy."

How and where had this intelligent woman gotten such phenomenally bad taste in men? Brenna shrugged into her jacket as the Rose Royce song faded away and Annette turned off the player. "Last song on the CD," she said.

"I guess I should head out."

"Thanks, Brenna. For everything. I mean that."

Brenna gave her a quick, tight hug. "You will be okay."

Annette nodded. "Crappy as this feels, it still beats the hell out of not knowing."

As Brenna was heading toward the door, Annette said, "Oh, did you ever hear from Lydia?"

Brenna turned. "Who?"

"Friend I made on this New York Families of the Missing chat room . . . She lost her daughter, years ago. She's had some bad luck with PIs, so I recommended you."

Brenna shook her head, her mouth dry. *Lydia Neff, Iris's mother . . .*

"That might not be her real name. Christ, I called myself AlbanyMarie. No idea where I got that one."

"We haven't had any new client calls for weeks."

"Weird. She private messaged me about a week ago, asking me if you were good at finding adults. She sounded like she was going to call you right away."

"Her daughter was an adult?"

Annette shrugged. "Don't know."

Brenna's cell phone vibrated at her hip. She held up a finger and answered it fast, without looking at the number on the screen. "Hello," she started to say. But a man's voice cut her off. A brittle, angry voice she'd never heard before. "Brenna Spector?"

"Yes. This is—"

"This is Nelson Wentz," the voice said, Brenna's eyes going big at the last name. "What have you done with my wife?"

5

"No disrespect or anything, Brenna, but you are seriously romping on my game."

"What's the big deal? You've done it for me before."

"Not when I'm playin'!"

Trent's voice, slathered in cool-dude lilt, was particularly tough to take at top volume through Brenna's Bluetooth, competing as it was with the thudding, shrieking din of Roseland or Lotus or whichever club Trent happened to be gracing with his presence tonight, no doubt working the room like a badger in heat. But Brenna was driving to Tarry Ridge for the first time in eleven years—Tarry Ridge, rife with tens of hundreds of potential memory triggers—and knew herself well enough to realize that in this case, biting her lip and reciting the Twenty-third Psalm wasn't going to do it. She needed live interaction, no matter how inane, to keep her in the present. The more inane the better, come to think of it—it was actually *harder* to get lost in a memory when she was baffled and annoyed. "Think of it as part of your job," she said. "Making sure the boss stays sane."

"Why can't you just sexually harass me?"

"Trent."

"Okay, fine." He sighed. "What do you want to know?"

Brenna passed a sign on the 287—"Tarry Ridge 4 miles."
She swallowed hard. She drove a 2002 gray Sienna minivan,
bought used three years ago, but when she inhaled now, on
this part of the highway, Brenna caught the new-car scent of
the maroon Camry she'd rented on October 16, 1998, from
the Avis on Twelfth and University.

*The steering wheel is smooth plastic. It feels strange
under her hands compared with the leather-covered wheel
in Brenna and Jim's Volvo—and it gives her a weird thrill,
that differentness.*

"Brenna? You there?"

*It's only one morning out of your life. Satisfy your curi-
osity and it's over . . .*

"Yo, Bren-na!" Trent said, and she was back in the
Sienna, on the night of September 30, 2009, with a dull ache
behind her eyes, and the Tarry Ridge exit looming five car
lengths ahead.

"Tell me anything," Brenna said. "What club are you at?
What are you drinking?"

"I'm drinking Bacardi and Coke. I'm in bed."

"You're in *bed*?"

"No, that's the club's name," he yelled. "Bedd! With two
Ds! It's in Brooklyn!"

Brenna's palms were sweating. "You scoring or what?"

"Not yet," Trent replied, as if she'd asked if he'd bought
tickets for tomorrow night's Rangers game. "But I'm about to."

"Who's the lucky girl?"

"Blonde in a pink tube top. Man, I love tube tops. They
like . . . do what *you* want to be doing, know what I mean?"

She rolled her eyes. "Oh yeah, I totally get that."

"This blonde . . . she's kinda got a Jessica Alba thing
going on."

"Jessica Alba isn't blonde."

"I'm talking from the neck down," he said. "And she is

massively checking me out . . . Hey baby. How about I buy
you another one of those cosmos—with chaser of *Trent*."

Brenna winced. "That couldn't possibly have worked."

"What's your name, gorgeous? Diandra. That is a name
that's made to be moaned in ecstasy. Know what I'm saying,
sweet thang?"

For several seconds, Brenna heard nothing but ambient
noise—a thumping bass pressing through super-powered
speakers, the whooping chatter of at least a hundred club pa-
trons . . . "Let me guess," she said. "Diandra's throwing up."

"Wrong, Miss Wiseass. She's giving me her digits."

"You've got to be kidding."

"What? No, baby, no I wasn't calling you wiseass I was
. . . Yeah, I'm on the phone with my . . . but . . . No, I'm telling you, this is *my boss*. I swear, I . . . Wait . . . Oh now don't
be like that . . . Damn." Trent groaned. "Completely *carpet-
bombing my game*."

"Sorry."

Trent sighed. "So tell me about this new client in Tarry
Ridge."

"His name's Nelson Wentz," Brenna said. "He's the
husband of Carol Wentz. That's the woman Morasco was
asking about."

"I remember. Just because I don't have your memory
thing, it doesn't mean I'm brain-dead."

"Yeah, well . . ."

"Why'd he contact you? Did Morasco throw him your
way?"

"Hardly."

Nelson Wentz had called Brenna's cell as she was leaving
Annette Shelby's hotel room, accusing her of abducting his
wife. Within twenty seconds, though, she'd been able to tell
he was grasping at straws. *Carol ran five searches on you
before she disappeared*, he had said. *She wanted your Web*

*site, your address and phone number, your career history.
She did a search with your name plus "missing adult"* . . .
But when Brenna had suggested that perhaps Carol had been
interested in hiring her—*Do you know anyone she might
have been trying to find?*—Wentz had caved, weeping into
the phone.

Brenna wasn't proud of it, but the sound of grown men
crying always made her skin crawl, and this phone conversation had been no exception. She'd offered up half a dozen
*I'm sorry*s. (Such an ineffectual phrase—as if Brenna was
to blame for Nelson Wentz's tears and could, by way of apology, make him stop.) But then he'd started telling her how no
one on the Tarry Ridge police force would help him look for
his wife, how he'd had the interest of one detective for about
five minutes, but now it was back to business as usual. *Your
wife left you. You'll just have to get used to it.* No one had
said that, of course, but it didn't matter. That was the *feeling*
Nelson had gotten from the police in his hometown—the
same feeling Brenna and her mother had gotten from Detective Grady Carlson of the Pelham Precinct on September 8,
1981—he of the bile-brown Members Only jacket and the
crumbs in his mustache and the statistics about unhappy
teenage girls who run away from home . . . "Would you like
me to help you find Carol?" Brenna had heard herself say.
And thus she and Nelson Wentz had struck a deal.

"He cried?" Trent said.

"He misses his wife."

"Whatevs. Seems a little dramatic for a phone call with a
stranger. You got his social? I can run a check."

"Already did," Brenna said. "Absolutely clean. Not even
a late credit card payment. Nelson Wentz misses his wife,
Trent. He loves her. He's at his wit's end."

"Hel-lo. Smokin' hot brunette at five o'clock."

"God, you're so sensitive."

"I am. See, most guys would only notice the double Ds. I notice the legs, too, and the face."

Brenna sighed. She was on Main Street now—3.5 miles away from Nelson Wentz's home according to Lee, the suave Australian voice on her GPS and for close to a year, the only man in her life. As Trent told his brunette that heaven must be missing an angel—*They still used that one?*—Lee requested Brenna make a right at the next intersection. She crawled toward it, checking out the retail space: Gap, Barnes & Noble, a Starbucks, plus an art-house theater, three galleries, a very high-end boutique, and a paint-your-own pottery store—all of them new to her.

Main Street was no time capsule, that was for sure. It was more like the Growing Dinosaurs Maya used to play with as a five-year-old. They started out as specks of sponge, but if you put one in a dish with a drop of water, it would expand overnight into a four-inch T-Rex—five hundred times its original size. For Tarry Ridge, it had been two drops—the ultra-exclusive Waterside Condominiums, brand-new eleven years ago, when Brenna had last been here, and the five-year-old Riverview Shopping Center, which was not so much a mall as Fifth Avenue with escalators. It had a Barneys, a Nobu, a Tiffany's with marble floors and chandeliers . . . The *New Yorker* had once done a Talk of the Town piece on the Riverview Shopping Center, referring to it in the headline as "Privilege under Glass."

Both were the brainchild of New York City developer Roger Wright—aka Donald Trump without the divorces, bankruptcies, Page Six mentions, and hair jokes. For sentimental reasons apparently, Wright had deemed his hometown a good place to build and, as ever, his instincts had proven correct. Over the past decade, this one-two punch of prime real estate had transformed the town from sleepy suburb into a glittering T-Rex of a bedroom community, with property values tripling and quadrupling on even the smallest of homes and more or less staying there, even with the housing bubble bursting. Nelson Wentz had made Brenna a very generous offer, yes. But unless he was leading a secret double life as a high-stakes gambler, the man was good for it.

"So, uh . . . Brenna?" Trent was saying. "You still need me to yap at you or what?"

"I'm fine. See you tomorrow. Have fun in Bedd."

"That would be the plan."

"Trent."

"Yeah?"

"Thank you."

Brenna ended the call. She saw one place she remembered—a stationery/candle store called Wax Attax—and pulled over to the curb to get a closer look. The last time she'd been here, it had been morning, and it was now more than three hours past the store's 6 P.M. closing time. Plus the window display consisted entirely of Webkinz—Internet-friendly stuffed animals that didn't even exist eleven years ago. But the spiky logo was the same—"Wax Attax!" rendered across the top of the window in thick, chrome-colored spray paint.

Looking at the name, Brenna returned to the morning of October 20, 1998, when she'd rung the bell on the counter and was greeted by a clerk with a halo of frizzy white hair, a black sateen blouse, and a name tag that said "Kaye."

The store had reeked of scented candles—vanilla mostly, with a little licorice worked in as if to intensify the headache. Kaye had been pleasant, though. Standing in front of the crepe-paper black cat and grinning cardboard jack-o'-lantern that had been tacked behind the counter for Halloween, she'd resembled a kindly witch. Seemed to know it, too.

"What spooky delights can I help you with?"

"*Actually*," Brenna says, "*I couldn't help but notice all the kids' items you have . . .*"

"*Are you a mom?*"

"*I have a three-year-old.*"

"*Oh, well you might be interested in our Sunday story hour! Do you live around here?*"

"*I live in the city.*" Brenna takes a breath. "*I was just wondering . . . Did Iris Neff ever come in here? For the story hours?*"

"*Are you a reporter?*"

"*What? No, I—*"

"*Because I really can't say anything. I know you're just doing your job.*"

"*I'm not a reporter.*"

"*Iris is a very smart little girl. With a wonderful imagination. My prayers are with her and her mom.*"

"*I'm not a reporter,*" Brenna says for the third time. She slips one of her old cards out of her purse—"*Brenna Spector—Errol Ludlow Investigations.*" She hasn't used these cards since marrying Jim, and that feeling seizes her again—that weird, guilty thrill.

With the pen from the counter, she crosses off Errol's number and writes down her cell. "*Sorry—we have to get new cards,*" she tells Kaye. "*I'm a private investigator. And actually, I'm just helping out with one tiny part of the case.*"

Kaye blinks. "*Okay . . .*"

"*Did you ever hear Iris mention anything about a blue car with a dent in the back?*"

Kaye shakes her head. "*No,*" she says. "*Certainly not that I remember.*"

"*Have you maybe seen a car fitting that description that you haven't—*" Brenna's sentence is cut off by the chirp of her phone.

"I'm sorry. We really don't allow cell phones in here," Kaye says. "People always speak so loudly on them."

"I understand." Brenna hurries outside the store to take her call, but by the time she does, it's gone to voice mail.

Brenna knows who it is before checking the message—she always knows when it's Jim calling, and again, this very specific sixth sense proves right.

"Can't wait to give you that surprise," he says. Brenna's stomach tightens. What would Jim say if he could see her here? What would he say if he saw her give that woman a card with Errol Ludlow's name on it? Go home. Now.

She puts the phone in her pocket and starts down the street toward her rental car.

She hears a rush of footsteps behind her. "Miss Spector?"

Brenna turns. It's Kaye. Her cheeks are flushed. "Listen, this is probably nothing," she says. "But I . . . I do remember one time in story group, Iris got into an argument with another little girl."

"Okay . . ."

"The girl said there was no Santa Claus, and Iris . . . strongly disagreed."

"So . . . Iris believes in Santa Claus?"

"She didn't just believe. Iris was adamant—argued it like a little lawyer. She said that when he wasn't in the North Pole, Santa came to Tarry Ridge. She told the little girl that our town is Santa's vacation home."

Brenna smiles a little. "Well . . . you did say that she has a wonderful imagination."

"Yeah, I know. And Iris did—does . . ." Her voice cracks.

"I'm sure this is very hard. A missing child is—"

"No wait. Here's the thing . . ."

Kaye closes her eyes for several seconds, puts her fingertips to her temples.

"Are you okay?"

The eyes open. "Yes," she says. "This . . . It's just a little weird."

Brenna nods, waiting.

"Iris said that when Santa visits Tarry Ridge, he drives a blue car."

A truck swooped past Brenna's parked Sienna, shaking her into the present. For several seconds she sat there, staring at that "Wax Attax!" sign, gritting her teeth.

Enough thinking. She would visit Nelson Wentz, get a look at that computer, collect her deposit, and call it a night. But when she started up her car and drove up the street and Lee again told her to make a right on Muriel Court, Brenna found herself turning left instead. And when Lee intoned, "Recalculating . . ." Brenna switched him off and kept driving. She didn't want to turn back.

6

It was something Brenna always did at the start of investigations—visiting the last place her missing person had been seen. She found it helpful to put herself in the shoes of that person, to retrace steps in reverse. But this was different. Carol Wentz had never been seen at 2921 Muriel Court. Only her *wallet* had been seen there—a flimsy tie to say the least, as wallets went missing a lot more often than their owners. It was very possible someone had stolen the wallet from Carol—or even found it somewhere—before leaving it in the Neff living room.

Yet Brenna was compelled to drive there—*yanked*, as if the Neff house was made of magnets. It all begged the question: *Who is my real missing person?* Brenna had no desire to answer that one, so she stared at houses instead.

Main Street may have been a Growing Dinosaur, but Muriel Court—at least the western part of it—was a true time capsule. Everything about that stretch of street looked exactly the way it had back in 1998—the uniformly square and manicured lawns, staid New England homes looming over them like reproachful aunts. No add-ons or swimming pools or studio spaces. Other areas of Tarry Ridge had been overrun with mini mansions and gated housing developments, all of them so new that gift wrap seemed fitting—but not this stretch. As far as Brenna could tell in the dark, even the paint jobs were the same.

Brenna passed the husky white colonial that Theresa and Mark Koppelson had shared with their five kids, two dogs, and, for a few hours on that overly hectic Labor Day afternoon, Iris Neff.

The Koppelsons still lived in the house. Brenna knew because she recognized the car parked in the driveway—a gray Subaru Forrester, license plate NYX319. It had been brand-new when Brenna had last pulled in behind it eleven years ago, but now it trailed a buff white MDX and a shiny black MINI Cooper—the newer vehicles' tired, aging relation. It was a good bet that the Koppelsons' youngest daughter, Claire—Iris's Labor Day playdate—was using it as a starter car. She was sixteen now, after all.

Harder to explain than the Subaru, though, was the swing set still standing in the front yard. The Koppelson children were far too old for jungle gyms and slides . . . *Maybe Theresa and Mark have had more kids since then* . . . Though Brenna couldn't help but see the swing set and even the car as attempts to stop time—to keep everything just as it had been the day a little girl disappeared from this house, so that Iris might return unchanged, unaged, unharmed, bringing the day back with her. Again she would bicker with six-year-old Claire over who got the last white chocolate chip cookie, feeling that righteous indignation only a first grader could feel. (*It's not FAIR! I'm the GUEST!*) Again she would storm out the front door. Only this time, Iris would stop at the swing set, linger by the glimmering silver slide, and start to climb to the top. Theresa Koppelson would then put her finger on a pause button, and everything in and around her house—from sprinklers to lawnmowers to TV screens to bees—would go perfectly quiet and still. Calm now, Theresa would walk out of the kitchen, the water she'd put on for macaroni and cheese caught at the point of boiling. She'd move around her frozen pets and family members and out her front door and into the breezeless air, past suspended hummingbirds and mosquitoes. She would approach the slide and take Iris Neff into her arms like a life-sized cardboard cutout. She'd bring the little girl back into her house and lock the door and call Iris's mother and never let her out of her sight until Lydia Neff came to pick her up. Then, only then, would she hit fast forward to tonight, to find the Subaru sold for parts, the swing set dismantled, other houses on her street changed, repainted, renovated, that one horrible mistake forever corrected . . .

Or maybe the Koppelsons were just procrastinators. Brenna had to stop projecting.

She had questioned Theresa Koppelson during the morning of October 20, 1998, but not for very long. Theresa hadn't heard anything about a blue car. All that Brenna now knew about that Labor Day afternoon—the macaroni and cheese, the girls' argument, the fact that Theresa was so busy, she hadn't noticed Iris's disappearance until two hours later, when she'd called Lydia Neff and left a message on her machine—all that information, Brenna had learned from the police report.

The only thing she'd gotten out of that five-minute conversation with Theresa Koppelson in the driveway of this house was "Blue car? No. Sorry." And, at the mention of Iris's name, that flash of shame. "She had walked home from our house twice before, you know. The news reports never mentioned that. She's a very headstrong and independent little girl, and when Lydia never called back, I . . . I assumed everything was . . ."

I know, Brenna had wanted to say. *I lost someone, too.*

Brenna fiddled with the Sienna's radio until she found a music station. Some boy band from half a decade ago was whining in harmony about filling their empty spaces with holes. She picked up the speed and forced her eyes back on the road and kept them there until she reached 2921 Muriel Court—thinking about nothing but spaces and holes and spiky-haired boy banders, spinning in slow motion.

Muriel Court ended on a cul-de-sac. The Neff property filled the left side, bounded by huge elms and pine trees. For a suburban house, it was very secluded and private—the row of tall hedges in front a few feet bigger, making the place look as if it were the home of a reclusive movie star. Ten years ago, Brenna had a clear view of the driveway from across the street and up—a good bead on the top story of the house, too, which at the time sported window boxes and curvy white shutters with cut-out hearts—awfully smorgasbord-restaurant-whimsical for a house so suddenly empty and sad. But now, all you could see of the house was the roof. The driveway was a tunnel of leaves.

Brenna pulled to a stop in front of the hedges, got out of her car. The house on the right end of the cul-de-sac, the neighbor's, was one of those split-levels—you just knew that at some point in its existence, the whole interior had been doused in wood paneling and macramé plant holders, that the rugs were shag and Tang-colored and felt stiff and oily to the touch. Even today, you couldn't look at it without getting the *Brady Bunch* theme song stuck in your head. Brenna thought they'd bulldozed most houses like that during the Reagan Administration, but there it was, standing out on this Tudor-infested street like a Brooks Brothers oxford in Trent's closet. She hadn't thought much of it the last time she'd been here, but now she understood the need for all the hedges and elms. Lydia Neff's way of avoiding guilt by association.

Brenna moved past the Neffs' "For Sale" sign and up the

path between the hedges. She'd never been this close to the Neff house. All she'd ever done was stake it out from across the road and up, and so this was all a new experience—no memories attached. The surprise of it kept unfolding.

Envisioning this visit, for instance, she'd never anticipated the smell of wet grass. She'd never expected the paint to look so fresh. She'd never expected the outdoor lights to be working, let alone *on*, nor had she expected a thick row of mums to be flourishing under the first floor windows. The word "abandoned" had conjured images of neglect, yet this home was anything but neglected. It was protected. Coddled.

And like the other houses on this street, unchanged. It was still the same pale yellow, with the same deep red roof and those cuckoo-clock shutters, red and white pansies spilling out of the window boxes, just like ten years ago.

She started to head around back, when she noticed something glinting out of the shadows between the far end of the house and trees bordering the driveway.

The closer Brenna got to it, the better she could make it out, and her heart began to pound. Explanations spilled into her head. *Maybe someone recently left it here—kids daring each other to sneak onto the property, the child of the Realtor or maybe a prospective buyer . . .*

That all felt like a plausible, if a sort of sick coincidence. But when she got close enough to put her hand on it, the skin pricked up on the backs of her shoulders.

It was a child's bicycle with the Strawberry Shortcake logo on the wheels, training wheels still attached. *This wasn't just left here*, Brenna thought, setting a new bar for stating the obvious. The bike's entire body was caked in rust. A spiderweb glistened across the handlebars.

And then there was the seat. On it, the name "IRIS" had been scratched, in the careful, rounded scrawl of a very young girl.

* * *

Brenna made her way around the house, where she was greeted by a sudden cold mist; timed sprinkler system. She hurried through the lawn and up to the back door, shaking the water out of her hair, all the while thinking about that bike . . . A rotting thing, hiding in the shadows of this coddled house. Over the phone, Nelson Wentz had told Brenna that after Lydia left town, she'd placed her home on the market fully furnished. *She wanted to leave it all behind*, Brenna had thought. *All the furniture, all the memories . . .*

But Iris's bike, standing in that spot like it hadn't moved in years . . . That was something different. Was it a provision of Lydia's? *Sell the house, do what you want with the furniture, but the bike stays.* Maybe Lydia saw the bicycle as something for Iris to grab on to, should she ever come back alive. *Something to tell Iris that her mother might have left, yes, but here, Iris, look at this. Kick the training wheels, run your hand over the seat, feel the imprint of your six-year-old signature. Here is your yellow ribbon, Iris. Here is your proof that you're still missed, still loved, still my child, always my child . . .*

Or again, maybe Brenna was projecting. She had a habit of attaching such deep meaning to inanimate objects when the truth was, sometimes a cigar was just a cigar—and the same could be said for swing sets and bikes. Things got left outside for years because they'd been forgotten—not remembered.

A sprinkler caught Brenna in the back of the legs. She moved closer to the window and peered in. The house was dark, but when Brenna pressed her face to it, she could make out a wooden kitchen table, a straight-backed chair at either end, a tall coat stand, and a dry sink, stacked with plates. *Fully furnished, all right.*

Brenna stepped back. To the right of the door was the

alarm system, its red light glowing over the keypad. She got her penlight out of her purse and shone it on the numbers. Odds were, the Neffs' alarm system was as unchanged as the rest of the house. And if that was the case . . . Well, most people used significant dates when coming up with combinations, so it was worth a try.

She would go back to the day she met Lydia Neff.

Brenna closed her eyes and took a few breaths. She shut out the crickets' chirping, the whisper of the breeze through the trees behind her. She focused her whole mind on the swish of the sprinklers, because it was water that was important to the memory, the controlled splatter of a fountain.

The date came to Brenna first—October 23, 1998. Soon after, she felt the air start to chill, for, as she recalled, the two-week-long heat spell had broken on October 22. Instead of the cotton skirt she was wearing, Brenna could feel her old black jeans hugging her legs, the tug of Jim's hooded Knicks sweatshirt, which she'd put on that morning for comfort and to cover the bruises on her neck.

Next, Brenna could taste the bottom-of-the-pot coffee she'd forced down before leaving her house. Her mind ticked off that morning's events: kissing Jim good-bye as he left for work, dropping Maya off at day care, taking the subway to a new car rental place—a Budget on Lexington and Forty-third; accepting a dark blue Chrysler LeBaron from a clerk named Cindy with a distractingly shiny nose; Cindy warning her that the previous renter had been a *smoker* and giggling before and after the word—as if "smoker" were some sort of euphemism.

Then she was behind the wheel and heading up Fourteenth Street to the West Side Highway and over the Major Deegan bridge and the Cross County Expressway, all the while trying to ignore the stale ash-stink in the car, how it brought out her headache, how it crept into her skin and made the damage from last night . . . the ache in her face and stomach, the cuts on her knuckles, the bruised flesh about her jaw and shoulders . . . how that smell somehow caused all that pain to come alive again, to *blossom* . . .

The freshness of the hurt makes her nervous—as if she'd managed to cast a disappearing spell on the wounds, but only for this morning, and now it's wearing off. Brenna checks the side of her face in the rearview. The jaw's a little swollen, but the bruise is still hidden under all the makeup she put on at 5 A.M., before going back to sleep.

Thank God.

Jim didn't notice the bruises this morning, but how long is that going to last? He's a journalist—a good one. How long before he figures out that last night, Brenna got chased ten blocks by a cheating husband after he caught her taking his picture, that the husband had yanked her into an alley, thrown her against a brick wall, grabbed her by the neck, punched her in the stomach? How long before he sees the cuts on her knuckles and figures out that instead of giving up her camera, instead of running, Brenna had fought back, hard? How long before he puts two and two together and it hits him that last night, his wife broke the one promise he'd ever asked her to make? "Stop." Brenna said the word out loud, followed by the first three lines of the Pledge of Allegiance. She needed to remember one moment, not the whole day. Why did her memory work this way? Why was Brenna's own mind so completely beyond her control?

She jammed her eyes shut. *The fountain. The goddamn fountain at the goddamn Waterside Condominiums complex. Late morning. October 23, 1998. That. Just that . . .*

The Waterside complex isn't as big as she'd thought it would be. Right next to the visitors' parking lot is the club area, with fenced-in tennis courts, meeting house, pool, gym, and then a dozen or so evenly spaced condos on either side of a wide empty road that stretches out to the west, overlooking the Hudson River, all of them so new you can practically still smell the paint.

Brenna gets out of the car. Her muscles ache when she stands, and the cuts on her hands sting from the cold.

She likes it here, though. She likes the quiet, the calm. No wonder Lydia Neff comes here every morning to "meditate." Brenna had thought it so strange when Lydia's neighbor told her that. Meditation among the mini-mansions. But now she gets it.

I'd do the same.

Brenna hears a distant lawnmower, then a staticky sound. Running water. The fountain. She moves toward the sound—past the club area to a marble sign that reads "Garden" in gold letters. It marks a path, running through a row of maple trees shading dwarfish, just-planted bushes.

Brenna heads up the path. She follows it until it widens into a circle, bordered by trimmed-down rose bushes, potted ficus, and Asian maples.

At the center of the circle is the fountain—made of a smooth white stone that makes Brenna think of sculptures and then, for the briefest moment, of her mother, sculpting.

Four wrought-iron benches stand evenly around the fountain. Everything so perfectly placed. So balanced, except . . .

A slender, black-haired woman sits alone on the farthest of the benches, her head down. She wears a long black coat. Her hands are folded in her lap.

Brenna moves closer.

On the back of the woman's right wrist is a tattoo: a dragonfly with a red body and blue and green wings.

When she looks up, Brenna recognizes the high cheekbones, the dark eyes, the down-turned mouth, laugh lines like faint parentheses . . . She recognizes Lydia Neff's face from an interview she saw on Good Morning New York, *three days after Iris's disappearance. And for a moment, Brenna has the strangest feeling, an almost starstruck feeling, and the question she's planned to ask this woman, the one she's rehearsed in her head and used on half a dozen other people, the one about Iris getting into a blue car, couched in the explanation that Brenna was an investigator, helping out with one small part of the case . . . those carefully organized sentences crumble and scatter, and instead Brenna hears herself say, "I know how you feel."*

Lydia stares at her.

Brenna clears her throat. She looks into the black eyes. "My sister got into a car. The car drove away. I didn't know who was driving that car, or why she got in, but it drove away, and she was gone. This person I woke up to every morning, who knew most all my secrets—this person who was such a part of my life that her presence in it was . . . It was like . . ." Brenna's gaze moves to the fountain—water hitting pale, sculptors' stone. And then back to Lydia's pale face. "It was like breathing."

Lydia's eyes cloud and glisten. A tear spills down her cheek. "Next Wednesday is Iris's birthday. I swear to God I don't know what I'm going to do."

"What are you doing here?"

A man's voice pulled Brenna out of the memory, the date ringing in her head. Next Wednesday. October 28. 10 28. But she couldn't punch Iris's birthday into the keypad—couldn't move at all.

Brenna knew the voice. It belonged to Morasco, and when she spun around, there he was, watching her hard-eyed through those thick glasses, his palm flat against the breast pocket of yet another tweed jacket, the tips of his long fingers grazing the opposite lapel, inches from where Brenna knew his shoulder holster would be.

7

Morasco walked Brenna off the property and to her car in silence. He'd come, he said, because a neighbor had reported a suspicious vehicle in front of the Neff house. But while he seemed to find Brenna's explanation reasonable enough—*Nelson Wentz hired me to find Carol. I figured, if I came to the place where her wallet was found, I might be able to talk to some of the police involved in the case*—he kept giving her odd, sidelong looks. She expected a follow-up question, and when they reached her car she got one. Of course, it followed up on nothing she'd ever anticipated: "Does Nelson Wentz know you used to be one of Errol's Angels?"

Brenna stared at him.

"Come on," he said. "You have to know they called you girls that. In fact, I think Ludlow coined the term himself."

"You know Errol Ludlow?"

Morasco shrugged. "Not personally, but as PIs go, he's legendary."

"And by legendary, you mean a flaming jackass."

Morasco smiled a little.

"It's okay. I worked for the guy for three years. I know his reputation, and let me tell you, it's well-deserved."

"Well . . . since you mentioned it."

"I am wondering two things, though."

"Yeah?"

"First, why would Nelson Wentz care that I used to work for Ludlow?"

Morasco shrugged. "He may have opinions on a PI who hires a bunch of pretty girls to do his dirty work." His gaze dropped to the ground. "Especially if ninety percent of it is trapping cheating husbands."

"I needed a job," Brenna said. "I'd just dropped out of college because I . . . I wanted to learn how to . . . to find people. There weren't a lot of options."

He gave her a long look. "Your sister."

"What?"

"You wanted to find people because of your sister, didn't you? She was never found."

Brenna stared at him. Her face felt hot, as if Morasco's eyes were two spotlights, burning her. "Okay," she managed. "That brings me to my second question."

"Yes?"

"How do you know I worked for Errol Ludlow?"

"It's not that hard to find out. Go to any private eye database, it'll have an employment history."

"I phrased that wrong," Brenna said. "What I should have said was '*Why* do you know I worked for Errol Ludlow?'"

"Well, I—"

"Why do you know about my sister? Why do you know so much about me and why do you care?"

Morasco adjusted his glasses, his eyes glittering in the dim light from the streetlamp, his lean face tinged with some emotion Brenna couldn't quite identify. "It's interesting," he said, finally, "how one word can completely change the meaning of a question."

Brenna exhaled hard. She stuck her key in her car door.

"I never knew Carol Wentz. Trent showed you our phone records. You saw yourself I haven't received a new client call in two and a half weeks."

"I know."

"I had nothing to do with Mrs. Wentz's disappearance."

"I know."

"So, then, Detective Morasco . . ."

"Nick."

"Nick. Why are you researching me?"

"Well . . ." He cleared his throat. "You've got to admit, you're kind of . . ."

"Kind of what?"

"Fascinating."

Her eyebrows went up.

"I mean . . . the disorder. I never heard of anyone having perfect memory until I read Dr. Lieberman's book."

Brenna stepped closer. More than anything she wished she could see inside his head, read his thoughts. She was usually pretty perceptive, but for the life of her, she couldn't figure out whether Morasco was being genuine, or whether he was completely playing her. And if the latter was true, what was he playing her for? Brenna felt her cheeks heating up again, and she was glad for the relative dark. "Maybe if you guys spent as much time researching Carol Wentz as you do researching . . . my disorder," she said, "her husband wouldn't have to waste his money on PIs." She opened her car door and slid into the front seat. "Bye, Nick."

Brenna started to close her window, but Morasco placed his hand over the frame and she stopped. He leaned down, put his eyes level with hers. "Carol Wentz never withdrew more than fifty dollars a week from her bank account, but the day before her disappearance, she went to an ATM and took out five hundred dollars."

"What?"

"I guess Nelson Wentz didn't tell you."

"No . . ."

"Interesting—because *we* told *him*," he said. "Oh, also three days before, Carol was seen at a diner in Mount Temple, sitting close to another man."

"Are you serious?"

He cocked an eyebrow at her. "You aren't the only person I know about."

She shook her head. "Nelson Wentz told me . . ."

"Let me guess. He had a happy marriage, and his wife would never leave him, but for some reason he can't get the cops to understand that?"

"Yes," she said. "In fact, that was almost word-for-word."

"Nelson Wentz is a nice guy, but he's not what you'd call a reliable narrator," Morasco said. "They had a crappy marriage, Brenna. Any of their neighbors would tell you that. And at least one of them would tell you that at her last book club meeting, Carol Wentz confessed—without going into detail—that she felt guilty and 'unfulfilled.' "

She stared at him through her open window.

He gave her a small, sad smile. "I'm telling you," he said, "because it helps to know what you're up against."

By the time she got her thoughts together enough to reply, Morasco was gone. And so she watched him, jogging up the block to where his car was parked, waiting.

Nelson Wentz was boyish, in the literal sense of the word. He was fifty-eight years old, which Brenna had learned from running the check on him, but sitting on an easy chair in his living room, he could have been twenty-five or fifteen or even five. So slight and delicate he was for a middle-aged man. Such a weak little shadow he cast—as if he'd managed to age half a century without making it all the way through puberty.

Nelson wore khaki pants and an off-white polo shirt, and the easy chair he was sitting on was of a grayish cloth, and in a way, it all camouflaged him. Like his wife, Nelson was pretty much completely beige—skin, hair, lips . . . They could have been brother and sister or even twins, save for Carol's startling eyes. Nelson's eyes, on the other hand, were small and pale and frustratingly restless. It made it hard to have a simple conversation with him, because whenever his gaze met Brenna's, it would dart all over the living room, landing on random objects—the framed seascape hanging over the TV, the wooden bust of Don Quixote on the mantelpiece, the orange striped cat stitched into the couch throw —and then it would stick there, as if Nelson was begging his own home furnishings to back him up.

And here Brenna had barely *asked* him anything yet. "How long have you and Carol been married?" was her latest.

Not exactly phone-a-friend material. Yet in response Brenna had gotten, "Fourteen years?" Delivered like the world's most embarrassing question. Directed at a book on the coffee table.

Okay, fine. You want to play tough . . . "Nelson?"

"Yes?"

"Why did you hire me?"

For the first time since she arrived, Nelson looked her in the eye. "To find my wife."

Brenna met his gaze. Briefly, she recalled Nero's Playground—the smell of sweat and old smoke, the blinging slot machines, the headachy taste of the white wine she was drinking, and the bachelor's glint in Larry Shelby's eye when he leaned in . . . *"You chained?" he asks, and all Brenna can think of is Annette, knowing in her heart her husband is alive, knowing that fact without question . . . but knowing so little else about him.* Brenna squeezed her eyes shut.

When she opened them again, Nelson was still watching her, his whole face twisted up like a question mark. "What are you going to do," Brenna said, "if Carol doesn't want to be found?"

"I don't know what you mean."

"I think you do, Nelson," Brenna said. "I'm thinking you weren't totally honest with me about the state of your marriage."

Nelson's gaze darted to Brenna's shoes. "I'm always honest."

"I spoke to Detective Morasco," she said. And that was all it took. Nelson seemed to deflate in front of her, the energy draining out of him and giving way to a type of hard weariness until, delicate as he was, he finally looked his age.

"Detective Morasco doesn't know the whole story."

Brenna stared at him. "Fine," she said. "But see, I *do* need to know it. If Carol took a significant amount of money out of an ATM right before she left, I need to know that. If she was talking to a strange man, I need to know that. If your marriage was . . . less than perfect—"

"It was fine. We were fine. Maybe we weren't . . . like other couples. Certain *overdemonstrative* couples . . . But I loved her and she loved me. We had a future together. We were going to spend our retirement in Provence. She wouldn't leave me."

He said it all quietly, but as he spoke, his face grew redder and redder.

Brenna nodded.

"We were fine."

"I understand." Brenna moved to the chair next to his—a spartan wood desk chair that seemed more a space filler than a piece of furniture, and angled herself toward him. "Now let me ask you something," she said. "Do you *want* me to understand—or do you want me to find your wife?"

"Both."

Brenna sighed. "Look, Nelson. I'm going to be asking you a lot of questions—some of them you might not want to answer because *thinking* about the answers—the honest ones—may hurt. Or maybe you've blocked certain things out of your mind . . . I need you to put all those feelings aside—to answer everything. Even if it means dredging up memories you'd rather stay buried." She pulled the chair a few inches closer. "Nelson," she said quietly, "do *you* understand?"

He looked at her for a long while, the red slipping out of his face, his features settling back to normal. "I promise," he said. "I'll tell you everything."

"Okay great." Brenna gave him a smile. "Now that that unpleasantness is over with, how about you give me her credit card number so we can see if there are any new charges . . . Any old bill is fine."

"I can do better than that," Nelson said. "I can give you her credit card."

"You have that?"

Nelson got up. "She has one credit card, and it's just for emergencies. We use my cards for all of our major expenses."

"Your cards."

"Yes. From my bank, and a few others."

"Your bank?" Brenna said. "You never combined your finances?"

Nelson looked at her as if she'd just socked him in the jaw. "No," he said. "We didn't."

"Why not?"

"I'm sorry . . . I have to get used to . . . probing questions."

Brenna hadn't considered that question particularly probing—*What's he going to do when I start asking about their sex life?* But because she could practically feel the anxiety flying off of him, Brenna pulled back. She nodded and said, "It's so hard, I know," and hoped that it put Nelson on the verge of at-ease.

"Keeping everything separate was easier."

"Sure," said Brenna. "So you're positive she didn't take the card with her?"

"She never takes it out of the house. She is very frugal."

Brenna followed Nelson into the kitchen, and as he moved toward the drawer beneath the stovetop, she couldn't help but step back and gasp. While the other rooms required few adjectives, other than "clean" or maybe "sufficient," the Wentzes' kitchen was a gourmet's dream come true—stainless steel fixtures, polished cherrywood cupboards, copper pots glimmering from a rack placed over a state-of-the-art gas stove, a good-sized island, complete with a Michelin chef–worthy block of knives and even a basket of fresh fruit, not to mention a refrigerator large enough to feed a kibbutz . . . Brenna loved this room, loved the bounty of it, the happy excess. It stood out like a Christmas tree in the Wentzes' otherwise prosaic home, and more than anything, it gave Brenna hope for their marriage. "Who's the cook?" she asked.

Nelson didn't answer.

"Nelson?" She pulled herself away from the fridge and looked at him, standing in front of the stovetop, staring into the open drawer beneath it as if it were a tragic headline.

Brenna went to him. That close, she was aware of his hands, which clasped the drawer so tightly that the tips of his fingers were white. "What's wrong?"

He took a step back. "Carol's credit card," he said. "It's gone."

"I was good to her," Nelson said. He was sitting in a small chair to the side of the stairs, gazing into the drawer of the sewing table, the drawer where he and Carol kept all the bills. He said it so quietly, Brenna could barely hear him. But it was the first sentence he'd uttered since discovering his wife's credit card was missing, and so Brenna jumped on it.

"You supported her."

"Pardon?"

"That's one of the ways you were good to Carol, right? You supported her in full."

"Yes."

"So, does that mean you also wrote the checks?"

"No," he said. "Carol handed the finances. She was . . . She *is* better with those things than I am."

Brenna moved a little closer, leaned against the stairs. "So if Carol wanted to keep a purchase hidden from you, she could."

"Ms. Spector, Carol would *not*."

"Remember, Nelson," she said slowly, "I'm on your side." She took one of Carol's credit card bills out of the drawer, texted her card number to Trent. "We should have her charges within the next day or so. My assistant has a very good source at this particular company. Now, you're sure she didn't have any other cards? Maybe one she told you she was canceling?"

Nelson didn't answer. Ever since he'd sat down here, he'd been worrying a spool of bright blue thread he'd plucked off the table and now he just stared at it, a thumb pressed into either side, pressing so tightly the thumbs quivered—the spool the only thing on earth that, at this moment anyway, Nelson seemed capable of controlling.

Brenna sighed. Clients like Nelson Wentz made her glad for the two years she spent at Columbia, working toward a psych degree. "Can you do something for me?" she asked. "Can you do something for me, Nelson?"

He looked up. "Yes."

"I want you to think back to your last night with Carol. Retrace your steps in your mind."

"Why?"

"We need to see if there's anything that stood out—strange behavior, maybe . . . something that might clue us in to her reasons for leaving. I mean—if she had any. We still don't know whether or not she was abducted."

"Okay," he said. "Where should I start?"

"How about breakfast?"

He gave her a blank look. "You want to know what I had for breakfast that morning?"

"Sure."

"I do not remember." He said it like he was in a court of law.

"Okay." Brenna sighed. "Well . . . it was a Thursday, correct?"

"Yes."

"Did you run any errands after work?"

"I do not remember."

"Try."

"I don't—"

"Sometimes it helps to remember what you were wearing."

Nelson closed his eyes. "A pair of very uncomfortable shoes," he said, finally. "I bought them at Target for twenty dollars. Half a size too small."

"Ouch," she said. "But if they were just twenty bucks, I can't say I blame you." She gave Nelson a smile, and he smiled back, and then his memory seemed to relax back into working order. He described his full day at the office and his commute home on the train and a brief stop at CVS to buy corn pads, and just as Brenna started to drift off into a bored stupor, Nelson said, "And then I came home, and I saw Carol in the living room."

"How did she seem?"

"Fine."

"Just fine?"

"Yes."

"Can you remember what she was doing?"

Nelson put his head in his hands, massaged his eyes.

"Take your time," Brenna said.

And he did. He rubbed his eyes for what must have been a solid minute. "I think she said, 'You startled me.'"

Brenna looked at him. "Where was she when she said it?"

Nelson took her back into the living room. "Here." He was standing a good twenty feet away from the couches, so she couldn't have just gotten up. He was far from the fireplace, too, but he was just about three feet away from a door Brenna hadn't noticed earlier.

"What's that door behind you?" she asked.

"Carol's crafts closet," he said. "She . . . uh . . . she might have just been closing the door when I came home. I'm not sure."

Brenna walked up to the closet. She opened the door. Nothing but craft supplies, it seemed, but she and Nelson started taking them out anyway.

Bolts of fabric and knitting bags filled to bursting with luxurious yarn, folded-up scarves and needlepoint kits and three latch-hook rugs that, Nelson informed Brenna, Carol had made back in college. Underneath it all, they'd found a small, black box. "What's in here?"

"I think that's where she keeps her quilting supplies." Nelson removed the lid. Sure enough, Brenna saw bright scraps of cloth, pincushions, thick needles and thread, scissors with handles shaped like strawberries, and several puffy squares, already sewn . . . She closed the box. "I guess that would have been too easy."

"Huh?"

"Nothing. It's just that when people have something they

want to hide, they usually choose a space that's theirs and theirs alone. So in other words, the kitchen drawer, the coffee table . . . even that sewing area judging from your familiarity with it . . . none of those would be ideal places. If Carol had something she wanted to keep from you, she would pick a place like her crafts closet. A place that belongs only to her."

"She doesn't," Nelson said.

Brenna turned to him. "What?"

Nelson stared hard at her, his jaw tight. "Carol doesn't have anything she wants to keep from me."

Nelson's wife didn't love him. Nelson's wife kept secrets.

After Brenna Spector left his home, Nelson sat on his couch for a long time without moving, barely blinking, until he started to remind himself of Anthony Perkins at the end of *Psycho*, sitting stock-still in the detective's office with his mother's voice coursing through him, refusing to move even as a fly crawled across his hand.

A ball of rage, trapped in a shell. That's what Norman Bates was, wasn't it? And that's what Nelson was turning into. He needed to stop. He needed to kill the rage before it overtook him and melted the shell and burned everything in sight.

The missing credit card, the crafts closet, and then, finally Nelson's own computer. Not Carol's *personal space*, as Ms. Spector had put it. Not by a long shot. It was her *husband's computer*. Yet according to the history check Ms. Spector had done, Carol had been sneaking onto this computer when her husband wasn't around. She had made several visits to a search engine called Chrysalis.org, yet she never seemed to use the site to search for anything. *Another secret.*

Nelson got up, and moved over to the oil painting of Sarasota Beach that hung over the TV. It had belonged to Carol's grandmother, and more than once—several times, Nelson could now recall—he'd come into the living room to find Carol standing in front of this painting, hands on her hips, a slight dreamy smile on her face . . . "What are you thinking about?" Nelson had asked her one time.

And Carol—typical Carol, with that brick wall in front of her thoughts, never letting you past: "The painting."

"You're thinking about the *painting*?"

"I just like it. That's all."

What had Nelson done to deserve this? For more than twenty years, he'd been good to Carol. He had given her everything she wanted. She never had to work. She'd done the cooking, yes, but only because she liked to cook. He'd never raised his voice, never hit or swore at or even threatened Carol . . . Nelson had been nothing but kind. Nothing like his own father and if Carol could have *seen* Nelson's father, full of Glenfiddich with a red face and meaty fists and a voice like a bomb exploding . . .

Nelson glanced at the clock over the fireplace. Midnight. He probably hadn't been up this late in twenty years. *At least it's a new day.* Quietly, he moved to the crafts closet, to that black trunk, still plunked in the open doorway. *When people want to hide things, they choose a space that's theirs and theirs alone.* But wasn't everything about Carol hers and hers alone? Wasn't her mind like this black trunk—hidden beneath layers and layers, the lid slammed shut?

Nelson opened it.

He saw bright scraps of fabric, spools of thread, a few pairs of scissors. Quilting supplies. He started lifting it all out, putting it on the floor, thinking, *That'll show you. That'll show you, Carol. I'm in your space. Your private space, and there's nothing you can do about it . . .* He didn't think that way for long, though, for the phone was ringing. Whose phone rang at midnight? *My phone is ringing at midnight.*

Nelson thought, *Carol*, and he was following the ring, rushing toward it. The nearest phone was in the kitchen. He leaped at the sound and by the time he got there, he was close to completely out of breath and feeling as if his heart might burst and not caring if it did, not caring about anything except getting her on the line . . .

Caller ID read "Unknown Caller." Nelson yanked the phone from its stand, pressed it to his ear. "Carol?" he said, on the edge of his breath.

There was no answer, just thick static, and Nelson thought, *Cell phone. Out of range.* But he kept talking, as though maybe his voice could bring her back into range and then pull her through the phone. "Carol? Is that you? Where are you?"

The static cleared enough for Nelson to hear her breathing. He said Carol's name again, but when she finally spoke, her voice wasn't the voice of Carol at all. "It's my fault," the voice said, before hanging up. And all Nelson could do was stand there, dead still, until the spell wore off and his tears finally fell. It was the voice of a teenage girl.

8

Clea stood over Brenna's bed—a shadow with a seventeen-year-old's body and a halo of yellow hair. She said nothing, but Brenna knew that Clea was leaving home. Again.

Brenna was dreaming. She knew she was dreaming. In her memories—those fallible, presyndrome memories—Clea was all different ages and emotions and actions, but in Brenna's dreams, she was always seventeen and always leaving. "Don't tell Mom," Clea said. "I'll call in a few days—promise."

"No you won't," Brenna said. "You will get into a car with a man I can't see. You will lean into the passenger's side window and tell him you're ready. He will tell you that you look pretty and call you by a funny name. You will get in the car and the car will drive away and I will never hear your voice again."

Clea moved closer. She knelt down beside her, and put her face so close that it was all Brenna could see.

"Oh my God."

Clea's entire face was wrapped in thick bandages—her eyes and mouth completely hidden, her nose and cheekbones gauze-covered slopes. *How can she breathe like that?* Brenna reached out to take the bandages off, but Clea slapped her hand away. "Please, Clea," she said. "Please let me help you."

Brenna heard her sister's voice, vibrating beneath the bandages. "I don't need to breathe."

"What happened to you?"

"Don't you *know yet*, Brenna? Shit, man, it's been *twenty-eight years*."

The section of bandages that covered Clea's mouth began to tremble. Brenna wondered if she might crumble into bits. Were the bandages the only solid thing about Brenna's sister? Was Clea the Invisible Man?

"It's your fault," Clea hissed. "You should never have let me go with him. You heard his *voice*. You heard his *deep, devil voice*."

You look so pretty, Clee-bee . . .

"Stop," Brenna whispered.

"You heard that voice."

"No."

"You heard it and *you did nothing*!"

"No, please!"

An enormous butterfly wing pushed out of Clea's bandaged mouth and another emerged from her forehead, and Brenna screamed herself awake.

"Christ," she said, once her screaming had subsided and her breathing calmed and she found herself alone in her apartment, hoarse and slick with sweat.

Brenna got out of bed. She went into the kitchen and poured herself a glass of water and gulped it down quickly, listening to the traffic sounds on Thirteenth Street, the dream still rattling in her head. She hated being awake at this hour, hated being alone after a dream like that. She hated being alone, period.

She thought about turning on some music, but that might make it worse, this feeling of one A.M. in this stretched-out apartment, Brenna the only living thing in it and her bare feet hitting the wood floors too softly as she moved from one end to the other.

The three days a week Maya was here, Brenna could wake up in the middle of the night and go to her doorway. She'd hear her daughter's heavy sleep-breathing—that whistling little snore—and it would relax her back to bed.

She walked back to Maya's room. Not a good idea now, she knew. Not when there would be no little snore, only the memory of it. Maya was at her friend Larissa's, after all. Larissa, whose mother had left those two girls alone in the apartment on May 4, 2001—and quite frankly Brenna didn't give a rat's ass whether it was just to get her mail or whether it was for three minutes or five minutes or twenty-eight years. *You don't leave little girls alone.*

Maya's room was dark. No one here to wake, so Brenna flicked the light on, her gaze floating from the manga posters on the walls to the bookshelves, lined with old schoolbooks and adventure stories and graphic novels, the top shelf stacked with filled-up sketch pads—Maya the artist, just like her grandmother, but with Clea's huge blue eyes that burned right into you, appraising . . . Brenna glanced at the clean white comforter on the bed, the silent bed, everything exactly where her daughter had left it, including the framed photo on the nightstand, the one Brenna never looked at, the photo of Jim and his second wife, Faith.

The quiet started to roar in Brenna's ears, so she shut the light off. She walked back to the living room, to Trent's desk. Even in his absence, her assistant always seemed to be around. It was the cologne. His leather chair, with all those beads and lacy garters draped across the back, tended to trap the scent and hold it, so that even on those rare occasions he took a few vacation days in a row, Brenna couldn't walk by his desk without feeling a migraine coming on. She didn't mind it so much now though. Pathetic as it sounded, the cologne smell felt sort of like company.

She noticed a new babe, pictured at the center of Trent's bulletin board—a platinum blonde with huge pillowy lips and the type of body that would stand out anywhere, except for maybe an inflatable doll factory. She had to be a porn star, or perhaps a really high-end bachelor party stripper—some kind of professional at any rate, because in the picture a shirtless Trent (nipple rings gleaming) was clutching her chin and licking the side of her face as if it were a giant Creamsicle. Yet the blonde was smiling, her eyes half closed . . . almost seeming to enjoy it. Brenna shook her head. *That woman deserves an Academy Award.*

Okay, so maybe the cologne was getting to her a little. Brenna made for the linen closet in the hall. She kept a twenty-pack of Ivory Soap in there, and she grabbed one fast and unwrapped it. She held it up to her face, feeling as if she were on a foreign planet whose atmosphere was made of Trent's cologne, and the soap was her only chance of survival.

Oh, that's much better . . . Brenna closed her eyes and inhaled, and without warning, she was back in her car in front of the Neff house, Nick Morasco leaning into her open window . . .

"I'm telling you, because it helps to know what you're up against."

He leans in and closes her door, his hand brushing hers, and for a half second, it registers that Nick Morasco smells of Ivory Soap, and that every man should smell of Ivory Soap. The skin warms at Brenna's neck, down the length of her back. Her gaze flicks onto his shoulders, across the opening of the white cotton shirt, and she's thinking, While we're on the subject of up against . . .

"Cut it *out!*" Brenna spat out the words, dissipating the

memory though her skin still felt warmish from it . . . *Unbe-lievable*. That really had passed through her mind tonight, hadn't it? Brenna's memory wasn't capable of playing tricks on her, and so there was no question.

A tweed-wearing cop who thinks I'm something out of Oliver Sacks. How hard-up can I possibly be?

Brenna headed over to her own desk and switched on her computer. She picked up the pearl-handled letter opener she kept on her desk—the only thing of her father's she owned—and twirled it in her hands, waiting.

Brenna wanted to believe she was at her computer by happenstance. That she had no idea what had brought her into this chair, but as long as she was here and awake, well, maybe she'd get some work done: Look into Carol Wentz, check out some of her interests, that search engine she'd visited, Google her again . . . But Brenna did know why she was on her computer. She'd known that she would be on it as soon as she'd woken up from the dream. Brenna knew the reason as well as she knew her own self, and Carol Wentz had nothing to do with it.

She heard a group of drunken girls passing by her apartment, their laughter drifting up to her open window, one shouting, "Stop, I can't breathe!" which reminded her of the dream again, of those bandages pressing against Clea's face . . .

Brenna hated her computer for taking so long to boot up, hated herself for being so impatient. She clutched the letter opener. Put it down. Picked it up again . . . But finally, she was able to get online, to go to her e-mail, and do what she'd wanted to do so badly, ever since she'd woken up.

According to her instant messenger, Jim was online. Of course he was. Jim had always been a night owl. He used to stay up till two, three in the morning writing his articles for the *Trumpet*, and then wake up at seven for his job. Brenna had thought maybe he'd get to bed earlier now that he was an editor and didn't have articles due—especially since Faith was a morning show host who left for work at 6 A.M. But as it turned out, Jim still burned the midnight oil. Or so Brenna had learned.

She'd been instant messaging with her ex-husband, after his new wife went to sleep, nearly every night for the past ten months. Brenna didn't know if that was healthy or not, but to be honest she didn't care. Seeing Jim Rappaport in person brought on memories so vivid, she had to turn away from him, couldn't look him in the eye or hear the timbre of his voice for fear of reliving a fight, or worse yet something tender and wonderful and still real under her skin. It was always Faith who brought Maya to her apartment, Faith she spoke to on the phone, all at Brenna's request—and as a result, she'd gotten to missing Jim terribly.

But as words on a screen, Jim worked. They could be friends this way. They could talk, and talking with Jim soothed Brenna, the same way Maya's breathing soothed her. It was proof he was alive, and it was something more than that.

Don't you ever sleep???? she typed.

His response was immediate: **Takes one to know one**.

Yeah, well. I had a bad dream.

Tell me about it.

You had a bad dream, too?

No. E-mail is a pain in the ass—no inflection. I meant: Tell me about YOUR dream.

Brenna smiled. For the dozenth time, it occurred to her that if they'd forgotten about marriage counseling and tried IMing instead, she and Jim might still be together. That was a pipe dream of course. Jim was better off with Faith, and Brenna was better off with Lee the GPS.

He wrote: **You there? Instant messenger says you stopped typing.**

Yeah, just a sec.

She wrote out the dream and sent it. After about thirty seconds, Jim started to type.

The words appeared: **Could mean a new beginning.**

Huh?

The butterfly. Out of the cocoon. You know? A new life where Clea is concerned.

Possible, I guess, she typed. **But I didn't feel that way. How did you feel?**

Brenna thought for a long time. Finally, she tried: **Suffocated. Scared. Confused.** Like most people who had been through a lot of analysis, Brenna knew all about dreams. The subconscious, as it turned out, was a terrible punster. For instance, the night after Brenna signed her first big-paying client—a Wall Street trader who wanted to track down his slacker younger brother—she'd dreamed that Mr. Howell from *Gilligan's Island* was chasing her around a haunted house.

When she'd told her then-shrink Sheila Shiner about it, Sheila had said, matter-of-factly, "Mr. Howell in a haunted house. You're afraid of wealth."

It was the same thing with this dream of Clea. Somewhere in that surreal scene lurked a bad pun, waiting to be groaned at. *A missing woman in bandages, wrapped up in bandages . . .*

Brenna recalled Nelson Wentz last night, sitting in his office with his face in his hands. *"I was so wrapped up in my own life,"* he says, his voice muffled by thick palms. *"I was so wrapped up I didn't pay enough attention." The room smells of Purell, and Brenna thinks,* Wrapped up in what? This? *She is not watching Nelson, though. She's looking at the computer screen, at Carol Wentz's search history. She is staring at the name of the search engine Carol had visited twelve times in the past week, but had never used for a search. The name of the search engine is Chrysalis.org.*

Butterfly wings. Brenna had been dreaming about the Chrysalis search engine.

Jim's words appeared on-screen: **Do you have a new client? Could the confusion have something to do with work?**

Brenna smiled. **How is it in my head? Comfortable in there? Can I get you a drink?**

Great minds . . .

Brenna typed: **Any reason why you would visit a search engine if you weren't going to search for anything?**

Your missing person visited Chrysalis?

Yep. How'd you guess?

If she'd visited Yahoo, you'd have dreamed of cowboys.

Brenna had checked out Chrysalis.org on Nelson's computer, and again on her own computer as soon as she'd gotten home, and she'd used it herself once. June 7, 2002. Google had been down for a few hours that day.

Really, she hadn't seen anything special about it—a simple homepage that consisted mainly of the search box and a swirly logo that was a little too unicorns-walk-among-us for Brenna's taste, but nothing to think about for more than a few seconds. To the left of the page, there had been a list of other services, all with "Chrys" as a prefix—ChrysNews, ChrysWeather, ChrysMovies . . .

Brenna went to Chrysalis, stared at the screen. It looked exactly the way she'd remembered it—of course it did. She told Jim, **I'm looking at it now. I still don't get it**.

Jim typed: **Go to the other services, and click on the bottom icon.**

It was simply a plus sign—Brenna hadn't even noticed it before—and when she clicked on it, ChrysBlogs, ChrysForSingles, and ChrysChats popped up. Brenna typed: **Interesting . . .**

Your missing person single?

No, but the chats look promising. Carol Wentz was a woman of many hobbies, that was for sure . . . Between the French cooking and the charity work and the book club and that damn closet full of crafts, it was no wonder she never had the time of day to give her husband. Sure enough, there was a chat room on Chrysalis for practically every hobby imaginable—all mixed together with chats for women going through menopause, single-parent families, infertile couples, and even victims of violent crime, all under the insanely inclusive heading of "Living."

Jim typed: **You're welcome.**

Sorry—Thanks! Just wading through about a million ChrysChats. Brenna paused a moment, then typed the words and sent them. **I'm really glad you're out there.** *Was that too much?*

As well you should be.

Brenna grinned. *Jim.* **So what should I try first? The French cooking chat?**

Two words: Boudin noir.

In an instant, Brenna was deep inside May 30, 1994, in a Paris bistro called La Muguet, some horrifying French version of the Beatles' greatest hits playing over the speaker system. *Brenna and Jim are four days into their honeymoon, and it's 9:15 P.M. Some French guy with one of those voices that sounds like he's crying all the time is belting out "Yellow Submarine" at far too loud a volume, but it doesn't matter because they're on their second bottle of chateau neuf du pape, and Brenna is savoring a bite of a crispy-skinned chicken that may be the most perfect thing she's ever tasted, trying to make it last forever. Meanwhile, Jim—who thinks it's exciting and spontaneous to order random items he's never heard of—is biting into a large cylindri-*

cal object the color of eggplant. He calls the waiter over.
"Qu'est ce que c'est?"

"Boudin noir, monsieur," the waiter says. "It is sausage,
made from the blood of pigs." A look crosses Jim's face—
much like Charlton Heston at the end of Soylent Green.
Brenna bursts out laughing.

Jim asked: **You remember?**

Brenna was laughing now, much as she'd laughed then,
her eyes blurring from tears, her head thrown back. She
caught her breath and wrote: **What do you think?!**

Jim replied fast: **I'd type you one of those smiley face
things, but you hate those smiley face things.**

Brenna double-clicked on the French cooking chat, but
when it asked her for a screen name and password, she wasn't
sure what she should call herself: *BoudinBetty? CrepeSu-*
zette? She typed at Jim: **Ever go into a hobby chat room?**

Uh, no. Wait—does bondage count as a hobby?

Good one. Want to join me?

In a French cooking chat room? Are you serious?

Brenna sighed. She supposed she could call herself something simple—NYCFoodie sounded okay. But what was she
supposed to do when she was in there? *Hey, sorry to bug*
you guys, but did you happen to see a woman named Carol
in here? About fifty, dirty blonde hair, beautiful kitchen?

Jim typed: **So anyway, I'm sorry.**

Sorry about what?

Why would these people talk to me about Carol, if they
don't even know me? Brenna started looking at the chat
room titles on either side of French cooking, as Jim put together his response.

Maya.

Brenna exhaled. *The sleepover.*

Jim typed, **She didn't ask me. She asked Faith. By the**

time I knew about it, she was all packed and Larissa's mother was at the door.

Brenna started to type a response, but she stopped when she noticed a series of chats titled "Families of the Missing." They were arranged regionally, and the sixth down was titled "Families of the Missing, New York State." Brenna stared at the name, her mind hurtling her back six hours and into Annette Shelby's hotel room.

"Oh, did you ever hear from Lydia?"

"Who?"

"Friend I made on this New York State Families of the Missing chat room . . ."

"Lydia," Brenna whispered.

Jim typed, **You still there?**

One sec.

Okay.

She grabbed her cell phone and texted Annette: *Not urgent, nothing to do with Larry. But if you are awake, please call.*

Brenna's landline rang seconds later. "'Sup?" said Annette, somehow managing to slur a three-letter contraction. Brenna wondered how many times the St. Regis staff had refilled the minibar tonight.

"Your friend from the Families of the Missing chat—Lydia, right?"

"Yeah?"

"Did she ever mention where she lives?"

"Hmmm . . . Westchester County, somewhere. Either Bronxville or . . . Oh, wait. It was Tarry Ridge."

"You're sure?"

"Her screen name is LydiaTR, and that's what it stands for. Lydia Tarry Ridge."

Brenna swallowed hard, thinking of Carol's wallet in the Neff living room, Brenna's phone number inside. "Did she finally call you?" Annette was saying. "I'm telling you she really sounded . . . I don't know . . . I was surprised she didn't call."

"Did she say anything else?"

"Like . . ."

"Did she mention feeling guilty or unfulfilled?"

"Uh . . . no."

"How about another man?"

"Nope. But more power to her if she's got one," Annette said. "Tell you the truth, I can't remember a fucking thing LydiaTR said, other than asking me if you were any good."

"When was the last time you were on?"

"Over a week ago. Ever since I found out that Larry's got a revolving door on his pants . . . Let's say I haven't been in a very *chatty* mood."

"Understandable."

"It's too bad, though," Annette said. "I really liked those people, and it was nice, being part of a group I could trust."

"A group you could trust . . ."

"I was totally honest with them—other than my name. And they were honest with me."

"Of course they were."

"Listen, Brenna. I hate to look a gift horse in the mouth, but I'm kinda changing my mind on that whole 'It's better to know' thing. I mean . . . why the hell did you have to be *so good* at finding Larry?"

Brenna could see Jim starting to type again. She fired off, **Still here—on phone**, an idea working its way through her mind.

"Brenna? Are you like, *texting*, while you're on the phone with me?"

"I'm sorry, Annette. I was just . . . taking care of some paperwork."

You're on the phone? At 2 A.M.?

Client.

"You're divorced, right, Brenna?"

"Yeah."

Jim typed: **Maya loves you, by the way.**

Brenna closed her eyes for a moment. Took a breath. She started to type, then stopped. Her throat was tight.

I know what you're going to type, B, and you're wrong. You do deserve that love. You deserve it more than you know.

"Are you still in touch with your ex?" Annette asked.

"Yes," Brenna said softly. "I'm in touch with him."

Thank you, J. Her eyes were welling up.

Stop crying, Jim typed.

Stop knowing me so well.

"I'll bet your ex has just one identity, too, right?" Annette sighed heavily. "Some girls have all the luck."

Brenna ran the back of her hand across her face, swiped the tears away. "Yeah," she said. "I'm pretty lucky." *We don't confide in strangers. We confide in the people who know us best. We tell them the truth.* "Listen, Annette. Can I ask you a favor?"

"Sure."

"Just for tonight, could I borrow AlbanyMarie?"

9

Oh Carol, Carol, Carol . . . Brenna woke up at 8 A.M., after five fitful hours of sleep, the name running through her head like a cheesy pop song. With the help of Annette's password (Larry4Ever, the poor thing . . .), Brenna had logged on as AlbanyMarie, and spent more than an hour in the Families of the Missing chat room, learning everything there was to know about LydiaTR—who was Carol Wentz, no question. *Carol, Carol . . . what you've been up to.*

As with nearly every other missing person Brenna had ever found, it was Carol's interests that had given her away. LIMatt61 had asked AlbanyMarie if she'd ever used the cassoulet recipe that LydiaTR had given her, while, on LydiaTR's recommendation, BuffaloSue had begun *Safekeeping*—the same book Brenna remembered seeing on the Wentzes' coffee table. WhitePlainsGreta22 had even mentioned Lydia's "marital problems" with her "noncommunicative" husband—and how DH had no idea Lydia knew how to use a computer. (That's what chat room and message board people always called their spouses—DH or DW for darling husband or wife, no matter how undarling they actually were. In fact, Brenna had first come across the abbreviation while working a case four years ago, skimming a message board for battered women.)

Though they all seemed thrilled—if a little surprised—

to see AlbanyMarie in the room after *her* missing DH had been found, the chat room members were also worried over LydiaTR—and eager to talk about her, even though talking seemed to stoke that worry. Lydia had been offline for a week, after all, which wasn't like her, not even a little . . .

Until finally, just as the digital clock over Brenna's computer had shifted to 2:49, Brenna thinking, *LydiaTR is Carol. I get that—but where did they both go?* someone with the screen name ClaudetteBrooklyn20 had logged on, lurked in the margins for ten minutes before dropping this shocker:

ClaudetteBrooklyn20: LydiaTR found her daughter.
AlbanyMarie: What, Claudette???
ClaudetteBrooklyn20: You weren't around, Marie.
        About a week ago. Late night. Lydia said her
        daughter called.
LIMatt61: I was there. Seemed like a prank to me.
ClaudetteBrooklyn20: She said she knew in her
        heart. And the girl sounded like a teenager.
SyracuseSue: She would be a teenager now, right?
        Wasn't she six when she went missing?
AlbanyMarie: You think that's where L is? With her
        daughter?
ClaudetteBrooklyn20: We can hope.
SyracuseSue: That would be so wonderful if true. I
        pray for Lydia's daughter every night. My mom's
        name was Iris, too.

The conversation had gone on like this, with LIMatt61 and WappFallsGordon joining, typing that they too hoped that the call Lydia had received really was from her long-lost child—but admitting to some cynicism about it. (*Teenagers make prank calls,* LIMatt61 had pointed out again. *Could have been an extortionist,* Gordon had chimed in.)

All the while, Brenna was staring at her screen with her teeth clenched, thinking, *You people don't know the half of it.* Why would Carol say that Iris had called Lydia? Why would she claim to *be* Lydia in the first place?

At three-ten, Brenna had tried, *You guys remember Lydia's daughter's case, right? Iris Neff? It was in the news.* In return, she'd gotten the chat room equivalent of blank stares: Silence for a solid three minutes, followed by SyracuseSue's *Marie, how is everything with your DH? Has he settled in okay?* Not a surprise. Of course they didn't remember the disappearance of Lydia's daughter—the disappearance of the *real* Lydia's daughter. Iris Neff had gone missing back when 24-hour news was just starting out, when Nancy Grace was still best known for her O.J. Simpson coverage, and missing kids were the domain of milk cartons—when there was a natural news cycle, headlines waxing and waning and retreating for good in two weeks, a month tops . . . especially when there was never a body, never a resolution. Eleven years on, no one remembered Iris Neff. No one except the girl's loved ones. And Brenna. And, apparently, Carol . . . *Why Carol?*

Brenna threw on a pair of jeans and a black long-sleeved T-shirt. She usually blew out her hair for work, but she was running so late today, she just combed in some conditioner and let it fall into curls. On cue, Brenna heard footsteps moving up the stairs to her front door. She knew it was Trent. After six years of his climbing those stairs five days a week, she recognized his footfalls—a fact that disturbed her, but a fact nonetheless. As Trent put his key in the door, calling "Yo!" into the crack once he opened it, just as he always did, it occurred to Brenna that his tenure as her assistant had lasted twice as long as her marriage. *Speaking of disturbing facts . . .*

Brenna picked up her desk phone and started to call Nelson. But then she thought better of it, recalled the morning of October 16, 1998, again and tapped in the number for the Tarry Ridge Police Department. One of the upsides to Brenna's condition was that she had no use for address books or speed dial. All she had to do was use someone's number once, and the memory of it was hers forever.

"Yo, yo, yo," Trent said, once he was in the room.

"A three-yo day, huh?" Brenna said.

"Triple your pleasure." Trent was wearing skinny jeans with an airy mesh tank top the color of peach yogurt, the nipple rings glittering through the holes. According to the thermometer on the kitchen windowsill, it was sixty-two degrees outside—far too cold for a getup like that—but then again it had to drop to at least forty before Trent would even touch a shirt that had sleeves on it. As the police department phone started to ring in her ear, Brenna asked her assistant, "So how was Bedd?"

Trent cocked an eyebrow.

"I walked right into that one, didn't I?"

"Way too easy, even for me."

Brenna heard the desk sergeant's voice on the other end of the line and held up a finger. "Detective Morasco, please. This is Brenna Spector."

Trent's eyes went big. "You're calling the military?"

Brenna nodded. "You'll see."

"What will I see?" said the voice on the phone, Morasco's voice.

She clenched her fists, flattening the bud of a memory. "Hi there."

"How's life in the world of Wentz?"

"Interesting," Brenna said.

"How so?"

"When you were working on the Iris Neff case, did you ever have reason to question Carol Wentz?"

"No." The smile dropped out of his voice. "Why do you ask?"

Brenna took a breath. "Carol has been impersonating

Lydia Neff in a chat room." Brenna looked directly at Trent as
she said it, watched his eyes widen even more. "It's the Families of the Missing, New York State room at Chrysalis.org."

"Do you know how long?"

Again, she said it to Trent. "I have no idea how long, or
what e-mail address she used to register with the site. Up
until a couple of days ago, her own husband thought she was
computer illiterate."

Trent mouthed, *I'm on it*, and made for his desktop.

"When was the last time she chatted?" Morasco said.

"Before she disappeared. The other people in the chat
room say she hasn't been on for a week," Brenna said. "Oh,
and you might find this interesting. Apparently, she was telling them that Iris had called her."

Quiet.

Brenna said, "Are you still there?"

"Yeah," he said. "Yeah, I am . . ."

"Any idea why she might be doing this?"

Morasco exhaled. "I don't know if I should tell you this,"
he said. "Because to be honest, I don't know what it has to
do with Mrs. Wentz's disappearance, or why she'd say Iris
had called."

"Irrelevant doesn't bother me. In fact, I'm a fan of it."

"Okay," Morasco said. "During the Iris Neff case, we
never questioned Carol Wentz."

"Yeah. You told me that."

"But we did question Nelson Wentz."

Brenna stared at the phone. "What?! *Why?*"

She heard a click. Morasco said, "I'm getting another
call. Hold on a second." And before Brenna could come up
with a question more articulate than *Why*, before Brenna
could even completely exhale, in fact, Morasco was back on
the line, his voice pulled tight enough to snap. "Brenna," he
said. "Carol Wentz has been found."

10

The clock struck 8 A.M. Nelson knew he wasn't going anywhere, so he called the voice mail of his supervisor, Kyle, and faked the stomach flu.

He thought about making himself breakfast, but he wasn't hungry. He walked downstairs anyway, though, his feet dragging the rest of his hollow shell body into the living room, to the phone lying on the coffee table—which was where he'd left it after receiving that strange call from the girl. *It's my fault*, she had said. Probably a prank. But such an odd and telling prank considering what was going on in Nelson's life. Such a strange choice of words—the girl might as well have been reading Nelson's mind. *It's my fault. My fault Carol is gone. My fault she was so unhappy, my fault she's never coming back, my fault . . .*

The trunk full of quilting supplies lay where he'd left it, too, bracing the open crafts closet door, half emptied, its contents strewn on the floor around it. This wasn't like Nelson at all. He liked everything in its place—in fact, it disturbed him deeply when it wasn't. He started to put Carol's things back in—the scraps of cloth and the thick spools of colorful thread—the squares she'd made (one bore a cheery daisy, another a red and green Christmas present), then the scissors and the pink and purple and yellow and red and pale blue bolts of ribbon.

As he replaced a tomato-shaped pincushion, though, his hand went very deep into the box and he touched cardboard. A layer of it, about six inches up from the bottom of the box. Nelson's hand flew out. *False bottom.*

He stared at the box, breathing in and out, and then his hands were back inside, acting on their own, yanking out all the fabric and thread and those charming little squares and satin ribbons and the strawberry-handled scissors and velvet pincushions, throwing it all to the floor. All of it props, all soft and colorful lies covering a false bottom. He slipped that out of the box, too, this piece of cardboard his wife had cut so carefully. *Cut it to fit, didn't you, Carol?* And then he stayed there on his knees, doubled over like an exhausted runner, panting deep into his chest.

Look inside. Look now. See what she's been hiding from you.

Nelson peered into the bottom of the box. He saw a stack of manila folders. The one on top had a Post-it on the front, a man's name and number written in Carol's careful hand. *Graeme Klavel.* Nelson's heart dropped. His hands trembled a little as he lifted the folder out.

But then the doorbell rang and his shoulders shot up and he dropped it to the floor, some of its contents spilling. Nelson glanced down thinking, *Love letters?* But no, the papers looked official, and as the doorbell rang again, he saw the stamp: *Tarry Ridge Police Department.* He saw the date, September 15, 1998, and then he saw the heading, "Interview Transcript: Lydia Neff." He stared at it, frozen.

Again, the doorbell. "Just a minute!"

Lydia Neff

He opened the door on a child. It took him a few seconds before he identified the child as Max, the eleven-year-old son of Gayle and Stephen Chandler, who lived a few doors up from them. The son of Gayle, Carol's book club friend. Gayle, who had told Detective Morasco she had seen Carol with a man in a Mount Temple diner.

"Is Carol around?" asked Max, a towheaded boy with the type of hard eyes that made it seem as if he was always challenging you. Max Chandler looked a lot like his mother, Nelson realized. And his mother had never liked Nelson much. Stephen was okay—a financial consultant who worked out of the home, always good with the stock tips and a genial smile, but Gayle . . . Gayle. Seeing Carol with another man must have made her so happy, though it was interesting she hadn't told her son about Carol's disappearance. Maybe she had. Maybe she'd sent Max over here to find out how Nelson was taking the whole thing—or maybe to goad him into anger so she could tell the police that, too? *Well, then.* Calling Carol by her first name—if goading Nelson was Max's goal, well, then, that had been a good start.

"Mrs. Wentz is not home," Nelson said. "Is there anything I can help you with?"

The boy looked him in the eye. Strange how deeply it affected Nelson, that look. At this child's age he could never meet the gaze of an adult without cringing, especially an adult man. Nelson couldn't help but feel his hackles rising, his anger growing toward Max Chandler—all four-foot-six of him—for being so confident as to look him in the eye like that, to stare at him with his mother's eyes, Gayle Chandler's eyes, as if he could read Nelson's thoughts and he didn't like what he was reading . . .

Lydia, Carol? You've been looking into Lydia? My God, it was more than ten years ago, and even then, it was nothing! I told you it was nothing. Didn't I tell you it was nothing? Didn't you believe me?

Max said, "I'm here to pick up your recycling."

"Right," Nelson breathed. "Friday. Right." One of Carol's many neighborhood projects was organizing a recycling drive, along with Gayle, for the sixth grade class at the local elementary school. Every Friday morning before their classes began, Max and his classmates would show up at each participating house, collect plastic bottles and cans, and redeem them at the Stop & Shop on Main, all proceeds going directly to the PTA's playground improvement fund. Nelson and Carol, of course, were childless and therefore had no reason to be involved with the PTA. But Gayle had asked Carol to help, and as with everything else her friends had asked of her, Carol had dived in one hundred and ten percent.

It just went to show how much care Carol put into her projects—whether it was the school recycling drive or her book club meetings or the knitted afghans she made for the old folks home . . . or whatever it was she'd been doing with this Klavel, this *research* she'd been conducting on Lydia Neff . . .

Max Chandler was still glaring up at Nelson. "So . . . uh . . . bottles and cans?"

Nelson realized he hadn't taken the recycling out all week. "I'll go get it out of the kitchen," he said. The boy started to follow him, but Nelson didn't want the boy following him, didn't want that ice-gaze on him for one single minute longer. "There's more bottles in the garage in the blue plastic crate. Why don't you go out there, and I'll meet you." The garage door opener hung from the line of key hooks next to the front door. Nelson plucked it off and pressed it into Max's hand in one quick movement. "Go," he said. He shut the door behind him.

Nelson sighed heavily. He headed in the direction of the kitchen, but again he was sidetracked by the file on the living room floor, and when he looked into the open trunk, he saw more files—a stack of them. He quickly pulled another one out. Inside this file was a collection of yellowed newspaper articles, all about Lydia's daughter's disappearance. Another held a series of posed family photographs—Lydia, smiling next to a man Nelson had never seen, the two of them holding a black-haired baby who must have been Iris. *What have you been doing, Carol?*

Nelson put the papers back into the folders, placed them back into the trunk. He stacked the quilting supplies on top of the folders and closed the trunk and put it back into the closet. He loaded the closet with the rest of Carol's crafts and closed the door. *There.*

Nelson needed to be practical. He couldn't think about all of this now. Later, he would call Ms. Spector. Forget the police; they didn't care. He would call Ms. Spector and he would tell her about Carol's apparent interest in Lydia—that was the phrase he would use, "*apparent* interest"—and he would ask her advice. He would tell her about these papers, and if she wanted to see them, he would show her. If it could help her find Carol, he would show her the papers. But for now, Nelson had to calm down and collect the recycling so he could send Max Chandler on his way.

Nelson hurried into the kitchen, and grabbed a small garbage bag full of plastic bottles and cans. *Take it, Max. Take it and go.*

From Nelson's doorstep, he could see that the garage door was open. He caught a glimpse of Carol's rear bumper, and a pang went through him, an extra shot of hurt. "Max?"

There was no answer. Seconds later, he felt plastic crunching under his foot, and the garage door started to close, then sprang back up. He picked the garage door opener off the ground. *Careless.* He started to get angry again. Out of the corner of his eye, he saw a small figure running down the center of the road, running fast, as if for his life. "Max?" *Where the heck is he going?* "Max!"

As Nelson neared the garage, he noticed a smell. *Dead mouse*, he thought. No, worse. Dead cat, maybe, trapped in the garage, which had been shut all week long . . . His anger lifted a little. No wonder the kid dropped the opener. No wonder he was running away.

He threw an arm in front of his face, breathed into the crook of his elbow, the bag of recyclables clasped in his other hand. He could empty out the bottles and cans. Put the dead animal in the bag. Throw it in the heavy trash can, get it out of here quick. Had he missed garbage pickup?

As Nelson neared the garage, he saw what looked like a moving black stain at the back of Carol's white Volvo. Closer, the stain revealed itself as flies. Maybe a hundred of them, crawling around the lock, over the car's logo, edging their way down to the license plate and back . . .

Maybe the dead cat was under the car. Holding his breath, Nelson crouched down and peered beneath the carriage. Nothing. He circled around to the front, peeking into the windows—nothing there, either. He checked the metal shelves that lined the sides of the garage—but the smell didn't seem to be coming from any of the cardboard boxes stacked on the bottom shelf, and the top ones were bare, save for Nelson's metal tool chests, with the largest tools—Nelson's Hoyt hammer, his biggest Phillips-head screwdriver, power drill, hedge clippers—hanging cleanly from hooks above them with one missing. Had he used the flat-head screwdriver recently?

The smell was definitely coming from the car. The flies were nowhere else except . . .

Nelson went back to Carol's car, reached through the open driver's side window, and used the button to pop open the trunk. The hum of flies grew louder.

He clutched the garbage bag, following the sound, the other hand over his mouth. *Just hold your breath and ignore the flies and get that animal into the bag as quickly as . . .*

How would an animal get into the closed trunk of a car?

The thought seeped through him at the same time as he reached the trunk and lifted it and stared inside. For a few suspended seconds, he just gaped at it without knowing. That ruined thing, oozing bugs. What was it? *It can't be, it can't be, it just can't . . .*

And then he saw the small white hand, fingers curved as if it were holding a wineglass.

Nelson heard sirens blaring down the length of the street, and cars screeching to a stop behind him. His face went numb and his ears throbbed, and he stared at that white hand and he knew. He knew why Max had run home to his mother and he knew why she had called the police, just as he'd known from the start that it was no cat, it was no dead animal, the smell was too strong for that. The way his shoulders had tensed, the way his skin had gone cold. Something inside him had known.

He was breathing in the smell and feeling that death hum—though he couldn't feel or breathe, not really. *Not at all.* Nelson's gaze stayed locked on the hand—on the plain gold wedding band, just like his own. And what little was left of Nelson's heart exploded to dust.

11

Nelson Wentz lay in the hospital bed, staring with stunned, glassy eyes, IV hooked up to an arm so frail and white it looked like it belonged to someone either much younger than him or much older than him, Morasco couldn't decide which.

Morasco hated questioning Wentz in the hospital. He felt physically at an unfair advantage and emotionally at a disadvantage—moreover, it was unnecessary. Wentz had suffered what the doctors here at Tarry Ridge General called a vasovagal syncope after finding his wife's body in the trunk of her car. Meaning he fainted. Meaning there was no reason why he couldn't be questioned later, at the station. He'd experienced a bad reaction to the sedatives the doctors had given him—hence the IVs and observation—but otherwise he was fine. Fit, even. They'd be releasing him before dinnertime.

Of course, when Morasco had tried explaining all this, the chief hadn't come close to agreeing with him. "The guy's wife has been moldering in the garage for a week, and if it weren't for that Chandler kid, she'd still be there," Chief Hutchins had said. "You want to invite Wentz out to brunch? Question him over banana pancakes?"

("Moldering," Morasco had replied. "Good word.")

So here he was, in Wentz's hospital room alongside Gil Pomroy—a red-faced, ticking bomb of a heart attack risk who took the role of "bad cop" way too seriously for anybody's good. There was no such thing as partners among Tarry Ridge detectives; too few of them for that. But Morasco got paired with Pomroy more often than anyone. Chief Hutchins's sense of humor, he supposed.

Pomroy hadn't said a word since entering the hospital room, but Morasco could tell he had a raging boner for Wentz. Driving over, he'd said, "You know how easy it is to fake a fainting spell?" So he knew what side the guy was on, as if there had ever been any question.

"How are you feeling, Mr. Wentz?" Morasco asked.

"Terrible."

Pomroy snorted.

"Thanks for letting us in to see you," Morasco said. "I know you've been through a lot. I'd like you to meet Detective Gil Pomroy. We're working together on Mrs. Wentz's case."

Morasco turned and glared at Pomroy until finally, he untensed his neck enough to nod.

"If you can find out who . . . who did that to my wife, I'll . . ." Wentz swallowed hard. "Anything I can do . . . to help."

Morasco took a breath. It was hard to look at Wentz in the hospital bed without thinking of his own father. Not that Nelson Wentz looked anything like Morasco's strapping, six-foot-one-inch dad. But he had been around the same age Wentz was now—felled by a sudden brain aneurysm—and Morasco had come home from college, camped out in his father's hospital room for weeks. Sitting next to the bed, holding the big hand as dry and cool as reptile skin, watching the barrel chest move up and down at the whim of the ventilator, begging under his breath, "Don't go, please don't go . . ." Begging and bargaining. His father never regained consciousness. That had been the last time Morasco had been in a hospital room for personal reasons—unless you counted Holly giving birth, and he never counted that. Not ever. He asked, "In the weeks before she disappeared, did your wife seem to be acting differently at all?"

"No."

"I know you told me she was using your computer. Did you find any strange e-mails she received?"

"No. As far as I know, she'd only used it to search for information on the woman I wound up hiring as my own investigator."

"Brenna Spector?"

"Yes. I don't think my wife had her own e-mail address."

"Do you have any idea why she'd want to hire an investigator?"

"No."

Pomroy said, "Are you sure?"

"Yes."

Morasco inhaled, let it out slowly. "Mr. Wentz," he said. "Was your wife ever aware that you were questioned in the Iris Neff case?"

"What? I was never questioned."

"You were. Maybe you don't remember, but I questioned you myself."

Whatever color remained in Wentz's face escaped fast.

"Lydia Neff," Pomroy said. "Good-looking woman. Well, back then anyway."

Morasco shot him a look. "Do you remember, Mr. Wentz?"

"You . . . you visited me at home," he said. "You never even came inside. We spoke for just a few minutes."

"That's what I'm talking about."

"You promised to be discreet. You promised not to tell anyone."

Pomroy let out a deep sigh with a little music in it, a mocking sigh. Morasco could sense the big lug nut flexing, mining his brain for the words with the most burn. Not for the first time, he wished he had the power to will Pomroy's mouth permanently shut.

"Mr. Wentz?" Morasco asked.

"Carol never knew about our conversation."

Pomroy said, "Did she know about anything else?"

Morasco's jaw tightened.

Wentz was sitting up in bed now, his eyes burning. "What do you mean?"

"Did Carol know about the affair you had with Lydia Neff?"

Wentz opened his mouth and closed it again, making a clicking sound.

"Did she?"

"Please," he said. "I don't . . . I don't feel well."

"Is 'affair' the wrong word, Nelson? How about 'youthful indiscretion'? Look, I know it was ten years ago, but women are funny about that stuff. They find out about it, even after all that time, and it's like it just happened."

"This is not helping," Morasco said, between his teeth. But Pomroy kept it up, as if someone were slowly turning up his volume.

"We know *women*, right, Nelson? They start *investigating*, they start *talking to people*. It's embarrassing and a *real pain in the ass*, isn't it? *Especially since you two didn't have the greatest marriage to begin with!*"

"I need the nurse . . . *Nurse!*"

The door opened fast—a short, silver-haired woman in a smock with pastel clouds all over it, asking, "Is everything all right?"

"We were just leaving," Morasco said.

He started out the door, but Pomroy wasn't moving. He stood a foot away from Wentz's bed, gaping at him. A human exclamation point. What information did he think Wentz would give him now? "I guess you're not gonna tell us where you put the . . . What was it that killed your wife? An ice pick? Maybe a spear gun?"

Oh Jesus Christ.

"Do you hunt, Nelson?"

Wentz's eyes were wide and wet. He was panting like an animal in a trap, the breath rushing in and out of his slack white mouth in pained little gasps.

"You both need to leave," the nurse said. And then, finally, Pomroy moved, Morasco following him out with his whole body tensed, frustration seeping through him and radiating out of his skin, his eyes . . . *Why all these posers in Tarry Ridge, these Dirty Harry wannabes with their suburban houses and their squeaky clean cars who wouldn't know how to question a human being if you took away their toys and put them in the South Bronx for a week, and man would I ever love to see that happen, would I ever love to make that happen to this tool right now . . .*

Nelson Wentz muttered two words under his breath.

Morasco turned around. "What did you say?"

"Nothing."

Once they were out the door, though, Morasco thought about it again, what Wentz had said believing no one was listening. He debated telling Pomroy about it, then the chief. But he wasn't sure he'd heard correctly. He only wanted to tell someone he thought he could trust, and there was no one on the Tarry Ridge force like that. In fact, there were few people like that anywhere. Morasco racked his brain for the name of a trustworthy person, someone he felt as if he could safely speak his mind to, but he couldn't come up with one. Not until he got to the waiting room and saw her there.

Brenna sat in the waiting room at Tarry Ridge General, staring at a six-month-old copy of *Vogue*—the Spring Fashion Issue, Cate Blanchett on the cover. A memory trickled into her brain—standing in line at the Rite Aid on University and Twelfth on March 14 at noon with a two-pack of Yodels and a large Red Bull, flipping through this exact issue, the woman in front of her complaining she's been charged fifty cents too much for the family-sized Garnier Nutrisse—but the memory didn't stay long.

"We'll be releasing him in just about fifteen minutes," a voice said, and Brenna looked up from the magazine to see a nurse—a chubby young thing with a sweet face and pink apple cheeks that matched her smock. "He asked if you could drive him home. That okay?"

"Sure." It was hard to say anything else to such a cherubic girl, though Brenna cringed a little as she said it, the memory of Nelson's home scrolling through her head—overrun with police and press and jostling murder fans. She'd been there five hours ago, when they'd towed Carol's car to the county's crime lab garage, medical examiner's van following close behind, the murder fans snapping pictures with their cell phones, gasping as if Carol Wentz's car were some visiting dignitary, waxing on about fiber and tissue evidence, so eager to display every nugget of forensic knowledge obtained from their vast libraries of *CSI* box sets . . . Brenna hoped that scene had dissipated since then because it had been hard to take, even for her.

Brenna put the magazine down. When she'd come to the hospital, she hadn't even expected Nelson would want to see her—what could she do for him now? Yet after he regained consciousness, she was the one person he'd asked for, and now he wanted her to drive him home. *He really has no one.*

The waiting room door pushed open. A man stomped past—red-faced, bug-eyed, gut straining against a cheap brown suit. It was as if everything within him were trying to ram its way out the front. Brenna had never seen a more obvious cop, and she knew he'd been in there talking to Nelson. *This is what it takes for him to get their attention*, Brenna thought, and then Morasco came through the door like a response. When he saw Brenna, his pace slowed a little and his eyes locked with hers and sharpened to points. "Call me," he said as he passed, so quiet only she could hear.

12

"I didn't kill my wife," Nelson said.

Brenna, who had just started up her car, put it back in park. "Did the police accuse you?"

"Please, Ms. Spector," he said. "I don't want to talk about it."

Brenna started up the car again. Morasco's face flashed into her mind, the sharpness in the eyes, the urgency—but then she put it away. Whatever he had to tell her could wait. Otherwise he'd have pulled her aside and said it right there.

Brenna would take Nelson home, pick Maya up at choir practice, and then she would call Morasco, from the normalcy of her own home. For now, though, she needed to focus on Nelson Wentz, whose home had no normalcy, not anymore. "You'll see your place looks a little different," she told him. "The garage is taped off—still considered a crime scene, but the house is all yours again."

"Again?"

"Yes."

"They went through my house?" Nelson's eyes were wide, his face even paler than usual.

"Looking for signs of a break-in—blood maybe," Brenna said. "They wouldn't talk to me much, but it seemed what

they were doing was pretty cursory. What happened to Carol
. . . That was most likely over a week ago, they said."

"Did they . . . did they take anything?"

Before pulling out of the hospital parking lot, Brenna
gave Nelson a long, careful look. Then she turned her eyes
back to the windshield and pulled out onto the dark, peaceful street. "What don't you want them to find?"

Nelson said nothing, but he didn't have to. At 12:30
P.M., Brenna had noticed Theresa Koppelson, weaving her
way through the cluster of neighbors. Theresa's hair was
shorter, with chunky highlights, there were a few more lines
around the dark eyes, and she'd gained the smallest amount
of weight, all over her body, as if someone had stuck Theresa with a bicycle pump and given it maybe three or four
squeezes. Immediately, Brenna had flashed on Theresa ten
years ago, tired and drawn, in the driveway of her colonial
home. Theresa, as expected, hadn't remembered Brenna at
all.

Assuming Brenna was a reporter, Theresa had answered
questions about Carol's giving nature and her involvement
in local charities, until Brenna had finally asked her if
Carol had any reason to be interested in the Iris Neff case.
Theresa had looked at her directly, that flash of shame long
gone from her eyes.

"The Iris Neff case?"

"Yes."

"That was a long time ago."

*"Someone told me that Carol's husband had been ques-
tioned during that case. Do you have any idea why?"*

"Well . . ."

"Yes?"

*"Around town, it was common knowledge, but you
should probably keep this off the record."*

"Of course."

"Honestly, I don't know why Carol stayed with him. It's not like they had kids to worry about."

"Turn left on Bahhhhnaby Lane," drawled Lee, the GPS.

"You know something funny?" Brenna asked Nelson. "I really don't need a GPS. The way my mind works, if I've been someplace once, I remember how to get there, down to the last hard right. I even remember which streets are one-way."

"Why do you have a GPS then?"

Brenna shrugged her shoulders. "I don't know. Company?" She smiled at him. "You understand, right?"

He stared out the window. "Yes."

"So," said Brenna. "I heard you and Lydia Neff had an affair."

Nelson's head snapped back around. "Who have you been talking to?"

"Does it matter? Apparently, it was common knowledge."

"It's . . . it's not true. I swear to God."

"Nelson," she said. "It's been one day since we met, and already, I can name several very important things you either lied about or neglected to tell me."

"That's different. Some things slip my mind."

"That may be, but if you're not going to tell me the truth about Carol withdrawing money from an ATM, why should I believe you when you say you and Lydia didn't have an affair ten years ago?"

"Recalculating," said Lee.

"I never cheated on my wife. Not with Lydia Neff, not with anybody."

Brenna made a U-turn. Nelson's eyes were moist, and she recalled the way he'd cried on the phone with her, begging her to find his wife. "I'm sorry for your loss, Nelson," she said. "I really am. I can't even imagine what you're going through right now."

"I want you to keep working for me."

"Doing what? You hired me to find Carol."

"I want you to find out who killed her."

Brenna made a left on Muriel Court. "I'm a missing persons investigator, not a homicide detective," she said. "The police are on it."

"No they're not," he said tightly. "They think I killed her."

Brenna was nearing Nelson's house. To her relief, she saw the news vans and squad cars gone, save for one car parked in front of the walkway—one of those tight silver muscle mobiles Brenna hadn't seen since the eighties. *A 1982 Pontiac Trans Am in the suburbs. Mid-life crisis much?* "When I was in high school, I dated a guy with a car like that one— only it was powder blue," Brenna said. "The license plate said Blu ID Soul, and the whole interior smelled like Polo cologne." She glanced at Nelson. "I had low self-esteem."

"Do you?" Nelson said.

"Not anymore. I mean, I'm not exactly self-help book material, but I know overcompensation when I see it."

"No," he said. "I'm not talking about that."

Brenna reached the front of Nelson's house. She pulled to a stop in front of the Trans Am, and its lights went on.

"Do you believe I killed Carol?"

She looked at him. "Nelson. I've only known you for two days."

"The police believe I did." Nelson was staring straight ahead, into the Z. The interior lights were on, too, and so Brenna saw him clearly. Red Face from the hospital waiting room. "Drives fast," she said. "Of course, some of those vintage Trans Ams can go from zero to sixty in 6.5 seconds."

"Huh?"

"I saw him leaving the hospital. Detective, right?"

He nodded.

"Of course he is."

Pomroy switched off his interior light, then started up his car and drove away, Nelson staring after him.

"You're home now," said Brenna. "Try and get some rest."

"This will not look better in the morning."

"No, but with some sleep, you may see it more clearly."

"Miss Spector, please. I know I've been less than forth-right about some things. But I never cheated on Carol. And I didn't kill her. I need to find out who did kill her and why, and you're the only one who can help."

"Detective Morasco is very capable."

"*Detective Morasco couldn't even find a little girl.*"

Brenna's hand dropped away from the car door. "What?"

Nelson exhaled. "Never mind."

"No," said Brenna. "What did you mean?"

"He was on the Iris Neff case. Much too young for the job if you ask me."

"You can't blame him," Brenna said. "Girls . . ." Her throat clenched up. "Children disappear all the time and are never found."

"Well, I'm not the only one who felt that way." He turned to her. "They demoted him."

"How do you know that?"

"Everybody did—though most probably don't remember. I just thought of it myself."

"Probably gossip."

Nelson shifted in the car seat. "No. It was a lot more than gossip."

"Really?"

"Carol's best friend, Gayle Chandler. She was very active in our Neighborhood Watch group and had many, many dealings with the police."

"She used to be Lydia Neff's neighbor."

"That's right." Nelson squinted at her. "How do you know that?"

"I just remember the name."

He took a breath. "Anyway, Gayle Chandler had it on good authority that Morasco was demoted for insubordination. There was a rumor, too, that he'd wasted police resources on . . . how did they refer to it? He was following up on the wrong clues. He was pursuing the wrong line of—"

"A bad lead."

"Yes! That's it."

Brenna recalled her phone conversation with a young Morasco, eleven years ago, too young for his job. Patronizing and dismissive, she had thought. But it wasn't that way. He'd been shamed. Morasco, perfectly friendly until he'd heard those two words and then his voice had gone cold. "Blue car." Two words that had ruined his career.

"That never should have been leaked to the press."

"No, I'm glad it was leaked because—"

"It was a bad lead."

"A bad lead?"

"It was false."

"People change," Brenna said. "Detective Morasco isn't young anymore." She got out of the car and opened Nelson's door.

"None of us are young anymore." Nelson's voice was small, defeated. He pulled himself out of the car without looking at her, and Brenna was overwhelmed with pity. She heard herself say, "I'll help you." Said it even before the idea had fully formed in her mind.

Nelson's garage, the door still wide open, was completely empty now—a big, hollow mouth trapped in a gasp.

As she and Nelson passed the garage, Brenna said, "Don't be surprised if the house looks a little different."

"Different how?"

"Well, police aren't exactly known for cleaning up after

themselves." By now, Nelson had flung open the door and switched on the light, and to Brenna's surprise, the house was in surprisingly good shape. There were a few open drawers and cupboards in the kitchen, but all the fixtures looked spotless, without a trace of fingerprint powder if there had ever been any—and even the block of knives remained intact. Nelson, though, was focused only on the answering machine—on the word "Full" blinking on the digital screen. "I don't think this answering machine has filled up since we bought it." He shut his eyes tightly and Brenna knew what he was thinking. *We.* He'd said the word so naturally, but now, it stuck in his throat.

"Probably reporters," Brenna said. "They can wait, right?"

Nelson pressed the button. Sure enough, the first call was from a young *Daily News* reporter, offering condolences in a voice much too chipper for the words she was saying. Nelson deleted the message without listening to the rest, only to receive yet another sympathy call—this one more sincere-sounding—from Steve Sorensen, the senior crime reporter at Jim's paper, the *Trumpet.* "I know him," Brenna said. "Nice guy."

Nelson looked at her. "Do you think I should talk to him?"

"Not yet," Brenna said. "You give interviews too soon, people will think you're being defensive. They think you have something to hide."

Nelson snapped, "I don't have anything to hide," just as Steve's message ended and the next one began.

"I know you don't, Nelson. But for now, the only people you should be talking to are me—and a lawyer if you need one."

Nelson's face was white. He was staring at the machine. Brenna stopped talking, aware now of the hoarse whisper coming out of it, the words. " . . . fucking animal. Murderer. You'll pay. I'll *make* you pay."

Nelson turned off the machine.

"Crank call," Brenna said. "You should get an unlisted number, soon as you can."

Like a sarcastic comeback, the phone rang. "Can you please pick that up?" Nelson said quietly.

Brenna answered the phone to static. "Hello?" she said again. "Is anyone there?"

No response.

Brenna glanced at the caller ID, which said, "Unknown Caller," then she looked at Nelson. "I think we have a bad connection," she said. "I'm going to hang up—"

"Please don't." It was a female voice—not a woman. A girl. A teenager. "Who is this?" the voice said.

"Shouldn't I be asking you that?"

"Is it a girl?" Nelson asked.

Brenna nodded. "I'm Brenna Spector," she said into the phone. "Mr. Wentz's investigator."

"I'm sorry," the voice said. "I'm so, so sorry."

"Why are you sorry?"

"I'm sorry about . . . Carol."

"Mr. Wentz accepts your condolences."

"No." The girl said something else, but static enveloped the words.

"What did you say?"

" . . . Carol. It was my fault."

Brenna froze. "Your fault?"

Nelson grabbed the phone from her. "Who are you? Please. This is Mr. Wentz. I lost my wife and I don't know why. But . . . but maybe you do? If there's anything you know, then please, please young lady, I—" Nelson stopped. Carefully, he replaced the phone. "She hung up."

"Who is she?"

"She called last night," Nelson said. "She said, 'It's my fault.'"

"Strange."

"I thought it was probably a prank, but . . . Maybe it was just the mood I was in. The loneliness . . . It stuck with me. Even in the hospital, when I was coming to, I could hear it in my mind. She sounded so sad."

"Did caller ID say unknown last night, too?"

"Yes." Nelson sighed. "I think I'm grasping at straws. Looking for meaning where there is none . . ."

Brenna was scrolling through the phone's call roll—all the incoming calls from today and the day before. "She said Carol's name to me."

Nelson's eyes widened. "She actually said—"

"It still could be nothing—Carol's name has been all over the news. But here's the thing I find strange." Brenna glanced up at him. "You didn't get any other calls today from Unknown Caller."

"So?"

"Even Mr. I'll-Make-You-Pay. He called from an actual number. Looks like a cell."

"Okay . . ."

"So this call from the young girl, which we got two minutes after we walked through the door. This call where she told me she was sorry about Carol. That was the first time Unknown Caller called, all day." Carefully, Brenna replaced the receiver. "You know what I'm saying?"

Nelson stared at her. "I'm starting to."

"Either this girl has amazing timing," Brenna said. "Or she knew we'd just come home." She gave him a long look. "I think she's been watching your house."

"She couldn't be watching the house," Nelson had said—not once but five times, the tension growing in his voice so that, by round three or so, the sentence's meaning had reversed.

She could be watching the house. A thought that clearly disturbed him to a surprising degree, considering everything else he'd been through today. But then again, this was a man who had said, "My house has been ransacked," over the tiny adjustments made by the police—the coffee table to the left by around two feet, the couch pushed back a few inches, the braided throw rug half a foot nearer the window . . . all noticeable only to someone with perfect memory—or chronic OCD.

"Why would she be watching?" he had said of the teenage girl. "I can understand her calling. But why would she be *watching*?"

Walking out to her car, Brenna could feel eyes on her—not from the neighboring homes or the small woods flanking all of their backyards, but from inside Nelson's house. When she turned, she saw his silhouette in the big bay window in the living room, a shadow, staring, terrified at the thought of someone staring back—terrified of some sad-sounding teenage girl.

Brenna was nearing the garage now. She walked up to the gaping door, and stared inside—at the empty hooks, all Nelson's tools removed and bagged and brought to the lab. Her gaze drifted from the lone band saw in the corner to the oil stain on the garage floor and then again, she recalled Carol's car, that grim procession headed for the county crime lab garage. She caught a hint of death smell, and gagged—unsure whether it was the scent of decay that lingered here, or just the memory of it.

Brenna backed away, headed fast for her car. She needed to pick up Maya at chorus practice, and that was all she thought of as she walked. She didn't turn to look at Nelson in the window, searching the darkness for his troubled young caller, nor did she pay much attention to the sound she heard, drifting from a pathway in the woods behind the house. It was a hissing, undermined by a slight, rusty squeak. And it wasn't until she was driving away, recalling the sound, that she identified it as the wheels of a very old bicycle.

13

Maya was not a performer. In the third and fourth grade, she used to play the clarinet—played it quite beautifully, in fact—but all Brenna had to do was bring that up, and her daughter would go into a frenzy of eye rolling. "Oh come on, Mom, you hated the way I played."

"Not true."

"I can't believe you would say that. It's not like you *don't remember*, so it can only mean you're *lying* to me." It got so Brenna stopped mentioning the clarinet altogether. Maya was an artist, after all, happier behind a canvas than on a stage—why should Brenna force her child up there, especially seeing as she'd never enjoyed the spotlight much herself?

But then this year, out of the blue, Maya had signed up for the school chorus—which rehearsed four nights a week—giving up both her cartooning class and the new *Dr. Who* on BBC America in order to fit it into her schedule. Brenna couldn't figure out why, and Maya never offered an explanation, but tonight, as she stood in the back of the brightly lit auditorium, watching the P.S. 125 All-Classes Chorus belt out "We Are the World," Brenna got it.

Maya's music was on a stand in front of her, but it might

as well have been in another school across the country for all the attention she paid it. No—as far as Brenna's daughter was concerned, every word, every note in the song was dedicated to a Justin Timberlake look-alike, back row center (easily six feet tall and with a beard—how old *was* this boy?), who gazed out into the spotlight as if he owned it.

Brenna caught Maya's eye and smiled. Maya nodded, but when Brenna cast a quick, quizzical glance at JT Jr. and then back, the girl's eyes went dead, then pointedly dropped to the music book. Brenna cringed into the shadows at the edges of the room—*Okay, sweetie. Won't mention it again . . .*

The boy was launching into a solo now, his fully mature, *American Idol*–ready voice urging, "Let's start giiiivvvv-vinnnng," with enough runs to give Beyoncé pause. He had to be at least sixteen, which—apart from being much too old for Maya—made Brenna start remembering Iris Neff again. Iris, who would be sixteen now if alive—sixteen and putting in calls to Carol Wentz, according to Carol's chat room friends. *About a week ago. Late night. Lydia said her daughter called*, ClaudetteBrooklyn20 had typed. Reading it, Brenna had assumed Carol had made it up, that Iris's phone call had been created in the depths of the same fevered and desperately lonely mind that allowed Carol to be Lydia Neff—her husband's rumored lover—online. But now, Brenna wasn't entirely sure that Carol had made anything up. Brenna recalled the teenage girl's voice on the phone at Nelson's house. *It's my fault . . .* She remembered the squeak of old bicycle wheels in the woods behind Nelson's house—woods that stretched all the way down the length of Muriel Court, ending at the old Neff home, where she'd seen Iris's childhood bicycle peering out of the shadows.

Stop. If Iris had come back to Tarry Ridge, why would she have called Carol instead of the police? How could a missing girl come home and stay hidden? Even as those thoughts came to her, though, others followed—Clea disappearing. Clea staying hidden. Hidden for twenty-eight years and yet still Brenna hoped, still Brenna *knew* . . .

Brenna closed her eyes, forcing her memory to bring back the days after Iris Neff disappeared—the news reports she'd listened to, the TV magazine segments she'd watched, rapt. Then she plucked her cell phone out of her bag and texted Trent: *September 14, 1998.* Dateline NBC *did a story on Iris Neff. Pls. contact NBC get a pic of Iris from archives and put it thru yr computer aging program.*

Trent immediately texted back: *On it.*

The song was over. When Brenna looked up, the chorus was dispersing and Maya was coming toward her, face red and her jaw tensed, eyes aimed straight ahead and filled with pain. It took Brenna only a few seconds to see why, for there was JT Jr., lit up like the Chrysler Building, running across the room to greet a wild-haired girl in very tight jeans—a girl five years and a boob job shy of Trent's bulletin board. He crossed right in front of Maya in order to do it, too, fell into the girl's arms and kissed her full on the mouth with that oh-so-embarrassing teenage directness—both of them so new to physical maturity that it was something to flaunt, to rev like a motorcycle engine on a peaceful street. Yes, she was more age-appropriate than Maya. But if her jeans were any tighter, she'd be wearing them internally, and Brenna hated her and him both.

"You're on time," Maya said. "What a surprise."

"Spare me the sarcasm." Brenna tried not to notice Maya's trembling lip. Still, she wanted so to hug her, the way she had during Hannah Friedman's fifth birthday party at the Tompkins Square Playground on May 17, 2000, when Maya had fallen off the jungle gym and lay on the dirt, crying "Mama!" and clutching her skinned knee. Brenna wanted to run to her daughter, just as she'd done then. She wanted to take her in her arms and stroke her hair and tell her, *Everything is okay, it's okay, it's okay, sweetheart . . .* But Brenna knew that wasn't called for and wouldn't be appreciated. She took Maya's backpack instead, slipped it over her shoulder. "You ready?"

Maya didn't answer. She headed for the door, and Brenna followed, both of them walking out and into the chemical purple twilight without saying a word. The whole way to Brenna's apartment, she and Maya walked in silence. Nothing new for them, but still her chest tightened, May 17, 2000, playing in her mind—leaving the party early, taking the 6 train to Serendipity, the pink cloth napkin tucked into Maya's collar and the banana split with two long spoons, little fingers patting at the Scooby Doo Band-Aid and *I feel all better now, Mama. I love you.* The whole day, start to finish, every sight and smell and emotion and sensation, the whole day as if it were happening now and wishing Maya could have that, too, wanting to share it with her so badly . . .

Once they got to the front door of Brenna's walk-up, she stood back and let Maya use her own key. It wasn't lost on her, the way her daughter's hand shook when she slipped the key into the lock, the way she swatted at her eyes. Brenna knew that there had been such different scenes scrolling through Maya's head during the walk home—but lucky for her, they were scenes she would one day forget. "He runs like a girl, you know," Brenna said.

Maya turned, and smiled, just a little.

Remembering Morasco's words at the hospital, Brenna pulled out her cell phone and tapped in his number once she was inside her building, following Maya up the first flight of stairs. He picked up fast. "About time."

"I had to pick my kid up at chorus."

"You're a mom?"

"Yes," she said. "I'm surprised that didn't turn up in your research."

He laughed. "I'm surprised, too."

"So . . ."

"So."

"Was there something you wanted to tell me?"

"Oh, right," he said, as Brenna rounded the final flight to find her daughter at the apartment door. "Actually it was something I wanted to *ask* you."

"Why am I not surprised?"

"Is Trent still here?" Maya said.

Brenna checked her watch. Seven-thirty. She shook her head.

Morasco was saying, " . . . when Detective Pomroy and I were speaking to Nelson."

"Pomroy," Brenna said. "Nice set of wheels he's got there."

"You've seen the ride!"

"You don't *see* a 1982 Pontiac Trans Am," Brenna said. "You *experience* it."

Morasco laughed. "You know your vehicles."

"Bet you guys call him Knight Rider behind his back."

He laughed harder. A grin pulled at Brenna's face. "I'm right, aren't I?"

"I take the Fifth."

Maya was staring at her. "Who *is* that?"

Brenna mouthed, *Work call*.

Maya raised an eyebrow.

What?

Maya pointedly turned away, got her keys out of her pocket, and set about unlocking the door. God, she could be infuriating sometimes.

"Anyway," Morasco said, "what I wanted to ask you about is Nelson's tool collection."

"His what?" she asked.

Maya pushed the door open.

"He had a pretty extensive one in his garage—and I'm wondering if he ever spoke to you about any of those tools in particular, maybe one that went missing . . ."

From the other side of the door, Brenna heard Maya scream.

"Gotta go." Brenna rushed into the apartment to find her daughter, frozen in the doorway, pointing at the man sitting in Trent's chair. "What are you doing here?" Maya said.

The man gaped back at her, mirroring her panic. "He let me in. The . . . the assistant. He told me to wait."

"Who are you?"

"It's okay, Maya." Brenna's gaze dropped to a small stack of files in the man's lap, the manila folders faded and beige as the face, the hair, the watery eyes pleading up at her. "This man is one of my clients. His name is Nelson Wentz."

Brenna suggested Maya go into her room and do her home-work, and for once she got no argument. Maya was through the kitchen and down the hall and closing the door behind her in a matter of seconds, without so much as one eye roll. *I should ask Wentz to come here more often.*

"Your daughter?" Nelson squinted after Maya, his eye-brows pressing into each other. "She . . . uh . . ."

"I know. She looks nothing like me." It was true. In fact, apart from inheriting Brenna's long, lanky build, Maya looked nothing like either one of her parents—a blonde-haired, blue-eyed shiksa goddess in their Semitic midst. "Switched at birth," Jim used to joke, and Brenna had never wanted to say it, knowing how much it would trouble him, the mention of the name. But the one person, the *only person* out of both of their families whom Maya looked remotely like was Clea. She looked more like Clea every day.

"What brings you here, Nelson?" Brenna asked.

He cleared his throat. "The trunk."

"What?"

"Do you remember Carol's trunk—the one with the quilting supplies?"

Brenna nodded.

"It . . . it had a false bottom," he said. "A piece of cardboard. I pulled it out, and underneath it . . ."

Brenna's gaze shot at the manila folders. "Those files?"

"Yes." He handed them to her. "I want you to have them," he said. "Not the police."

Brenna flipped open the first file. She began to read the first page and for a moment, she was sitting across from Errol Ludlow in the Skyline Diner in White Plains on October 23, 1998, *Errol sliding a manila folder across the Formica-topped table, smiling that oily smile, and Brenna looks into the eyes, dull like black olives, guilt heating up the backs of her ears* . . . Brenna gritted her teeth, closed the file fast. "The Neff police report."

Nelson nodded. "That's what was in Carol's trunk. Nothing but pictures of Iris, her family, old newspaper clippings . . ."

"Really interesting . . ."

"At first I was thinking she was obsessed with *Lydia* because . . . Well, you know."

Brenna nodded.

"But after you left tonight I looked through these files, Ms. Spector. I looked through all of them."

"Yes?"

"I think she was trying to find Iris."

Again, Brenna recalled the girl's voice on the phone, the squeak of bicycle wheels behind Nelson's house. *It's my fault* . . . Yes, it seemed bizarre. But still . . . Still. "I think so, too, Nelson." Brenna cleared her throat. "And you know what else?"

Nelson gave her a long look, a strange emotion working its way into his eyes—a mixture of hope and dread and growing knowledge. "What?"

"I think she may have found her."

Brenna convinced Nelson to let her show Carol's papers to Morasco—only to Morasco, no other police—with the added caveat that she would memorize them first. She told him that by tomorrow, she would have a perfect age-enhanced photo of Iris, and she would bring him a copy, plus she and Trent would canvass the neighbors, post it on the Web . . . if anyone had actually seen Iris Neff wandering around Tarry Ridge, they would soon know.

After hearing this, he seemed to relax a little, but as he was making for the door, Nelson's body stiffened again. "I hate going back to that house."

"I know. It must be so difficult for you."

"Not that," he said. "I mean, it's awful going back there, knowing what happened to Carol . . . But the phone calls, Ms. Spector."

"Reporters?"

"Yes, and worse. So many hateful calls . . . They think I killed her. They think I had an affair with Lydia and she found out after all these years and confronted me and I . . . I can't believe they would think that. People I don't even know . . ."

"Nelson?" Brenna said.

"Yes?"

"Is there anything I should know about your collection of tools?"

Nelson's lips tightened. The blood drained from his face until he looked the color of skim milk, and he shook his head, very slowly. "Why would you ask that?"

"Well . . . they've all been bagged and removed from your

garage. I'm just wondering if you've noticed any of them missing in the past few weeks."

"No." He turned and left Brenna's apartment, shutting the door hard behind him. Brenna heard Maya's door opening, light shuffly footsteps as she approached. "He's gone?" Maya said.

"Yep."

She exhaled. "Weird guy."

"His wife was murdered," Brenna said—a halfhearted protest. She looked at Maya. "But yeah. He's definitely weird."

14

Brenna fixed spaghetti Bolognese for dinner. She plugged her MP3 into the speakers and put on some Rachael Yamagata—one of those rare artists she and her daughter both liked—and the two of them sat at the table, eating and listening to Rachael's sad, yearning voice and not saying a word. Typical for them, but that didn't make it right, did it? More and more, Brenna and Maya brought to mind those zombie couples you see in restaurants, eating entire meals without speaking, without looking at each other directly, without even chewing in unison.

Maya didn't seem to mind the lack of talk, but really, how was Brenna to know that? Perfect memory or not, Brenna still viewed the world through her own eyes, no one else's. For years, she'd thought of Maya as quiet and laconic, not one for the spotlight—but was that really her daughter's personality, or was it simply the effect Brenna had on her? "So what's his name?"

Maya looked up from her plate. "Who?"

"You know. Back row center. Mr. Vibrato."

Maya put her fork down. She gazed at Brenna with those eyes—Clea's eyes, blue as a baby's, yet so full of knowledge you wanted to look away. "Miles."

"As in, Miles to go before he grows up?"

Maya swallowed hard. "Apparently."

"He'll be sorry."

"You think?"

"If he has half a brain."

Maya rolled her eyes and went back to her plate. Brenna thought, *I tried*. For quite a while, there was nothing in the room, no sound at all but forks clinking on china and Rachael want, want, wanting to be your love and Brenna's thoughts, teetering on the edge of a memory, wishing back to a time when she knew the right thing to say.

"Mom?"

Brenna wasn't sure whether Maya had said it in her mind or here at the table. She put her fork down and waited until her daughter spoke again.

Maya said, "When you were my age . . ."

"Yes?"

"Did anything like Miles ever happen to you?"

Brenna nodded. "Dave Handly. But I wasn't your age. I was sixteen. And two months."

"Was he older?"

"Yeah . . . He was one of those guys you hear about. Nineteen years old, and they still hang around their old high school, go to all the parties . . ."

"You mean a total loser."

"Yes, honey. But I wasn't as sophisticated as you, and so to me he was . . . a man."

"Did you go out with him?"

"Honestly? I didn't even talk to him. I pretty much just stood across rooms from him, staring," Brenna said, her mind reeling back . . . "Until this one party at Lisa Minor's house. October 7, 1986. It was 10 P.M. I'd been there for an hour. I was sitting on the couch with my friend Becky Joseph. She was telling me how she'd gone to third base with

Kenny D'Amato, and . . . I probably shouldn't have told you that."

"I know what third base is, Mom."

Brenna sighed. "Anyway, Becky is talking, and then this song starts playing on the stereo . . ."

"What song?"

"'And She Was' by the Talking Heads. It caught me by surprise and it . . . it triggered a . . . sad memory . . ." Brenna's eyes went hot, her throat clenched up. *Damn.* Brenna dug her fingernails into her palms . . . *Get it together . . .*

"You okay?"

Brenna took a breath and blinked . . . "Fine . . . Anyway, like an idiot I start crying, right in the middle of Becky's story. She says, 'What the hell is wrong with—' But before she can finish the sentence, there's Dave Handly on the other side of me—right there on the couch, handing me a Kleenex." Brenna swallowed some ice water. "Seriously, Lou Reed could have been handing me a Kleenex, I wouldn't have been more starstruck."

"Lou who?"

"Funny."

"So then what happened?"

"We . . . uh . . . we spent some time together." Brenna cleared her throat. "And Dave said some wonderful things . . ."

"Like?"

"He told me to tell him all the songs that make me cry. He wanted to know my favorite books, favorite movies, if my heart was ever broken and by whom . . . He said, 'I want to know everything that makes you *you*.'"

"Wow."

"Yep. But then two days later, I was waiting for the bus to take me home from school. He pulls right up in his black Karmann Ghia, picks up Lizzie Karp . . . and completely ignores me." Brenna could feel the chill fall air at the back of her neck and on her cheeks, the waistband of the black corduroys she'd been wearing, *Lizzie Karp's giggly "Hi!" and the crunch of drying grass under her sneakers as Brenna shifts her weight, back and forth, back and forth . . .*

"That sucks," Maya said.

"Sure does." She drank more water, forced a smile. "Like your grandma says, 'Beware of men who can string words together like pearls.'"

Maya nodded slowly. "You know what Miles told me?"

"What?"

"He said even our first names are a perfect fit."

"God help you."

"And he said they should call us M&M—because we're so *sweet together*." Maya rolled her eyes. Then she started to cry. Brenna moved around the table and took her daughter in her arms, and Maya let her—not quite hugging back, but resting her head on her shoulder, allowing Brenna to comfort her and that was enough . . .

"Why did you have to give me a name that starts with M?" Maya said.

Brenna smiled. "You can change it if you want." But then the smile froze and died. She saw the letter M in her mind, typewritten on a page, the letter taking her back to October 23, 1998, meeting Lydia Neff for the first and last time at the Waterside Condominiums, then driving to the Skyline Diner in White Plains for the appointment with Errol Ludlow and hoping with her whole mind that no one would be watching, no one would see . . . *The Skyline lot is nearly empty. She parks and walks up to the front door, the envelope in her hand . . . She can't yank the image out of her mind— an image of herself, walking through the door, as viewed through the scope of a telephoto lens . . .*

"Mom?"

The diner door is heavy and she pushes it open and her eyes go right to him—Errol Ludlow, third booth from the back, and peering up at her over black half glasses, smiling like a friend. Errol Ludlow with his oversized head and his tree-trunk limbs and oven mitt hands, too big for the booth, too big for the diner, and smiling at her, six-foot-eight-inches of unadulterated bullshit. Errol Ludlow, meaty hands resting on a manila folder—the Neff police report, Brenna knows—and the cuts on her face sting, each bruise aches . . . the sight of him pulling at her wounds, waking them up. I could leave now, *she thinks.* I could turn around and leave.

"Hello? Mom?"

Brenna approaches the table. "Here." *She places the envelope in front of him.*

"Nice gree-ting af-ter four years." Errol overenunciates. He doesn't speak so much as spit words, syl-la-ble by syl-la-ble. He's always done that. It drives Brenna nuts. She goes for the folder. "Ea-sy now. Don't grab. You'll get your po-lice re-port after I make sure these pho-tos are clear . . ."

"Mom. Are you . . . Are you remembering something?"

Brenna could hear the hurt in Maya's voice. "No, honey," she said. "I'm here." But she could still feel Errol's oily gaze on her, could still smell the green tea on his breath, in the cream-colored cup in front of him.

"Nice pho-tos," Errol says. "Not that I'm surprised. You've always been good at your job." She moves into the seat facing him. He slides the manila folder across the table . . .

Maya said, "You know what's weird?"

Brenna looks into the eyes, flat like black olives, guilt heating up the backs of her ears, but still she slips the papers out of the folder, her hands shaking.

"What you'll be in-ter-ested in," Errol says, *"is the Q and A with 'M.'"*

"You know what's *weird*, *Mom*?" Maya was standing up now, her dish in her hands.

"What . . . what's weird?"

"In order to get your full attention, you have to be something that happened in the past."

"Honey, that isn't true," Brenna said, with the Skyline Diner still in her brain, Errol's gaze on her, his thin lips pursing together to make that letter . . . *M*. Brenna said it again, but Maya was bringing her plate to the sink. Then she walked out of the kitchen, back to her room, and closed the door. Brenna knew her well enough not to follow, much as she wanted to, much as she didn't want to admit that Maya was right.

The Q&A with M was on page 18 of the police report. Brenna had a feeling she would have remembered that, even without hyperthymesia. Alone at her desk, with Maya now asleep in her room, Brenna opened the beige file. Strange how blurred the type now seemed on the Xeroxed page— type that was forever fresh in her mind.

Brenna started to turn to page 18, when a Post-it sailed out and onto the floor—*Graeme Klavel* written in what she now recognized as Carol Wentz's neat handwriting, plus a phone number with a Westchester County area code.

Brenna called the number. A machine picked up after one ring: "You've reached the offices of Klavel Investigations and the home of Graeme Klavel . . ."

Another PI. "Hi, Mr. Klavel, my name is Brenna Spector. I'm an investigator from New York City, and I'm looking into the death of Carol Wentz. I don't want to interfere with the police investigation, but if you could just let me know if you had any dealings with her, I'd appreciate it."

Next, she put in a call to Morasco. When she got his voice mail, too, she left a message asking if he'd come across a PI named Graeme Klavel and telling him she had some papers to show him. Then, she let herself turn to page 18 and read the Q&A with M. The questioner, back then, was Detective Nick Morasco. M was a three-and-a-half-year-old girl. Brenna's gaze slid down the yellowed page, and she recalled how she'd felt the first time she'd skipped to it, reading it quickly on Errol's dubious advice, thinking, *An interview with a preschooler. Yet another example of Ludlow's stellar sense of humor . . .* until she'd reached the middle of the page, and then she understood.

> **M:** Iris left with Santa. They drove away.
> **NM:** What did Santa's car look like?
> **M:** It was blue.

The car, as remembered by M, was "happy," because it "had round eyes and a smile." It "looked like a toy," therefore M was "pretty sure elves had made it." Santa and Iris looked happy, too, and after they both had gotten into the car, it flew away, "up to the North Pole." When Brenna had finished page 18 ten years ago, she'd thought, *That's one hell of a bad lead all right.* But this time, she found herself struck more by Morasco's questioning technique—the patience and respect he showed this little girl.

> **NM:** Did Santa scare you?
> **M:** Nobody's scared of Santa.
> **NM:** Good point. Now, would you say he was taller or shorter than your dad?
> **M:** Rudolph wasn't there.

NM: No Rudolph? Really? I bet Santa missed that big red nose.

M: You're funny.

Morasco talked like a dad. A good one. It made Brenna wonder if he really did have kids, and if so why he hadn't mentioned that on the phone today—after all, he'd asked with such interest if she was a mom. *It might be time to do a little research of my own.*

But as she flipped to the next page and then the next, her current thoughts dimmed, the back of her neck began to sweat. She was nearing page 22, and soon, Brenna knew, she would be reading that same page again in her mind, reading it for the first time in her old apartment on Fourteenth Street . . . She would be cross-legged on the soft, pale red couch Jim had inherited from his parents, with Maya's deep sleep-breathing floating out of her room and Brenna's face still throbbing slightly from the previous night's cheating husband and the black standing lamp shining down on her like an accusation, a judgment, the light bouncing off the page, hurting her eyes.

Brenna muttered the Pledge of Allegiance and then the lyrics to "Somewhere Over the Rainbow" and then a few lines of Salt-N-Pepa's "Shoop"—anything to stop her mind from going there.

Page 22 of the police report was another interview, a brief one between Ray Griffin, the police chief at the time, and a friend of Lydia Neff's, a man who went by the name of John Doe.

Nothing remarkable, really. What got Brenna was not the interview itself, but what had happened when she was reading it.

Brenna is reading the words "TAPE ENDS" when she

hears Jim's voice. Her stomach drops. She doesn't know when Jim got in or how long he's been standing over her, but his tone shakes her. The hollowness.

"I just got back from Ludlow's office. I know what you did last night."

"Errol, wait, I—"

"Errol. You just called me Errol. I can't believe this."

"Jim, I just needed the police report. It was a one-time job. I'll never speak to him again, I promise."

"What good is a promise from you, Brenna? What the hell good is a promise from you?"

Brenna was holding her breath, her eyes closed tight, Jim's words echoing in her head. *"You worked for Ludlow. You put yourself in danger. You put Maya in danger . . ."*

"I didn't put Maya in danger."

"I don't think I will ever be able to forgive you."

Holding her breath always worked. Always chased the memories away because breathing was something you needed to do in the present. No getting around breathing, no matter how powerful the memory . . . Brenna gasped. *Good . . . good.* She turned the page and opened her eyes.

Page 22 was gone.

What she was looking at—the interview with Theresa Koppelson about the events leading up to Iris's disappearance—had been pages 24 and 25 of the previous police report. In this version, it was 22 and 23, the two final pages.

Brenna turned on her computer, opened up a blank Word document. She saw the time in the lower right of the screen—11:14 P.M. Later than she'd thought, and close to the same time it had been on October 23, 1998, when she'd read the missing page. Her mind didn't want to go back there, but she pushed it—and within seconds she was back on the red couch, alone in the room, assuming Jim was working late, not knowing what was about to happen . . . She read the interview in her mind, then came out of it and typed the words on screen:

INTERVIEW WITH "JOHN DOE" CONDUCTED
BY CHIEF RAY GRIFFIN

RG: How were you acquainted with Lydia Neff?

JD: We have done some work together. I would sometimes see her on the train.

RG: When you spoke, did she ever mention being frightened of anyone—anyone close to her who might want to harm her daughter?

JD: No . . . We didn't speak very much.

RG: It appears you did, sir.

JD: What, uh, what do you mean?

RG: In Ms. Neff's phone records, there are three calls to your home phone during the week of September 1, all late night.

JD: I don't know what to tell you. I don't know why she called. I barely knew Lydia Neff.

RG: This call, on September 3 at midnight. It lasts twenty-five minutes. And it came from you.

JD: I don't know. I don't, I don't, uh, remember any such call.

RG: You don't remember what was said.

JD: I don't remember any such call.

RG How well did you know Lydia Neff?

JD: I, uh, already told you. Enough to say hi. That's all.

RG: How well did you know her daughter?

(TAPE ENDS)

Why would someone remove that page? Brenna tried to think, but then the rest of the night came rushing at her again too fast and soon she was sobbing, the pain so fresh and raw again, tearing at her.

Brenna's screen beeped. She looked up to see an IM from Jim: **How did the Chrysalis chat room treat u?** The words blurred thick.

She typed: **Speak of the devil.**

Huh?

Nothing. I was just having a memory.

A good one, I hope.

Brenna drew a long, ragged breath. "You could have forgiven me," she whispered. "You just didn't want to."

Hello?

Brenna typed: **Gotta go.** She turned off the computer before he could ask for an explanation. Then she walked to Maya's room—softly, because Maya was a light sleeper. She cracked open the door, listened to that whistling snore, the room dark and warm with it, her daughter's breathing. She stood there for quite a while, thinking about Jim and forgiveness until she was finally able to make herself stop. Then her mind shifted to missing things—tools, pages from police reports, women like Carol Wentz . . . Trust, too. So many things, you noticed only after they disappeared.

15

The Wentz house was an entirely different animal the following day—and not a cuddly one, either. Driving here this morning at the request of Nelson, who'd left a message on her voice mail, Brenna had expected more or less the same as what she'd seen here the previous night— a few shreds of crime scene tape, maybe a persistent reporter or two, and at most a handful of murder fans—the dwindling remnants of local tragedy.

What she saw instead was a media circus that rivaled June 17, 1994—okay, maybe that was an exaggeration, but still . . . The number of news vans and cameras seemed to have tripled from the previous day, which Brenna couldn't figure out at all. Carol's body was gone. The police had left. What more could be gained from a few yards of yellow tape and an empty garage?

Brenna scanned the crowd for Trent. He was supposed to meet her here with Carol's credit card info, the age-enhanced photo of Iris Neff, and anything else he'd been able to pull together, but it was hard to pick out anyone in this melee—even a tangerine-skinned vision in sleeveless mesh and hair care product who routinely barked, "Yo" at the top of his lungs.

Brenna parked her van a block up the cross street behind

a thick line of cars, some double-parked—she half expected a tailgate party—then headed back toward the melee, eyes peeled for Trent the whole time. As she got nearer, she saw them all setting up their cameras and testing their microphones and jockeying for the best positions, shoving into one another like this was a subway platform at rush hour. Brenna's stomach dropped. *He didn't. He did not. Nelson did not . . .*

Before she could even finish the thought, she recognized Jim's wife, Faith Gordon-Rappaport, anchor of the popular morning news show *Sunrise Manhattan*, and she knew. Brenna knew. No way would Faith show up anywhere unless she'd been invited. *Oh, Nelson. What were you thinking?*

Faith was talking to her cameraman—skinny and serious in a vintage green and black plaid shirt and one of those huge scraggly beards that guys in their teens and twenties were suddenly sporting—the latest hipster look, along with those god-awful cereal bowl haircuts, guaranteed to make their wearer at least eighty percent less attractive.

Quite a foul night this cameraman was, next to the sunny day that was Faith. Brenna couldn't help but wonder how they got along, but then Faith got along with everybody. Brenna approached Jim's wife, coifed and shiny from the back in a cream wool suit, her gold hair pulled into a matching clip. If this were a soap opera, Brenna would have hated Faith for stealing the heart of a man whom she could literally never forget—or at the very least for being a former Miss Georgia whose suits always matched her hairclips.

But the truth was, Faith was a genuinely nice person. She was a great stepmom, and so considerate of Brenna, handling every drop-off and pickup of Maya for the past seven years—ever since she and Jim had gotten married— because she'd understood Brenna's condition, understood how painful it was for her to look Jim in the eye without ten years rolling back like tide, without her heart aching and shattering all over again. It was quite a skill, having such an obvious advantage but not rubbing it in. And judging from Faith's life, from the whole upward trajectory of it, it was a skill she'd honed via plenty of practice.

Brenna tapped Faith on the shoulder, and she turned, her whole face erupting into a smile. "Brenna!" she said in her soft Southern accent. "Not the first person I'd expect to see at one of these! What brings you here?"

"By *one of these*," Brenna said, "you mean a press conference, don't you?"

She nodded.

Brenna sighed. "Damn."

"Is Nelson Wentz a friend?"

Brenna shook her head. "A client," she said, "who doesn't seem to know how to listen to advice."

"Oh my."

"Took the words right out of my mouth—minus a few expletives."

"If you don't mind my asking, who'd he hire you to find?"

"Carol," Brenna said.

"Oh *my*."

Brenna nodded. "He called me last night, said to come to his place because he wanted me to see something—I didn't know that *something* would be this."

"I'm sure he'll do fine."

"Said like a true, bloodthirsty TV reporter."

"Guilty as charged."

"This is all off the record, by the way," Brenna said. "Except the bloodthirsty reporter part."

Faith smiled, but just for a second. She took a quick glance in the cameraman's direction and moved closer. "Listen," she said quietly, "I'm sorry I let Maya spend the night at her friend Larissa's the other night."

"That's all right."

"No," she said. "No, it really isn't. Jim reminded me you'd just come back from your Vegas assignment and probably missed Maya more than usual. He said it was thoughtless of me."

She looked at her. "He said that?"

"Yes, and he was absolutely right. It *was* thoughtless. I didn't *think* at all."

"Faith," Brenna said. "No one is perfect."

Faith started to say more, but then a mumbling erupted from the group of reporters, and a push forward, and sure enough, there was Nelson leaving his house in a plain gray suit, accompanied by a stooped, ancient gentleman with a thin parcel of white hair—one of the few living men who could make Nelson seem robust by comparison.

The reporters rushed toward the duo—who probably weighed less than 250 pounds cumulatively—their cameras switching on, microphones jumping out from the ends of rigid, insistent arms. It made Brenna uncomfortable, this feeding frenzy with such a paltry, frail catch. She moved closer so Nelson could see her.

The old man stepped forward. Carefully, he removed a sheet of white paper from the pocket of his black suit coat, as well as a pair of super-thick Ben Franklin–style reading glasses that Faith's cameraman no doubt coveted. It took him more than a full two minutes to accomplish this task, and watching was agonizing.

"I am Malcolm Fischbein," the old man read, in exactly the voice you'd expect to come out of him—a sort of extended, rattling gasp. "Mr. Wentz's attorney." Shocked stage-whispering from the reporters. Brenna could pick out the words "retirement" and "fossil." She heard Faith's cameraman mutter, "You've got to be kidding me," and she thought, *At least Fischbein knows how to shave.*

The man coughed deeply, then continued. "Mr. Wentz would like to thank you all for coming. As you know, he has been through a very difficult time, and would appreciate your cooperation as far as giving him the privacy he needs in order to grieve the death of his wife, Carol. Mr. Wentz will now read a brief statement, after which there will be no questions."

The crowd emitted a collective sigh. Brenna felt relief edging through her, her shoulders starting to settle. *No questions. Thank you, Mr. Fischbein.*

Nelson caught Brenna's eye and gave her a brief nod as he unfolded his own piece of paper. "Good morning everyone," he said in a tremulous voice. Brenna couldn't look at him. She was too nervous. For several seconds, it was June 10, 2005, and she could feel the cold metal chair pressing into her back as she sat in the front row of Maya's first clarinet recital, sweat pooling at the backs of her knees. *The Blue Danube. Why did she pick the Blue Danube when she can play Beethoven's Ninth so perfectly?*

" . . . a credit to her community and a wonderful wife. We had plans. We were going to retire to Provence. I loved Carol, and finding her the way I did was devastating . . ."

Nelson didn't seem to be doing that bad. Brenna checked out the reporters' faces. They were all listening respectfully—some even appeared to be moved.

Nelson said, "I understand your need to report the news, but I also ask for your consideration."

Out of the corner of her eye, Brenna saw a tight, acid yellow muscle T. Sure enough, it was Trent standing next to her, folder in hand, gaze riveted to Faith's cream-suited ass. Brenna gave Trent a swat on the arm, breaking the focus. "Oh, hey." He gestured at Nelson. "What the hell?"

Brenna shrugged. "Your guess is as good as mine," she whispered. "But at least he isn't humiliating himself."

Nelson was saying, "Please try to put yourself in my position. I've lost everything I held dear. Allow the police to continue their investigation, and allow me to mourn in peace." Nelson looked up from his paper. "That's all," he said quietly. Brenna glanced around. Respectful silence. *No harm done.* She wanted to kiss Nelson and his lawyer both.

And then, Nelson smiled.

Brenna was sure it was reflexive—a symptom of his nervousness—but for whatever reason, Nelson Wentz, who had remained composed and sober throughout his speech, broke out in a shit-eating grin that lasted long enough for every photographer in the tristate area to get a shot of it in glorious high def.

"Uh . . ." Trent said.

"Nicolai, you're getting this, right?" Faith asked her cameraman.

Go, Nelson. Go back inside.

Nelson's lawyer took him by the arm and led him back into the house, no doubt beating himself up inside for allowing a press conference. Brenna couldn't stop shaking her head.

Nicolai switched off his camera and began taking it apart. Faith turned to Brenna. "Well, I thought he did a very good job," she said.

Brenna rolled her eyes.

"How you doin', Faith?" Trent was trying what he must have thought was a seductive pout, with his arms crossed over his chest in a way that purposely accentuated his flexed biceps.

"Fine . . . Brent, is it?"

"Trent. But my special ladies call me TNT."

Faith just looked at him.

"TNT," he repeated. "It's Trent but, uh, without a couple of letters. Follow me?"

"As far as I'd like to. See you soon, Brenna."

After Faith and her cameraman left, Trent said, "Looks like the Pointer Sisters got a face lift."

"You're saying you think she had a boob job."

"Yep."

"And I knew exactly what you meant. I didn't need a translation." Brenna sighed heavily. "Trent, you and I spend too much time together."

"Aw, you'd be lost without me." He handed her the folder. "I'm thinking Faith needs glasses though."

"Because she wasn't checking you out."

"Bingo!"

"You see what I'm saying? You understand the *problem* here?" Brenna had the folder open now, and was staring at Trent's age-enhanced photo of Iris Neff—a raven-haired teen, with prominent cheekbones and a mysterious little smile. It broke her heart a little. Trent's photos always did. They were so real, all you could see in them was potential. "Wow," Brenna said. "She looks a lot like her mom."

"Not anymore."

"Huh?"

"Check out the next photo."

Brenna flipped to a picture underneath—a heavyset woman with frizzy gray hair and a wan, sad mouth. Only the eyes were the same, glittering darkly out of that tired, unremarkable face, as if they were slumming it. "Where did you get this?"

"I captured it off her Web site."

"Lydia Neff has a Web site?"

"She did two years ago. I guess she was trying to be a life coach. She was all certified and everything. Nice Web site, too, but it hasn't been touched since she left town."

"Lydia really changed."

"Well, if you ask me, she was eating her grief."

"*Eating her grief?* Where the hell did you get that? Oprah?"

He shook his head. "Tyra Banks. She did a whole show on food and love a couple of weeks ago, and— Stop looking at me like that. It was very *informative*."

"Do we know where Lydia Neff is living now?"

"Nope," Trent said. "Do we need to?"

Brenna thought back to the police report, the missing interview with John Doe . . . "We might."

"On it."

"Me too."

Trent stared out at the dispersing crowd. "What was up with Wentz's smile? May as well gift wrap his ass and leave it on the DA's doorstep with a nice box of chocolates."

Brenna winced. "I'm hoping maybe some bigger news will eclipse it. Maybe Brad and Angelina getting married, Mayor Bloomberg declaring a state of emergency . . ." She removed a printout from the folder—Carol's credit card charges from the last three weeks before her disappearance. "There are no charges after the twenty-fourth."

"The lady wasn't killed for her card. Look at September 22 though."

On September 22, Carol had eaten at the Blue Moon Diner in Mount Temple. Brenna recalled what Morasco had said. *Carol was seen at a diner in Mount Temple, sitting close to another man.*

But it hadn't been a very romantic meal, had it? Only ten dollars—and Carol had paid . . . A thought crept into Brenna's mind. "You have a reverse directory app on your smart phone, right?"

"Yep. Whatcha need?"

"One sec." Brenna thought back to the previous night— walking home from chorus with Maya and finding Nelson at Trent's desk, handing her the files and spaghetti Bolognese and Dave Handly, the whole night, right up until she'd opened the file containing the Neff police report and the Post-it had sailed out . . . "Okay. Look this up for me." Brenna rattled off Graeme Klavel's number as Trent tapped it onto his screen and waited. "Klavel Investigations," he said. "2920 Columbus Avenue . . . Mount Temple." He looked at Brenna. "Guess maybe it was a business lunch?"

"Uh-huh," Brenna was reading the charge right after the one from the diner. "Forty-two dollars and eighty-nine cents. To where? Sammy's?"

"It's a convenience store."

"Where?"

"Buffalo."

Brenna frowned at him.

"I know, right? I called, but they weren't open. I'll try again." By now, the crowd of reporters had thinned out considerably. "We should go in."

Just as she and Trent headed up Nelson's walkway, though, Brenna felt a tingling at the base of her neck, across her shoulders. *Someone is watching me*, she thought. And then . . . *Iris*.

But when she spun around, the face Brenna saw, staring out at her from the group of reporters, was not that of a raven-haired teenage girl. It was a face she remembered. A face she didn't like.

Brenna turned back around and grabbed Trent's arm, leading him quickly up the walk. "So what about the chat room membership? Do we have an e-mail address for her yet?"

"Yep," Trent said. "I'm running it through this new hacking program I've come up with. It puts through all combinations of letters and numbers until the account recognizes the password. But it would help if Wentz could tell me some of her likes and dislikes, lucky numbers maybe . . . so I could narrow down the field. This way, it's gonna take weeks."

"We'll ask him. I doubt he'll know anything, but we can ask." Brenna ventured a glance at the street. *Gone.*

She took a breath. "So," she said as they reached the door, her pulse finally slowing. "What was Carol Wentz's account name?"

Trent scrunched up his face. "It's a weird one," he said. "OrangePineapple98."

Brenna stole another glance up the block.

"What do you keep looking for?"

"Just someone I recognize from eleven years ago," she said. "A cop."

"Must be a pain in the balls to never forget a face."

"*Total* pain in the balls." Brenna scanned the sidewalk. She didn't see the cop anymore, didn't see that face. But still, she felt watched.

16

He shouldn't have watched her for that long. Humans are animals after all, equipped with thousands of sensors to protect that delicate, impractical flesh. Stare at anyone for an extended period and the tiny hairs stand up at the back of the neck, the stomach churns, the skin perks into goose bumps, the mind knows your intent.

No one understood that as well as Adam Meade, yet even after she turned and spotted him, he felt compelled to stare. He knew her from somewhere, this woman who was working for Nelson Wentz. Brenna Spector, her name was. Meade had learned that from listening in on Mr. Wentz's phone conversations. But it wasn't the name that was familiar—it was the face. Meade found it so irritating, this gap in his memory, this *Where do I know her from?* He so rarely asked himself questions he couldn't answer.

Use your strengths, son, Meade's father used to say. And Adam, the firstborn and only son Adam, who always took his father's advice . . . Adam Meade possessed a battery of strengths, and used them well.

He was observant. The moment he'd noticed the look Nelson Wentz had exchanged with the tall, thin woman at the front of the press group, Meade had set about working his way around all the mumbling bodies and bulky camera equipment and rigid microphones, until he'd gotten close enough to hear the woman's assistant call her by name. *Brenna*. Bingo.

He could blend in. Tall and striking as he was, Meade had been able to stand right behind Brenna Spector during and after the press conference, overhearing everything she said to her assistant—even taking notes on the steno pad he'd brought along to look like a typical earnest reporter.

He was fast. Now, Meade left Brenna Spector's line of vision, brushing quickly past the dispersing press. He headed down three blocks, then up the quiet side street where he had parked his car. He'd parked near a willow tree, browning in the fall chill, and in its shade he pulled the pad out of his pocket and went over his notes. *Buffalo convenience store*. He didn't care much about that—he'd already taken care of Buffalo. What got his attention here was *Klavel Investigations*—a name he'd never heard Nelson Wentz mention over the phone.

He ran his gaze over Klavel's phone number, then the address. Another thing Meade's father had taught him: *When it comes to doing business, face-to-face meetings are always best*. Meade pulled out his iPhone and transferred the address into his GPS. Only twenty minutes away. He could drive there now, start acclimating himself. On the street behind him, a squeaky bicycle passed. He glanced up and saw the rider—young girl in a yellow helmet. He paid her no notice. Another of Meade's strengths was his ability to focus, exclusively, on the matter at hand. And today, the matter at hand was a face-to-face meeting—its planning, and execution.

He was loyal. He was very loyal.

Brenna and Trent were greeted at the door by Mr. Fischbein—though "greeted" was perhaps too generous a term. The old man pushed open the door and moved past them, muttering something in the process that might or might not have been "Hello." Once inside, Brenna called out Nelson's name but heard nothing in response. Eventually, they found him—a small beige lump on the living room couch, head in his hands as if his neck was on strike.

"Nelson?" Brenna said. "How are you?"

"My lawyer quit."

"Mr. Fischbein?"

Nelson nodded into his hands.

"'Cause you smiled?" Trent said. "What a pussy."

Brenna shot him a look.

"What?" Trent said.

She glanced around the room. Apparently, Nelson had done more than schedule the press conference last night, because the braided rug was once again flush with the fireplace, the couch was moved a few inches forward, the coffee table was back in its original position, the faint residue of fingerprint powder on the windowsills was wiped clean. Again, these changes were something only someone with perfect memory would notice, but still it was a significant amount of work. "I see you cleaned up," she said.

"I can't stand things out of order." Nelson glanced up at Trent. A look of horror crossed his face, as if he'd just found a man-sized dust bunny under his couch that happened to be wearing the Ed Hardy catalog, but if this registered with Trent at all, it wasn't showing.

"You've met my assistant, Trent, right?" Brenna said. "At my office."

"Oh, right. Yes. Hello."

"Hey, Nelson. If you could show me where your computer is, I'm gonna do a bit by bit transferal of your hard drive."

"Excuse me?"

"Oh, I'm just gonna copy the shit off your computer, see

if we can find anything your wife may have downloaded and deleted."

Nelson stared at him, anxiety building in his eyes.

"Don't worry, man. I'm like a doctor. You got porn on there, I'm not gonna say nothin'."

Nelson's gaze shifted to Brenna. "How do you think I did out there?"

"I'm the wrong person to ask. I warned you against talking to the press in the first place."

"I know, but . . ."

"It isn't important what we think. And the sooner we figure out what really happened to Carol, the sooner your name will be cleared."

"I laughed at my grandma's funeral," said Trent.

"Nelson's office is upstairs. First room on your right."

"Okay. Fine. Jeez."

Once her assistant had left, Nelson looked at Brenna. "I was hoping she might be there," he said under his breath.

"Who?"

"You know . . . Iris."

"That reminds me." Brenna opened the folder, removed the photo, and handed it to Nelson. His eyes widened.

"It's the age-enhanced photograph of Iris Neff. Remember? I told you Trent was making one?"

Nelson exhaled. "She looks so . . ."

"Like her mother."

"Yes." His voice was choked.

She stared at him. "Nelson?"

"Yes?"

"Is there anything you haven't told me?"

"What do you mean?"

Brenna took a step closer. "About you and Lydia," she said quietly. "About Carol, and any fights you may have had. About any tools you noticed were gone from your garage . . ."

She took a breath. "But especially, Nelson, about you and Lydia."

"No."

"Trent is upstairs. Whatever you tell me will be just between you and me. I promise."

His gaze dropped to the floor. "I've told you everything."

"All right." The words sighed out of her.

Nelson was looking at the picture. "You know, I haven't seen this girl," he said. "But that doesn't necessarily mean anything. I haven't been out much. I think Iris is alive, Miss Spector. I think Carol was trying to save Iris, and that's why she had all those files. I think maybe she found Iris, and was trying to track down . . . Iris's mother, so she could . . ."

Nelson kept talking, about how possible it all was, how it would all make so much sense. After all, no one had ever found Iris's body, and what if she was like that girl, you know, the little blonde girl in California who had been held captive for eighteen years . . . But all Brenna could do was recall the phone conversation she'd had with Morasco the previous day.

"During the Iris Neff case, we never questioned Carol Wentz."

"Yeah. You told me that."

"But we did question Nelson Wentz."

Nelson had not told her everything. She wondered if he ever would. Nelson was saying, ". . . and that young girl sounded so upset about Carol. What other young girl would be that upset about—"

"Did Carol have any connection to Buffalo?"

His smile dissolved. "What?"

"We have her credit card bill," Brenna said. "It looks like she spent $42.89 at a Buffalo convenience store."

"She has an aunt in Buffalo." The spark faded from his eyes. "Carol never spent that kind of money."

"You didn't know everything about her," she said. "So what?"

Nelson's gaze dropped to the floor.

"What you *didn't* know about her isn't important, Nelson," she said. "What you *did* know. What you *do* know. That's what I need."

Above them, Trent's heavy footsteps moved toward the stairs.

"It's not that I didn't know everything about Carol," Nelson said. "I knew *nothing* about her." And Brenna knew her words had been lost.

"And Carol knew . . . she knew very little about me."

Brenna stared at him.

"Dude!" Trent called down from the top of the stairs. "Are you aware that you've got Mailkeep?"

Trent arrived in the room and said it again.

"I don't know what that is."

"You get some work done on your computer on August 29?"

Nelson thought for a moment. "Yes. At least I'm pretty sure that's the date. I've had some spyware issues, and the Kleins' oldest son, Jonathan, took a look at it."

"Did he download any new programs for you?"

Nelson nodded. "Some antivirus programs to allegedly erase the spyware. None of them very good . . . Oh, and he said he threw in a few extras—word processing and the like."

"Well, one of those extras is Mailkeep. It automatically makes a copy of all e-mails and saves it to the hard drive." Trent grinned at Brenna. "So in other words, we can check out everything OrangePineapple98 wrote without having to hack her password."

Nelson looked at Trent. "OrangePineapple98?"

"Your wife's screen name for her e-mail account. I was gonna ask—any idea what that might mean?"

Nelson's eyes were flat as quarters. "I didn't even know she had an e-mail account."

The phone rang. The three of them turned toward it. The machine picked up right away, and Brenna started for it, hoping it was the girl calling again.

The machine beeped and the caller began speaking before Brenna reached the kitchen—not a girl at all but a grown woman, the voice shrill and angry and more than a little off-balance. "I saw you on TV, you evil smiling piece of shit. Smiling after you *butcher* your wife. You're gonna die. *Die and rot in hell, scum.*"

Brenna picked up the phone and disconnected on the caller, but the voice still hung like a fog in the house. She went back into the living room, hoping Nelson hadn't heard. But she saw the look in his eyes and she knew he had. The phone rang again. "It's only the beginning," Nelson whispered. "Only the beginning."

17

Nelson seemed a little better by the time Brenna and Trent left his house. Of course that was like saying someone with a terminal illness who'd tripped and fallen seemed a little better—simply on the basis of his having gotten up off the floor.

After the third hate message (didn't these people have anything more productive to do with their lives?), Brenna had tried convincing Nelson to get an unlisted number, but he refused. *If I do that*, he'd explained, *Iris will never be able to call me.* So she'd set the answering machine to pick up after only one ring and turned the volume all the way down, and then she'd made Nelson call Phil Reznik, a good criminal defense attorney she knew, and set up an appointment with him for 5 P.M. Next, she'd gone into his immaculate upstairs bathroom, found some sleeping pills in the medicine cabinet, given him one, and made him go to bed. Mission accomplished.

Throughout it all, Trent had remained quiet. Strange for him, but Brenna hadn't really thought about his reasons until they were on Nelson's front step with the door closed behind them, the few remaining reporters shouting questions from the curb. "Excuse me, ma'am? Sir? Are you relatives?"

"How do you know Nelson Wentz?" "Can you answer a few questions about Mr. Wentz's current state of mind?"

"No comment!" Brenna said. But as she started to step down onto the walk, Trent took her arm and said, through his teeth lest reporters read lips, "What makes you so sure he didn't do it?"

She stared at him.

"Don't go all Pollyanna on me, Spec. People do bad things. No one knows that better than you."

"Excuse me," said Brenna, "but did you just call me *Spec*?"

"New nickname I'm trying out. You likey?"

"I hatey. It's even worse than TNT, which— *Christ, why can't you just talk like a normal person?*"

"Hey, chillax."

"You think Nelson killed his wife. You think he stabbed her to death, shoved her body in the trunk of her own car, then begged the police and me to find her."

"I'm just telling you what's on my mind. The cops think he did it."

"No they don't."

"Some of them do. The press thinks he did it . . ."

"So therefore you think he did it, too?"

"I'm just saying I don't know. He's one of those little guys with the psycho eyes. One of those dudes his neighbors always say, 'He was such a quiet man,' and 'He kept to himself.' " Trent surveyed the reporters across the street, then leaned in closer. "And not for nothin' but his wife takes a shitload of money out of the bank and doesn't tell him, but tells her *book club* she is feeling 'guilty' and 'unfulfilled'? She doesn't even tell him she can work a computer? Come on. Even *I* know that's a sucky marriage."

"He reported her missing. He begged the police to investigate. He hired *me*. Twice."

"It's a good cover."

Brenna sighed. "I don't want to talk about it."

"Just sayin'."

"I hate that expression."

Trent gave her a little nod, then started to head down the walk, reporters shouting at him again. Midway, though, he stopped and spun around, as if he'd forgotten something. "Brenna?"

"Yeah?"

"You're not mad at me are you?"

"Not any more than usual."

"Okay because . . . I don't know if you know this, but you're more than just a boss to me."

She looked at him.

"I mean it. You're like my hot female brother."

Brenna smiled. She couldn't help it. "I'm not mad at you."

"Cash." Trent turned and took the rest of the walk quickly, then jogged out onto the street, past the news throng to his car—a surprisingly staid gunmetal Ford Taurus he'd inherited from his parents.

Brenna headed down the walk. Several of the reporters asked for her name and how she knew Nelson Wentz, and Brenna said, "No comment" again, grateful to Faith for not having told them who she was. There was safety in anonymity. They were directing their stares and shouts at Brenna, but she wasn't being watched or spoken to, not really. She could escape into her thoughts.

Brenna had reached the end of the walk and the reporters' shouts were getting louder now, more insistent. She heard, "Ma'am, did Nelson Wentz kill his wife?" A familiar voice. She turned. The reporter's name was Cyrus Whitney. She'd seen it six years ago, in white letters, sandwiched between the New York 1 logo and "StormWatch '03!" He'd been covering the nor'easter on February 22, heavy parka shielding his face, shouting over the sound of pelting ice. Brenna smiled at him and said, "Moved up in the world, huh?"

He squinted at her.

She sighed. "Never mind." She turned back toward the street.

"Ma'am?" Cyrus Whitney said again. "Did Nelson Wentz murder his wife, Carol?"

Brenna didn't reply. She couldn't. She was staring through the windshield of a passing car. *The cop.*

As the car turned up the next street, Brenna stayed still, ignoring the reporters around her, remembering the morning of October 21, 1998, smelling the clean of the rented car, feeling the unseasonably warm sun through the windshield, one hour into her second morning of watching the Neff house, waiting for a blue car to pass . . .

Brenna watches the two white-shuttered windows, sneering out of the yellow paint. She sees a shadow pass through one and draw the shades. Lydia. *Brenna whispers the name. Can she feel Brenna watching?* Get out of the car. Knock on the door. Speak to Lydia Neff. Ask her about a blue car, and put this day, this week, this feeling behind you . . .

Brenna puts her hand on the door.

There is a crashing knock on the passenger's side. Her hand flies away, and her heart pounds, and when she turns toward the knock, his face fills the window . . . thick and angry, and . . . weird. He has a button nose, a small cupid's bow mouth, a black beauty mark, square on the left cheek . . . It is a face ugly in its prettiness, with features too delicate and small for the meaty jaw and square forehead, for the eyes—flat and mean as shark's eyes—and for the hand, moving toward the breast pocket of the brown polyester jacket—a cop's jacket.

She swallows hard. Opens the window. She tries to

put on a smile, but her mouth twitches. Her palms sweat.
"Hello, Officer. Can I help—"

"You need to leave." His voice is deep and hollow.

Brenna's stomach clenches up. Her skin feels cold. "Am
I doing something illegal?" As she says it, Brenna no-
tices a uniform standing behind him—fortysomething and
bulky, with a surly thin mouth buried in beard scruff. The
muscle, presumably, though at least to Brenna he's far less
threatening.

"You need to leave," the big, pretty one says again, and
of its own accord, Brenna's hand turns the key in the igni-
tion, starts the car.

"Has Mr. Wentz thought about turning himself in?" one
of the reporters called out. A stupid enough question to
bring Brenna out of the memory. She nearly thanked him,
but instead managed to stay quiet, slowing her breath as she
walked to her car, putting the cop's strange, pretty face out
of her mind.

It wasn't until Brenna was getting into her Sienna that it
hit her that, when the cop had driven by, she'd never even
glanced at his license plate. Or that his car had been blue,
and at least eleven years old.

Nelson found it so strange—this desire people had to put
the grieving to bed. The more hopeless the situation was,
the more they wanted you to sleep it off. *You need your rest.*
Go in that room and turn out the light. Take this pill. Every-
thing will be so much better once you're unconscious and
can't infect me with your depressing existence.

"Please get some sleep," Ms. Spector had said after
giving him the pill and a Dixie cup full of water. She'd even
gone so far as to turn down Nelson's covers, her homosexual
assistant standing behind her with his big arms crossed over
his chest like a bodyguard. *Get some sleep, or else.*

"Thank you," Nelson had said, not meaning it at all.

The thing was, sleeping pills didn't work on Nelson. You'd think a five-foot-seven-inch, 133-pound man would be no match for a single Ambien, but for whatever reason, it took two or even three to make him slightly drowsy. He hadn't bothered letting Ms. Spector know this, though. She thought he needed rest, let her believe he was getting it. Anyway, he could use the peace and quiet.

Nelson was reading in bed. Trying to, anyway. He had that book Carol had been reading for her club—*Safekeeping*. The book was a memoir, and Nelson thought it might help him with his online course.

But there was another reason, deeper and less logical and so much harder to admit, even to himself. Especially to himself. Nelson wanted to hold something Carol had held. He wanted to put his hands where hers had been only a week and a half ago, turning pages with blood coursing through them, a pulse beating in the wrists. He wanted to put his eyes where hers had been, see the words she had seen. He wanted to climb into that mind and think those thoughts. So badly, he wanted to be with Carol. The living Carol. He wanted to know her.

But it wasn't working. He couldn't read a sentence of this memoir without recalling Carol's lifeless eyes, Carol's face, rotting on the bone, Carol's paralyzed hand, still wearing the wedding ring. Was this the memory he'd take with him for the rest of his life? From now on, would he hear Carol's name and envision that thing in the trunk?

His wife.

How could they believe Nelson had killed Carol? Detective Pomroy, those reporters . . . *She was his wife*. How could they have thought he'd gone to his garage, taken his flat-head screwdriver, and shoved it into the heart of his own wife, who hadn't been having an affair to get him back for Lydia, who hadn't been preparing to leave him, who had simply been trying to find a lost little girl . . .

Nelson cringed. *Don't think on that, don't think, don't think . . . think about the living, think about Iris . . .* At the thought of that name, Nelson bolted up in bed and the book dropped to the floor. And then the phone rang. Or maybe it was the screeching phone that made him drop the book. The timing was so close, Nelson wasn't sure.

The phone was on Carol's side of the bed. Nelson grabbed the receiver and saw "Unknown Caller" on the ID screen, and hit the talk button, cutting off his own voice on the pre-recorded message: *The Wentzes aren't in right now . . .*

"Iris?"

There was no answer. No static, either—she must have been calling from an area with better reception, or else she'd charged her battery.

"Is that you?" Nelson was on the edge of tears. "It's okay. Whatever it is that happened, whatever you . . . you think you did to Carol . . . I'm not angry with you. Please. I could never be angry with a child." Nelson took a breath, aware of how tightly he was grasping the receiver. Like a lifeline. His fingers hurt.

"Mr. Wentz, this is Graeme Klavel, returning your call."

Nelson sighed, the air falling out of him. "Oh, yes," he said. "Sorry. I . . . I thought you were someone else."

"Right, well . . . in answer to your question, I did do some work for your . . . uh . . . your late wife."

"Can you please explain to me what that work was?"

There was a long pause on the other end of the line.

"Mr. Klavel?"

"Do . . . do you hear a . . . a clicking sound?"

Nelson swallowed. "No."

"Listen, I . . . I've been getting a lot of phone calls about your wife. Yours is the only one I've returned."

"Yes. I appreciate that."

"I'm calling you, Mr. Wentz, because I was married once, too, and . . . You sure you don't hear that?"

"Hear what, Mr. Klavel? Please, I . . ."

"I don't feel comfortable discussing this with you over the phone."

"*Mr. Klavel, did you and my wife find Iris Neff?*" He fairly yelled it, but it didn't matter. Mr. Klavel had already hung up.

Nelson felt light-headed. His gaze drifted up to the wall over the bed—to the picture of Carol and himself on their wedding day—May 26, 1995. They were standing in front of city hall in New York City—Carol in a sensible cream-colored dress, Nelson in the suit he'd worn to work at Facts of Note that day. They had been married during his lunch hour. Carol took the train in for it, then commuted back to their house once the judge had finished with the ceremony. The picture had been taken with a disposable camera, by a stranger on the street, a black man. Nelson couldn't even re-member whether the man had been young or old. But he did know that Carol had bought her own flowers, from a bodega on Chambers Street. *I remember my wedding day*, Nelson thought. And then the phone rang again.

18

The pretty-faced cop had been driving a Subaru Vivio. Ever since her older sister had disappeared into a car that Brenna had only been able to describe as "light blue," she'd made a point of learning about cars, noting the model and make of most vehicles she came in contact with. And this tendency, combined with her memory, made it possible for Brenna to look at most any car and identify, with reasonable certainty, the year as well. This particular Subaru Vivio was in the Bistro series. Most popular in '95–96, it had a sort of retro, European feel for a K-car, with a rounded front like a MINI Cooper. Brenna and Jim had looked at Subarus in 1997 before settling on their Volvo four-door, so that's how she knew. She also knew that the Vivio, introduced in 1992, was discontinued in 1998. Translation: The car that had driven by Nelson's house today was definitely around when Iris Neff had disappeared.

Could it have been the same blue car Iris Neff had gotten into? Could Morasco have placed his job in jeopardy by implicating a fellow police officer in the disappearance of a little girl?

Brenna would have written off the whole idea as an Olympian jump to conclusions, but for one detail: Two of the more distinctive features of the Bistro were the round, evenly spaced parking lights directly under the headlights, and the slight curve to the bumper—*round eyes and a smile*. It was a *happy* car. A car that *looked like a toy* so that any child—particularly a three-and-a-half-year-old like M— might be safe to assume that *elves had made it*.

Brenna tapped the Tarry Ridge Police Department number into her cell phone and asked for Morasco. Again, she got his voice mail. Was he just not picking up?

She had been to the Tarry Ridge Police Station once— October 21, 1998. She'd stood at the tiny building's front desk for all of six minutes, talking to a very young female uniform with frizzy blonde hair, a thick body, and a name tag that said "Fields."

"I have some information regarding the Iris Neff case." Brenna's face is flushed. She barely has enough breath to get out the words because she's parked her car three blocks away and jogged all the way here. What kind of a police station has no public parking?

"You can give me the information, ma'am." Fields has a shiny face, a thick layer of acne on her cheeks. Brenna puts her age at twenty-one, tops.

"I'd rather speak to Detective Morasco, if that's all right."

"He isn't around, ma'am. I can take your information."

"I'm . . . I'm a private investigator. Yesterday, I spoke to Kaye at Wax Attax—she runs the children's story hour?"

Fields gives Brenna a look like she's just recited page 78 of The Brothers Karamazov *to her, in its original Russian.*

"Anyway . . . at story hour, Iris once told Kaye that Santa visited her house. And that he drove a blue car."

"Santa?" Fields spits out the name, with as much attitude as someone with a name tag/acne combo can muster.

"Um, the important *information here would be* blue car *and* visited her house." *Brenna hands Fields her old busi-*

ness card, Ludlow's number crossed off and her cell written in its place. "Could you give this to Detective Morasco, please?" She doesn't bother waiting for a response—just pushes open the door, leaving Fields standing there, in the corner of her eye, twirling the business card between her stubby child's fingers.

"Fields better have quit since then," Brenna said out loud as she turned left on Clements, crawling along the street until she got to 3721—the address of the police station.

Former address. 3721 Clements was now a Talbots. Brenna turned Lee the GPS on, looked up Tarry Ridge points of interest, and found "Police."

The station was listed as being on 4549 Main. Brenna let Lee guide her, but when she got to the address, she stopped in front and leaned on her wheel gawking at the building and doubting for the first time her perfect, suave piece of machinery. Was her honeymoon with Lee finally over?

But no, there was "Tarry Ridge P.D." out in front in elegant gold letters—the same gold letters Brenna had seen eleven years ago, on the white marble slab in front of the Waterside Condos.

God only knew what those condos were like today, if this was how Tarry Ridge was coddling its municipal buildings. The police station could have easily been a high-end art museum or a rare books library or possibly a branch of Saks. Ultra-modern, with big windows and a sparkling white paint job, it was at least three times the size of the previous station. Needless to say, it had its own parking lot now. A big one.

Brenna was getting honked at. She pulled into visitor parking and headed for the station, and that was when she noticed the garden. A police station with *landscaping*. There was a row of hedges out front, and a stone path leading up to the door, white primroses and mums planted on either side, a small, neatly trimmed lawn. To the right, a small

Japanese maple shaded a white wrought-iron bench, ideal for finger sandwiches and sonnet reading. The bench bore a gold plaque. Brenna moved closer in order to read it: "In Memory of Lily Teasdale."

Inside the station, the first thing Brenna noticed was an enormous, gold-framed oil portrait hanging over the front desk—a silver-haired matron in a high-collared black dress with a closed, Mona Lisa smile, rounded eyes, and a very high forehead. The woman's features struck Brenna as oddly familiar. She read the brass inscription at the bottom of the painting out loud: " 'Lily Teasdale 1920–2000.' "

The uniformed officer at the front desk turned. "What?"

Brenna immediately recognized her. Fields. Minus the acne, the hair straightened and highlighted, the waist a bit slimmer, but still in uniform, still with that expression on her face—bored to the brink of agony. *The building may be brand-new, but the desk sergeant is merely renovated.*

"Lily Teasdale," Brenna said. "She looks like someone I know. Was she married to a police officer?"

Fields rolled her eyes. "The Teasdales are the oldest family in Tarry Ridge."

"Okay, but what does that have to do with the new police station? Did the family have an interest in law enforcement, or—"

"They built it. I don't know."

A font of information. Brenna was about to drop the topic and ask for Morasco, but then the word "built" settled into her brain and took her back to 5:30 P.M. on September 18, 1998, to chopping a freshly peeled carrot into a romaine and tomato salad and Jim's voice in the other room, competing with the sound of the TV news, ordering a large cheese pizza over the phone.

"Extra cheese!" Maya shouts.

"Can you make that extra cheese? Thanks."

*Brenna hears the news announcer say, "Tarry Ridge,"
and Jim calls out, "Look at this, honey! Roger Wright's
building in the suburbs, now."*

*Brenna dries off her hands on the lobster dish towel that's
hanging off the oven handle. Then she heads into the living
room. "Tarry Ridge is where that little girl disappeared
from," she says, watching the image on TV. Roger Wright—
ageless features, golden hair, the type of jaw people call
proud. The whole of him gleams with health, as if he grew
up in a magic bubble, and no harm could ever touch him.*

*"The man who brought the Wright Shopping Center to
Manhattan is moving to the suburbs," the announcer says, as
the camera focuses on Wright, cutting the thick red ribbon.*

*The newscaster intones, "A native of Tarry Ridge, Mr.
Wright says he's thrilled to give back to his hometown."*

*"Give back," Brenna snorts. "Like those condos are
low-income housing." Roger Wright gives the camera a
thumbs-up, and Brenna glances at the woman next to him,
a woman who must be his wife—wide-eyed and perfectly
coifed and smiling. Smiling with her mouth closed, as if she
wants to keep all her happiness inside her . . .*

The eyes, the face shape, the smile of Wright's wife—
all identical to that of Lily Teasdale. "Did Roger Wright
build this station?" Brenna asked Fields, who, predictably,
shrugged.

"Was Lily Teasdale his mother-in-law?"

"Something like that."

Brenna sighed heavily. *A bubbling font.* "I'm here to see
Detective Morasco."

For the first time, Fields gazed directly at Brenna's face.
She cocked her head to the side and squinted. Brenna knew
the look. She'd seen it a lot: *Do I know you from somewhere?
No, probably not.* "Detective Morasco is in a meeting."

"I can wait."

"I don't think that's possible, ma'am. If you leave your name and number, I can have him call you."

"No, no," Brenna said. "It's absolutely possible. See?" Brenna stood there, smiling at Fields for a good ten, twenty, thirty seconds, until finally, Fields picked up her phone, tapped in an extension, and said, "Detective Morasco, it's Sally."

"Sally?" said Brenna. "Your name is *Sally Fields*?"

She ignored her. "I'm really sorry to bother you, but there's a woman here to see you, and she refuses to leave." She paused for a moment. "I didn't get her—"

"Brenna Spector."

Fields repeated Brenna's name into the phone. "Right. Yep." Then she hung up. "He's coming out."

"Shouldn't you be saying something like, 'He likes you, he really likes you'?"

Fields rolled her eyes, went back to her computer. "It's *Fields*, not *Field*," she muttered. "Get the name right."

"In the Iris Neff case, why was the blue car a bad lead?" Brenna asked Morasco. They were sitting in a Starbucks, five blocks up from the police department. They'd walked there together, making small talk about the fall weather, the new police station (which, in fact, had been standing since 2001), the effect of the recession on the Riverview Shopping Center, and the Yankees' chances of winning the World Series, all the while Brenna's brain working overtime, rehearsing how she was going to lead into the question, trying to figure out the best way to bring up what was obviously a sore topic without the detective closing up on her or, worse yet, walking away.

And yet *this* was the best she could come up with—two seconds after they'd sat down at a table by the window with their cups of black coffee (No skinny decaf soy milk lattes for either one of them—only the basics; they'd small-talked that topic to death, too . . .), the question thrown into Morasco's face like a gallon of ice water, no foreplay whatsoever, before he'd even so much as put his cup down on the table.

"Well," he said, "I guess I don't have to ask you why you wanted to see me."

"Sorry. Like I told you before, I'm a blurter."

Morasco's eyes filled with some emotion—she couldn't tell whether it was caring or hurt or just the thickness of the glasses. Then he smiled a little and took a sip of his coffee, and Brenna thought, *At least he isn't getting up and leaving.* "It was a bad lead," he said, "because I was *told* it was a bad lead."

"Who told you?"

"The chief. The chief at the time. He passed away a couple of years ago."

"Ray Griffin?"

"Yes. How did you know . . . Never mind."

"What were his reasons?"

Morasco shrugged. "It came from a little girl."

"Some of the best leads come from little girls."

"Not everyone feels that way." Morasco turned his gaze out the window. He was quiet for a while, but Brenna could tell he wanted to say more, and so she just sat there, waiting. "I got accused of McMartinizing."

"Of what?"

"There was a preschool, back in the eighties, the McMartin school. The people who ran it were falsely accused of molesting the kids . . ."

"I remember the story."

He smiled. "Of course you remember . . . Anyway, you know how the McMartin preschool kids were coerced into accusing the adults because the investigators asked them leading questions?"

"You got accused of leading the little girl into saying she saw a blue car."

"Yes."

"But you didn't lead at all. You were . . . very kind, actually."

"How do you know?"

"I saw the interview."

"You did?"

Brenna nodded. "I read the whole police report."

"When?"

"Eleven years ago."

He smiled at her.

"But, uh . . . also last night." Brenna opened her messenger bag, removed the small stack of files Nelson had given her. She slid them across the table. "I told Nelson I would only show these to you," she said. "He doesn't trust the police. Or maybe he just doesn't trust middle-aged dudes who drive Trans Ams, I don't know . . ."

Morasco was paging through the folders—the yellowed news articles, the kindergarten pictures and family portraits, and then, finally, the police report. "Where did he get these?"

"They were Carol's," Brenna said. "She'd hidden them, at the bottom of a craft and hobby box."

"Quite a hobby."

"She was looking for Iris."

He gazed at her. "Weren't we all?"

She took a sip of her coffee, scalding her tongue. No matter how long she seemed to wait at these chain shops, the coffee was still too hot. She took the lid off and blew on it and said, "I think they might be related."

"Carol and Iris?"

"No," she said. "Carol Wentz's murder and the Iris Neff case." She told him about Carol, calling herself Lydia and telling her friends in the Chrysalis chat room that her missing daughter had called. She told him, too, about the calls Nelson had received from the young girl saying it was her fault—but she didn't put two and two together. She let him do that.

"You think Iris Neff came back to town and killed Carol."

"No," she said. "But I do think it's possible that they may have been in contact."

"Carol and Iris."

"It's possible."

"And you're thinking that . . . this *contact* . . ."

"Could have been the thing that got Carol Wentz killed," she said. "Yes."

Morasco said nothing. He swallowed his coffee and gave her a long look—that same look he'd given her outside the Neff house two nights earlier, and again she wanted to get inside his brain, to read his thoughts. "We found the murder weapon," he said.

Brenna stared at him.

"Large flat-head screwdriver. From the same set Nelson Wentz has in his garage."

Brenna felt numb. "Where . . . where was it found?"

"Wrapped up in a garbage bag and thrown in the trash can of the Lukoil station on Van Wagenen and Main." He placed his cup on the table and looked at Brenna. "Cheapest gas station in town. Owner says Nelson Wentz goes there all the time."

Brenna's jaw clenched up. She felt as if the floor were shifting, listing under her chair like a rickety boat, about to capsize.

"Is there anything I should know about your collection of tools?"

"Why would you ask that?"

"Well . . . they've all been bagged and removed from your garage. I'm just wondering if you've noticed any of them missing in the past few weeks."

"*No.*"

She focused on the song seeping out of Starbucks' speaker system. Death Cab for Cutie. "I Will Follow You into the Dark." Yet another song about the romance of dying, and it was one of Maya's favorites. This disturbed Brenna. Of course, every generation entertained this notion, and sometimes when Brenna closed her eyes and focused, she could hear Clea blasting "Don't Fear the Reaper" and singing along at the top of her lungs, though the memory wasn't as clear as she'd like it to be. No memory of Clea was as clear as she'd like it to be.

"When Pomroy and I were questioning Nelson Wentz at the hospital," Morasco said, "Pomroy asked him about a murder weapon. Nelson didn't seem to know what he was talking about, but as we were leaving, I thought I heard him say something under his breath." He took another swallow of his coffee.

Brenna watched him.

"Flat-head screwdriver," Morasco said softly. "That's what I could've sworn I heard him say."

Over the speaker system, the singer assured his love that they would be holding each other soon, in the blackest of rooms. Brenna thought about Nelson—his frightened face, the plain gold wedding band on the small hand. She thought of a screwdriver, coated in Nelson's dead wife's blood, and hard as she tried, she couldn't picture that hand, holding that screwdriver. Brenna took a deep breath and released it slowly, placing her hands on her coffee cup, just to feel the warmth. "McMartinizing," she said. "Isn't that some kind of dry cleaning?"

"You're changing the subject."

"No, I'm not."

"I'm telling you that Nelson Wentz is a person of interest who is getting more interesting by the hour."

"And I'm telling *you*," Brenna said, "that you know what it's like to be wrongly accused."

Morasco swallowed. She could see his throat moving up and down under the striped button-down collar of the rumpled shirt he was wearing beneath his tweed jacket—the same one he'd worn to her office three days earlier. She could feel his eyes working behind the glasses as he watched her face. Brenna kept her expression neutral, hoping hard that he couldn't see through her, couldn't see this gnawing doubt. She needed Morasco on her side right now. The doubt she could deal with later, on her own.

Morasco said, "Why are you so convinced Nelson Wentz didn't kill his wife?"

Brenna exhaled. "Why are you so convinced he did?"

"I'm not."

"I knew it."

"Not *entirely*."

"But others are, right?" She leveled her eyes at him. "Your coworkers. Probably some of the same ones who told you to leave the blue car alone. It wasn't worth pursuing. As if *anything* wouldn't be worth pursuing when it came to a missing little girl . . ." Brenna was going back to September 8, 1981—to the feel of hard vinyl against the backs of her legs as she sat across from Detective Grady Carlson's desk in the Pelham Precinct House, to stale cigarette smoke worming into her sinuses and Detective Grady Carlson's voice, so slow it had reminded Brenna of a 45 record played on 33 . . . *"You saw your sister getting into a light blue car, but you didn't say anything about it for two whole weeks?"*

"Clea said not to tell."

Brenna forced the coffee to her lips and drank with her eyes squeezed shut, pulling herself back, pulling herself away from the headachy smell of the precinct house, from the crumbs in the detective's mustache, the deep lines in his face, framing that smirk.

"You were very nice to that little girl," Brenna told Morasco. "You showed her respect."

Morasco gazed at her. Brenna became aware that her eyes were hot, her vision slightly blurred. He didn't mention it, though—didn't even ask if she'd been in a memory—and she couldn't figure out whether it was out of kindness or if he was simply too lost in his own thoughts to notice that her eyes were filled with tears.

"I'll look into the Wentzes' phone records," he said.

The Neff police report—the missing page, specifically— wasn't something Brenna felt comfortable asking Morasco about, especially after watching him read through the entire thing, making no remark other than "This brings back memories." Either he didn't realize the John Doe interview was missing, or he'd been instrumental in its removal. She might learn in time, but not now; it probably didn't have much to do with what happened to Carol, unless . . . "You said you questioned Nelson in Iris's case," Brenna said, as they left Starbucks. "Why?"

"Nelson didn't tell you?"

Brenna shook her head.

"I'd rather not say."

She looked at him.

"If it had any bearing on your case, I would, Brenna. But it was just about some . . . rumors. I don't feel comfortable gossiping about people."

"You asked Nelson about his affair with Lydia."

He opened the door for her. "Why did you ask me if you already knew?"

She stopped on the sidewalk, facing him. "Nick?"

"Yeah?"

"Did Chief Griffin ever question Nelson? Anonymously or otherwise?"

Morasco's eyebrows went up. "No," he said. "Why do you ask?"

She started walking. "No reason."

Brenna felt her cell phone vibrating, and picked it up to a text from Trent: *TNT charm strikes again. CW's carrier will e-mail me her records, subpoena-free.* "Yes," Brenna whispered.

"Huh?" Morasco asked.

"Oh, my assistant," Brenna said, realizing halfway through the sentence that Trent's illegally obtaining Carol Wentz's cell phone records wasn't something she wanted to share with the police, even one she was starting to trust. "Uh . . . he ordered us Cajun for lunch."

Morasco shrugged. "Not a big fan of burnt food, especially when they call it blackened." He looked at Brenna. "Don't throw euphemisms at me. You burnt it, say so. Tell it like it is."

"Good point."

"Brenna?"

"Uh-huh?"

"We can't tell each other everything."

She looked at him.

"That's okay. Far as our jobs go, it's the nature of the beast, but . . ."

"But what?"

"I'm pretty sure we're on the same side."

She started to smile, but something in his eyes stopped her. "Not many of us on this side, are there?" she said.

"Nope." They were in front of the station now. Morasco's gaze drifted to a car edging its way into the police parking lot—a silver BMW 360i.

"That's some fancy cop car," said Brenna.

"It's the chief's."

Brenna and Morasco watched the BMW pull into a re-served space. A chunky man slid out. He wore a charcoal gray suit that looked expensive, even from a distance. He strode past Morasco and Brenna and into the station without saying hello. He had that look on his face, like a celebrity shopping for groceries. *I know you recognize me but please don't talk to me.*

"That's seriously the chief?" Brenna said, once the station door had closed behind him.

"Yep," said Morasco. "Chief Lane Hutchins. Under-stated, isn't he?"

But Brenna hadn't asked the question because of the pompous figure the chief so obviously cut. She'd said it be-cause she honestly *had* recognized him, and her mind was reeling back once again, taking her to October 20, 1998 . . . To that knock on her passenger window, and the pretty-faced cop peering in at her with his shark's eyes, the bulky, scruff-faced uniform standing behind him.

"Lane Hutchins rose up the ladder pretty damn fast," Brenna said.

"Huh?"

"During the Iris Neff case, he was a uniformed officer."

Morasco gave her a half smile. "I'm not even going to ask how you know that," he said. "But yeah. You're right. Lane doesn't come from money but he's always seen himself as a bigwig. Made him a little hard to work with back then, the attitude. He hated taking orders—always said, 'I do better without people standing in my way.'" Morasco took a breath, his eyes drifting away from Brenna's, into some middle distance over her shoulder. "I've got to hand it to him, though. He knew how to make the right people happy."

"Such as?"

"Teasdales," he said. "You make them happy, you make

the mayor happy. Lane hasn't worked past five a day in his life, but he golfs with Roger Wright at 7 A.M. every morning. Around here, that's what you call a work ethic."

"So, listen . . . What's the name of the detective who drives the light blue Vivio Bistro?"

"Huh?"

"I saw him at the Neff house ten years ago with Hutchins, actually. And he was just at Nelson's press conference. Big guy in his forties, brown hair, pretty-boy features?"

Morasco looked at her. "Doesn't sound like anybody I know," he said. "You sure he's with the Tarry Ridge PD?"

"He's got a black mole, right here." Brenna pointed to the side of her face.

Morasco's eyes were blank. He shook his head.

"Are you sure?"

"We had a dozen plainclothes officers and twenty uniforms when I started working here," Morasco said. "Thanks to the Teasdale funding, we've now got five more of each. I know all of them very well. Not one of them fits that description."

Brenna took a step back. "But I saw him . . . with Hutchins. I was staking out the house and they knocked on my window. Told me to leave."

Morasco shrugged. "No idea."

She looked deep into his eyes, wishing again that she could see what was going on behind them. "Nature of the beast," she said.

"No, Brenna. I honestly don't know who you're talking about." Morasco said good-bye to Brenna with a handshake and a quick smile. He left her standing outside the station, alone with her doubt.

19

The press had all left by the time Brenna made it back to Nelson's house. A good thing for him, too, because if any news outlet had been there, they'd have gotten the photo op of their lives: Nelson Wentz's investigator, leaning on his bell, pounding on his door with the side of her fist, shouting his name like some spurned wife in a Lifetime movie.

It was Brenna's fault, of course. She was the one who'd insisted he take the sleeping pill, then unplugged his upstairs phone, set his machine to pick up after one ring, and turned the volume way down, so that it was now just as impossible to wake him with a call as it was to accomplish the task via the too-thick front door, or this maddeningly feeble electronic bell.

Brenna backed up for a few moments, eyeing the bay window that made up most of Nelson's living room wall. The pristine white draperies were drawn shut, as always. She moved closer and put her hand on the glass, gave it a tentative knock. The sound resonated. She wondered how hard she could bang on the window without breaking it, her gaze shifting to the small garden at the base of the window—a bed of impatiens, atop which staid white mums flowered at evenly spaced intervals, all framed by a line of smooth, fist-sized rocks. For a few moments, she imagined picking up one of the rocks and winging it at the bedroom window. Brenna had a good arm—she'd pitched for her high school softball team and even played for the *Trumpet*'s team as a ringer two years in a row, forcing the rival *New York Post* to insist on a "no spouses" clause for company games—but these rocks looked like they could do some serious damage. She wanted to *talk* to Nelson, not face him in small claims court.

Her gaze went to the rock at the center—slightly larger and rougher, with an odd, bloated shape. A familiar shape . . . Brenna grabbed it. Sure enough it was plastic, the same brand Brenna's mother had bought from Ellory Hardware at 2975 Ocean Street and placed under that hedge by the side of the house twenty-three years ago. *If you need to use the key, fine. But this rock needs to be our secret, Brenna. You make sure no one sees you opening it!*

Brenna twisted open the rock, pulled the key out, unlocked Nelson Wentz's front door, and hurried upstairs, following the sound of his snoring.

She found him in his bed, flat on his back in the type of deep sleep that ages you—blanket up around the chin, mouth wide open, cheeks sunken in. He could have been eighty or ninety years old. This could have been his death-bed. On the nightstand next to him, Brenna saw the book she'd noticed on the coffee table—*Safekeeping: A Memoir*. She put her hand on the cover, and Nelson gasped as if she'd touched a limb. His body jerked, and when Brenna turned, she saw him, sitting up in bed, his eyes wide open and confused. "What are you doing here?"

"Let myself in."

He stared at her. "What's wrong?"

"We need to talk, Nelson," Brenna said. "They found the murder weapon."

He closed his eyes for a moment.

"You know what was used to kill her."

He nodded slowly.

Brenna made herself look him in the eye. "How do you know?"

Nelson took a deep breath. "When I found Carol. I . . . I saw her wounds. I saw that my screwdriver was missing from its hook."

"*Well then why the hell didn't you tell the police?*"

Nelson sat up, and the blanket slipped, revealing the plain white T-shirt, the one he'd been wearing under the dress shirt and bow tie for the press conference. There was something indecent about it. He looked vulnerable and exposed. "They were . . . they were already accusing me. I was frightened."

"Why didn't you tell *me*?"

He cleared his throat, pulled the blanket closer to him. "I don't know."

"We had an understanding, Nelson. You promised to tell me everything—no matter how difficult or embarrassing it was to say."

"I was afraid."

Brenna exhaled, watched his face. Nelson's mouth twitched. He returned her gaze, but his eyelashes kept fluttering. Brenna didn't know whether to take that as evasiveness or nerves—with Nelson, they so often went hand-in-hand. She said, "They found the screwdriver at the Lukoil station on Van Wagenen and Main."

"That's . . . that's where I always get my gas."

"So you understand the problem here," she said between her teeth. "You understand the situation that you're in?"

Nelson collapsed, as though someone had put a lead weight in his chest and then ripped out his spine. He rested his elbows on his knees and sank his head to his wrists. He stayed like that for quite some time, his shoulders trembling.

"Why would someone," he kept saying, "why would some-one do this to me, why would someone be so cruel, why would someone, why . . ." His voice was muffled and slightly wet. Brenna wasn't sure whether Nelson was crying until he looked up at her. His eyes were dry.

"Nelson?"

"Yes?"

"Did you kill your wife?"

"No. I swear to God I didn't. I wouldn't . . . I would never hurt Carol."

Brenna searched his face. "I believe you," she said. And she meant it—for those same simple instinctual reasons that had made her believe him in the first place. And because for the life of her, she couldn't picture a man as frail and anal retentive as Nelson Wentz committing such a violent and messy act.

But Nelson *was* hiding something from her—she knew that much. "Can I make you a cup of tea?" she said.

Nelson pulled his head up. "I think I need a Scotch."

In Nelson's luxurious kitchen, Brenna mixed him a Scotch/water so weak, she could have served it management-approved at a shopping mall chain restaurant during two-for-one happy hour. She fully understood Nelson's desire for a good strong drink, given the circumstances. But she was afraid of how it might interact with the sleeping pill he'd taken earlier, and she had no desire to pick Nelson up off the floor and carry him upstairs.

Brenna handed him the drink and poured herself a glass of water, and the two of them walked into the living room. He took the same chair he'd been in the night he'd hired her. As she sat down in the hard chair next to him—the same one for her as well—her mind briefly shifted back to that night, two nights ago, Nelson looking her in the eye. *I promise. I'll tell you everything.*

She waited for Nelson to take a swallow of his drink. She put her glass of water down on the coffee table, making sure to use a coaster so that he wouldn't jump out of his skin. "Nelson?"

He looked at her.

"There's something you're not telling me," she said, "about you and Lydia Neff."

Nelson's face flushed at the name. He took another enormous swallow. "I don't know what you're talking about," he said.

Brenna exhaled hard. "I'm sorry, but I can't work this way."

"What do you mean?"

"We've been through this dance about a dozen times in the past two days, and I'm tired of it. I have no use for evasiveness or white lies, or if-you-don't-have-something-nice-to-say or whatever you want to call it. It's all bullshit. You want me to work with you, I need facts. All of them. And if that's too much for you to handle, then I suggest—"

"I was in love with Lydia Neff."

Brenna's eyebrows went up. She stared at Nelson for what felt like a full minute, unsure of how to respond. "So," she said finally, "you did have an affair?"

"No." His eyes were starting to cloud.

"You had feelings for each other?"

He shook his head.

"I don't understand."

"Lydia had her own PR firm," Nelson said. "She ran it out of her house, but she had to go into the city a lot. There was a period, a dozen years ago, when she was working on a major event—the opening of the Rose Building on Fifty-seventh. She was taking the train into the city almost every day for a few months." He took another huge gulp of his drink, draining it, Brenna glad for all the water she'd put in.

"And . . ."

"And you know, I take the train in to my job at Facts of Note. We'd be on the platform at the same time. At first, we just said hello, but at some point, we started sitting together and talking."

"What did you talk about?"

"Politics, religion, scientific discovery . . . You name it. Lydia would always ask me about whatever article I happened to be editing, and the conversation would sort of . . . take off from there." Nelson set his glass down on a coaster, and sat down again. He ran a hand through his wispy hair, gazing up at the ceiling. "She was so . . . interested."

"Not like Carol."

"No. Not like Carol."

"You fell in love with Lydia during these train rides?"

He nodded.

"Couldn't wait to get to the train station every day."

"That's right."

"Do you think Lydia felt the same?"

Nelson shook his head. "I was just someone for her to pass the time with," he said. "I think part of me knew that, even back then—but I didn't care. Do you have any idea what it's like to have a woman—a woman like Lydia Neff—hanging on your every word? Looking into your eyes like you're the only man on earth?" The hand went back into the hair. "She started to confide in me, too."

"About . . ."

"Her past. Her wild college years. Her ex-husband, Iris's father. A genius, but wrecked his brain with drugs—methamphetamine, I think . . . He was in an institution back then. I don't know that she told anyone else about him, other than me."

Brenna looked at Nelson. "She trusted you."

"It was never an affair. We weren't doing anything wrong—just talking."

"Sometimes, talking is more intimate."

Nelson stared down at his hands

"Especially if no one else is talking to you."

Nelson picked at a thumbnail. For the briefest moment, he lifted his gaze to Brenna's face, and his eyes looked different, bright—as though someone had suddenly flicked the switch behind them. "Timothy O'Malley."

"Huh?"

"Timothy O'Malley. Lydia's ex-husband—that's his name." He looked up at Brenna again, his eyes still blazing. "She went to Syracuse, majored in art history. Her freshman roommate was a prudish girl from Harrisburg, Pennsylvania, named Marianne Stanhope. I remember everything she ever told me, Ms. Spector. Every single detail of her life— I've kept them all in my head like . . ."

"Souvenirs."

"Yes." He breathed in and out. "Souvenirs."

"I understand," Brenna said, and she did. Probably more than anyone, though her mind didn't pick and choose the way Nelson's did. She knew what it was like to be a human time capsule—to be the only one in a conversation to remember its details. She knew how one-sided that could feel, how terribly lonely it could make you, especially when those details held within them that feeling—that crumbling of the heart . . . "Did Carol know about your friendship?"

"She never asked," he said, "so I didn't say anything."

Brenna's mind went to the folders under Carol's quilting supplies, the photographs and police reports and the secret chat room life she'd been leading as LydiaTR . . . "She suspected something."

He nodded. "The funny part was, the whole thing—

whatever you want to call the thing that was going on between Lydia and me . . . By the time Carol said something about it, it was more or less over."

"How so?"

"Lydia's train rides started tapering off, till they were around once a week at most," he said. "Lydia was still friendly, but she seemed more distracted. My feelings, thankfully, started to fade."

"Okay . . ."

"Then one night . . . God, I remember it like it was yesterday. It was a Saturday night, and I was watching the ten o'clock news and Carol walks into the room. She says, very matter-of-fact, 'Someone told me that you and Lydia Neff are having an affair.' "

"What did you say?"

"I told her that it was completely untrue, of course," Nelson sighed heavily. "Carol told me she'd heard it from her friend Gayle Chandler. She said Gayle had heard it from Lydia herself. Can you imagine? Why would Lydia tell a lie like that?"

"That's horrible."

He nodded. "I told Carol the whole story. She seemed to believe me, but still I was bothered. After Carol went to sleep, I drove over to Lydia's house. There was another car leaving, just as I was getting there. It made me feel . . . strange."

"Jealous?"

"Maybe. Anyway, I knocked on the door, and it was the weirdest thing. Here I'd driven there at that ungodly hour to tell Lydia what Gayle Chandler had said and ask her if it was true . . . But I didn't wind up saying any of that." He cleared his throat. "I asked her about the car."

"The car," Brenna repeated. "The one leaving the house."

"Yes, and she acted so . . . so bizarre, I forgot everything else I'd been planning to say."

"Bizarre?"

"She told me to forget I saw the car. Forget I was ever there. Tonight never happened. I left pretty quickly—Iris was sleeping upstairs and I didn't want to wake her, and besides . . . Lydia frightened me."

Brenna leaned in closer. "Your feelings for Lydia . . ."

"They went away that night." Nelson's gaze dropped to the floor. Brenna knew he wasn't telling the complete truth about that, but she wasn't going to call him on it. It wasn't important. The phone rang once in the kitchen, and the machine picked up silently. Neither one of them moved. That wasn't important, either.

"I thought Carol was over any hurt feelings or suspicions she may have had," Nelson said finally. "It was more than a decade ago, and it was nothing to begin with. We never talked about it . . . But then seeing . . . seeing everything she'd been up to before she went away . . ." Nelson's voice cracked. "If it was my feelings for Lydia . . . If that was the reason why someone *did that* to Carol, I don't think I'm going to be able to live with myself."

Brenna put a hand on Nelson's shoulder. It felt delicate as a bird's wing. "It'll be all right," she said. "Don't worry. It'll be okay . . ."

Finally, he caught his breath. "I wish she would call again."

"The young girl."

"Iris. Yes."

Nelson reached for his glass, sucked down a piece of ice, and chewed it up. They sat there for several seconds, the crunching sound filling the air around them. "You want to know something weird?" Nelson said finally.

Brenna looked at him.

"The car—the one leaving Lydia Neff's house that she seemed so frightened over . . . Carol and I had just been at the Subaru dealership that day, looking at the exact same model."

"Subaru dealership?"

"Yes. Coincidental, huh?"

Brenna opened her mouth, then closed it again. Her throat was dry. She grabbed her glass of water off the table and took a long, draining gulp. *No. No it couldn't be . . .*

"Are you all right, Ms. Spector?"

"Nelson," she said. "Do you happen to remember the color and model of the Subaru you saw?"

Strange, there were dozens of Subaru models available twelve years ago, ranging from the rugged Forester station wagon to the citified Impreza sedan. Yet before Nelson spoke, Brenna knew exactly what he would say.

"It was a Vivio Bistro. Light blue."

20

Meade wouldn't have chosen the car for himself. It was too compact for a man his size, and getting into and out of it was a process that bordered on arduous. Over the years, though, he'd learned to appreciate the unfolding of his powerful legs and arms, the tilting of his broad shoulders to maneuver them out the door, the pushing back against the seat to propel himself out of this tiny sedan—*propel* himself, like a missile. The effect was surprising—onlookers would often double-take, wide-eyed. Adam Meade thrived on surprise. So Meade was grateful for this undersized vehicle. It reminded him of his place in the world.

When Meade parked the Vivio this time, though, he made sure there were no onlookers. He found a quiet residential street a few blocks up from his destination, the sidewalk shaded by maple trees ablaze with dying leaves. He pulled beneath a tree with especially thick and remarkable foliage—a bright orange distraction. Before getting out of the car, he checked the sidewalks, then the windows of the modest apartment buildings and brick row houses. Finally satisfied that he was alone, Meade propelled himself out of his metal cocoon of a car and walked through this neighborhood in Mount Temple as if he were another, less remarkable person. He could not afford to surprise anyone today. Surprise made people remember and Meade did not want to be remembered.

Columbus was a busy avenue where the buildings all appeared somewhat sea-worn, as though the constant whooshing of buses, trucks, and speeding SUVs had eroded their facades. The apartment house was by far the most forlorn on the street, and to make matters even worse, Graeme Klavel's office was in the basement apartment. Meade had yet to meet Klavel in person, but he felt as if he had a good sense of the man, eking out his living under a city street, buried and forgotten, as if he were already dead.

Meade wasn't fond of most of Mount Temple. But he did like the Blue Moon Diner. He'd eaten a late, leisurely breakfast there, and, as always, it reminded him of a place his father used to take him when he was a little boy—a coffee shop near Dad's base back in Jacksonville, where "the men of the house" would go for biscuits and gravy every Sunday morning while his mother and sisters were at church . . . It pained Meade to think of those times now, but still he enjoyed the Blue Moon, where he could brush up against his past without going all the way in.

While he'd been eating, he'd stared at the sports section of the *Daily News* without reading it, listening instead to the two women at the next table—Mrs. Bloom and Mrs. Archibald, discussing their lives while lamenting the rash of switchblade murder/robberies that had hit the town and surrounding areas in recent months. "Just when we thought it was safe," Mrs. Bloom had sighed. And Meade had sat there with his ham and eggs, nodding at a photo of Alex Rodriguez sliding home and thinking, *How true, Mrs. Bloom. How true.*

Meade reached the front door of the apartment building without passing so much as one other human being on the sidewalk—a gift. Life often worked in his favor, he realized. He needed to take note of those happy coincidences, to focus on what he had rather than what had been taken from him. Meade needed to remember to always be grateful.

Klavel answered his buzzer. "Klavel Investigations."

"Hi, Mr. Klavel," Meade said into the speaker. "I was referred by Mrs. Bloom from Patterson's Dry Cleaners?"

"Oh yes . . . Elaine's a good friend."

"Nice lady. Anyway . . . I have some work for you. It's kinda personal though. It, uh . . . it involves my wife."

"Yes. Yes of course." Klavel buzzed him in.

Meade walked down the stairs. Within moments, he was inside the shabby office, the barrel of his Glock .45 pressed against Klavel's forehead. Klavel's rodent face was bathed in sweat. His breath, as you might expect of a man who lived and worked underground, smelled like sewage. Right now, it was coming out of him in short, popping gasps.

"Where did Carol put it?" Meade asked quietly.

"Wha . . . what did you . . ."

"Carol Wentz."

"Y-y-yes. I know," Klavel cleared his throat. His body was trembling. He swallowed, the way a dying man would when offered the smallest sip of water. "I know Carol, but I . . . please take that gun away."

"Tell me."

"Tell you what? Christ, I can't even think. I'll tell you anything you want if you would please . . . please . . ." His eyes were slick. "I . . . I don't know what to say."

"Where did Carol put the drawing?" Meade waited. Ninety-nine percent of the time, the Glock could make people do whatever you wanted—whether it was getting into the trunk of a car, setting fire to their own hair, or telling the truth. You just needed to be patient, to watch.

"The what?" Klavel asked.

"The *drawing*."

"I . . . I don't know what you're talking about. God help me, I don't." Klavel's eyes had gone big. Gazing into them, Meade knew he was being honest.

"That's a shame," Meade said, meaning it. "It's a shame that you don't know." Without taking his eyes away from Klavel's, he reached into his jacket pocket with his free hand, touched the handle of the switchblade. Another of Meade's strengths was his ability to make the right decision.

"Please," Klavel whispered. The word half dissolved in his sewer breath, an assault. "What do you want me to do?"

Meade thought.

Klavel said, "Anything you want," and Meade cut him off, if only to get him to close his mouth.

"I want you," he said, "to make a phone call."

"Before I forget," Brenna told Trent over the phone, "I need you to contact car dealerships in Tarry Ridge—find out if any light blue Subaru Vivio Bistros were sold there in 1996, '97, and '98."

"How exciting is my job? Jay-Z got nothing on me."

"You know, sarcasm and nipple rings really don't mix."

An explosive "Sssh!" cut her off.

"Man," she whispered.

"Why can't you just buy a freakin' iPhone?" Trent said for the third time this conversation. His voice in Brenna's earpiece had a whiny edge that made her want to slap him, but he did have a point. She was at a computer in the Tarry Ridge library, trying to go over Carol Wentz's forwarded phone records with her assistant, but the enormous librarian kept truncating their conversation with these abrupt, spastic shushes—it was almost like a form of Tourette's.

Brenna had just gotten shushed for the fifth time in five minutes, which would have made a lot more sense if there were anyone else besides the two of them in the computer room.

Brenna glanced at the librarian—who glared back as though she couldn't wait to bite off her head and spit it into the book return box. "Just so you know," Brenna muttered into her hand, "somebody around here could really use an anger management class and about fifteen Xanax."

"I'm serious, dude," Trent said. "If you had an iPhone or a BlackBerry, you could access your e-mail anywhere—your car, a nice park . . ."

"Can you please not call me dude?"

Trent sighed audibly. "You watch your movies on a Betamax, too?"

"All right, fine, point taken." Brenna went back to the list of numbers on her screen. It covered Carol Wentz's last two weeks of phone use, with nothing at all after 9 P.M. on September 24—the last day Nelson had seen her. "She made a decent amount of calls here," Brenna whispered. "Did you check out all these numbers?"

"Yep. All except that last one—looks like a Westchester area code. She called it a few times that week—five on the 23rd."

"I see it," Brenna whispered. "One ten-minute call and four three-minute ones, all less than thirty seconds apart."

"Like she kept remembering stuff she'd forgotten to say."

"Or she kept getting hung up on."

"Sssh!"

"Yo, even *I* heard that," Trent said.

Brenna turned to the librarian. There was a name tag pinned to her sprawling bosom, but frankly, Brenna couldn't make herself keep her eyes there long enough to read it. "Look, I know you're just doing your job," she tried. "But this is important business. I'll be out in five minutes, promise."

"I'm not *just doing my job.* You want to conduct business, go to Starbucks." Her voice sounded exactly like the serial killer's from *Silence of the Lambs.*

Trent said, "Hey, is she one of those librarians with the cute little glasses and the tight skirt with the garters underneath?

"You mean a librarian from a porn movie?"

"Uh . . ."

"No. No, she is not."

"Sssh!"

Brenna went back to the list. The Westchester number, the one Carol had called so many times. "It's Graeme Klavel—the PI she hired."

"Damn, you are so good with phone numbers," Trent said. "I should take you to clubs. Chicks could give me their digits, they'd go right into your brain . . . I wouldn't even have to break eye contact to put 'em in my phone."

"I can only remember the numbers, Trent," Brenna said. "I can't make them give you their *real* ones."

"Hilarious."

"So anyway, it looks like he was working for her recently—not just whenever it was he got her the police file. There was that lunch at Blue Moon, but all these calls before and after."

"She had him looking for Iris. Explains why she never called you."

"I'll call Klavel again after we hang up." Brenna was now looking at the three calls Carol had made to Buffalo. If this bill were any indication, she didn't like to spend a lot of time on the phone—most all her calls lasted five minutes or less, yet the ones to the Buffalo number were thirty, twenty-five, and thirty-five minutes respectively.

"You looking at Buffalo?" Trent said.

"Read my mind."

"Sssh!"

Brenna looked at the librarian. "Careful—you might break a tooth."

"I checked those Buffalo calls," Trent was saying. "They're all to someone named Millicent. Bet it's that aunt Wentz told us about."

Brenna said, "Did you ever find out what she spent forty-two eighty-nine on at that convenience store?"

"Yep."

"And?"

"Carton of cigs."

"*Really*?"

"Hey, she was a charitable lady. Cigs are expensive. The owner says somebody picked them up. I assume Aunt Millicent." Trent went back to the phone bill. "That one at the top of page 2 is to Carol's friend Gayle Chandler and the rest are mostly errand calls—dry cleaners, beauty salon, some French grocery store in Bronxville. Except for this one Tarry Ridge number—7651."

Brenna scanned the list. During the last few days of her life, Carol Wentz had called the number eleven times, each call lasting ten seconds or less. "Why does she keep calling and hanging up?" Brenna said.

"Got me."

"Do you have information on it?"

Trent gave her a name: Willis Garvey. An address: 225 Morning Glory. Not anyone Nelson had ever mentioned, and not a neighbor. In fact, once Brenna Google-mapped it, she saw that Morning Glory Road was located in the Waterside Condominiums complex—about as far away from the Wentz house as you could get and still be in Tarry Ridge.

After ending her call with Trent, Brenna printed out the phone records and placed them in her bag, along with a few more copies of the age-enhanced Iris Neff photo.

"In a library, we observe library rules!" the librarian shouted after her, her voice echoing.

Brenna turned, gave her a "Ssshhh" that lasted a solid ten seconds as the hulking woman stared, saucer-eyed. "Hypocrite," Brenna said.

Once outside, Brenna tapped Graeme Klavel's number into her cell phone. Again, she got the answering machine with the Klavel Investigations message. *Some business this guy must do, never answering his phone.* She left him another message and headed for her car, ready for her next step. A simple one.

If Brenna were a fan of conspicuous consumption, the Waterside Condominiums would have blown her out of her chair. As it stood, the place gave her a headache. Apart from maybe a handful of trees and the marble sign out front, the property was virtually unidentifiable as the dozen luxe but understated homes she'd driven to ten years ago—the peaceful, out-of-the-way spot Lydia Neff liked to visit every morning in order to, as her neighbor (and apparent town gossip) Gayle Chandler had put it, "meditate by the fountain." The marble sign that read "Garden" was gone—along with, Brenna imagined, the garden itself and all the other elements of the complex that had been somewhat restrained. There were still grounds here, yes—but they were endlessly rolling, painstakingly landscaped grounds that would have been at home in Versailles. The gated recreation area was now the size of a country club, with tennis courts that rambled on for acres.

There was something grotesque about the Waterside Condos now—the residential equivalent of that once-beautiful actress with the overzealous plastic surgeon. And while Brenna couldn't help but remember the original, she doubted many others did. With this type of rapid, unfettered expansion, the people living with it tend to suffer from post-traumatic amnesia. *What are you talking about? It's always looked like this . . .*

Following Lee's polite orders, Brenna winded her way past malachite lawns bedecked with rose bushes and topiaries, past mini mansions with multiple chimneys and bulbous turrets and chandeliers glistening from behind bay windows that stretched up three, four, sometimes even five stories. But her mind wasn't on any of it . . .

Willis Garvey. The name kept taking Brenna back to tenth grade, to the smell of Pine-Sol mingled with her history teacher Mrs. Carmody's rose hips perfume, the cold, hard waddle of Brenna's hinged metal desk pressing into her knees as she watched Sophia DelVechio start her oral report on Marcus Garvey . . . Completely pointless memory, but the syndrome didn't discriminate, with Sophia Del-Vechio as alive in Brenna's mind as Jim ever was, or Morasco, or Grady Carlson, and all of them more so than her father, more so than Clea . . .

225 Morning Glory Road crept up on Brenna and slapped her in the face. She'd been driving on autopilot, following Lee's instructions with Sophia DelVechio's yawn-inducing oral report running through her mind from start to finish. (Too bad an in-depth description of the Pan Africa movement wasn't something Brenna needed right now, or she'd be in great shape.)

Brenna pulled to a stop in front of the Garvey home. Like all the others in the complex, it was white and muscular, flexing out of its smallish lot in a way that was almost obscene. The car in the driveway was a car you'd expect at a house like this—2008 black Esplanade, assiduously waxed. Brenna had no doubt she'd be able to use the hood as a makeup mirror should she so desire.

Brenna recalled the Wentz house—so decidedly non-showy, save for the kitchen. She thought about Carol Wentz's 2002 Volvo, a car known for its good mileage and high safety ratings that had probably never seen a coat of wax since its showroom days. Why had Carol been calling these people and hanging up? Why had she been calling them at all?

She rang the doorbell, and a maid answered, in uniform. It was one thing to hire a housekeeper, quite another to make one wear a blinding white dress and bib apron. What was this, *Masterpiece Theatre*? All she needed was a doily on her head. The maid was very short and of Hispanic descent and could have been anywhere from thirty to sixty. "Can I help you?" she said, eyeing Brenna warily, her gaze moving from Brenna's hands to her pocketbook and resting there, no doubt expecting the stack of Jehovah's Witness flyers.

"I need to speak to Mr. or Mrs. Garvey, please." Brenna dug around in her purse for her wallet and slipped out a business card. "Is either one of them home? I noticed the car in the driveway."

The maid's eyes narrowed. "There is no Mrs. Garvey," she said. And as if on cue, a Greek sculpture of a man appeared behind her—golden hair tousled just so, bright green eyes glittering out of his chiseled face like the chandelier in his gargantuan window, sparkling white polo shirt setting off a perfect tan—he could have been a CEO, but only if real CEOs looked like CEOs as described in romance novels, so perfect and gleaming that Brenna couldn't look him in the eye without blinking repeatedly. *This is who Carol Wentz called and hung up on eleven times?* "Mr. Garvey?"

"Yes?" His smile was bright enough to make Brenna's pupils contract.

"I'm Brenna Spector." She handed him the business card. "I'm working with the police on the Carol Wentz murder."

"Yes?"

"Did you know Carol Wentz?"

"No. I mean, I've certainly heard of her, on the news and all. But no." He frowned at her. "Why?"

Brenna said, "She seemed to know you."

The frown deepened. "Would you like to come in?"

"Please."

Garvey nodded at the maid. She promptly left. Brenna followed him into the great room and gasped—she couldn't help it. Everything in the entire space was white—from the chandelier, staircase, and balcony to the puffy chairs and handwoven rug, to the sparkling floorboards, to the Ionic columns framing the white brick fireplace. All of it tailor-made to show off Garvey's tan, it seemed, save for the two Emmys on the mantelpiece and the small collection of pictures—Christmas card–worthy photos of the same boy and girl at different ages, the boy younger and always with a goofy grin, the girl more serious and straight-backed, both of them immaculately dressed, with Garvey's golden good looks.

"My kids," Garvey said. "Justin and Emily. I'm divorced, but I get them most weekends—they'll be here tonight, in fact."

"Actually," said Brenna, "I was looking at the Emmys."

He smiled. "Daytime Emmys. They're a dime a dozen."

"You're on a soap?"

He nodded. *"The Day's End."*

"My mom's favorite!"

"Well, you can tell her you met Dr. Shane Kirby."

"I will." Brenna went back to her purse. "To tell the truth, I don't talk to my mother all that much. But next time I do . . ."

"I will have eliminated an awkward silence."

"Absolutely."

"That's what soap operas are for." Brenna heard the smile in Garvey's voice, the smoothness. He knew she was about to ask him questions about a murdered woman and yet here he was, grinning and calm, interview-ready. *Actors*. She wondered what his ex-wife thought of that quality, but more she wondered what Carol Wentz had thought of it. Carol, with her haunted eyes and her sad little marriage and her secret obsessions, buried beneath quilting supplies and community work . . . "Willis?"

"Will. Willis is my given name, but I can't hear it without thinking of that kid on *Diff'rent Strokes*. Remember that show?"

"Sure I remember it," said Brenna. "Did you ever know Lydia Neff?"

He blinked at her. "I thought you came here to ask me about Carol Wentz."

"I did."

"Well, I didn't know Carol Wentz. And I don't know . . . what was the name you just said?"

"Lydia Neff."

"I don't know her, either."

Brenna removed the phone records from her purse, her gaze moving up and onto his calm face, the green eyes placid as glacier water.

"You've got to understand," Garvey said. "I just moved out from L.A. in January to be closer to my kids. I barely talk to anybody out here except the *Day's End* people, let alone anybody from Tarry Ridge."

"How do you know?"

"How do I know what?"

"How do you know Lydia Neff is from Tarry Ridge?"

The eyes went harder. "I assumed."

Brenna unfolded the phone records and pointed out the 7651 number. "This is your number, right?"

He swallowed. "Yes. How did you . . ."

"Carol Wentz's phone bill from right before her death," Brenna said. "Help me out here. Why would she make eleven calls to you in three days if you don't know her?"

He stared at her. "I have no idea."

Brenna gave him a good, long look. Some of that icy perfection melted off him. His eyes were no longer hard. In fact, Garvey looked a little frightened.

"You sure you never met Lydia Neff?" she said. "She has a daughter named Iris who disappeared around eleven years ago?" Brenna removed one of the age-enhanced photos of Iris Neff from her bag and showed it to him. "This is the way Iris would look now, but she also looks very much like her mom."

He stared at the picture, and then back at Brenna—as if she'd just presented him with a test in advanced physics, written up in ancient Sanskrit. "No . . ."

For now, at least, Brenna believed Garvey. It was hard not to, helpless as he looked, this facile actor at a complete loss for words. Maybe Carol was calling Garvey for reasons that had nothing to do with Iris. This was real life after all—not *The Day's End*. Not everything made sense. Not everything fit together. Maybe Carol Wentz was a woman with more than one secret, with more than one obsession. "She could have been a fan," Brenna offered.

Garvey shook his head. "I never received any of these calls."

"They look like hang-ups," Brenna said. "Maybe your housekeeper answered them."

"Nobody answered them," he said slowly.

"What do you mean?"

"This is my second line. Only my agent uses it." Garvey took a breath, stared at Brenna. "My second line is a fax machine."

* * *

As she was driving out of the complex, Brenna called Trent. "I need you to check the Tarry Ridge directory, come up with a list of phone numbers one or two digits off from Willis Garvey's."

"Oh man. First the thrill of talking to Subaru dealers and now *this*."

"What'd I tell you about sarcasm?"

Trent sighed. "So that number from the phone bill . . ."

"It's a soap star's fax machine."

"Oh. My. God. You're telling me that Willis Garvey is *the Will Garvey*? Dr. Shane Kirby?"

"You watch soaps *and* Tyra Banks. Excuse me but do you actually do any work over there when I'm not around?"

"Hello, it's called TiVo."

Brenna exhaled. "So, what's the word from the dealerships?"

"Nada, señorita. Ten years ago, it was all about SUVs in the 'burbs—no wussy little K-cars. I found maybe half a dozen Vivios sold per year at those dealerships, three tops would be Bistros—none of 'em light blue."

"That sucks."

"Yeah, but I hear they were cash in Europe so maybe somebody bought one there and shipped it out."

"You'll go over registration records?"

"I am on it like it was Kim Kardashian's ass," he said. "Oh and don't forget your meeting with Sarah Stoller. Four P.M."

Brenna winced. Sarah Stoller was her newest client—a psychiatrist who lived in a cottage on the grounds of the Cornell Medical Center in White Plains. Brenna was dreading the visit. It might have been the probing gazes she usually got out of them when they found out about her condition—or perhaps it was the way Dr. Lieberman used to pick her brain monthly when she was a kid—but for whatever reason, psychiatrists made Brenna nervous. "I'll be there."

After ending the call, she phoned Nelson. She got the answering machine after one ring—of course. Nelson still hadn't changed it back and she didn't blame him. Back at the library, she'd checked out a link Trent had sent her—the *New York Post* online—a huge picture of Nelson's press-conference grin, accompanied by a scathing article about the discovery of the murder weapon, entitled simply, "SCREWED."

Brenna called again, got the machine, ended the call, tapped the number in again, got the machine . . . *"Pick up, Nelson, please. I have a question for you, please pick up,"* she shouted, as if shouting made a difference with the volume turned all the way down. She was about to end the call yet again when she heard Nelson's voice, calm and quiet, on the other end of the line. "Yes, Ms. Spector."

"Nelson," she said. "I'm so glad you answered. Listen, we have Carol's cell phone records from the last two weeks."

"Ms. Spector, I don't recall ever saying you could call me Nelson. I'm old enough to be your father. Please afford me the simple respect of calling me Mr. Wentz."

Brenna's eyebrows went up. "Oookay. Sorry about that."

"Apology accepted."

Brenna glared at the phone, as if it were to blame for the strange chill in Nelson's voice. She would assume he'd had a few more Scotch/rocks since she left—not so diluted this time around—only he wasn't slurring his words. If anything, he sounded a little too sober.

She pressed on. "I'm calling because I need to know if Carol . . . if Mrs. Wentz ever had an interest in soap operas, especially *The Day's End*."

There was a long pause.

Brenna said, "Are you there?"

"Carol never watched soap operas."

"Okay. I didn't think she seemed—"

"I appreciate everything you've done for me, Ms. Spector."

Brenna was reaching the end of the condominium complex. She saw the marble sign and pulled over to the side of the road and put the car in park. "Excuse me?"

"I'm not going to be in need of your services anymore."

"But . . . Ne— Mr. Wentz—"

"Please send me a bill. I will remunerate you in full."

"I don't understand," she said.

But he had already hung up.

For a long time, Brenna stayed in her car staring out the window, the conversation replaying in her head again and again and again. It wasn't what Nelson Wentz had said that bothered her so much, or even the words he had used to say it. It was that tone. Each time the call repeated in her mind, Brenna would hear it again, hear it anew, and it would fill her with the strangest sense of dread. She would hear Nelson Wentz's voice in her earpiece, so flat, so hollow. It was as though someone were holding a gun to his head.

21

Over and done with, Nelson thought as he hung up the phone. But the discomfort clung to him, with all its symptoms—sweat pooling and pressing against the back of his neck, sweat trickling under his jaw and down his shirt, beneath his pants legs, sweat crawling all over him until he felt more wet than dry—a man turning to liquid.

Answering the phone when Ms. Spector called had not been easy for Nelson. He hated being abrupt with people. At work, the firings he had to do were few and far between, and even then, he usually let HR handle them alone.

But it was over now. Nelson had fulfilled his end of the deal. As Mr. Klavel had requested during their second phone conversation, he'd called up the defense lawyer, Phil Reznik, and canceled his appointment with him as well. He didn't need to speak with anyone now—no one at all until 10 P.M. when Mr. Klavel would do as he promised. He would tell Nelson—and show him—what Carol had known.

Nelson hadn't told a soul about speaking with Mr. Klavel, even though this had been quite a confessional day for him. *I was in love with Lydia Neff*, he had told Ms. Spector, and it wasn't until he'd said it out loud that he realized it to be true. But interestingly, saying it out loud—admitting it to another person . . . It was kind of freeing, wasn't it? To let them go, those feelings—to box them neatly into words and toss them out there for others to see . . . In a way, it took the bite out.

I was in love . . . Interesting that he'd stuck his love in that safe place—the past tense—without even thinking about it first. *Was, not am, Carol. I* was *in love.* Nelson felt a lightness now, a sense of calm.

This must be why people write memoirs.

Nelson recalled Carol in her straw hat, smiling. He pictured her face, her living face as he'd first seen it, turning to look at him. How he'd gasped at his first glance of those huge gray eyes . . .

He didn't think of the thing in the trunk at all—only his wife, living and young and smiling at him, and he was grateful for that. He was grateful for a lot, now. His strength was coming back. The phone rang again. He checked caller ID to see if it was Unknown Caller—strange that the only two people he wanted to speak to both had blocked phones—but it wasn't. It was Tarry Ridge Police again, and they could wait. He would speak to them tomorrow when he could really help them, when he'd spoken to Mr. Klavel and had learned about his wife.

"I'm going to know you, Carol," Nelson said. His voice bounced against the kitchen walls, off the tile and stainless steel and copper and pewter—all those hard, shiny things Carol had picked out herself for this room, this one room she truly loved.

Nelson was about to go back upstairs again and try for another nap, but instead he walked into the living room and up to the painting of Sarasota, Florida. He stood there, gazing at it. For the first time, he noticed the soft flecks of sea foam on the cream-colored sand, and how the sun reflected off the sapphire ocean in glints. He noticed the whispery seagulls in the blue sky and the clouds, thin and harmless as cotton candy, rays of sun streaming through them that looked so real, it made you feel warm.

He imagined Carol, standing where he was, staring up at the picture with that dreamy look on her face. And after all these years, he understood.

"Lovely," Nelson whispered. "Just lovely."

Brenna nearly forgot her 4 P.M. meeting with Dr. Sarah Stoller—and would have missed it entirely if Trent hadn't programmed it into the electronic calendar he'd given her for Christmas last year—a torturous little device complete with a reminder bell that sounded like a miniature air raid siren.

For Brenna, perfect memory didn't translate into keeping to a set schedule. She missed appointments if she didn't have them in writing—especially (and rather ironically) if she happened to be caught up in a particularly detailed memory at the allotted time.

Or if she'd just been fired for no apparent reason.

Best not to think about that now. Easier said than done, of course, with Nelson's hollow voice replaying in Brenna's mind, that whole final phone conversation unspooling start to finish as Brenna drove, much like Sophia DelVechio's Marcus Garvey report, only so much harder to comprehend. *What is going on with him?* Brenna wondered, though she knew thoughts like that were pointless with the likes of Nelson—*Mr. Wentz*, that is. Best to keep her mind on the road.

Cornell Medical Center, where Dr. Sarah Stoller worked and lived, was one of the more elegant mental health facilities in New York State, with landscaping not unlike the old Waterside Condos, pre–plastic surgery and wealth bloat. Brenna had heard of it, of course, but this was her first time here, and as she drove past rolling green picnic areas and tennis courts, Brenna was a lot less antsy than she'd anticipated. It looked nothing like an insane asylum. The buildings were all Tudor and Georgian brick, and once you got onto the main campus (it actually was called a campus, as the hospital was also a teaching institution), you could have easily fooled yourself into thinking you were on the grounds of an Ivy League college—were it not for the discreet bars on the windows.

Dr. Stoller's cottage was nestled at the far end of the eighteen-hole golf course—a two-story Tudor with lots of windows and sunny white floorboards and house plants—easily a hundred of them hanging from the high ceiling, sprouting out of cheerfully painted urns, crawling up mini trellises, and filling nearly every available square inch of space in the aptly named sunroom, which was where Sarah Stoller and Brenna were taking their meeting. The room smelled of fresh dirt and moist leaves and pasty stargazer lilies. The couch and chair they were sitting in were of a bright green cloth and soft as spring grass so that they, too, seemed botanical—a whole room more outdoors than in. "So many beautiful plants," Brenna had said as they walked in, breathing deeply. Sarah Stoller had shrugged. "I like things with roots."

Like the medical center, Dr. Stoller wasn't anything like Brenna had expected she'd be. There was none of the probing shrink-stare about her, none of that cocky intensity. On the contrary, Dr. Stoller was tiny and diffident, with a graying Dutch boy haircut and a shy smile. She rarely made eye contact, and when she did, there was a flatness to her gaze, like a bulb had burned out. Brenna couldn't figure out, though, if this had always been an aspect of her personality or if it was that type of grief she'd seen in so many families of the missing—the type that steals the part of you that lives behind the eyes.

Right now, Brenna was looking at pictures of Dr. Stoller's

mother, Elizabeth—a pretty, seventy-five-year-old woman who suffered from severe Alzheimer's. Elizabeth had disappeared from her Princeton, New Jersey, assisted-living facility four months earlier, sometime in the middle of a Saturday night. Reported missing by her nurse the following morning, Elizabeth hadn't been seen or heard from since.

Do you think you could find her? Dr. Stoller had asked over the phone two weeks ago.

Brenna had given it to her straight: An adult with dementia was the worst type of missing person to track down next to a very young child, and for similar reasons. Like children, their actions were rarely logical. They didn't use credit cards or check into hotels or join clubs or even make phone calls very often. In fact, the best you could hope was that they'd get arrested somewhere. The worst . . . Brenna hadn't gone into the worst over the phone, though when Sarah had called again a week later to set up the appointment, she'd said, very pointedly, "I'm not expecting a miracle. Just hoping for one."

"Mom always liked to go for walks," Sarah said now.

Brenna flipped through the stack of pictures—Elizabeth smiling broadly in a pink sweat suit with Sarah at her side, Elizabeth and Sarah in her room at the facility, flanked by a young volunteer and a golden retriever. Sarah and Elizabeth on a park bench shaded by peach blossom trees, both of them smiling—such happier pictures than the ones she'd looked at three days earlier in her own office, Morasco flinging open that folder on her desk, tapping pictures of a sad, beige woman Brenna had never seen in her life—a woman on her wedding day, standing alone in front of an office cubicle, clutching a bouquet of carnations bought from a bodega.

"You and your mother seem very close," Brenna said, careful to use the present tense.

"Mom was the only person I ever really talked to."

Brenna nodded.

"No, I mean literally the *only person*," Sarah said. "I'm a Freudian analyst. I spend my whole life listening to people, saying nothing. I've never been married, and my friends— well, maybe we talk politics, movies. We might discuss trends in psychiatric care, but I don't open up to them." She leaned back into the couch, pulling her thin legs beneath her. "That's an interesting phrase, isn't it? Open up. Like you rip yourself open and let others see your insides."

"It can be nearly that painful," Brenna said.

The doctor gave her a smile. "You're not big on analysis."

"No."

"Me neither. All psychiatrists have to go through it, of course, but back when I was seeing a therapist, I'd find ways to talk about more general topics . . . My whole life, my mother was the only person I felt comfortable talking to— even after she got sick."

"Why is that?"

"I think," Sarah said, "that she's just a good listener."

Brenna looked at her.

"Everybody needs that one person, you know? The one person they can talk to."

Brenna thought about Nelson, falling in love with a woman he barely knew, a woman he commuted into the city with for just a few weeks. Falling in love with her via that simple, rare act of talking and listening. She thought of Jim, whom she hadn't laid eyes on in seven years, but whom she still needed so much, to read the words she typed on the screen, to see her thoughts, to listen . . . Then she thought of Maya, who last night had let go of the eye rolling and the silence and the contempt and spoken to Brenna, really *spoken* to her for the first time in so long . . . yet much as Brenna knew that need, much as she could feel it, her mind had abandoned Maya. It had abandoned them both.

Brenna swallowed hard. "Every mother should be a good listener, Sarah."

"Excuse me?"

"What I'm saying . . . is that I'll do everything I can to find Elizabeth."

Over the next hour, Brenna and Sarah discussed Elizabeth's likes, dislikes, passions, and pet peeves. They talked about her favorite foods (garlicky pasta, fresh tomatoes, crème brûlée) favorite types of music (Sinatra, Rimsky-Korsakov), sense of humor (Marx Brothers, Woody Allen), pets (a series of panicky Chihuahuas, a cat, fussy and obese)—the high and low points of her long, complicated life. Unlike Nelson, Sarah could answer any question Brenna threw at her. She knew everything about her mother and clearly loved relaying the details—from her tiniest quirk to her most important belief, all those things that put flesh to the idea that was Elizabeth Stoller, that made her live again. By the time Brenna was ready to leave, it was as if Elizabeth was in the room with them. And Sarah was smiling, some of the color back in her face. "You've given me a lot to work with," Brenna said.

"Me too." Sarah put a hand on her shoulder. "Thanks."

As Brenna started up her car, her thoughts moved back and forth from Nelson and Lydia, to Jim and herself, to Sarah Stoller and her mother . . . *Everybody needs that one person.* And then she thought of Carol Wentz. She and her husband barely spoke, her chat room friends only knew her as a fictionalized screen name. Gayle Chandler, whom Nelson had referred to as Carol's "best friend" . . . Brenna had met Gayle Chandler ten years ago, and at that time she'd positioned herself as *Lydia's* best friend. "*Check the new condos. Every morning, Lyddie goes there to meditate by the fountain. She's a very spiritual woman, you know . . .*"

Gayle, who, two years prior to that, had falsely informed Carol—for whatever reason—that Lydia was screwing her husband. Brenna didn't know Gayle Chandler, but she knew a crisis queen when she saw one—a woman with very little life of her own, dying to insinuate herself at the center of any tragedy . . . No, Gayle wasn't *that one person*, either.

It wasn't until she was pulling out of the medical center and onto busy Bloomingdale Road that Brenna found herself recalling Carol Wentz's phone bill—those three thirty-minute calls to Buffalo buried amid all the seconds-long errand calls and brief chats with friends. It hit her that two of the three Buffalo calls—presumably to Carol's cigarette-smoking aunt Millicent—took place right after a conversation with Klavel, her private investigator.

That one person. Carol could have been telling Millicent everything she learned that week. *And what exactly was it that Carol Wentz had learned?*

Images flooded Brenna's brain—announcing themselves one by one like a line of light switches flicking on . . . The blue Vivio Bistro at Lydia Neff's house twelve years ago: Lydia urging Nelson, *Forget you ever saw the car. Forget you were ever here*. Three-and-a-half-year-old M from the police file, telling Morasco that Iris had gotten into Santa's "happy" car, which had "round eyes and a smile." The big, pretty-faced cop, in front of the Neff house eleven years ago; driving by the Wentz home this morning, staring through the windshield with his shark's eyes, his predator's eyes. Staring through the windshield *of Santa's happy car.*

Then, Brenna recalled the voice of the girl over Nelson's phone, buried in static but still clear enough. *It was my fault.* The voice of a teenage girl. A sixteen-year-old girl, taking the blame for Carol's death.

That one person . . .

What if the girl on the phone really had been Iris Neff?

What if Iris had been taken away in that Vivio Bistro eleven years ago and had returned two weeks ago? What if, in a bid to escape her captor, she'd phoned Mom's old confidant Nelson Wentz? What if Carol had answered instead? What if Carol had become *that one person* for Iris—that one person who could listen. The one who might help.

Carol hadn't called the police . . . Of course she hadn't. Brenna thought of Lane Hutchins, ten years ago in uniform, standing next to that pretty-faced cop, the cop even Morasco claimed not to have known. Lane Hutchins. Now, chief of police. Then, the muscle. *Of course Carol hadn't called the police.*

She had called her own "one special person."

Brenna pulled into a gas station and parked. She closed her eyes and took herself back to the computer room at the Tarry Ridge library—to the smell of Windexed plastic, to Trent's voice in her earpiece, *"You looking at Buffalo?"* and the scroll of telephone numbers on the screen in front of her . . .

Brenna dug her nails into her palms and she was back in the present, Aunt Millicent's number still fresh in her head. She picked up her phone and tapped it in. *Okay, Aunt Millicent. Tell me what you and Carol were talking about.* She hit send.

"We're sorry. The number you have reached is no longer in service at this . . ."

Must be some mistake. Brenna stared hard at the phone, and tapped it in again, making sure she got each number right.

"We're sorry . . ."

Could she have seen it wrong on the screen? Brenna called Trent, asked him to read the number back to her . . .

"Same one I remembered," she whispered.

"There a problem?" Trent said.

"It's disconnected."

"The aunt's phone? But she was just talking to her last week."

Brenna said, "Can you do a reverse directory on that number?"

"You gonna go up to Buffalo now?" Brenna could hear his fingers clacking away at the keyboard.

"Don't know."

"You sound kinda weird. You on to something, Spec?"

"Not sure. And don't call me Spec."

He sighed. "The address is 811 Mulberry Street, Buffalo."

Brenna's breath caught. Her mouth went dry. "Mulberry."

"I don't see any apartment number."

"That's because it's the whole house."

"How do you know that?" Trent said, with Brenna's mind already answering, already pulling her back into the Las Vegas airport at 1 A.M. on September 30, returning home after finding Larry Shelby, the air-conditioning chilling her bare arms as she approached her gate . . . *Brenna glances up at the two TVs flanking gate A23 as she nears it. CNN coverage of a fire in upstate New York. On each TV, the image of a blazing, four-story house at night. The screens glow like devil eyes.* Why is cable news so pyromaniacal?

A female voiceover intones, "A fire claimed the lives of five residents of 811 Mulberry—a group home for recovering addicts in Buffalo, New York, early this evening, with two more rushed to the hospital in critical condition. Firefighters are still trying to control the blaze, believed to have been set by one of the residents . . ."

Brenna flips her MP3 player back on, Iggy Pop singing about his Chinese rug, as an elderly black woman appears on the screen . . .

"You there?" Trent was saying.

"What is Millicent's last name?"

"You mean the aunt?"

"Millicent," Brenna said. "The one with the Buffalo number."

The elderly black woman is talking animatedly, tears in her eyes, her head shaking and shaking, as if she's in her own world—a world of no-this-can't-be-happening—as if she doesn't know the camera is there.

"Her name is Millicent Davis," Trent said.

Brenna said the last name along with him, her mind still in the airport, with Iggy Pop shouting about success in her ear and white letters appearing under the distraught woman's face "MILLIE DAVIS, OWNER, 811 MULBERRY."

"Millie Davis isn't Carol's aunt. She's the owner of a group home for addicts," Brenna said.

"Huh?"

"A week after Carol called her there, the whole place burned down."

"What?"

"You heard me," Brenna said, another idea gaining strength. *A group home for addicts . . .* "Trent, did you get anywhere on that search for Lydia Neff?"

"Nope—very weird. I've run traces on her credit cards, her phone—nothing's been used in the past two years. It's like she dropped off the planet."

"Look on other planets then."

"Huh?"

"I'm serious, dude."

Brenna ended her call. She was ten minutes away from the Tarry Ridge library, and it closed in twenty. She needed to get there, fast.

The library was of the same smooth white stone as the police station, with Ionic columns out front as some kind of symbol of higher learning. The architecture was that cold blend of classical and modern—synagogue-meets-mausoleum. Like

most other buildings in Tarry Ridge, it seemed just a little
too big for its own good—as Brenna recalled from her previous visit, there weren't anywhere near enough books in the
place to justify its sprawl. Out front, a long table stretched
out, laden with pies, cookies, and stacked-up brownies,
three middle-aged socialites lined up behind it, pimping
the library bake sale at the top of their lungs. "*Pleeeease*
donate to the library!" yelled one—a barrel-chested blonde
in pink shirtdress. "Lemon Lulu cake is only seven dollars!"
hollered another—this one younger and skinnier, her style
somewhere between high school cheerleader and subway
panhandler. "The Lulu cake is *spectacular*! You will *not* be
sorry." It always amazed Brenna how enthusiastic the rich
were about raising money. They could be fighting tooth and
nail against the estate tax, but give 'em a tin can and a relatively pointless cause—more money for an already overly
endowed library, for instance—and they were on you like
Lincoln Tunnel hookers.

Brenna rushed through the marble foyer, around the expansive checkout desk, her footsteps echoing—through the
reference section, left at Books on Tape, and back into the
computer room, the super-sized librarian standing up at her
desk to give her the stink eye.

Brenna smiled up at the librarian. She had to be at least
six-foot-five. "Have you grown taller since the last time I
saw you?"

The stink eye intensified.

"Computer password, please," Brenna said. "Sorry I can't
chat, but I'm in a hurry."

The librarian handed her a piece of paper with a password
typed on it and crashed back down on her chair, glaring.

Brenna took a seat at the first computer, the idea burning
through her as she logged on. *Why was Carol having half-
hour-long conversations with a group home owner?* Brenna

went to Google News and typed in 811 Mulberry. A slew of articles about the fire popped up. She clicked on the one from the *Buffalo News*, reading it all the way through, her heart pounding. When she finished, she closed her eyes. *I was right . . .* For several seconds, she was back in Nelson's living room, just a few hours ago, Nelson expounding on Lydia, the Scotch floating off his breath . . .

"Her past. Her wild college years. Her ex-husband, Iris's father. A genius, but wrecked his brain with drugs— methamphetamine, I think . . ."

Five residents of 811 Mulberry—all recovering addicts— had perished in the fire. *". . . Timothy O'Malley. Lydia's ex-husband—that's his name . . ."* One was listed in critical condition, at Sisters of Charity Hospital in Buffalo. His name was Timothy O'Malley, and the fire was believed to have originated in his room.

"He was in an institution back then. I don't know that she told anyone else about him, other than me."

Brenna went to Google images, typed in O'Malley's name and then the address 811 Mulberry. In a follow-up news article, she found a picture—the face gaunt, the long hair thinning, dark circles under the eyes like bruises, but still . . . it was the same young man from the family portraits in Carol's folder.

811 Mulberry was a group home. All residents shared a phone. Carol had been talking to Iris's father. She'd bought him a carton of cigarettes, probably to get him to talk more.

Brenna picked up her cell phone and started keying in the number. The librarian stood up.

"I'm calling the police so you'd better not freakin' shush me," Brenna snapped.

The librarian sat down so fast the room shook a little.

Brenna asked Fields to connect her with Morasco, and he was on the line fast, his voice strange, cold.

"Nelson didn't kill Carol," she said. "Her death was a part of something else. Something bigger."

"How do you know?"

"Iris's father spoke to Carol on the phone. Less than a week later, Nick, five days after Carol's death . . . Iris's father's home burned down."

"Timothy O'Malley?"

"Yes. He's in critical condition."

Morasco inhaled sharply. Brenna could hear his breathing shake as he let the air go. "My God," he whispered.

"Listen," she said quietly. "I know you don't want to do any more damage to your job than you've already done. I get that. But if you could just give me the name of that cop I told you about—the one with the mole . . ."

"I don't know who you're talking about."

Brenna pressed on. "I'm not asking you to get involved, Nick. But I think that cop might have had something to do with Iris's disappearance. And since he seems to be the only one around here who can still *talk*—"

"I swear to God, Brenna. I don't know who that is."

"Christ, are you that afraid? You said yourself we're on the same side."

"You don't understand." Morasco said it through his teeth, and so quietly she had to press the phone to her ear. "I need to ask you something."

Brenna exhaled hard. "What?"

"Graeme Klavel. The investigator whose number you found in Carol Wentz's files."

"Yes?"

"Did you ever talk to him? Find out if he'd done any work for her?"

"No," she said. "He never called back." She closed her eyes. "We have Carol Wentz's cell phone records, though."

"You do?"

"Don't ask how," she said. "Carol spoke to Klavel repeatedly—five times during the last week of her life. His office was in Mount Temple. He was probably the man she met at the diner."

Morasco took another deep breath, and Brenna listened— a slow inhale and release, as if he was trying to calm them both. "Coincidences happen all the time."

"What do you mean?"

"This isn't some movie. Real life, things happen. They don't really fit together—they just look that way. That's why you have to look at the facts. Houses burn down for all sorts of reasons. Tim O'Malley was a chain smoker. Carol Wentz wasn't Klavel's only client. Mount Temple has a high crime rate."

"Nick."

"Yeah?"

"What the hell are you talking about?"

"Just a second." Brenna heard the shuffling of feet. When Morasco spoke again, his voice was barely above a whisper. "Brenna, Graeme Klavel was murdered."

22

Brenna stood just outside the open door of Graeme Klavel's basement apartment/office, crime scene techs swarming his wrecked body so that she was only able to see it in parts—an outstretched arm here, a foot there, shoeless and sallow, and blood, so much of it, the rotting smell so thick she had to breathe into her shirtsleeve. As with what few other crime scenes she'd been to, Brenna hated to look, yet there was that car-crash curiosity that made it impossible to turn away. It was sick, yes, but it was also instinctual. *You're the only species that knows it's going to die, you will stare at the preview. You can't help it.*

Though Brenna was technically outside the apartment, she still felt trapped. Klavel's space was so small to begin with, and with all his files upended, his closets emptied, clothes and papers strewn all over the floors as if the apartment itself had been assaulted, it was a wonder all those cops and crime scene techs could fit in there.

Brenna's gaze slid from the body to the tipped-over kitchen table to the pulled-out drawers—Klavel seemed to do all his living in two small rooms—then rested on the dark window over the sink, a window looking up at the street. *Sad*. Brenna heard her name then, and saw Morasco, moving through the room toward her, a stocky, silver-haired guy at his side in a navy blue blazer and a checkered oxford that dug into his neck. Brenna assumed it was the Mount Temple cop who'd heard her message on Klavel's answering machine. As Morasco had told Brenna on the phone, one of the detectives on the case had called him because her message had mentioned Carol's name.

The two men made their way out the door, Morasco touching her arm lightly when he greeted her. "Brenna," said Morasco, "this is Detective Wayne Cavanaugh, Mount Temple Police."

"Good to meet you."

Cavanaugh nodded. "You too."

Oddly, Brenna's gaze settled on his nose—the tiniest afterthought of an Irish nose buried in his meaty face, bright blue eyes hovering over it. "You're a PI?"

Brenna nodded. "I work out of the city."

"So . . . I'm taking it you didn't have much contact with Mr. Klavel?"

"Never spoke to him," she said. "In fact, I was getting a little annoyed he wasn't returning my calls."

"What were you calling him about?"

"He had done some work for Carol Wentz. Her husband, Nelson, is my client."

The blue eyes narrowed, and for a moment he reminded Brenna of her mother's cat, Rodin—overfed and milky-eyed, always teetering on the brink of a nap. "You mentioned that on the machine," he said. "Do you know what the work was?"

"You didn't find it in his files?"

"Please answer my question."

"Yes," Brenna said. "I know what the work was."

He sighed. A heavy sigh with a wheeze attached, which again made Brenna think of Rodin. Twenty-two years old and so fat he could barely stand up, so uncomfortably bulbous his skin seemed a size too small, yet still that cat was alive, proof that nature made no sense, never did, never would . . . "Gimme a break."

"Hey, I answered your question."

"You go to law school or something?"

"Nope. I studied psych."

"Great."

"Now my turn," she said. "Did you find Klavel's files regarding the work he did for Carol Wentz, or were those files missing?"

Another massive sigh. "All of his electronic equipment was stolen," Cavanaugh said, as Morasco made his way back to them. "He kept all his files on a laptop, so, to answer your question, yes, Carol Wentz's files were missing. All of Mr. Klavel's files were missing." He looked at her. "My turn."

"Yes?"

"You know the friggin' question."

Brenna smiled a little. "Klavel got Ms. Wentz the police files for the Iris Neff case."

"That little girl? From eleven years ago?"

"Yep."

"Weird." Cavanaugh looked at Morasco. "But it's probably more interesting to you guys in Tarry Ridge."

"Uh-huh."

"Four of these in less than half a year, I can't get one fuckin' witness, one latent print, nothing . . . this guy is too smart," he told Morasco, between his teeth. "You're lucky."

Brenna said, "Why is he lucky?"

Cavanaugh gave her a tight smile. "No more questions," he said.

* * *

Morasco and Brenna walked away from the crime scene, the silence between them somehow punctuated by the near-constant roar of traffic. It was dark already, with that insidious fall chill in the air—another year beginning the slow fade to black—and that added to the feeling.

Brenna had spent a decent amount of time on Columbus Street back when she was working for Errol. She'd stood in the doorway of number 2034—then a boarded-up building, now a vacant lot—haunted it for a good two hours, all so she could snap pictures of a cheating husband by the name of Victor Gomez getting some afternoon delight from one Sam McFarlane, who lived in 2037, directly across the two always-busy lanes. Sam had not been a Samantha but a Samuel—a mountain of a New York City bus driver, and Brenna had used her telephoto lens to capture images of the two men in the doorjamb, Victor standing on tiptoe to kiss big Sam good-bye. It had been one of her sadder assignments—Brenna had always viewed men who cheated on their wives with other men to be acting not so much out of selfishness or even weakness, but out of physical need . . . Anyway, Columbus had been a crap street back then and it was still a crap street now—the type of street the real Columbus would say, "Thanks a whole hell of a lot" over, maybe reconsider that whole claiming-of-America thing, if this crap street was all it was going to get him.

Morasco started to walk toward the nearest cross street, where his car was parked. Brenna thought for a moment he was just going to leave her there, without saying another word, when he stopped and turned to her. "Nelson needs a good lawyer," he said.

"That's why Cavanaugh called you lucky. Because your murder is already solved. You're going to arrest him."

Morasco nodded.

"Unbelievable."

Morasco took a step closer. "Here's the thing, Brenna," he said. "Cavanaugh told me Klavel's killing was identical to the other switchblade murders in the area—stabbed in the neck and gut in the exact same way. That information was never in the papers."

Brenna looked at him. "What was stolen from Klavel?"

"You heard Cavanaugh. Same thing that was stolen from all the switchblade victims."

"Electronic equipment."

"TV, recording stuff, speakers, spy cams . . ."

She gave him a flat look.

"And yes," Morasco said. "The iBook that Klavel did all his business on."

"If someone wanted to find out what he'd told Carol," Brenna said, "then these particular robberies were an excellent cover."

"Yeah, but—"

"Just like a chain-smoking addict could easily burn down a group home."

"Right."

"And an unhappy marriage could end in murder."

"Yes," he said quietly. "So we've either got one supergenius killer, desperate to cover up an unsolved disappearance from eleven years ago . . ." His gaze dropped to the sidewalk. "Or, seeing as this is life, Brenna, we've got what's known as a rotten coincidence."

Brenna put a hand on his shoulder. She watched his face until finally, he looked back up, into her eyes. "Which do you think it is?" she asked.

"Does it matter?"

"Yes."

Morasco said nothing. He didn't need to.

"So," Brenna said, a smile coming on. "We *are* on the same side."

As Morasco walked Brenna to her car, they discussed Carol Wentz and Iris Neff, searching for connections beyond the gossip that once swirled around Nelson and Lydia. There was the blue car, of course. The Vivio Bistro, which had cruised by the Wentz home following Nelson's press conference and had obviously been parked outside Lydia's house more than once. But Brenna was now convinced that Morasco truly didn't know who its pretty-faced cop driver was—or if that driver, the one with the mole, had ever been a cop at all.

There was Carol's wallet, found in the Neff home, and the files and files of research Carol had kept on Iris's disappearance and Carol's claim to her chat room friends that her "daughter" was alive and back in touch . . . but beyond that, there wasn't much that tied together this middle-aged, murdered woman and this eleven-years-missing girl. Except, of course, for another vanished person. "We've got to talk to Lydia," Brenna said as they turned up the street where her car was parked.

Morasco shook his head. "We'd have better luck finding Jimmy Hoffa than Lydia Neff. No one around here has seen or spoken to her in two years, and that includes her Realtor."

"Hoffa. Timely reference there."

"Hey, it's a classic."

Brenna smiled. He smiled back.

"Listen, Nick. If you were concerned about sharing facts with me because I work for a possible murder suspect, you don't have to worry anymore."

"What are you talking about?"

"Nelson Wentz fired me a couple of hours ago."

"What? *Why?*"

"I have no idea."

Her phone chimed, and she answered it, well aware he was still gaping at her. "Brenna Spector."

She heard a choking noise on the other end of the line—a cutting off and releasing of the breath in drawn-out, trembling whispers. "Who is this?" Brenna said, before she recognized the sound. *Crying.* "Hello?"

And then she heard the voice. "I'm a terrible person," said the voice, the wet, choked voice of a teenage girl. The same girl who had called Nelson. "I'm so sorry, so, so sorry."

"Who are you?" Brenna whispered.

The girl ended the call. Brenna looked at Morasco. "We need to find Lydia Neff," she said.

Visiting the last place a missing person had been seen. Retracing steps in reverse. It was something Brenna had always done at the start of investigations—but not this one. And she knew she had to. Lydia Neff hadn't been heard from in two years, but her furniture was in her old house—pretty much everything she owned was in that house—and, as Morasco said, "Far as information on Lydia goes, that's as good as it's gonna get."

Brenna wasn't working for Nelson, true, but she couldn't turn back now. She owed it to Carol and Timothy O'Malley and Graeme Klavel and to the girl on the phone. She owed it to all those pieces of information shoved into her head, from eleven years ago and from today, all those bits of knowledge bumping into one another, like a machine full of bum parts, nothing really clicking.

On what was probably the last night of her life, Carol Wentz had gone to the Neff house. What had brought her there? What had made her leave that house in such a hurry that she left her wallet behind, never wanting to go back—

this practical-minded woman choosing instead to replace her driver's license? What had she been so frightened of?

"I'm going to the Neff house," Brenna told Morasco once they reached her car.

"I figured."

Brenna opened the car door and the light switched on, illuminating the age-enhanced photo she'd left on the passenger's seat. Morasco picked it up, his gaze soft on the girl's face. "Iris?"

"Yes."

"It's funny, I had one of these made up every year, from when Iris would have been ten through fourteen, maybe fifteen. Every year. I'd fax or e-mail the photos to the hospitals, the missing children's organizations, FBI, every place that might be able to track her down . . . I did it behind the chief's back—it was a closed case by then, after all, and hell, I wasn't even supposed to be on it when it was open."

"I'll bet Lydia appreciated it."

"She never knew," he said. "I figured, why get her hopes up, you know? But the thing is, Brenna, *I'd* get my hopes up. Every time I sent that damn thing out I'd imagine Iris walking through the station door, asking for her mom."

Brenna said, "I know exactly how you felt."

"You do?"

She studied the soft gaze, the way his hands held the picture, that tenderness . . . "You felt like, if Iris were to come back, then anything would be possible," she said. "Anyone could come home."

Morasco swallowed hard. He looked up from the picture and into her eyes, and she saw that his eyes were clouded—not with tears but with the threat of them. "Yes," he said softly.

"By any chance," she said, "are you a father?"

"No." The word sounded dry enough to crumble in the night air. Brenna knew there was something Morasco wasn't telling her—a pain under his skin he couldn't talk about out loud, and she wasn't going to make him. She had pain, too.

She put a hand on his arm. "Would you like to come with me to the Neff house?"

"Yeah," he said. "Yeah, I really would."

Iris's childhood bicycle was still propped up at the side of the Neff house, frayed handlebar streamers glinting in the garden lights.

Seeing the bike for the second time, in the exact same spot as it had been three nights ago, Brenna couldn't help but picture Iris herself—sixteen-year-old Iris—sneaking onto the grounds of this house after so many years away. She pictured this long-captured girl knocking on the front door and whispering her mother's name, searching the grounds for anyone alive but finding only her own bike, splayed in the dirt, dripping with cobwebs and rust. Brenna pictured Iris righting the bike, wishing there were so much more she could right with that blue car lurking somewhere, its engine running, waiting to take her back.

"You coming?" called Morasco, who was already around the side of the house, moving toward the back door.

Brenna hurried to catch up. Before meeting her here, Morasco had stopped at the Realtor's place to get the alarm combination. At the back door, Morasco fished the paper out of his pocket and started to key it in.

"1028, right?" said Brenna.

He turned to her. "The Realtor changed it after the break-in, but that was the old combination. How did you know that?"

"Iris's birthday. October 28. Lydia Neff told me."

"When?"

"Eleven years ago."

He smiled. Pushing the door open, Brenna noticed the

smell first—a mustiness. It brought her for a few seconds to October 19, 1985, day two of a five-day family trip to Florida, to walking through the haunted house at Disney World with her twin cousins Liz and Deb . . . She recounted the first three lines of the Pledge of Allegiance to pull her back, but that same scent was still here—not manufactured and sprayed into the air to give you chills as it had been back then, but real. The smell of ghosts. "Why did Lydia Neff leave?" Brenna asked Morasco. "Where did she go?"

"That would be the sixty-four-thousand-dollar question."

"Another incredibly dated reference," she said. "How old are you, anyway?"

"Sometime I'll do my Jack Paar impersonation for you." Morasco turned a light on, and Brenna looked around the kitchen—that long wooden table, the dry sink stocked with plates, the refrigerator humming. If it weren't for the smell, you'd think someone still lived here and they simply were out for the night.

"There were renters here for a while," Morasco said, reading her thoughts. "Three sets of them, six months apiece. It's only been totally vacant for four or five months, and I think the Realtor still has high expectations."

Brenna nodded. "Do you know exactly where the wallet was found?" Brenna asked Morasco.

He nodded. "This way."

Brenna followed him through the kitchen, then through a small room with hard floors and creamy white walls, empty, save for a bamboo yoga mat. On the wall facing the mat was a dark wooden plaque, painted with white letters:

CONQUER THE ANGRY MAN BY LOVE
CONQUER THE ILL-NATURED MAN BY GOODNESS
CONQUER THE MISER WITH GENEROSITY
CONQUER THE LIAR WITH TRUTH

Over the doorway, one more: "The greatest achievement is selflessness."

Brenna said, "Lydia liked to meditate."

"Yeah," he said. "I don't know whether that was a real interest, or just how she was coping with her grief, but back when I was working on the case, we had to work around the meditation and the yoga classes." They entered the formal dining room, the walls painted a forest green, with white trim over the doorways. There was a fireplace against the wall and a dusty table lined with chairs, a pewter dish at the center filled with smooth, yellow stones that had been cut to look like pears. Brenna's eyes went to a framed photo over the fireplace—a larger version of one of the family pictures Brenna had seen in Carol's folder: a posed black-and-white of a longer-haired Lydia, smiling in a sundress, baby Iris in her lap. A young man stood behind her, hand on her shoulder. He had wavy brown hair that grazed his collarbone, a thick beard, but she recognized the eyes from the later pictures in Carol's folder—the troubled eyes. Timothy O'Malley.

"I questioned Tim just once—he was living at a rehab up in Albany." Morasco said. "He wasn't a great source of information back then, but if he wasn't . . . Well, if the situation were different, he'd be able to help us now."

"Why?"

"He knew Lydia. Probably better than anyone. When Iris disappeared, he was in lock-down rehab. He wasn't reacting well to the methadone. Couldn't have weighed more than a hundred ten pounds and half of what he said made no sense at all, but Lydia was still visiting him regularly—telling him her problems."

"Wait. *She* was telling *him* problems?"

Morasco nodded. "Her 'strong shoulder.' She told me that herself."

Brenna looked up at the picture again—the pain in the young man's eyes, the young woman, so pretty but so serious, and the baby, smiling, all of them touching each other, his hand on her shoulder, her hand covering his, both of them holding the baby's chubby arms. *Support*. "They're all gone," Brenna said. "A whole family."

"Yes," he said. Then, "Life."

She turned to Morasco. He was staring at the picture. "Life," he said again, and again Brenna sensed it, that pain behind the skin, behind the eyes, held back by the thinnest of threads. She had an urge to touch the side of his face, but bit it back like a memory. "Where was the wallet found?"

"The living room," he said. "Next room over," and they both moved toward it in silence.

The living room looked instantly familiar—the couch with the cream and brick red Southwestern print, the soft chair beside it, dark green cloth, placed against a wall the same brick shade as in the couch. Brenna moved toward it. ". . . exactly where the wallet was found," Morasco was saying, but his voice was fading even as he said it, Brenna careening back to September 10, 1998, three days after Iris Neff disappeared, to the taste of black coffee in her mouth and the feel of the hot mug in her hands, the cold, smooth hardwood floor beneath her bare legs as Brenna sat in the living room of her Fourteenth Street apartment wearing Jim's long-sleeved "Ski Aspen" T-shirt, her back propped up against the couch, watching *Good Morning New York* at 10:15 A.M. . . .

"It's every mother's worst nightmare," the newscaster's voice intones. Lydia Neff appears on screen, staring at a framed picture. Brenna looks at the pale face, the raven hair—a woman both striking and strikingly sad. The image fades into a snapshot of a smiling little girl. Pigtails. Purple

overalls. The newscaster says, "Lydia Neff's six-year-old daughter, Iris, wandered off from a playdate on Labor Day. She has not been seen or heard from since."

Brenna takes a swallow of her coffee. The screen blinks, and now Lydia Neff is seated in a dark green chair, three framed pictures behind her. "I know she's out there somewhere," Lydia says. Her eyes glisten. Tears. Brenna can't look at Lydia Neff for too long. Every time she does, she flashes back to her mother two weeks after Clea disappeared—the same pain in her eyes as Brenna told her, "Yes. I saw her leave. She told me not to tell you, Mom . . ."

Lydia says, "A mother knows these things. I can feel it."

Brenna focuses on the framed pictures behind her head—all crayon drawings on white paper, hung in a vertical line. On top, a stick figure standing beside a puffy green tree; at the center, a round, smiling face with long eyelashes and black hair—"MOMMY" below it in a child's scrawl; at the bottom, a pink Valentine with a rainbow hovering over it, surrounded by stars. Iris's artwork. Framed.

"If your daughter is watching right now, Lydia, what would you like her to know?"

Lydia Neff looks directly at the camera. Her upper lip trembles. "Just that . . . that Mommy loves you and . . ." A tear trickles down her cheek. "Please be safe. Please come home . . ." Brenna stares at Lydia Neff's eyes. She can't look away from them. She clutches her coffee cup, slipping back into July 29, 1985, 9 A.M., finishing a bowl of oatmeal in her kitchen, bringing it to the sink and looking out the window as Ricky D the deejay says "Next up, Talking Heads!" and Brenna notices Mom in the garden, cross-legged on the grass, staring up at that sculpture she made after Dad left. Staring at the sculpture as if it could talk, as if it was talking to her, as if it was telling her why . . .

" . . . Brenna?" Morasco was saying. "Are you all right?"

Brenna bit the inside of her cheek so hard she tasted blood. "I'm okay," she said. She was still gazing at the chair.

"I don't know if you heard me. But right where you're standing," he said. "That's the exact spot where Carol Wentz's wallet was found."

Brenna didn't answer. Not right away. On the wall behind the chair, the three pictures were still hanging. "She left Iris's artwork behind." As Brenna said it, though, she realized the order had been switched—the Valentine drawing was now at the center. Mommy was on the bottom. "Carol's wallet was found under these pictures?"

"Yep."

She walked up to the pictures, gently lifted the three of them off the wall, and placed them on the table next to the window. Compared to the other two, Mommy felt light. Brenna turned it over, and sure enough, the drawing pressed against the glass, unprotected. The back of the frame was missing. When she looked down, she saw it lying there at the base of a table—a thin square of black cardboard. Brenna picked it up. "Whatever Carol took from this house," she said, "I'm pretty sure it was hidden in the back of that frame."

23

They were just outside the door, Brenna keying the alarm back on, when the thought hit her. "That girl who's been calling. If she actually is Iris . . . or if she's someone who knows her, then maybe she was the one who asked Carol to get whatever it was that was hidden behind the frame. I mean . . . who else would know it was there?"

"Maybe," said Morasco. "Or it could have been something that Tim O'Malley told her about."

The alarm light flashed on. Brenna stepped away from the door. "You don't believe Iris is back."

He shrugged. "I'd *like* those calls to be coming from her," he said. "But sadly, too good to be true usually is."

"God, you're a nihilist. Lighten up. Let's hear some of that Jack Paar."

Morasco smiled, but then a car was screeching into the Neffs' driveway—the door slamming, footsteps crashing around the hedges and up the walk.

Brenna looked at Morasco. His hand went to his lapel. She thought of Carol, a woman nearly as meticulous as her husband, leaving this house so fast she left the pictures in the wrong order. Never to return, even for her wallet, even for her license. What had scared her off so fast?

Footsteps.

They grew louder. Brenna's heart pounded . . . and then she heard a voice. "Hello!" She recognized it. Immediately, Brenna's shoulders relaxed. Annoyance blotted in her chest. "What's she doing here?" she said.

Morasco frowned at Brenna. He started to call out, "Hello," and then sure enough, there she was, tromping around the corner of the house, Coach bag clutched in both hands as if someone might pry it away at any moment. "Hello, Detective," she said.

Morasco said, "Brenna Spector, I'd like you to meet—"

"Gayle Chandler," said Brenna.

Gayle's eyebrows shot up. "Do I know you?"

"We've met."

Morasco said, "Gayle is the Realtor." He glanced at her. "Brenna is a private investigator, working for Nelson Wentz." He smiled a little. "She never forgets a face."

But honestly, Gayle looked almost exactly the same as she'd looked eleven years ago, when Brenna had approached her in front of her house. The hips might have been a little wider, and there were a few more lines around the mouth, but otherwise, she was unchanged down to the frosted coif and the big gold knot earrings and the smug, placid smile. "I just wanted to make sure you were able to get in okay."

Brenna said, "So you were the one to find Carol's wallet in the house."

Gayle's smile dropped away. "Yes . . . Poor Carol."

"You were her best friend."

Gayle glanced at Morasco. "I wouldn't say that. I did like her very much, though. We were in the same book club."

"Nelson said you were."

Her eyes went hard.

"Nelson Wentz said you were best friends," Brenna repeated.

Gayle Chandler turned to Morasco. "Well then, I'll just check the door and be on my way."

Brenna said, "What did Carol call you about during the last week she was alive?"

"Huh?"

"There was a call from her to you on her cell phone records. One and a half minutes."

"Oh, right," she said. "She called to ask if I'd finished our book club book. *Safekeeping*."

"Because you were *book club friends*."

Gayle eyed her. "Yes."

Morasco frowned at Brenna.

"Lydia Neff, on the other hand," Brenna said. "You were *very* close to her."

Gayle blinked. "I haven't talked to Lyddie Neff in two years."

"I said *were*. You *were* close to her."

"Yes . . . So what?" She looked at Morasco. "Is this official police business?"

Brenna said, "Can I ask you something?"

"Do I have a choice?"

"Why did you tell Carol that Lydia and Nelson were having an affair?"

Gayle's face went slack. "What?"

"You were friends with Lydia Neff. Such close friends that you knew her daily schedule. After Iris disappeared, you knew that she went to the Waterside Condominiums every morning at nine to meditate."

"And you know this about me because . . ."

"During the week of October 18, 1998, you stopped by Lydia's house four times that I know of. At 11:30 A.M. on the twenty-first, you brought a bag from Dunkin' Donuts and two large coffees and stayed two hours. On the twenty-second, you brought her a casserole and stayed an hour and a half . . . You were close."

Gayle gaped at Morasco. "What is wrong with her?"

He shrugged. "She has a good memory."

"But one year earlier than that, you told Carol Wentz that Lydia was having an affair with her husband."

"I don't—"

"Let me tell you something, Gayle. If there's one thing I know for sure, it's that time doesn't have an eraser on it."

"What is that supposed to mean?"

"It means that when you tell a lie, it's still as much of a lie five, ten, twenty years later as it was on the day you told it."

"I didn't tell any lies."

"You do the wrong thing, you hurt someone, you figure, 'Well, time will pass. People will forget. It'll be just like it never happened.' Right?" Brenna gritted her teeth, her anger building. "It happened, Gayle. The whole world can forget, that still doesn't change the fact. Twelve years ago, for whatever petty reasons, you told an awful, malicious lie."

"I didn't."

"Oh please."

"I did *not*!"

"Your lie hurt Carol Wentz more than you ever could have imagined. It led to an obsession that probably killed her." Brenna glared at her. "Time doesn't heal wounds, Gayle. Sometimes, it infects them."

Gayle's eyes were watering. Brenna cast a quick glance at Morasco, who was looking at her in such a way, she couldn't tell whether it was admiration or shock or fear or a blend of all three. "Why did you tell Carol that Nelson and Lydia were having an affair?"

Gayle swallowed, visibly. When she spoke, it was very quietly, between her teeth. "Because they were."

"Oh now, *come on*."

"Lydia told me. She said it had started one night, when he'd given her a ride home from the train station. They stopped and had a drink and the wine got the best of them. It was supposed to be just a fling, she said, but it kept . . . happening." She cleared her throat. "By the time she told me, it had become very serious—overwhelmingly serious, *too serious for her.* Lyddie knew she should end it, but she didn't know how."

"Lydia Neff . . . and Nelson."

"I told her she could do a lot better than him," Gayle said. "But Lyddie told me . . . they could talk to each other."

Brenna stared at her. *Everybody needs that one person . . .*

"It sounded to me like he'd gotten obsessed with her, though," Gayle said. "Lyddie was a mess. I didn't want to get involved. Why would I? I told Carol for one reason: to help Lydia. I told her so that Nelson would have to let Lydia go."

Brenna said nothing. She just watched her, this woman whom she'd figured for a crisis queen, shallow to the bone. For a few moments, she flashed on Gayle eleven years ago, with her frosty pink lipstick and her popped collar, the two Range Rovers in the driveway, one black, one white, so gleaming-new you expected bows on them. *"Every morning, Lyddie goes there to meditate by the fountain. She's a very spiritual woman, you know . . ."* And Brenna had thought, *One of those.* One of those people like Roger Wright the developer. One of those shiny people who never wanted for anything, raised under glass so that pain never touched them . . .

Gayle swiped a tear from her face. In a few seconds' time, she seemed to have aged ten years, all that shine and smugness melting away. "There is a lot of anger in Nelson Wentz," she said.

Brenna was starting to believe her.

Gayle started toward the door, then stopped, turned. "If you want to talk about wounds," she said, her voice still shaking, "I suggest you talk to your client. I imagine he knows a hell of a lot more about them than I do."

Brenna and Morasco walked to their cars without saying a word. Once they reached her Sienna, she leaned against it, facing him, Gayle's words swirling through her head.

Gayle wasn't a crisis queen. Her friend had told her about an affair she'd begun—an affair she was trapped in and couldn't leave. An affair with Nelson Wentz. *There is a lot of anger in Nelson Wentz.*

"You okay?" Morasco said.

"Just because I remember everything, it doesn't mean I'm right about everything." She looked at him. "Correct?"

"You're honest. You expect other people to be the same. That's a *good* quality."

"You sound like my shrink," she said. "Well, this shrink I went to fourteen years ago, actually. I don't see anybody now . . ."

"I questioned Nelson Wentz when I was working Iris's disappearance, Brenna. He told me he and Lydia had never had an affair. I believed him, too. Okay?"

"So we're both gullible."

"Hey," he said. "At least you're not alone."

She felt herself smiling a little. "I still don't think he's a murderer. Does that make me extra-gullible?"

"Maybe."

"Am I alone?" Brenna said, and then a switch went off in her head, and again she *was* alone, in her kitchen the previous night after Maya had gone to sleep, looking through Nelson's folders and then remembering the missing page of the police report . . . "Remember when I asked you if Chief Griffin ever interviewed Nelson?"

"Yeah. I told you no."

"Were you telling me the truth?"

He frowned at her. "I talked to Nelson in his own driveway. He said he'd barely ever spoken to Iris. He said he hadn't had an affair with Lydia—it was just a very close friendship. I promised to keep it between us, and it didn't go beyond that."

"So he wasn't John Doe?"

Morasco frowned. "John Doe?"

"Page 22. Well, it was page 22 eleven years ago. Now the first page of the Theresa Koppelson interview is page 22 and . . ."

Morasco was staring at Brenna as if she'd suddenly burst into Greek opera.

"You have no idea what I'm talking about."

He shook his head.

"Something from the Neff police file. I transcribed the interview from memory. I'll e-mail it to you later."

"Okay." He looked into her eyes, gave her a small, sad smile.

"What?"

"Brenna," he said. "Do you ever feel like you're a better person than everybody else? Not just smarter. But more genuinely good?"

"No."

"Well, you should." He touched her arm, so lightly she could barely feel it. He didn't say anything more, but the gesture, the utter gentleness of it . . . *Don't look at me like that, Detective Nick Morasco. Do not look at me like that because I will remember and it will hurt.*

They stood there, staring at each other for a drawn-out

moment. Until finally, Morasco spoke. "There must be a better way of making a living than this."

Brenna blinked. "Huh?"

Morasco said it again, with an accent—an effete lockjaw. "My Jack Paar impersonation," he explained after.

They both forced themselves to laugh.

24

Brenna arrived home at six twenty-five—maybe twenty minutes late at the most, but she knew Maya would be angry. "It's hostile you know," Maya had once said of Brenna's lateness. She'd said it on June 20, to be exact, when Brenna had met Maya for brunch at the Cowgirl Hall of Fame at ten forty-two rather than ten-thirty—and all Brenna could think at the time was, *Hostile? Where did she get that word?*—and then, in the middle of their eggs Benedict, Maya had said, "Faith is *never* late," which had struck Brenna as pretty hostile right there, and so she'd pointed that out, and then the two of them had spent the rest of the meal in icy silence.

Brenna expected the cold stare tonight. She'd texted Maya an apology but hadn't heard back—of course.

And once Brenna opened the door to her apartment, she was greeted, not by Maya at all, but by her backpack, sitting on the kitchen table like a bulky centerpiece. "Maya!" Brenna called out. No answer. She noticed a Post-it on her computer screen:

CHECK YOUR E-MAIL
TNT
P.S. Buy an iPhone.

She started to turn the computer on, but realized Trent's e-mail would have to wait till later because from here, Brenna noticed that there was another backpack next to Maya's. She moved closer, put her hand on it. A black Jan-Sport. Completely unfamiliar.

"Maya?"

She heard a man's voice. "You really are so good," the voice said, and then, "Where did you learn?" Brenna moved toward Maya's bedroom, she could tell the voice was coming from behind the door—a deep, young voice. *You look so pretty, Clee-bee*. Brenna gritted her teeth. Knocked. "Maya?"

The door opened, and there was her daughter, flush-faced and with that crooked, embarrassed smile—so young and so old at the same time. "Hi, Mom," she said. "I was just working on my art project."

Brenna peered past her daughter, at the source of the deep voice, sitting cross-legged on her bed . . .

"Hi, Mrs. Rappaport. My name is . . ."

"Miles," said Brenna.

"That's right."

"It's Spector. Not Rappaport."

The smile dropped away. "Uh . . . Sorry."

Brenna heard herself say, "What are you doing here?"

Maya cleared her throat. "Mom. I told you. We're working on an—"

"Art project," Brenna said. "I know . . ." She closed her eyes for a moment, counted quickly in her mind from twenty to sixty-four, shutting the memory out of her head—*September 8, 1981, the cold metal chair on her bare legs and the smell of pine soap on the wood-planked floors of the gym at City Island Elementary. Brenna sitting in morning meeting like a ghost. First day of sixth grade. First school day without Clea. The principal talks about a fundraising*

*drive for underprivileged youth in the South Bronx, and
Brenna feels eyes all over her. Cold, staring eyes. Aaron
Spiegel right behind her whispering to Katie Johnson.
Brenna doesn't want to hear, but still she strains to listen . . .*

"*. . . Talk about total sluts! My brother Steve said she was
humping the whole football team at George Washington.*"

"*Gross!*"

"*Clea-mydia. That's what Steve calls her. I bet she's one
of those runaway hookers now.*"

Brenna bit her lip.

"*Maybe she's doing pornos.*"

"Mom?"

"I'm sorry, Miles, but you need to leave. It's getting awfully late, and Maya's got homework to do."

"Mom. This *is* my homework."

"Maya." Brenna took a breath. "Please."

"That's okay. Bye, Ms. Spector. Bye, Maya." Miles got
off the bed. It wasn't until Miles passed her that she noticed
he actually *was* carrying an artist's notebook and a set of
pencils. *Nice prop.*

After Miles left, Brenna turned to Maya, and for several
seconds, they stood staring at each other, saying nothing.

Finally, Maya said, "Should I order pizza?"

"What the hell is going on in your brain?"

Maya stared at her. "Chinese?"

Brenna closed her eyes for a moment. "Can I talk to
you?" she said. "Please?"

Maya followed her to the kitchen table. After they both
sat down, Brenna said, "I don't want to see you get hurt."

"I don't understand."

"Yes you do. Just yesterday, Miles broke your heart, and
today he's in your room? Number one, he doesn't deserve
you. Number two, it's totally unacceptable to have a boy on
your bed with the door closed."

"I wasn't . . . I mean . . . Mom . . ." She sighed heavily. "What part of 'We were working on an art project' don't you understand?"

"Grandma used to tell Clea, don't sell yourself short. Only be with boys who deserve you, and who will show you respect. And Clea rolled her eyes at her. Just like you're rolling your eyes at me right now."

"I'm not Clea."

"No, you're not. Clea waited till she was fifteen before she started acting up."

"That isn't fair!"

"Life isn't fair," said Brenna. "He was all over that girl last night, Maya. Do you really think *that little of yourself*?"

Maya was staring fire at her. Fire and bullets, the arms crossed over the chest, the face bright red, the jaw thrust so far forward, it looked as if it hurt, but that didn't matter. Feelings didn't matter. This was life.

"Do you understand me, Maya, because I swear if this happens again, I'll take the lock off your door."

Maya pivoted away from the table, stormed down the hall.

"Don't you walk away from me!" Brenna said, her own mother's voice coming out of her mouth, Clea's feet stomping away . . .

Brenna heard more footsteps, and then Maya was back, an artist's notebook in her hands. Her whole body trembled, and when she spoke, her voice shook, too. "Miles and I are partners in art class. I didn't pick him as my partner. The teacher assigned it. We were doing homework." She slammed the notebook on the table in front of Brenna. "I was telling the truth."

On the notebook was a detailed sketch of a bearded young man with a slight, mysterious smile, light glinting off his eyes. *Miles*. Brenna turned the page. Another detailed rendering. Miles, contemplative, in profile. On the next page was a slightly different angle, the beginnings of a sketch—just the basic lines, but it was the same pose, the same boy, the same background on all three drawings: the headboard of Maya's bed. Brenna looked up at her.

"I'm not Clea."

"Oh Maya. I'm sorry . . ." She closed her eyes. "It isn't you. I'm having trouble believing that anyone is telling the truth today. It's this client of mine. I just found out he lied to me about something very important."

Brenna heard the slam of Maya's bedroom door, and when she opened her eyes, the girl was gone. Brenna looked down at Maya's sketch—a likeness of the boy she used to love and now hated, of course she hated him. Brenna didn't need to *teach* her to hate him . . . A perfect likeness. "You're very talented," Brenna said to no one.

Then she ordered pizza, walked over to her desk, and turned on the computer. She called up her e-mail—a new one from Trent, one titled "Subaru 411." She was about to open it when an IM from Jim flashed on her screen: **You okay?**

Brenna sighed. **Sure. Why?**

You were so abrupt last night.

I was just tired, Brenna typed. For several seconds, she stared at the words without sending them, the previous night swirling through her mind, start to finish. Brenna deleted the sentence. In its place, she typed: **I lied**.

About what?

Being okay.

Do you want to tell me about it?

Brenna exhaled hard, her eyes starting to blur. **It's hard. Not being able to move on.**

No answer for three, four, five seconds. Then: **From me? Yes.**

Jim didn't type back. He didn't want to have this conversation, she knew. Even after all these years, he still didn't want to talk about everything that had happened after she'd done that job for Errol—the stony silences, the useless months of counseling, the late nights he spent at work, the way he'd turn away from her in bed, unable to forgive, unable to trust. He didn't want to go there now, and who could blame him? He had the luxury of forgetting, of putting the past behind him and creating a new life with another woman while Brenna . . . But that wasn't Jim's fault, was it? Being normal?

She tried: **Not just you. Every mistake I've ever made.**

Jim still wasn't typing. Brenna exhaled hard, blinked the blur out of her eyes.

I'm sorry, she typed, but then the message came back. **JRapp68 is offline**. She stared at the screen. Jim's icon was now an X. "Okay, Jim. Thanks for checking in." A tear spilled down her cheek. Then another. She put her head down on her desk and before long she was sobbing, audibly sobbing, tears hot on her face, her shoulders shaking, her throat raw.

Brenna felt a tentative hand on her shoulder, and then another. "Mom?"

She wanted to tell Maya to go back to her room, because she shouldn't see her mother like this, should she? Mothers were supposed to be strong, but Brenna wasn't feeling strong and she didn't want to cry alone, and so she leaned on her thirteen-year-old daughter, put her arms around her, and the two of them stayed like that for a long time, holding each other, neither one of them, for now, alone.

The pizza arrived and Brenna and Maya ate it in front of *Psycho*—tonight's installment in AMC's October Halloween Countdown. They'd both seen the movie repeatedly so they knew what was coming, but that didn't make it any less scary, Maya burying her face in Brenna's shoulder as soon as Detective Arbogast put the first foot to staircase. They didn't talk to each other much during the movie, but it was a comfortable silence. Sometimes it was good to just watch something.

After Maya went to bed, Brenna switched her computer on. Jim was still offline, but she wasn't going to think about that. Maybe he was out or busy and if he wasn't, she didn't want to know. She clicked on her e-mail: Trent's "Subaru 411," plus a new one, from Morasco, titled "Memory."

She opened Morasco's:

> Hi,
>   So the last time I talked to Lydia Neff, it was right before she left town. She stopped by the station, told me she wanted to thank me for everything. I asked her what her plans were, and she said she was going to visit an old friend first, and then "relocate." She didn't say where. I didn't press her. No one ever heard from her again. But here is what I just remembered: Do you know where the old friend lived? Buffalo.
>   Yours,
>   N
>   P.S. Just FYI, I also do a mean Eisenhower.

Brenna smiled. She hit reply, and typed:

> Thanks for the Buffalo info. It is "verrrry interrresting," as Arte Johnson would say.
>   Speaking of outdated material, see attached. It's page 22 of the Iris Neff police report—it

was in the file I obtained in '98, but missing
from it now.
    Enjoy,
    B

She attached the page she'd typed and sent the e-mail,
all the while thinking, *Buffalo.* Just before she disappeared,
Lydia had obviously planned to visit Tim O'Malley. As
Brenna had learned from the articles she'd read, he'd moved
to 811 Mulberry from Albany two and a half years ago,
which would have made him a relatively new Buffalo resi-
dent when Lydia made her decision to leave Tarry Ridge.

Her strong shoulder. The man she told about all her problems.

Brenna made herself remember the library, the news
articles about the group home fire . . . She looked up the
number of Sisters of Charity Hospital and called and asked
for intensive care. When she got a nurse on the line, Brenna
said, "Is Tim O'Malley able to speak?"

"Ma'am, I told you, I can't release any information about
his condition unless—"

"I'm an investigator."

"Buffalo Police? I'm sorry. I talked to a male detective
before."

Brenna mulled it over for a couple of seconds. "That's all
right," she said.

"He's still critical, still unconscious, Detective . . ."

"Spector. Thanks."

"We'll let you know as soon as there's any change."

"Appreciate that." Brenna started to hang up, then
stopped. "By the way," she said. "Why did you say, 'Ma'am,
I told you'? Have you been getting a lot of press calls?"

"No," the nurse said. "I just saw the blocked number and
I thought you were that lady."

"Lady?"

"Yeah. Asks how Mr. O'Malley is, and I keep telling her she has to be a relative. Ten minutes ago she called again, tried saying she was his wife and you know as well as I do, he doesn't have a wife."

Brenna's mouth opened, then closed again. She tried, "You mind my asking the lady's name?"

"She calls here all the time. Never gives her name. That's why I thought you were her. She's the only one who—"

"Can you do me a favor?" Brenna said.

"Ummm."

"Next time the lady calls for Mr. O'Malley, can you please tell her to call Brenna Spector? Can you tell her it involves both Mr. O'Malley and Iris and it's urgent?"

"Iris?"

"I know it's . . . it's strange," Brenna said, anxiety building in her voice. "I'm . . . I'm in New York City right now. On business. Let me leave my number."

There was a long pause on the other end of the line. Brenna waited for the dawning knowledge of *You aren't with the Buffalo Police*, waited for the *How dare you*, for the click of the disconnecting phone. "Sorry," said the nurse. "Just getting my pen. What's your number, Detective Spector?"

Okay . . . Brenna thought, after she hung up. *Okay* . . . It was now officially beyond her control. The only thing Brenna could do now as far as O'Malley's caller was concerned was possibly her least favorite activity: waiting for a phone call.

Brenna closed Morasco's e-mail, opened Trent's.

Hola Spectorita,
    Attached: all registration records for Subaru Vivio Bistros in Westchester County—1996, 1997, 1998— minus dead people. As you'll see, I organized the list

*with men first, then women. Good thing the Bistro is
(was?) a jank ass ride—so the list isn't too long.*
  Later,
  TNT

  *P.S. List of phone numbers similar to Will Garvey's
TK first thing manana. I've got a computer program
working on it.*

  *P.P.S. Elizabeth Stoller's picture e-mailed to all hos-
pitals and businesses w/in a thirty-mile radius of the
Walter P. Klein Assisted Living Facility.*

  P.P.P.S. I know. I rock out loud. You're welcome.

Brenna downloaded and opened the attachment. A list
to go over. This was good. It would keep her from looking
at the phone, from waiting for the woman who'd been repeatedly phoning Sisters of Charity to call her, from believing that the woman would almost certainly be Lydia Neff,
because who else would be calling about Tim O'Malley's
condition without leaving a name? Who else would claim
to be his wife?

Amazing, Brenna thought. Wentz had fired her six hours
ago and lied to her repeatedly and yet here she was, eye-
deep in his case, so painfully close to answers and wanting
those answers, so badly . . .

Calm down. Look at these names.

Trent was right—there weren't that many Bistro owners
on the list. Just a dozen counting the women. She went into
Google images and began typing in names, plus towns. The
first Bistro owner, Russell Chesney, was a radiologist from
White Plains with a Facebook page. She couldn't get into the
page, of course, but his profile pic showed her she didn't need

to—a man and a woman and a dog, none of whom looked remotely like the pretty-faced, supposed cop Brenna had seen. Next up was Percy Bridges—a smiling bald accountant from New Rochelle with his own Web site. Then there was certified yoga instructor Samson Moore—a sculpted, heavily tattooed black man who offered classes five days a week at the Equinox Gym on Eighty-fifth and Lex.

It was incredible how easy it was to find people on the Web now. Really *find people*—their faces, their professions, their life stories . . . If Brenna had been looking for, say, the next man on the list, Martin Wickham, all she'd need to do was Google the name and look at his online résumé to learn that he was now the chief financial officer of Los Angeles Orthopaedic Hospital, having moved from his home in Scarsdale six years ago. Just yesterday, Martin's daughter Phoebe had won a short film competition at USC. Martin was very proud. Brenna knew because he'd tweeted about it, posting a link to the film on YouTube . . .

It was a basic human desire, wasn't it? To be seen and heard? And now there were so many opportunities for that—a giant, pulsing, electronic memory out there, created so that anyone at any time could show his face, share his life, send up a flare, get known. It made Brenna's job easier. But it also made it so upsetting when, in spite of all that opportunity, a person insisted on remaining invisible . . .

Call me, Lydia.

For the hell of it, Brenna typed Lydia Neff's name into the search bar. Very little came up—a few CNN transcripts from eleven years ago, plus an item from a missing children's Web site. The story was too old for there to have been that much Web coverage, and it seemed that Iris's disappearance was all Lydia Neff was known for—all she wanted to be known for, anyway. Except . . . Brenna typed in "Lydia Neff" plus "Life Coach" and got Lydia's old Web site—Lydia's sad, heavy face with the words, "Free yourself!" underneath it in flowery cursive script, like some kind of sick joke. Scrolling across the bottom of the page were three words:

Relearn
Renew
Reinvent

Followed by a number for appointments, which Brenna called, again for the hell of it. Disconnected. Of course it was.

She went back to the list of Bistro owners with that last word wedged in her head. *Reinvent.* She thought of the old Lydia—those sharp cheekbones, that shining black hair, those lively eyes. The type of woman who turned heads, stopped traffic. The type who could find her way into a man's mind and stay there, haunting him.

Yet in the last few years, she'd let it all go, the cheekbones swallowed up in that doughy face, the silken hair faded to gray fuzz, with only the eyes remaining, sparkling out from folds of unfamiliar flesh. Party crashers, those eyes—and such a sad, dull party . . .

She is. And then she was. Just like that.

Brenna closed her eyes, Lydia's old face and new face blending in her mind. *Reinvent.* Was that what Lydia had been doing? Not letting herself go, not "eating her grief," but *freeing herself*? It could have been all conscious—Lydia wrapping herself in layers of fat, like a cocoon, and then . . .

The greatest achievement is selflessness.

Leaving her old self behind. Walking away from this town plain and unmissed. A quick visit to Buffalo to see her "strong shoulder" one last time, and then she was a new person free to start a new life—away from the ghost of her missing child, away from the man in the Vivio Bistro.

She went back to the list: *Roger Wright Industries (company car).*

Brenna froze. She closed her eyes, revisiting her conversation with Nelson this morning, the hard chair beneath her, the Scotch on his breath, the story . . . Nelson and Lydia, taking the train every day . . . *There was a period, probably a dozen years ago, when she was working on a major event—the opening of the Rose Building on Fifty-seventh.*

Brenna Googled the Rose Building. She scanned through dozens of listings until she got the bright idea of adding "opening," "new," and "launch." She skipped to the last page of listings, and that's when she hit pay dirt. The original press release. She read it quickly. There were quotes in the release from the building's architect, from the decorator, and from the developer—Roger Wright. "The building's name, Rose, is in honor of my wonderful mother-in-law, Lily Teasdale. Lily is far too humble to want her name on a building, but I do feel that both the building and the name are a fitting tribute to the grace, beauty, and elegance of both Lily and her daughter, my lovely wife, Rachel."

The press release had been written by Lydia Neff.

Brenna stood up, backed away from the computer. She walked down the hall to calm herself and then she stood in the doorway of Maya's room, listening to her sleep . . . *Company car.* For several seconds, Brenna was back behind the wheel of the rental car on October 21, 1998, that pretty-faced supposed cop at her window. *You need to leave,* with the bulky uniform at his side—the uniform she now knew as Chief Lane Hutchins.

She could hear Morasco's voice in her head: *I've got to hand it to him, though. He knew how to make the right people happy.* And was that ever true. The pretty-faced, supposed cop, the man in the blue car, the man who had been haunting Lydia Neff's house before Iris disappeared, the

man outside Nelson Wentz's house this morning, staring at
Brenna as if she were prey, the man who no doubt was *Santa
Claus* . . . He wasn't a cop. Never had been one, supposed
or otherwise. He worked for Roger Wright Industries. And
so did Lydia.

Brenna leaned against the wall, thinking, *And so, apparently, does the current chief of police.* Okay, that might
have been a stretch. Standing next to someone doesn't mean
you're employed by them. But still . . . *What was Lane
Hutchins doing eleven years ago, standing next to a Wright
employee, acting as if kicking me off Lydia Neff's street was
official business?* Brenna's head hurt. She felt a slight ringing in her ears, as if too much information were flooding
her mind, too much at the same time, and if she didn't rest it
might even explode.

Brenna headed back to her work area. It was well after
11 P.M., after all. She would turn off her computer, get some
sleep, approach all this information fresh in the morning,
when she could really think.

But as Brenna neared her desk, the ringing in her ears
grew louder. And she realized it wasn't in her ears at all, but
her cell phone, turned down low.

25

Brenna picked the phone up fast, checked the caller ID. An unfamiliar number, but with the same area code as Sisters of Charity Hospital. *Buffalo.* She cleared her throat, thinking, *Calm. Professional.* "Brenna Spector."

"The ICU nurse. She said you wanted to talk to me." The voice was small, frail. Nothing like the voice Brenna remembered from the fountain at the Waterside Condominiums, but then everything else of Lydia Neff's had changed since then. Why not her voice, too?

Brenna took a breath. "Listen, you've been anonymous for two years," she said. "That won't change. No one will know where you are, but I need to ask you a few questions about a man you used to know."

"I don't know what you're talking about. Anonymous?"

"Please, Lydia—"

"My name isn't Lydia," said the voice. "I thought you were going to tell me about Tim."

Brenna's breath caught. "You're the woman who has been calling the hospital."

"Yes."

"What is your name?"

"Millie," she said slowly. "Millie Davis."

Brenna exhaled hard. "The group home owner."

"Yes."

"You've been calling the hospital, not leaving your name."

"Yes."

"Why?"

"Because I'm worried about Tim," she said. "And I'm scared."

Brenna sat down at her desk. She clutched the phone to her ear and spoke very softly. "I understand," she said, though honestly, she didn't understand at all.

"I know you're not a Buffalo cop," Millie was saying. "The nurse told me Spector. I looked the number up online. Saw your Web site. You're a private investigator."

"That's right."

"This number. It's your direct line. The Web site said, 'Confidential calls.' "

"Right . . ."

"So this call, Ms. Spector," she said slowly. "It's confidential."

"Yes."

Brenna heard her exhale—a trembling wave of breath. "Good."

"Ms. Davis?"

"Yes?"

"Why are you scared?"

Another long, shaking sigh. Brenna half expected her to hang up. Then she said, "I don't think Timothy set that fire."

Brenna's eyes widened. "Did you see anybody coming or going?"

"No. It happened after three in the morning. All of us were sleeping till the flames got big."

"So then what makes you think someone else started it?"

"The way Tim had been acting. Very nervous. High-strung. You'd knock on his door, he'd say, 'Go away!' That wasn't like Tim. He was usually very friendly, very welcoming."

"How long had he been acting that way?"

"Just about two days," she said.

"Did he have any visitors around that time?"

"None that I knew of—of course, I wasn't always there. He did get a couple of phone calls from some lady earlier that week. I picked up the phone. She sounded very nice. I know it wasn't her he was scared of."

Brenna said, "That was Carol. Carol Wentz."

"Oh," said Millie. "I was thinking it may have been his ex-wife."

"Why?"

"Because when she asked to speak to him, she said it was about Iris. I knew Iris was his little girl. He kept a picture of her in his room."

Brenna closed her eyes for a moment. *The single bed, the framed picture, the wild-haired man, sitting there alone with his haunted eyes, hoping . . .* Brenna said, "Did Tim ever mention what it was that Carol told him about Iris?"

"No."

"Okay," Brenna said. "Thank you for calling me back, Ms. Davis."

"Listen, Ms. Spector, there's one more thing that might help."

Brenna waited.

"The day the house burned down, Tim asked me something strange."

"Yes?"

"He asked if I could put a new lock on his door."

"Ms. Davis, are you sure he didn't have any visitors? You didn't see any strange cars around your house?"

"No," she said. "Well, wait . . . Come to think of it, I

did pass one car when I was coming home from the market. It was leaving our street, but they could have been visiting anybody. There were ten people living there, quite a few who got more guests than Tim."

"What kind of car was it?" Brenna asked. "Would you know the model and make?"

"I don't know cars," she said. "But it was blue. And teeny tiny. Looked just like a little toy."

After hanging up with Millie Davis, Brenna turned off her computer and went to bed with such frustration coursing through her . . . *So close and yet so far.* Carol had been talking to Tim O'Malley about Iris. He'd been frightened before the house burned down. He'd been hiding from someone— but who? Who was this man who worked for Roger Wright Industries, this man who had known both Lydia Neff and Lane Hutchins, this man who drove a blue car that looked like a toy?

She managed to fall into a swirling, dreamless sleep, but then at 5 A.M. she'd woken up with a start, a memory racing through her mind . . . *The cool fall air is at Brenna's back and the sun glints off Morasco's glasses as he speaks, Chief Lane Hutchins's BMW in the parking lot, the silver fender in the corner of her line of vision . . .*

". . . Lane hasn't worked past five a day in his life, but he golfs with Roger Wright at 7 A.M. every morning. Around here, that's what you call a work ethic."

Brenna got out of bed. First, she went to the kitchen, packed a lunch for Maya, then wrote up a note: *I'll be gone for most of the morning. Work. Love, Mom.* She placed it on the counter next to the lunch, then added: *I am very proud of you.* Then she taped a ten-dollar bill to the paper. *In case the lunch is too lame.*

Next, she went to her computer, switched it on, and, in

the solitude of approaching dawn, spent an hour researching both Wright Industries and Tarry Ridge.

Wonder how many holes they play. Brenna had been in the parking lot of the Tarry Ridge Country Club for a little more than fifteen minutes, continuously shifting her focus between the club entrance and Lane Hutchins's silver BMW 360i, a cup of gas station coffee in her hand. Nick had been right about Lane Hutchins's work ethic. It was seven-thirty now, and when she arrived, Hutchins's car was already comfortably in its space. She checked her watch again and texted Trent so he wouldn't wonder where she was: *I think the Viv. Bistro is the Wright company car. Checking that out now in Tarry Ridge—hope to talk to Wright himself.*

Thirty minutes later, just after she'd finished the last of the coffee, Hutchins appeared at the back exit with his golf bag over a shoulder, slouching his way through a conversation with the one and only Roger Wright. Brenna watched the two of them for a few moments: Wright in all his preppy, vacation-tanned perfection, the mirror image of himself eleven years ago at the Waterside Condominiums ribbon cutting—absolutely untouched by time—teeth gleaming, skin glowing, living proof of what wealth could get you, chatting with Hutchins, this bulky social climber in his mint green polo shirt and plaid golf pants—expensive clothes but also the slightest bit ill-fitting, as if they somehow objected to the body that wore them. From this distance, she couldn't tell whether Hutchins was sweating, but if he wasn't, she knew he was making a concerted effort not to, that he'd trained the sweat out of himself in order to achieve his goal. *What could those two possibly be talking about?*

As for Brenna, she was doing her best Faith Gordon-Rappaport imitation—bouncy, blown-out hair, a pink and green Ralph Lauren shirtdress and cashmere cardigan she'd bought at an Upper East Side consignment store two years ago for those very special occasions when she needed to look moneyed and content, tasteful gold earrings, oversized sunglasses, and a smile she'd been practicing all morning.

As soon as Hutchins and Wright began to move apart from each other, Brenna slapped on the smile and strode toward the two men, channeling one of those library bake sale women, waving like a lunatic. "Roger?"

Wright turned, the bright smile belied by flat eyes, *Am I supposed to know you?* written all over his face, albeit in tasteful calligraphy.

"I'm sure you don't remember me." Brenna held out her hand. "Candy Bissel. I write a column for the *Sleepy Hollow Press*?" She felt Hutchins's glare on her and gave him a grin. "It's an honor to meet you. You're doing a wonderful job, Chief."

His face relaxed into a politician's smile. "Sixty percent decrease in crime in less than five years."

"Don't I know it! And might I say, imposing an 11 P.M. curfew on Tarry Ridge teens was a stroke of genius."

The smile grew broader. "I get a nice salary from this town," he said. "I make it my business to give the taxpayers their money's worth."

"I don't know where we'd all be without Lane," Wright said.

"You're one to talk, sir!" Brenna beamed.

"Miss Bissel, I'm sorry, but I'm finding it hard to place your face."

Brenna laughed. "1996. Opening of the Rose Building. I covered it for the paper—I was just out of Brandeis and oh-so-enthusiastic?"

Wright exhaled. "Of course."

"The thing is, I never forget a face, and if you don't mind my saying, you haven't changed a bit."

"You're too kind."

Brenna turned to Hutchins. "It was a fabulous opening," Brenna said. "African dancers, tuna tartare . . . Oh, I could go on and on. The publicist was a doll, too." She turned to Wright. "What was her name again?"

"Claire Goodman."

"No. No, that wasn't it."

"Claire's been doing all our PR for years."

Brenna blinked a few times. "No, it was Linda or something like that. Very pretty woman . . . Wait . . . Lydia!"

Again with the flat eyes.

Brenna cleared her throat. "Anyway, sorry to bug you, but—"

"That's quite all right."

"Seriously, it's kismet I ran into you guys because I literally just . . . well, not just . . . but yesterday, in the library parking lot, I saw one of your employees I met at the Rose opening, and for the life of me, I could not remember his name." She turned to Hutchins. "That ever happen to you? You have a whole conversation with someone and you know them, but you can't remember their name to save your own soul?"

"Nope." He gave her a wink and pointed to his forehead. "Steel trap."

Brenna sighed. "That's why those taxpayers give you the big bucks," she said. "Faces I don't forget. Names, not so much."

"What did this employee look like?" Wright asked.

"About your height, maybe a little bit taller. Dark hair—a little gray now. Broad shoulders. Good-looking. A mole right here." She pointed to her cheek. "Oh! And he drives a Subaru Vivio. One of those little K-cars they used to make in the nineties? Cute!"

Brenna took a look at Wright. The smile was gone.

"Something wrong?" she asked.

"You had a conversation with him."

"Yes . . ."

"You met him at the Rose Building opening?"

"Yes."

Wright cast a look at Hutchins. He wasn't smiling anymore, either.

"I don't know of anyone in my employ who fits that description," Wright said. His voice was cold.

"But—"

"Mr. Wright doesn't know all 180 of the people working for him."

"He only had thirty-eight employees thirteen years ago," Brenna said. They both stared at her. Brenna cringed. "I mean . . . uh . . . more or less."

"Who *are* you?" Hutchins said. "Why are you here?"

Brenna cleared her throat. "I'm sorry to have bothered you." She walked back to her car, with their ice-stares on her back, her cell phone buzzing SOS in Morse code from the inside of her purse—the vibration she'd chosen for text messages, and ridiculously appropriate, given the way she was feeling right now, but still . . . *Why that reaction? The guy with the mole drives a company car. How can he be anything other than a known Wright employee?*

Once she exited the parking lot—hoping the whole time Hutchins wasn't taking down her license plate yet knowing he was, of course—Brenna finally checked her cell phone screen. The message was from Trent. *Re: Wright Company car. Just found out registration changed in 1999 to ADAM MEADE. Call me.*

"Now he tells me," Brenna whispered. "*Now* he freakin' tells me."

* * *

"Adam Meade is not a dude you want to think about this close to Halloween," Trent said, just after Brenna called him.

Brenna sighed. "That's a great movie tagline. How about a few specifics?"

Trent rattled off everything he'd learned about Meade. The son of Vietnam war hero (and posthumous Congressional Medal of Honor recipient) Forrest Meade, Adam Meade had graduated from high school in Jacksonville, Florida, and spent many lost years before getting a job as an orderly at the VA Medical Center in the Bronx. Described in three complaints filed by patients as "emotionally abusive," Meade still managed to find employment as a security guard at Wright Industries from 1996 to 1999. His tenure with Wright ended, when, according to Trent, "He got his psycho ass fired."

"Why?" Brenna said.

"Well . . . on paper, it was a layoff," he said. "A reorganization of the security team."

"What wasn't on paper?"

"I don't know."

"Okay," she said. "So, how do you get 'fired' from 'layoff,' and 'psycho ass' from 'reorganization of the security team'?"

"Wright Industries is hardly laying anybody off now, let alone in the friggin' late nineties," Trent said. "And as far as that security reorganization goes, do you know the total amount of guards that were, uh, *laid off* that year?"

"Let me guess," said Brenna. "One."

"Yep."

"Very perceptive, Trent," she said. "I'm impressed."

"My biggest strength is still my bod," he said. "But I'm learning."

"So the big question is, who has Meade been working for for the past ten years?"

"Your guess is as good as mine. I'm thinking maybe he must hire himself out—private security, maybe? I *can* tell you that he's tried to join the army four, five times, both before and after he got fired by Wright. But he never made it."

"Why?"

"Psych test. Flunked the thing every time."

"How could Lydia Neff get involved with a guy like that?"

"Really?" Trent said. "When she was hot? Or, uh . . . more recently?"

Brenna sighed. "I gotta go, Trent."

Brenna ended the call as she hit the stoplight on the corner of Main and Muriel Court, Lydia Neff on her mind—or rather, Nelson Wentz's description of Lydia Neff twelve years ago, just after the Bistro had pulled out of her driveway . . . *She told me to forget I saw the car. Forget I was ever there. Tonight never happened. I left pretty quickly—Iris was sleeping upstairs and I didn't want to wake her . . .* Then, she thought of the question she'd asked Trent—*How could Lydia Neff get involved with a guy like that?*

Brenna knew the answer, of course she did. She'd known it when she'd asked, and it was an easy one. When it came to love, people were crazy. People were self-destructive and self-punishing and irrational and sad. They didn't look for what was good for them, but for qualities they wanted, needed for whatever sick, shoot-yourself-in-the-head reasons. They looked for those qualities again and again because they were adults and it was their absolute right to look for those qualities, to ruin the lives that were theirs to ruin . . . No, that wasn't the question at all. The question Brenna had really wanted to ask was this: *How could Lydia Neff let a guy like that near her daughter?*

Brenna's cell phone vibrated in her lap. She looked at the screen. Morasco. "Hey, listen. I have a name for you on the Bistro owner, and you're right. He isn't a cop."

"Who is he?" Morasco's voice was very quiet.

"Adam Meade," Brenna said. "He used to work for Roger Wright Industries."

Morasco was silent.

"Hello? Nick? Are you still—"

"How did you get the Neff police report, Brenna?"

"I told you. Nelson Wentz—"

"Not the new one. The old one. The one with page 22. How did you get that?"

"Errol Ludlow got it for me. Why?"

Morasco took a breath. "I never saw that page."

"But you were in charge of the case."

"I never knew that interview had been done. Chief Griffin interrogated this John Doe guy—this guy who had been talking to Lydia Neff on the phone—without ever telling me."

Brenna pulled over to the side of the road, turned the car off. "I think John Doe was Meade," she said. "He was a security guard for Wright Industries. He was fired—or laid off—after Iris's disappearance, and he seemed to have been involved with Lydia."

"Unbelievable."

"Actually, it is pretty damn believable," Brenna said. "One of Wright's employees is questioned by the police in a child's disappearance because there's late night phone calls from him to and from the kid's house . . . he's going to want to keep that quiet. God, wait a minute . . ." She took a breath. "It would explain why they didn't want you pursuing that lead. The little girl you interviewed. She described Meade's car perfectly . . ."

"Brenna, I don't want you working this case anymore. It isn't safe."

"What are you talking about?" she asked, but even as she said it, the image clicked into her brain yet again—Meade at her car window ten years ago, Hutchins at his side. "When Hutchins was a uniform, he was working the Iris Neff case," she said.

"Yes."

"He was working under you."

"Yes."

"What job did you assign him?" she asked, though the answer was obvious, her skin bristling with that knowledge, even before Morasco told her himself.

"He was going over Lydia Neff's phone records."

Why was Hutchins allied so closely with Adam Meade? Why had the chief called him "sir" in the interview? What type of sway did he hold—a former security guard? Whatever the answer, he did hold sway, and the best Brenna could do would be to do as Morasco said, get out of this now, leave it to him—a police officer himself—to get to the bottom of this.

But what about the girl who had called Nelson? What if Iris was out there somewhere, alive and needing help? Brenna gripped the steering wheel. *Carol tried to help. Tim O'Malley tried to help. Klavel, too . . .*

Past Muriel Court was the entrance to the 287 South, and that's where she needed to go—cross Muriel Court, take the entrance, leave Tarry Ridge. Leave with a woman dead in the trunk of her car and something missing from the back of Iris's framed drawing, leave with Lydia Neff invisible and Adam Meade everywhere. Leave without knowing.

She saw Nelson Wentz in her mind, Nelson Wentz, lying in bed, fragile in his undershirt. Nelson, whom Lydia had clearly used as a smoke screen. Oldest trick in the book— spread rumors you're screwing the unimportant little guy, it steers everyone away from the big guy you're really screwing. During her tenure with Errol, she'd seen five different mistresses pull the exact same scam, yet still she'd assumed Lydia had been telling Gayle Chandler the truth.

You're honest. You expect other people to be the same.

She stared out her window, recalling her conversation with Nelson. *I'm not going to be in need of your services anymore,* he'd said, without explanation, his voice so hollow and still. *You hire a PI because you need answers, Nelson. Did you find the answers? Is that why you fired me?*

Brenna squeezed her eyes shut, focused on the road. She would leave Tarry Ridge. She would leave Nelson Wentz. She would leave Nick Morasco and all the ghosts that haunted Lydia Neff's house. She would try to not think about the past three days. She would try to move on. She would fail miserably.

It is July 29, 1985, 9 A.M., and Brenna is finishing a bowl of instant oatmeal she made for herself. Ricky D the deejay says, "Next up, Talking Heads!" and then the song. "And She Was." About a girl slipping into thin air. Brenna's friend Carly says it's about an acid trip, but Brenna thinks it's just about disappearing.

In the garden outside, Mom is sitting cross-legged in the grass. She is staring up at the sculpture she made—an exact replica of Ammannati's Neptune. Nude and burly and bearded, looking over his left shoulder like he just heard someone sneaking up on him. Neptune is embarrassing, but he's been here so long he's also sort of a comfort.

Mom carved him out of a huge slab of expensive marble that arrived at their house one week after Dad left. Brenna had been just seven years old at the time—she can barely remember her dad's face now—but she can remember that marble slab, five men unloading it from the back of a big truck.

"What are you going to make with that, Mom?" Clea had asked.

And Mom had replied, *"Someone that won't ever leave."*

Now Clea's gone. She's been gone for almost four years. Brenna knows she's alive because she has to be. Brenna wonders if Clea's heard this song. "And She Was." She pictures Clea, closing her eyes and listening to those words and singing along about a world of missing persons . . .

Brenna wonders if Clea ever pictures her. She wonders if Clea ever pictures Mom, sitting cross-legged in her garden, not having spoken to Brenna in three days. She wonders if Clea has any idea how much it hurts to watch Mom out the window, staring up at Neptune's face as if he can talk, as if he is telling her why everyone here seems to leave but him.

"I'll find her," Brenna whispers. *"I'll find Clea for you, Mom."*

Brenna put the car in park and turned off the ignition. She hadn't crossed Muriel Court as she'd told herself she would. She had made a left, driven down four blocks, and pulled up in front of Nelson Wentz's house—what she'd wanted to do all along. *Fire me if you want, but I need the answers, too, Nelson. You don't have to pay me. I just need to know.*

Brenna leaned on Nelson Wentz's doorbell for a solid minute. No answer. Nelson was home, though. His car was in the driveway, so he was either (a) avoiding her or (b) zonked out on sleeping pills. Brenna wasn't going to let him get away with either. She walked over to the plastic rock by the bay window, twisted it open, and took out the key.

Once Brenna got inside the house and closed the door behind her, she called out Nelson's name. No answer, but she did hear water running upstairs. "Nelson?" she yelled again.

"It's Brenna!" She took a few steps into the living room. "I need to talk to you!"

No answer. He obviously couldn't hear her down here. She'd wait in the living room until he finished his shower.

She walked over to the couch. It had been moved a good foot back from its usual position. The throw rug, too, was against the window rather than in front of the fireplace, and the wooden bust of Don Quixote at the center of the coffee table rather than on the mantelpiece. Weird . . . for Nelson, anyway. Did he think he was turning over a new leaf? Was this barely noticeable redecoration part of that? She sat down on the hard wooden chair—her usual chair, she realized, and that's when she noticed something under the easy chair, Nelson's chair. A book. *A book on the floor? In Nelson Wentz's house?* The water was still running, the pipes above her groaning. Brenna crouched down, peered under the chair, and slipped it out. *Safekeeping: A Memoir.* She flipped it open and started to read, sliding a fingertip under the dust jacket on the back cover . . .

There was something taped back there. Brenna removed the dust jacket and saw it—a slim envelope, stuck to the inside of the back cover with what looked like an entire roll of Scotch tape, like Nelson was figuring on sending the thing off into space. *No, not Nelson. Carol.* This was Carol's book club book. This was the book Carol had called Gayle about, the book Nelson had seen Carol reading on the last night of her life. Brenna's mouth went dry. Her heart pounded. The envelope was slim enough to fit under the jacket of a book. Slim enough to fit behind a picture, in a frame.

She pulled the tape off the envelope, freeing it. Then she held it in her hands for a few moments, debating the ethics of all of this before finally she succumbed. She had to open it. Of course she had to open it.

In the envelope was a piece of paper, neatly folded. Brenna's eyes went to the lines, drawn in red crayon. A stick-figure girl at the center of a giant flower, with squares drawn in the background, a sun poking out from the upper left corner . . . Another drawing of Iris's . . . It was more detailed than the others yet it made less sense. Why was the girl trapped inside a flower? What were those squares supposed to be? Carefully, Brenna unfolded the drawing, wondering, *Why was this hidden behind a picture frame?*

Three snapshots fell out, onto the floor.

Brenna picked them up, turned them over . . . She gaped at them, these three happy vacation photos, all with a digital date of August 20, 1997. And then she took a breath and closed her eyes and looked at them again, one by one, staring hard into each, as if it might somehow turn to dust and poof away, as if she were stuck in some strange dream . . .

The first was of Lydia Neff, tanned and young and smiling. She wore a white T-shirt and cutoffs, and leaned against the hood of a light blue Subaru Vivio Bistro. The second was of Lydia on what looked like a hotel bed, under the covers, an arm thrown over her eyes, sleeping. And the third . . . The third was of a naked man, on the same hotel bed. He was lying on his stomach and staring into the camera lens with an emotion so raw, so serious and true that Brenna herself could feel it, twelve years later and in the living room of a house where neither she nor the photo belonged. She could feel it, tightening in her chest until she could no longer look at him. It wasn't her place to look. The emotion belonged to the man, and it was for the woman behind the camera, for her and her alone . . . The emotion was love. The man was Roger Wright.

Not Meade. Wright. That was the affair Lydia Neff was trying to cover up by telling Gayle she was sleeping with

Nelson. It was Roger Wright who'd been driving the company car before Meade had bought it. Lydia Neff hadn't invited a gun-wielding psychopath into her house as her daughter slept. She'd invited a very rich, very powerful, very married man. A man who, at least for one moment in time, had looked at Lydia as though he would give it all up for her—his family, his fortune, all that and more. He loved her.

Iris said that when Santa visits Tarry Ridge, he drives a blue car. It had been Wright leaving Lydia's house when Nelson had gone to talk to her. Wright whose car Lydia told him to forget ever seeing, Wright whose car Iris had clearly seen as well. Brenna could imagine the conversation. She could practically hear it.

Whose car was that at our house, Mommy?

Nobody, honey.

No, Mommy, no. I woke up in the middle of the night. I saw a blue car, leaving our driveway.

Oh. That was . . . It was Santa, sweetheart.

Santa? Really?

Yes. Sometimes he visits our house. But you mustn't tell anyone or he will never come again.

Brenna shoved the drawing and the pictures into her bag and ran upstairs. "Nelson!"

No answer. Just the sound of running water.

Brenna walked through Nelson's bedroom to the bathroom and pounded on the door. "Nelson! It's Brenna! I need to show you what Carol found."

Still no answer. She put her hand on the knob and the door drifted open. Steam poured out. The mirror was completely fogged. She stepped inside. It was like stepping into a rain cloud. How long had the water been running?

"Nelson?"

She caught sight of the note first, face up on the sink.

Black pen on pale blue stationery, its edges curling from steam. Brenna read.

"No," she breathed.

The smell registered, gripped in the steam, flat and foul. Why was she noticing it only now, that smell? Brenna didn't want to turn around, but she did. She turned, and she saw him there, the poor man, poor sad Nelson Wentz, hanging from a towel hook right next to the shower, his own belt around his neck. Brenna felt the ripping pain of her own scream, but all she could hear was running water.

26

It was the face that would stay with her—the pale skin, the two black eyes, the mouth wrenched open in a sick parody of a smile. *Halloween makeup.* That had been Brenna's first, irrational thought, her mind trying to come up with excuses for what she was looking at—the lifeless body, hanging from the thick hook, one foot pushing against the faucet, the water running and running, hot and then cold for what must have been at least twelve hours. *The water bill.* That had been Brenna's second irrational thought, which had lasted all of half a second before she'd started shrieking.

Nelson Wentz was dead—the apparent cause of death strangulation from hanging. And though Brenna still couldn't wrap her mind around it—so much of it didn't make sense—the police seemed ready to rule it a suicide from the moment they arrived at the house. There had been no outward signs of a struggle or a break-in. Nothing different about Nelson's home at all, save for the slightly rearranged furniture, which had gotten Brenna nothing but blank stares when she'd brought it up.

And then, of course, there was the note.

*I can no longer live with the guilt. I killed my wife,
Carol. I beleived her to be having an affair. I let my
anger get the best of me. I am so sorry. God have
mercy on my soul.*

Nelson Wentz

As you would expect, Nelson's handwriting was meticulous. Perfectly formed block letters, evenly spaced. The note was now in a clear evidence bag on the coffee table, surrounded by Morasco, Pomroy, and two other detectives whom Brenna had never met—a thickly built, red-haired woman in a plain navy blue wrap dress, and an older guy in a tie with anchors all over it, neither one of whom had bothered introducing themselves. Brenna, who had been briefly questioned by the group, now leaned against the crafts closet, watching them wait for the chief to arrive.

The detectives said very little. Wrap Dress and Anchor Tie were sitting next to each other on the couch, their hands folded in their laps. They looked like a married couple being interviewed for a very boring documentary, with Pomroy, the meaty host, leaning against the window frame behind them. Morasco was at the edge of Nelson's recliner, both feet on the floor. Throughout their sparse conversation, he kept glancing over at Brenna, which she found both a comfort and a distraction.

" . . . should be here any minute," Pomroy was saying, and then Hutchins strolled in, the cue so obvious-seeming, Brenna half-expected a laugh track. He'd changed out of his golf togs and into a three-button, pinstriped suit—cut to fit him maybe five pounds ago, the back of the jacket tight and shiny through the shoulders.

"How are we doing, men?" Hutchins said. "I hear we got a suicide note, no signs of a B&E, body discovered this morning . . ." Pomroy lumbered up to him and began rattling off specifics, and Brenna watched these two heavy men, her eyes dry and flat.

Odd the way death settled into your system. After that initial panic, you went a little dead yourself, your heartbeat slowing, your emotions going numb. It was a coping mechanism, but it was also, Brenna thought now, a form of empathy . . .

"Miss Bissel?"

It took Brenna a few seconds to realize Hutchins was addressing her. She swallowed hard. "Hello."

He pointed to his forehead. "Like I said at the club, steel trap." He gave her a tight, hard smile. "I never forget a name, even a fake one."

"Oh, well, that was—"

"You know it's against the law to misrepresent yourself to a police officer."

Brenna said, "I was doing my job."

Hutchins and Pomroy stared at her, that statement, in all its lameness, echoing in Brenna's ears.

"You've got to understand—"

"Oh, I understand," said Hutchins. "Just like you should understand that when I ran your plates after you accosted me in the parking lot, I was just *doing my job* as well."

Brenna said nothing. She was clenching her teeth so tight her jaw hurt.

"You can leave, Ms. Spector. You've given us all the information we need."

Three crime techs walked out of the house with their metal briefcases, and then two more emerged from the bedroom, carrying Nelson's bagged body downstairs on a stretcher. It looked so small, almost like the body of a child.

Brenna turned and followed, but she stopped when she got to where Morasco was sitting. He looked up at her.

"He spelled 'believed' wrong."

"What?"

Wrap Dress said, "I think the chief just asked you to leave."

Brenna ignored her. "Nelson Wentz," she told Morasco. "He was one of the most anal people I ever met—a total perfectionist. And not only that, he edited encyclopedia articles for a living. Don't you think it's a little odd that a person like that would spell a word wrong in his own suicide note?"

Brenna felt five sets of eyes on her, but she looked only at Morasco. "Think about it," she said quietly. And then she walked out the door, and to the sidewalk, where she waited.

Across the street, press cars and news vans kept arriving and parking until they formed a small herd. Cameramen were starting to unload their equipment, reporters checking their reflections in rearviews. Brenna watched them, flashing back for several seconds to Nelson's press conference, until Hutchins strode out of the house and moved toward them, everything about him so broad—the smile, the wave, the body, doing battle with the expensive suit. He was the exact opposite of Nelson, and it brought Brenna back to the present. The other detectives followed—a Greek chorus with their smug expressions, all in perfect step except for Morasco, who headed straight for the sidewalk and up the street where his car was parked so quickly, he didn't even seem to see Brenna as he passed.

Brenna tore off after him, reaching him just as he was about to get into his car. She tried to say his name, but at that point she was so winded that all she could do was slap him on the shoulder.

He spun around. "Brenna." There was a flicker in his eyes—a warning.

"I know you told me to drop the case," she breathed, "but seriously, Nick, how could I?"

She started to say more, but he cut her off. "When people

are under stress," he said, "they do things they normally wouldn't."

Brenna moved closer, her breathing slowing. "What do you mean?"

"Spelling words wrong."

She exhaled. "Oh."

"Normally, people aren't stressed when they kill themselves. They've been through all of that already and the body creates a sense of calm." He took a breath. "But as you and I both know, Nelson Wentz was not a normal man." He sounded as if he were reading from a script.

"Listen. We have to talk. I have something important to show you."

"I'm sorry. But we really can't open an investigation based on one misspelling."

"Nick, what the hell—"

"Sssh."

He glanced both ways, then stared pointedly into her eyes. "Washington Playground," he said between his teeth. "Parking lot. Ten minutes."

The Washington Playground was clean, but surprisingly small and unassuming when compared to everything else Brenna had seen in Tarry Ridge—refreshing in a way, in its normalcy. There was a curving slide, a swing set, a dome-shaped jungle gym, and a huge sandbox, all of it perched on a neat green lawn surrounded by park benches, not a Teasdale plaque or statue in sight. The park was nearly empty. Two blond kindergarten-aged boys took turns on the slide, two middle-aged Hispanic women watching from one of the benches, chatting. That was it.

Yet when Morasco walked up to her window and said, "Car or playground?" Brenna opted for the car. Better to be safe.

Once inside, Morasco said, "Candy Bissel? From the *Sleepy Hollow Review*?"

"*Press*. Not *Review*."

He gave her a look.

"I don't have a badge to flash. I get my information any way I can."

He sighed heavily. "What were you doing at Wentz's, Brenna? I told you—"

Brenna put a hand up, cutting him off. She took the envelope out of her bag and handed it to him. "This," she said, "is what Carol took out of the picture frame."

Morasco looked at her. "How do you know?"

"Open it."

Morasco slipped open the envelope, removed the crayon drawing of the stick-figure girl, trapped inside the flower. "Another picture by Iris?" he said. Then he saw the photographs and said nothing. He stared at each one, no sound in the car at all but his breathing, until finally, he spoke. "Wright and Lydia Neff."

She nodded. "The Vivio Bistro was a company car back then. It didn't transfer over to Meade until 1999."

"A company car. Not easily traced."

"That's right. The perfect vehicle for secret meetings."

He turned to her. His face was pale. "Wright has worse secrets than that."

"What do you mean?"

"I researched Meade a little. I spoke to the director of the Bronx VA Hospital. I read some of the complaints made against him, Brenna. Withholding food and pain medication, overloading them with laxatives, suspected cutting, burning. In one report, he denied any wrongdoing, but claimed the patient 'deserved agony' because he no longer wanted to fight in the army. He's a sociopath. Inhuman."

"Yes."

"And yet Wright hired him, after that. He must have seen the records."

"He did wind up firing him."

"Did he?"

Brenna stared at him.

He stole a quick glance at the chatting nannies, then moved in closer, his gaze fixed on her face. "Chief Griffin retired five years ago. Moved into the Waterside Condos. No one ever asked how he could afford a place there. Just like no one asked how Hutchins can afford his 360i, his country club membership, those ridiculous shiny shoes . . ."

"Not to mention the police department building."

"The Teasdale Station House," he said. "Yes."

"But what does that have to do with—"

"Chief Griffin was a widower. No kids. No one to talk to, really. Lydia Neff used to go to the condos pretty often."

"To meditate."

"Right. They already knew each other because of Iris, of course . . . But maybe three, three and a half years ago she and Chief Griffin struck up a friendship. Not like they were dating or anything, but you'd see them together, Lydia and the chief, out at a diner maybe, walking through the shopping center . . ."

"Someone to talk to." Brenna looked at him. "A strong shoulder."

"Chief Griffin was big into bike riding. He took the same route, around the reservoir, every morning at 7 A.M. You could set your clock by him." Morasco's gaze darted to the rear window, and then it was back on Brenna's face, burning. "No more than six months after he and Lydia started talking, Chief Griffin's body was found, dead from a massive brain injury, the bike destroyed . . . Looked like he'd run into a tree, but there were no witnesses."

Brenna's eyes widened. "Was there any sort of investigation?"

"Are you *kidding* me?"

Brenna's mind went to Hutchins, promoted to chief by an appreciative mayor, the mayor of a town built by Teasdale money. Wright and Hutchins, the world's oddest pair, golfing every morning for years. *Not so odd.* The Lily Teasdale Police Station—elegant beyond reason. Named after the mother of Wright's wife. Wright's wife, who never knew a thing. Rachel Teasdale Wright, so patrician-calm at the Waterside Condos ribbon cutting, living in her glass bubble, smiling with her mouth closed, keeping all that happiness to herself . . . Happiness she *could* keep, always, as long as people like Hutchins accepted Wright's money, Wright's funding, as long as they did their jobs and kept his secrets and made sure that bubble never broke.

People like Hutchins. And the mayor. And Meade. "You think Meade is still working for Wright off the books," Brenna said. "You think he's still keeping Wright's secrets."

Morasco stared into her, through her, his jaw set. "I don't want you working this case anymore."

Brenna swallowed hard. She tried a pout, a squeaky Lucille Ball voice: "Waa, Ricky, I wanna be in the show!"

His face didn't move.

"Oh, come on. Was that one too current for you?"

"I mean it."

"I know you do, Nick," she said softly. She disengaged her hands from his. "But really. Is that something you say to a grown-up?"

He sighed. Then shook his head.

She took back the envelope. "If you don't mind, I'm going to put this somewhere that's safer than the Tarry Ridge Police Department."

"And that would be pretty much anywhere on the planet."

She slipped her arms around his neck and gave him a hug, inhaling the Ivory Soap, feeling how close he held her for those few racing seconds, feeling safe. Brenna knew she would remember, and she was glad. She wanted to keep this.

Once she pulled away, Morasco said, "Promise me you'll be careful."

"I will."

"And you'll call. Often."

"I will."

"And you'll tell me everything, keep nothing from me, let me help you, whether you think you need it or not."

Brenna gave him a long, steady look. "Will you do the same?"

"Yes."

"Then okay. I will."

He opened the door and left the car, his gaze never leaving her face. "I'll hold you to that," he whispered. As Brenna pulled out of the space and drove away, Morasco sat in his own car, hands on the wheel, watching her go.

He wasn't the only one.

27

When Morasco arrived at the station, Lane Hutchins was out by the fountain giving a press conference. His second of the day, but that wasn't unusual for Hutchins. Public appearances of any sort were what he liked best, and the *way* he spoke . . . Not like a police officer or even a politician. More like Charlton Heston auditioning for *All My Children*.

Passing behind the TV cameras, Morasco heard the chief say, ". . . little did anyone know, Nelson Wentz harbored some dark secrets . . ." *That's right, Chief. Tell us about secrets.*

". . . a little man, with a giant rage . . ."

"Who writes this crap?" Morasco muttered. One of the cameramen turned to him, eyebrows up. Morasco kept his head down and slipped into the station thinking about secrets, how long they could keep before they rotted and stank and killed everything around them.

The station was mostly empty, most of the other detectives flanking Hutchins at the press conference, the uniforms who weren't on patrol making sure the chief saw them standing among the reporters, watching. Morasco walked to his desk—such a large desk, polished to a sheen by the cleaning crew and so much like most everything else in this station—oversized and gleaming and completely unnecessary. His old desk had worked fine. His old desktop computer had been perfectly sufficient, and his old phone, too, without the headset, without the reflective space-age surface and the voice dial that constantly called wrong numbers.

You work in a place like this long enough, you get used to it, the pointless waste. The hypocrisy. But all you have to do is look at it directly and it doesn't matter how long it's been. It socks you in the face, just as hard as the last time you took a good, long look. What was he doing here? Why hadn't he left eleven years ago?

There were no pictures on Morasco's desk, not anymore. Before the divorce, he had one framed photo—a small one of Holly and himself, taken during one of their camping trips upstate. He didn't remember specifics, but he could recall the look of the photo—smiling, arms around each other, surrounded by evergreens or maple trees—at this point, he wasn't sure which. What he did know—what he would always know—was that Holly had been three months' pregnant when the picture had been taken. Morasco had kept that picture on his desk for a very long time—after the baby's birth and death. Even for a good three months after the divorce became final, the picture stayed there, next to Morasco's computer. The department relocated to this new address, the enormous desk arrived. He stuck the picture in the drawer for a few weeks. Then he threw it out.

There are statistics, overwhelming ones, about the divorce rate among couples who lose a child. Experts say that after such a death—a SIDS death, beyond either parent's control—it is nearly impossible for that couple to look at each other without feeling a sense of loss and powerlessness. Counseling might have helped, but Holly was never one for counseling. She just wanted to forget.

Iris Neff disappeared four months after Matthew died in his bassinet. At the start of the case, Lydia Neff had given Morasco a picture of Iris—a little girl in purple overalls with a big smile, her black hair pulled into pigtails. Morasco had made color copies of the photo, and then he'd put the original in the top drawer of his desk. Every day he'd crack the drawer, look at Iris's face, and think, *I'll find you. Don't worry.* He'd kept the picture in that drawer long after it had outlived its usefulness, nearly as long as he'd kept the framed camping trip photo on top of his desk. Morasco wasn't one to forget. If anything, he held on to memories too tightly.

He buzzed Fields. "Did you ever get those phone records for me?"

"Carol Wentz? Yes—the phone company sent them over a couple hours ago."

When he picked them up at her desk, Fields said, "I'm sorry. I would have given them to you myself, but I figured you didn't need them anymore, what with Nelson Wentz . . . You know."

"Sure, Sally. No worries." Morasco took the files back to his desk and started skimming through the numbers, made to and from the Wentzes' landline in the two weeks before Carol's death. There weren't many calls at all—just two pages' worth.

When he got to the start of the second page, though, he stopped. He read the number a couple of times, just to make sure he hadn't gotten it wrong.

There was a roar of conversation at the front door just then—the chief coming back to work, along with the dozen detectives who had been standing behind him during the press conference. They all filed in, talking and laughing. Morasco heard Wentz's name a few times, along with some bad pun-riffs on the word "hung." Gallows humor. Literally. Pomroy walked up to Morasco's desk. "Where were you?"

"Taking care of some paperwork," he replied, the phone number he'd seen still swirling around in his head. "Be right back—I gotta go ask Sally something."

Morasco headed back to the front desk. "It says here," he told Fields, "that Carol Wentz called this police station on Monday, September 21, 9:30 A.M.?"

Fields looked at the list, nodded. "Yep."

"I mean . . . I'm assuming it was Carol, not Nelson, because he would have been at work. Right?"

"Just a sec." Fields jiggled her mouse and her computer screen lit up. She'd been on her Facebook page, but Morasco pretended not to notice. Fields kept very precise records of everyone who called the station and whom she connected them with. For that, in Morasco's opinion at least, she was allowed all the social networking she wanted. Fields called up her phone log file and stared at the screen. "You're right—it was Carol," she said. "See? She asked to speak to the chief. She was on for ten minutes."

Morasco exhaled. "Thanks, Sally," he said, his body moving of its own accord, around Fields's desk and into the chief's office suite, past his assistant and through his polished mahogany door, her whispery protests hanging in the air behind him, just motes of dust. Hutchins was on the phone. Morasco heard him say, "Gotta call you back, Eugene."

Hutchins hung up, looking at Morasco as though he were something he thought he'd successfully wiped off the sole of his shoe this morning, only to find it still there, clinging.

"Was that Eugene Conti, editor of the *Gazette*?" said Morasco. "Or Eugene Phillips, the mayor?"

Hutchins gave him the crack of a smile. "I'm busy right now, Detective Morasco. If you have any business, discuss it with Detectives Pomroy or Fleiss."

Hutchins's desk was sprawling and decorated with a sky-line of expensively framed photos—Hutchins with Mayor Phillips, Hutchins with Donald Trump, Hutchins with Conan O'Brien and Mayor Bloomberg and some actor from *Law & Order* whose name Morasco couldn't remember. Hutchins with Derek Jeter and Hutchins with Matt Lauer and Hutchins with Roger Wright, golf clubs in hand. In each picture, the chief wore the same practiced smile—the mouth stretched wide and the eyes flat and the shoulders squared. Hutchins could have substituted a cardboard cutout of himself for half these photo ops, it wouldn't have made any difference. Morasco walked up to the front of the desk. He put both hands on the smooth surface and leaned over it, staring into Hutchins's eyes. "What did you talk to Carol Wentz about?"

"Excuse me?"

"On September 21, Carol Wentz called here. She spoke to you for ten minutes. What did you talk about?"

"None of your business, Detective."

"Twenty minutes after she called you, she called Graeme Klavel, a private investigator she knew. What couldn't you help her with that Graeme Klavel *could*?"

Hutchins stood up at his desk. He was a big man—same height as Morasco, but he easily had forty pounds on him. He used to be quite the bar brawler back in the day, before he became a "public official." And when he met his gaze, Morasco saw a glimpse of that Lane, the old Lane with the meaty jaw and the crazy eyes, Lane the asshole, who had once broken a guy's nose at Yankee Stadium for rooting too loudly for the Sox. *Did his photo op pal Jeter know that story? Doubtful.*

Lane Hutchins stared into Morasco's eyes for a solid minute, saying nothing.

Morasco stared right back. "It's an easy enough question, Lane," he said quietly. "What did you not want to look into for Carol Wentz?"

Hutchins squared his jaw, the bones pressing against his skin. "She asked me to speak at the Methodist church," he said finally. "She thought it would be interesting for members of her women's group to hear how they could become involved in the Neighborhood Watch program." His voice was like ice cracking. Morasco left the office knowing there were changes to be made.

Hutchins hadn't thought Morasco had noticed, but he had. That glint of recognition in the eyes, the slight blanching of the skin at the mention of Klavel's name. *Changes to be made.*

When Morasco got back to his desk, Pomroy was leaning against it, talking to Fleiss. "We're thinking about ordering from Frankie's," he said. "You in?"

"Not hungry." Morasco left his desk and then the station, taking the phone call list along with him.

"Maybe she joined a convent," said Trent by way of greeting, just after Brenna walked through her apartment door. He was staring at his computer screen, uncharacteristically intent, a look on his face as if he wanted to climb into whatever it was he was reading, yet despite all that, despite everything she'd seen and learned today, Trent's shirt still stopped Brenna in her tracks.

"Shirt" was a generous description, to be honest. It was more of a sports bra, with the profile of a roaring tiger thickly rendered on the front in what looked like spray paint and mustard, red sequined tears dripping out of its angry yellow eyes.

Wow. Like what Christian Audigier would see in his nightmares after a twenty-four-hour appletini bender.

Brenna shook herself away from the garment, started toward his desk. "Maybe *who* joined a convent?"

"Lydia Neff."

"Doubtful." Brenna looked over his shoulder at the screen.

"Lydia's credit card bill from two years ago," he said. "Last charge she ever made was for thirty dollars, at a gas station." He looked up at her. "In Buffalo."

"So she did make it up there."

"And, oh, wait—before I forget, someone called for you a few minutes ago, but I let it go to voice mail."

"Trent." She took a breath. "I've got a few things to tell you about, and you're gonna need to prepare a little."

"Oookay . . ."

Brenna waited for him to tear himself away from the computer, give her his full attention.

"First of all. This." She removed the slim envelope from her purse and put it on the keyboard in front of him. "Carol was hiding this," she said. "She took it out of the Neff house. Taped it in a book."

He opened it up, removed the drawing and then, the pictures. He gaped at them. For a moment, he appeared to swallow his own tongue. "Well, wax my ass," he said, once he began to collect himself.

"Also . . ." She cleared her throat. "Nelson Wentz is dead."

"*What?*"

Brenna talked him through the entire day, from her run-in with Wright and Hutchins to discovering Nelson's body to everything Morasco had told her about, including Chief Griffin's untimely death, Wright's probable involvement, everything . . . Then she left Trent there, uncharacteristically silent, his jaw practically unhinged, while she walked over to her desk to check her voice mail.

"I don't usually like to, uh, pull out early," Trent finally said as the electronic voice told Brenna she had one message, "but in this case, it would seem like the smart thing to do."

"Huh?"

"We should get out of this. Leave it to Morasco. I mean, come on. Our client is dead. Meade seems to be killing people left and right. The police looking the other way, and Roger freakin' Wright seems to be in on it . . ."

"And you think Morasco can handle all that alone?"

"Brenna."

"I'm not pulling out, Trent. Early or otherwise." Brenna started to say more, but the words died in her throat once the voice mail message began.

"I want to give you my name and number but I feel like, if I do, things will happen that I won't be able to stop. I know what happened to Mr. Wentz. I want to say something, but I'm so scared. I wish I could take back what I did, but . . . they're going to be so angry with me. Oh my gosh, I've got to go."

The teenage girl. The electronic voice announced, "End of new messages."

"She called," Brenna whispered.

"Who?"

"We need to find Lydia Neff." Brenna's cell phone rang. She answered it fast, without looking at the ID. "Yes."

"It's Nick."

She exhaled hard.

"You were expecting someone else."

"That girl. She called me again. Left a message, and I was hoping . . . I just want to *know*."

"Well," he said slowly, "this might help."

"What?"

"I finally got hold of the Wentzes' landline records, Brenna. I'm looking at three calls, made to the Wentz home, at three, three-ten, and three-fifteen in the morning on September 21."

"Before she started calling Klavel."

"Before she started calling anybody," Morasco said. "I'm thinking these calls might have been what set her off in the first place."

My fault. "Okay," Brenna said. Her heart was pounding, and she wished she could slow it, slow down her whole body, the speeding pulse, the racing thoughts . . . *Don't get your hopes up.* "Do you know who the calls were from?"

"I haven't had a chance to do a reverse directory," he said. "But they're all from the same number—555–7651."

Brenna's mouth went dry. "You don't have to do a reverse directory," she said, "I know the number."

"Who does it belong to?"

Brenna took a deep breath, let it out slowly. "It belongs to a soap star's fax machine."

28

Traffic was vicious. It couldn't be helped, though. Brenna was headed to the suburbs at 6 P.M., along with enough commuters to successfully overthrow and re-populate a good-sized third world dictatorship.

Brenna wondered if Will Garvey himself was among this throng. She'd seen more than a dozen shiny black Espla-nades while crawling up the West Side Highway to the Cross County, the SUVs multiplying by tens and twenties as she left the city behind.

Garvey was supposedly through shooting *The Day's End* at 4 P.M. today, after which he would come directly home, as it was one of his nights with his son and daughter. At least, that's what his housekeeper had told Morasco over the phone—far more amenable, apparently, to a policeman's voice in her ear than to some strange woman at her door, asking about her boss's possible connection to a murdered woman.

Four P.M. Morasco and Brenna had figured on maybe forty-five minutes to remove the TV makeup and get into his street clothes, another half hour to say good-bye to his castmates, pick up his car, and get on the road. He ought to be home by six, they'd assumed. The timing worked for

Brenna. Maya had texted her at five, wanting to spend the night at Larissa's again, and this time, Brenna didn't argue about it. *Be good*, she'd texted back. *Mind her mother.*

After arranging to meet Morasco at Garvey's house at six, she'd gotten her car out of the garage, said good-bye to Trent, and hit the road, only to be stuck in this hell for more than forty-five minutes, with some goddamn gold Chevy Cavalier riding her bumper like a Brahma bull in a state of extreme arousal. "Any closer, you'd be in the front seat," Brenna muttered into her rearview.

Brenna looked at her watch: six-ten. She sighed, called Morasco on her cell, and got his voice mail. "Better go on into Garvey's without me if you haven't already," she said. "The Cross County is a nightmare."

No sooner had she hung up, though, than Brenna saw the light at the end of the tunnel. About half a mile up, the highway branched off—Whitestone Bridge traffic to one side, Merritt Parkway to the other. Most of the cars were headed for the Whitestone, but Brenna wanted the Merritt. A get-out-of-traffic-hell-free card. *Praise be.*

As soon as the road ahead cleared up, Brenna accelerated, but wouldn't you know the Cavalier was right behind her, reaming her Sienna as though it still had no other choice. "Use the fast lane!" she yelled.

Brenna sped up even more, and the Cavalier chose that moment to take Brenna's advice and try the fast lane on for size, clipping her in the right rear bumper. "Goddamn it!" Brenna pulled onto the shoulder and flipped her hazards on. She just could not get a break today. She checked her rearview, fully expecting the Cavalier not to be there—a hit-and-run, on top of everything else. Okay, at least it was pulling over, too.

Has to be a rental car, she thought as she opened her passenger's side door and got out to inspect the damage. *Some jerkoff from out of town, paid the collision insurance and obviously wants his money's worth.*

She sensed a tall body behind her—the rental car driver—and anger barreled through her. This was the worst time for something like this to happen. The absolute worst. "What were you thinking?" Brenna snapped. She started to spin around to face him, but stopped when she felt cold metal at the small of her back. The barrel of a gun. She turned her head just enough to see the shadow of a face behind her, clear for a few seconds in the lights from a passing car. The pretty features. The thick jaw. The mole.

Adam Meade slipped the cell phone out of her front pocket. "Get back in your car," he said. Brenna obeyed. She had no other choice, Meade directing her behind the wheel and sliding into the passenger's seat, Meade and his gun, forcing her back onto the highway, telling her where to drive, leaving his rented Cavalier behind.

Morasco got the message from Brenna just as he was arriving at Willis Garvey's overdone wedding cake of a mini mansion. She was caught in traffic. Going to be late.

Morasco sighed. He took a look at Garvey's house. The shades were drawn in front of the enormous great room window, but Morasco could see shadows moving behind them, all the lights in the house blazing. He rang the bell, and within seconds, the door opened—answered by a guy who looked like he'd walked off the cover of a drugstore romance novel, minus the puffy shirt and the breathless woman in the corset. "Mr. Garvey?" Morasco said.

He frowned. "Yes . . ."

"Detective Nick Morasco. Tarry Ridge Police Department."

Garvey stared at him for a full twenty seconds. "I'm sorry," he said finally. "Am I supposed to know what this is regarding?"

"Just a few quick questions, if you don't mind."

Garvey nodded.

Morasco followed him into the house, through a hallway and into a great room that turned out to be a housekeeper's nightmare—all of it white. From somewhere up the stairs, music blasted—bass that shook the floor above them and a woman's voice: "That's not my name," over and over and over, punctuated by uproarious, girlish laughter. Morasco felt like he was in a nightclub's basement.

"My daughter has a friend over," Garvey said, stating the obvious.

"Mr. Garvey," Morasco said, "how is it you knew Carol Wentz?"

Garvey's face went to stone. "Listen," he said. "I already told that investigator you're working with, I don't know Carol Wentz. Outside of the news, I've never heard the name in my life."

"Then why did you call her?"

"She called me," he said. "I never called her."

Morasco cleared his throat. "You called Carol Wentz three times on September 21, starting at three in the morning."

Garvey stared at him. Above them, the singing woman asked if you'd been calling her darlin', and someone cranked the volume up even more. "Girls, would you turn that down, *please*!" Garvey shouted. Then he looked at Morasco. "I'm sorry, but I have no idea what you're talking about."

Morasco removed the phone call list from his pocket. "These are all the incoming calls to the Wentzes' phone." He pointed out the September 21 calls. "This is your fax number, right?"

Garvey stared at the page, his tanned skin going pale. "I . . . I honestly don't know how that could have happened."

"It happened three times in a row."

The girls had turned the music down, but the bass prevailed. *Bump-da-dum, bump-da-dum*, like being trapped in a giant metronome. Garvey took the paper from Morasco. He held it in both hands, staring at it for a long while, as if he expected the numbers to suddenly change. Was this acting? If it was, Garvey was really, really good.

"Mr. Garvey, if you could just explain to me what you told Carol Wentz, then—"

"Wait a minute. September 21. . . . That was a Monday."

Morasco nodded. "Just about ten days ago. Shouldn't be that hard for you to remember."

"Girls!" he hollered. "Come down here please."

"Just a minute, Dad!"

"Right now!"

Mercifully, the music switched off. And within moments, two young teenage girls appeared at the top of the stairs—one tall and blonde and bearing a striking resemblance to Garvey; the other smaller, with brown hair and glasses.

"What, Dad?" said the Garvey look-alike.

"Detective Morasco, this is my daughter, Emily," Garvey glared at the girl and her friend. "You girls had a sleepover last Sunday."

"Uh, yeah." Emily looked at Morasco. "Is that against the law?"

"Don't be rude, Emily."

"Sorry."

Garvey took a breath. "Emily, were you two making prank calls from my fax machine?"

Emily's smile dropped away. "No, Dad. Of course not—"

"I mean it."

Emily turned to her friend. The girl looked stricken, Morasco had to say—a look of crippling guilt crossing through her face. There was something familiar about that face, too, something in the eyes . . .

"It wasn't me," Emily said.

"I will not tolerate lies."

"I'm not lying, Daddy," the blonde girl said. "I swear."

"I have the proof right here, Emily. I have the phone—"

"It was Maggie."

Maggie . . . Oh my God . . . Morasco stared at the big eyes, the worried little mouth, the wispy brown hair . . . and he remembered blue plastic barrettes. Tinker Bell barrettes. He remembered pink sneakers with Velcro straps, dangling a foot off the floor . . .

"I'm so sorry," Maggie said, tears forming in her eyes. "I'm so, so sorry. It's my fault."

Sitting on the metal chair in the interview room, the chair dwarfing her, the yellow T-shirt with a fluffy white cat on it. Little fingers clutching the plastic cup of water. Three and a half years old. The squeaky voice. The shy laugh. *Nobody's scared of Santa.*

"I prank-called Mrs. Wentz. But it wasn't my idea. It was Emily's idea."

"It was *not.* You were the one who told me about the chat room!"

"I can't believe you girls," Garvey said. "I mean I honestly cannot believe you."

"I told her not to do it."

"You did not, Emily. Stop it." Maggie had tears in her eyes.

Emily said, "Mrs. Wentz thought Maggie was . . . was somebody else."

"I'm sorry. I'm so sorry . . ."

Mrs. Wentz thought you were Iris. We all thought you were Iris. Morasco shook his head, staring speechless at this girl, seeing the passage of time in her face, from three and a half to fourteen, the same little girl, causing so much trouble . . . "Maggie?" he said finally. "Maggie Schuler?"

* * *

Brenna drove. Meade kept his arm against the back of her seat, the barrel at the base of her neck. He'd taken the safety off—made her watch him take the safety off and then placed the barrel there, just above her collarbone like a cold, extended kiss. Brenna's mind would try to rescue her—it would take her, for instance, to April 18, 1994, to the roof of the Fourteenth Street apartment building at midnight with REM on the boom box, Jim's fingertips against Brenna's cheek and his lips moving to touch hers, but no sooner would she feel those lips, that impossible tenderness welling up in her chest, no sooner would she hear Michael Stipe sing about corrosives doing their magic slowly. Brenna would feel the metal against her skin, and she would return, again, to Meade.

"Get off here," Meade said. They were on the Deegan expressway now, the 230th Street exit. The Bronx. Brenna did as she was told. "What do you want from me?" she said.

He didn't reply.

Meade had her turn down a long avenue, and then make a left on a smaller side street. Another left and two quick rights, and they were on a desolate stretch of road, where if you looked down, you could see the dark murky water. Pelham Bay. *God.* Was this some kind of existential joke, or had Meade planned it this way? Brenna could see City Island from here.

"Stop the car."

After she pulled onto the shoulder, Meade grabbed the keys out of her hand. "Get out," he said, and as she got out of the car and let him push her around it, looking down at the bay, the gun now between her shoulder blades, Brenna felt herself step into the night of September 7, 1981, Meade's calm, quiet voice morphing into her mother's shrill one . . .

"Get out of my house."

"Clea told me not to tell you, Mom. That's why. Because Clea made me prom—"

"Two weeks ago, Brenna. Your sister could be dead right now."

"I'm sorry."

"If she is dead, it is your fault. It's your fault she's gone. Get out of my house."

Brenna's watch says 9:45 P.M. It is September but the air is still warm and wet and thick, like breath. Brenna opens her front door and walks down to the sidewalk. She turns left, heads toward the bay.

"Where did you put it?" Meade said.

Brenna passes the Lindens' house, the Moskovitzes', the Mangiones', the Conrads' . . . She opens the gate to the Center Street Beach. She takes off her shoes and feels the cool sand under her toes. Pelham Bay is a black mirror, city lights reflecting off the surface. She walks into the water until it is past her ankles, past her knees. She will not swim. She will not fight. The water is cold but she will keep going in . . .

"Where?" He jabbed the gun in her ribs.

Brenna heard herself say, "I don't know what you're talking about."

"You do."

The water is at Brenna's waist. The current tugs at her. I will not fight, *she thinks.* I will not fight.

"I don't understand."

It is up to her neck now. She pushes against the current, seaweed brushes against both wrists, wraps around her waist. It makes her cringe. She sees the lights of the city in front of her. "Good-bye," she says. Brenna closes her eyes. She is about to go under when she hears something behind her, a splashing . . .

For a moment, the gun lifted away from her back.

A splashing in the water and then her mother's voice.

"Brenna! Brenna! Don't, sweetheart, please! I'm sorry! Come back!"

Meade punched Brenna in the stomach with the side of the gun. The air rushed out of her, and she fell to her knees gasping. Back in the present. "Where is it?" he said.

He wants the picture of Wright. Brenna wheezed. Her hands scratched and grasped at the concrete beneath her— tiny bits of gravel, shards of glass. *Yes. There* . . . She struggled to her feet, a good-sized glass shard clenched in her palm. He grabbed her by the arm, forced the barrel of the gun to the base of her chin, and held it there. "The question is not going to change. The drawing wasn't yours to take. I know you have it. I will get it back."

"The *drawing*?" The cold barrel pushed against her throat. It was a big gun. A .45, and if he fired it, right now, at this range, her head would explode. Yet in spite of it all, he was using euphemisms. Not the picture of Lydia Neff with Meade's car, not the picture of Meade's naked, very married boss. Not the evidence of Lydia and Roger's affair. The child's drawing those pictures came wrapped in. "You're talking," she said slowly, "about the items Carol Wentz removed from the Neff home."

"Yes."

Brenna couldn't fight a gun, but she could fight a man. After the beating from the cheating husband eleven years ago, she'd learned how to fight, learned good. Made Errol pay for the classes. It was the least he could do. She could fight a man, even if he was a hired killer, standing behind her, holding a gun to her throat. She just needed to know exactly where his eyes were . . .

"I've seen the photographs. I know everything." Brenna shifted the shard of glass from the palm of her hand, clutched it tight between her thumb and her index finger. "You know I do," she said. "So why would you ask for the drawing?"

She could feel his breath at her temple. "Because I *want* the—" he hissed, and that was enough. *Don't let him finish the sentence.* Brenna's arm shot up and back, back to where she'd felt his breath, the hand aimed just a few inches above. She felt his eyelash at her wrist, perfect. She dug the sharp end of the glass in, dragged it . . .

Not the eye, but close enough. A sound came out of him and his grip went lax, the gun clattering out of his hand. It went off when it hit the sidewalk, and for a moment, the sound deafened them both.

Meade backed away, clutched his eye. "Goddamn it!" he yelled, the other eye scanning the sidewalk, as if he could spot the bullet and retrieve it.

Brenna kicked the gun away, her ears still ringing. Meade charged at her. She saw him coming in slow motion and balled her hand into a fist and punched him hard in the groin. He wheezed, falling forward. She started to look for the gun, but then he slugged her in the side of the face. It was like a door slamming into her, little flecks of light in front of her eyes. She started recalling the cheating husband eleven years ago, his fist in her face—the shock she'd felt, more shock than pain, because she'd never felt such focused hate. She tasted the salt of her own blood, just as she had back then, and started to recall more—the sewer smell of the alleyway, the calloused hands, grabbing for the camera . . . *Stop remembering. Stay here.* "Four score and seven years ago," Brenna whispered, "our fathers brought forth on this continent . . ."

Meade frowned.

Brenna raked the shard of glass down the length of Meade's cheek.

He yelled. Blood spurted down the side of his face, but Brenna kept at it, kept scratching and cutting—again across his brow, his chin, his thick neck, bleeding him for Nelson, for Carol, for Klavel, for . . . "Where is Iris?" she heard herself scream as she swiped at him. "Where is she?" He grabbed her by the wrists, and shoved her away. She fell backward onto the concrete. She put both hands behind her, bracing herself, and felt steel against her fingertip. The gun.

Meade dived for it, but Brenna got to it first. She aimed it at him and he froze. She pushed herself up, pressed it to his chest. She reached into the pocket of his cheap brown jacket, felt her key chain and yanked it out, something else falling to the pavement. Her cell phone. She kicked it aside, keeping the gun on him as he glared, his face covered in angry slashes, blood dripping down his neck, pooling against his collar, silent now but for the growl of his breathing.

There was a picture on her key chain. A miniature of a drawing Maya had done in first grade. A big round head with a stick body, long curly hair, and a smile. It had been during her princess-loving phase and so Maya had graced the head with a crown. On the crown she'd written "Mommy."

Brenna jabbed the gun into the hollow of his neck. "You're still working for Roger Wright, aren't you?" she said, her face throbbing, words slurred from blood.

He said nothing.

"How many people have you killed to cover up his affair?"

Meade glanced down at the gun, then back at Brenna. His breathing had slowed now. She could smell the blood on him, the sweat—yet Meade's face was strangely calm, the hate drained out of it along with the pain of his wounds. Meade was a statue, now. Cold, unblinking. *He will never leave.* "You have a gun," he said. "Why don't you use it?"

Brenna felt a punch in her gut, then a barreling rush of pain. Meade backed away and her grip on the gun loosened, her head felt light. She saw it in his hand—a blade, covered in blood. Her vision blurred. She held up the gun with faltering hands, pulled the trigger. The gun exploded, threw her back onto the pavement, the keys dropping. Her ears ringing with the sound but still she could hear the clattering of the keys. *Strange.*

Was Meade dead? Had she shot him?

She felt pavement against her back, salt and copper filling her mouth. Her thoughts swam, her memories . . . *"She's crowning," says Dr. Abrams. Brenna is wet with sweat. Her hair sticks to her forehead and her body is slick against the sheets and the pain—the wracking pain like a forest fire inside her and then . . . the baby's shrieking cry, and the hot tears on her face and Jim's hands grasping her shoulders, his lips on her cheek. Jim's voice in her ear. "Do you hear her, honey? Oh God, oh my God she's beautiful . . ."*

Remembered pain flipped back into real pain. Breathing was hard now, Brenna's breath frail like a baby breathing, her body needing more air than she was able to give it. Brenna put her hand to her pain and felt her shirt—wet, sticking to her. She brought the hand up to her face and saw it black with her own blood. *I'm dying.* The cell phone. She reached for it, touched it . . . *Call 911.* She pressed the numbers, and she heard a tinny voice . . . "Help you?" But she couldn't answer, couldn't speak. Her breath was so shallow now. Goldfish breathing. As if her throat was a single gill and she was floating atop murky water, floating on her back and then turning on her side. And then over again, to the blackness.

29

"She's moving now. I think she's waking up," a voice said.

Brenna opened her eyes to holes. Hundreds and hundreds of black pinholes in white squares—soundproofing tiles. Long fluorescent lights. She was lying in a hospital bed. Her eyes went to the IV in her arm; she raised her other arm and touched the side of her face and felt a thick bandage.

"She's awake," said the voice again. Iris's voice from the phone, and Brenna struggled up in bed and saw Morasco, sitting against the wall, next to a young girl Brenna had never seen in her life.

Brenna's mouth was very dry. She started to cough. Morasco took a paper cup from her bed stand, plucked something out, and slipped it between her lips. An ice chip. She sucked on it and chewed it up and caught her breath. "How did you find out about me?" she croaked.

"Police radio. Don't try to talk any more, though. Okay? It's 9 P.M. You're at Columbia-Presbyterian," he said. "You needed a few stitches for the knife wound, a transfusion, but you're in surprisingly good shape, considering . . . Brenna, what happened?"

"Meade," she said.

"Oh my God."

"He . . . He wasn't . . . I didn't get him?"

"No. Meade wasn't there."

Brenna closed her eyes. "I shot at him. With his .45."

"I'd say I told you not to get involved, but that might make you talk again," Morasco said. "I don't want you to talk, Brenna."

Brenna's gaze moved to the girl, still sitting against the wall. She wore square-framed glasses. She had a shy, heart-shaped face and silky brown hair, parted in the middle.

"I'm Maggie," she said in Iris's voice.

Brenna looked at Morasco.

"That's Maggie Schuler. She was a friend of Iris's when she was very young. She used to live in the house right next door to the Neffs'. The split-level."

"The *Brady Bunch* house."

"Sssh. Yes."

"She was in the police file," Morasco said. "She was M."

Brenna's eyes widened. She sat up in bed, and the stab wound seared. She put a hand to it, touched bandages.

The girl looked down at her hands. "I'm so sorry," she said, and Brenna flashed back to standing in Nelson Wentz's kitchen. "Another ice chip," she said.

Morasco gave her one and said, "Start with the chat room."

The girl cleared her throat. "Back in August, I heard my brother, Eric, talking to his friend Jonathan Klein."

Brenna sucked at the ice, Nelson's voice running through her head, talking to Trent, just after the press conference *. . . Some antivirus programs to allegedly erase the spyware. None of them very good . . . Oh, and he said he threw in a few extras—word processing and the like . . .*

"Jonathan had been doing some computer work for Mr. Wentz," Maggie said. "One day, Mr. Wentz was out at work or something, and he told Jonathan that if nobody was home, to use the spare key. He did, but when he went up to the computer room, he caught Mrs. Wentz on a chat room called Families of the Missing." She tugged at her lip. "She freaked out—told him not to tell anyone."

"I know that chat room," Brenna whispered.

Morasco looked at the girl. "Maggie started lurking on it."

"I did," she said. "I don't know why."

Morasco said, "You don't remember being interviewed by me."

"No. Not really. But I do remember Iris. I was so little and she seemed so big. I don't have any sisters. Just my brother, and I guess, when I was a kid I just . . . I looked up to her."

Brenna nodded.

"Anyway, Mrs. Wentz was on that chat room a lot, pretending she was Iris's mom. It was so obvious it was her—she's the only one from Tarry Ridge and she was always talking about Iris and how she would never give up on her. I . . . I don't know why, but it made me kind of mad."

"Because it made you miss Iris," Morasco said.

"Yeah. Maybe. I also felt bad for Iris's real mom. I mean, what if she went into that chat room and saw some lady imitating her?" She looked at Brenna. "Anyway . . . I was over at my friend Emily's last Sunday and I told her."

"Emily Garvey."

"Yes. And Emily dared me to call Mrs. Wentz. Pretend I was Iris."

Brenna stared at her.

Maggie's eyes glistened. She took her glasses off and rubbed her eyes with one hand. When she spoke, her voice shook. "I called three times," she said. "You know how it is when you start telling a lie and then you start to believe it? After a while, you're writing this whole movie in your head, and you're kind of . . . you're not inside yourself anymore.

You're like an actor, playing a part. I was Iris. I told her to stop pretending she was my mom. I told her to leave me alone."

"Maggie," said Morasco. "What did Carol say to you?"

Maggie swallowed hard. "She said, 'Please let me help you, Iris. And then she said she was sorry." She took a deep breath, released it. "She kept telling me she was sorry, over and over again."

Brenna stared at her, all of it hitting home. Carol hadn't spoken to Iris. She hadn't found a missing girl. Carol had received a prank call, and overreacted. God only knew why she was sorry—but did that matter now?

Morasco said, "Carol's first call on Monday morning was to Hutchins. She probably told him about the phone call and said she believed Iris was alive. Maybe she thought he could help her find Iris."

"Or Lydia," Brenna said.

He looked at her. "Yes," he said. "Hutchins wouldn't help her, so she called Klavel, who tracked down Tim O'Malley. Tim spoke to her a few times, and during one of those conversations he told her something that made her break into Lydia Neff's old house and take . . . the items that had been hidden in the frame."

Maggie sank lower in her seat. "I've been going back to my old neighborhood," she said. "I've been riding my bike on the path behind the houses. I've been looking at my old house, trying so hard to remember it, to remember Iris . . . Remember more than I do, but I can't. Not really."

"Maggie's family moved the year after Iris disappeared. Her parents were able to make an offer on one of the Waterside Condos." He gave Brenna a pointed look. "Got it for a steal."

Brenna shook her head. "Amazing."

Maggie said, "There's one thing I do remember. Nobody thinks I remember it, but I do."

Brenna looked at her.

"I was with Iris on the day she disappeared."

Morasco said, "You never told me that."

"I never told anybody." Her lip trembled. Her eyes welled and sparkled. A single tear slipped down her cheek, and Brenna wanted to wipe it away, Maggie was still that young. "I had been with my parents at one of the Koppelsons' neighbors—don't remember the name. But I was in the yard and I saw Iris on the sidewalk and I followed her." She took a breath and stared up at the ceiling, losing herself. "I remember Iris telling me Santa was in town and we could visit him and get our presents early. I remember walking with her, and then I remember being scared because the sun was setting and we didn't know where we were. We were lost. I saw Mrs. Wentz, coming out of her house. I remember seeing her in her yard and . . . and just running at her." Maggie shut her eyes. "Mrs. Wentz picked me up and took me inside and called my mother. Iris stayed on the sidewalk. Mrs. Wentz never saw her. I never told her she was there."

"You think you left Iris," Morasco said.

"I know I did. I mean . . . I *remember* it. I remember going into Mrs. Wentz's house and looking behind me and seeing Iris, running away."

Brenna kept her gaze on this young girl, with her baby-fine hair and her chubby cheeks, the same age as Maya, just three years older than Brenna herself had been when her sister had gotten into the blue car.

"I'll always remember it."

Brenna's chest tightened. Her knife wound burned.

"Her parents are in the waiting room," said Morasco. "You ready to go, Maggie?"

"Yes," she said quietly, and Brenna couldn't help but think

of the years and years Maggie Schuler would spend looking back rather than forward, of all the things Maggie might give up—her education, her happiness, even the people she loved most—all to try and take back one mistake, to fix one unfixable thing. "It isn't your fault, Maggie," Brenna whispered, as much to herself as to the stranger who stood in front of her. "It isn't your fault. You were only a little girl."

30

Dr. Glassman was an excellent physician. Meade had met him while working at the VA Hospital. He was good back then—skilled and considerate. Yet he was too distracted by everyday things to be truly great. Little League games, anniversaries, tennis lessons for his daughter . . . He'd often leave work early for something as mundane as a school play—a school play, when there were lives to be saved. It didn't make sense, but then again, human behavior rarely did. Meade didn't begrudge Dr. Glassman that, his humanity. But still he saw the weakness—that flaw, thin as a nerve, that kept him from becoming the great thing he was meant to be.

Then one day, a fire struck the Glassman home while the doctor was at work, killing his entire family. After a long mourning period, Dr. Glassman emerged changed. He was now a man without emotions, a man who lived only to save lives, to fix bodies—sew them up and send them out. Dr. Glassman never asked questions. In fact, he rarely spoke. He worked out of his small apartment in Morningside Heights, plucking bullets out of chests, sewing up knife wounds, sometimes stabilizing the erratic beat of a dying heart. He seemed to get no pleasure out of this, no joy, no sense of accomplishment. He healed, quite frankly, because he could do nothing else. Dr. Glassman was the closest thing to a machine Meade had ever met. For that reason, he trusted him.

Dr. Glassman attended to the bullet wound first. It had struck Meade in the shoulder, and it burned when removed, but he stayed stoic, as he knew his father would have done. *Soldiers don't cry*, Dad had told Adam, Adam at ten years old, a different Adam than the world saw now. Dad had said that to young Adam as he left their house at dawn, walked out that front door for the very last time, on his way to his sixth and final tour. *"Don't worry, son. Hanoi's got nothing on me. Hey, what's that in your eye? A tear? Soldiers don't cry, Adam. You must be strong. I need you to take care of the ladies while I'm gone."*

"Yes sir."

"Atta boy."

As Dr. Glassman sewed up the gash on the side of Meade's face, treated the cuts over his eyes, bandaged the shoulder, and disinfected the glass wounds, Meade put his father out of his mind. Instead he thought about machines—the simple beauty of them, the singularity of purpose. The Glock, of course, was a perfect example, and in a different way, Meade's car. So was the tracking chip he'd stuck beneath the carriage of Brenna Spector's van after the press conference, while she and her assistant were visiting Nelson Wentz.

The doctor was a machine now—a machine that saved lives—and though he might not care enough to realize it, this made him great. Tragedy had transformed him. Just as it had transformed young Adam.

Before he left the apartment, Meade put the money on the kitchen table. As usual, the doctor didn't look at it. Instead of just leaving, though, Meade put a hand on his shoulder, looked him in the face. "Some fires," Meade said, "happen for a reason."

Dr. Glassman said nothing. His eyes were dry as stones.

"You do realize I hate hospitals," Morasco said. He was standing next to Brenna's bed at 10 P.M., just about to leave.

"Then you must be miserable at this point."

"Not really. In fact, I kind of like this hospital, if only because it's keeping you from going out and getting attacked again." He smiled, and Brenna flashed on Wright, naked in the photograph, staring at Lydia . . .

Amazing what love did to the eyes. It made them light up in the same way pain made them light up, the same way tears did. How could anyone be capable of that much love and that much hate at the same time?" Brenna said, "How do we know?"

"How do we know you won't get attacked here in Columbia-Presbyterian?"

"No," Brenna said. "How do we know that Meade is still working for Wright? How do we know he's not going after these people of his own accord?"

"Are you serious?"

She looked at him. "I'm not saying Wright didn't bribe the Schulers and Chief Griffin with homes in the Waterside Condos. And I'm not saying he didn't make sure Hutchins took that interview out of the police file. I'm just saying . . . Maybe he isn't responsible for the *killings*. Maybe Meade is a stalker. Maybe he somehow found out that Carol Wentz had the photos, and he's doing this out of some weird loyalty to Wright."

Morasco stared at her.

Brenna sighed. "I know," she said. "I guess I just don't understand why any sane human being—even an entitled asshole like Wright—would be able to destroy that many innocent people. Seriously, how could you live with yourself?"

Morasco glanced away for a moment. "People make all kinds of excuses, Brenna. They tell themselves lies. They repeat those lies in their heads over and over until they become memories," he said. "That's how they live with themselves."

"I still don't get it."

"Of course you don't," he said. "Your memory never lies." Morasco touched the bandages on her cheek. "Please don't get attacked by goons anymore."

"Goons." Brenna smiled. "That sounds like a word Jack Paar would use."

"Wiseass." His gaze stayed locked with hers, and for a moment, she might have seen it in his eyes—that spark, love or pain, she wasn't sure which.

Or maybe she was just remembering the picture.

Trent showed up per Brenna's call at 10:30 P.M. with a packed bag that included a change of clothes, toothbrush, plus Brenna's laptop and the envelope containing the three pictures and the drawing, all of which Trent had scanned, downloaded, and copied. He'd come in just after Morasco had left and must have passed him in the hall, because the first thing he said when he saw Brenna was, "You and Morasco. Huh? Huh?" accompanied by a hand gesture she hadn't seen since fifth grade.

"Uh, no."

Trent gaped at the bandages on her face. "Man," he said. "I hope you gave it to Meade fifty times worse."

"I tried."

By now, doctors had informed Brenna that her tests had all come back within normal range and she didn't need another transfusion, but that they'd like her to stay the night for observation. Fine with her—the hospital was as good a place to figure things out as any, and, as Morasco might have said, a place where she wasn't likely to get attacked.

She took the laptop from Trent and flipped it open, connecting to the hospital's wi-fi. Then she placed the pictures over the screen like a lightboard, stared at Wright's face. What did a man like him do with a great love once he was through with it? Did he throw it into his work? His marriage? His children? How could he just turn and aim that laser elsewhere? How could he ever forget?

How could any man ever forget?

She stole a glance at her home screen. Jim wasn't online. *Fine.* She'd call Faith tomorrow morning, arrange for her to pick up Maya at school, explain to her that she was laid up for a bit but it was nothing serious . . . Brenna shut her eyes tight, as if by doing so, she could squeeze the pain out of her mind. *Forget.* "Thanks for all this, Trent," she said. "I'll probably be out of here sometime tomorrow, so I'll see you."

"Wait. There's something I need to show you."

She gave him a look.

"I didn't get anything else pierced. I swear."

"Okay then."

Trent edged next to her on the bed, minimized her home screen. "If you go to the control panel, you'll see I downloaded Nelson Wentz's Mailkeep."

"The program that saves copies of all e-mails."

"Yep."

Brenna found the Mailkeep icon and clicked on it. She saw a long list of e-mails, all of which seemed to be from Nelson's address. "Have you looked at these yet?"

"Nope. I just transferred it before I came over."

There were some e-mails from as recently as two days ago—one from Nelson to what looked like an online memoir-writing course, another to his boss, Kyle, titled "Taking personal day. Back next week." It struck her anew, the strangeness of his death.

Trent's cologne pressed into her sinuses, and she turned to find him leaning to the computer, a pec against her back, his head practically on her shoulder. "A little space please," she said.

Trent put a finger to the bottom of the list. "Look."

He was pointing at one e-mail—the only one that wasn't from Nelson. It was from OrangePineapple98, dated September 24, 11:30 P.M. The subject line read: "HOW DARE YOU." The recipient was rwright@wrightindustries.com. "Her last night alive, Carol e-mailed Wright."

"Oh, Mommy."

"You can say that again," Brenna whispered. She clicked open the e-mail. No message beyond an attachment—a jpg, which Carol had named "neff." *The pictures*, she thought. *Carol e-mailed him the pictures*. Wright had learned who Carol was from the e-mail address. That was easy enough for someone as powerful as him. He had learned who she was, and then he had sicced Meade on Carol, on everyone she had spoken to, everyone who might know, all just to keep a secret.

She stared at the subject line, anger bubbling up inside her, pressing against her wounded skin until she thought she might explode from it. *How dare you?* she thought. *How dare you, you sick, selfish . . .* Then she opened the attachment. Her eyes widened.

"I don't get it," said Trent.

Neither did Brenna. Carol hadn't sent Wright the three incriminating photos. The attachment was a scan of Iris's strange drawing—the stick-figure girl, trapped in a flower.

Trent left twenty minutes later, when a nurse came in to remove Brenna's IV. "Yikes. Nast. Needles. Gotta go," said

Trent, who less than a week earlier had paid someone to stick silver hoops through his nipples during his lunch hour. Trent LaSalle, ever a mass of contradictions.

Brenna said good-bye as he hurried out the door, her mind still fixed on Carol's e-mail to Roger Wright. *How dare you*, she had written to Wright—not over his affair with Lydia, but over a missing child's drawing. What could it mean? She cut and pasted Carol's e-mail, tacked on the attachment, and sent it to Morasco's personal e-mail address, along with a message: *From Carol Wentz to Roger Wright. Last night of her life.*

"How's your pain?" said the young nurse, surprisingly stoic for someone with pink clouds and rainbows all over her smock. "Scale of one to ten."

"I'd say about a two, maybe three."

"We'll hold off on the painkiller then. Buzz me if you feel worse."

After the nurse was through removing the IV and had left the room, Brenna stared first at the downloaded image and then at the original drawing, wishing she'd completed the psychology degree she'd begun at Columbia, if only to be able to interpret the meaning behind the crayon lines. What had driven Iris to draw this?

Of course, she did know of someone who could probably tell her . . .

Brenna hadn't spoken to Dr. Lieberman in years, but his e-mail address was safe in her memory and, whimsical ties notwithstanding, she knew of no better child psychiatrist than him. Quickly, she fired off an e-mail to Lieberman, keeping the small talk to a minimum, as he tended to analyze even the most mundane of sentences. *I need your professional opinion*, she typed, *on this drawing by a missing, six-year-old child. Could you please interpret and get back to me ASAP?* Then she attached the downloaded image.

Brenna had just sent the e-mail when an IM flashed across her screen:

JRapp68: Hi.

Jim. Brenna inhaled sharply, her knife wound burning with it. The skin around her left eye began to sting and she was sorry now she'd turned down painkillers, though she knew deep down they wouldn't have done much good. Her jaw was throbbing, the bones in her face ready to split, yet she had no sense of the bandages she wore now. That's how she knew: the pain in her face wasn't real but remembered. It was pain from eleven years ago, from a cheating husband whose name she'd never known, bursting to life on October 23, 1998, one night after the husband has inflicted it, with Brenna's own husband glaring her in the eye, Brenna's own husband saying, "*I don't think I will ever be able to forgive you.*" Brenna's own husband crushing her heart. Brenna typed: **Hi.**

I'm sorry I disappeared last night.

Brenna stared at Jim's words. She started to type, **That's okay**. But then she deleted it. It wasn't okay. Why should she say it was? She went for the keyboard: **I wasn't saying that I blamed you for moving on. I don't blame you at all. I like Faith. She's good to Maya, and I'm glad she makes you happy. I was just saying: It isn't as easy for me. The memories I have of us are still alive in my head, and sometimes they hurt bad. That isn't your fault. It isn't mine, either. It's the disorder.**

Brenna sent the paragraph without reading it. She didn't receive an immediate reply. IM said he wasn't typing. But Brenna wasn't sorry she'd sent it. It was something that needed to be said, whether he wanted to hear it or not. He could ignore it in the future, forget she ever said it, but she needed to say it now. She still felt it—that love, that ache. She would always feel it and he ought to know.

Jim typed: **What's my excuse then?**

Brenna stared at the screen. Typed a question mark.

He typed: **I remember, too, Brenna. I hurt, too.**

Brenna started to reply but stopped herself when she saw that Jim was still typing. His next message flashed on-screen: **I can't keep doing this**.

Doing what?

IMing every night. I've come to look forward to it— probably more than I should.

Her breath caught. *Don't leave me*, she wanted to type. *I need you*. She thought about telling Jim where she was right now. Thought about saying, *Can we at least wait until the stitches from my ABDOMINAL KNIFE WOUND are removed?* But she didn't. It wasn't fair. **Whatever you need to do**, she typed instead.

Jim typed: **Thank you**. Then he signed off. Brenna read the two short words on the screen—the last words she would see from Jim in a long time—and tears crept into her eyes. She felt someone nearby and looked up to see the stoic young nurse standing over her. Brenna hadn't even heard her come in.

"Are you in any pain?" the nurse asked.

"You don't wanna know."

"Excuse me?"

Brenna swatted at her eyes. "Kidding. I'm good."

The nurse frowned at her, but thankfully the phone rang at Brenna's bedside before she had to explain anymore.

The nurse reached for the phone, but Brenna grabbed it first. "Hello?"

"Hey." It was Morasco. "How are you feeling?"

"Not bad, I guess."

"Listen," he said. "I got the e-mail."

"What do you think?"

"I think," he said, "that I would very much like to nail Roger Wright's ass to the wall."

Brenna smiled a little. "Great minds."

There was a short pause, and then he spoke again. "I've got a plan."

"Am I in on it?"

"I'd like you to be. The thing is, it would mean checking out of the hospital and leaving, very early in the morning." As he told her about the plan—a simple one—the remembered pain dissipated, replaced by a strange and very real excitement. *This could work.* "I'm in," she told Morasco. "I'm in no matter what."

31

"You look like a movie star, ducking the press after undergoing her fifth face-lift."

Behind the oversized sunglasses she'd picked up at a Rite Aid near the hospital, Brenna rolled her eyes. That would teach her, she supposed, for asking Morasco how she looked. Doctors had removed the bandages at five this morning, and though the bruises were nowhere near as bad as she'd imagined they'd be, the sunglasses were a necessity, especially considering where she and Morasco were going and whom they were about to see. She had her hair pulled back, and she was all in black—black jeans, black boots, black turtleneck sweater (Trent's idea of a change of clothes, which, considering what he could have brought, was a fine choice). Morasco, on the other hand, was wearing one of his tweeds, this one with actual shoulder patches, a rumpled white oxford, jeans. Very postgraduate Camus scholar. She imagined they made an interesting-looking pair.

It was 6:30 A.M., and they were in the unmarked car Morasco drove—brown Impala, because they figured such an obvious cop car would help their cause. When your goal was, after all, to make Roger Wright sweat, appearances needed to be seriously considered.

They were on Wright's street now—a parade of turrets, Tudor and spiraling brick chimneys, all tucked away behind downy sprawls of green. "Fancy area," Brenna said.

Morasco nodded. "You nervous?"

"A little."

He pulled up to an enormous gate—Wright's gate—and turned to her. "I can't tell you how impressed I was by the way you questioned Gayle Chandler."

"You're just saying that to make me feel better."

"No, I'm not. You use the memory to your best advantage. And your technique is just amazing."

Brenna felt herself blushing a little, and was glad for the sunglasses. "Thanks."

He spoke into the intercom. "Detective Nick Morasco. Tarry Ridge PD."

A Spanish-accented woman's voice replied, "Can I ask what this is regarding?"

"I need to speak with Mr. Wright, regarding an ongoing case."

A full ten seconds elapsed before the woman said, "One moment." Three solid minutes before the gate finally opened.

Morasco pulled up a very long driveway, lined with evergreens atop a lawn that could have easily doubled as a golf course. He drove past a thatch-roofed carriage house to an enormous, stately colonial—white brick, black shutters, Ionic columns that brought to mind the Tarry Ridge library, with its unwieldy librarian and screaming bake sale debutantes. Brenna blinked that scene away—hard to believe it had been only yesterday—as Morasco pulled in front of the house and removed the folder from the glove compartment, and they both slipped out of the car to find Wright—Roger Wright all suited up for his morning golf game, Roger Wright in his madras pants and his pink polo, his graying gold hair gleaming in the bright sun and his blue eyes surprising spikes of concern—Roger Wright striding toward them, because this was a man who didn't simply walk, he strode. "Can I help you?" he said to Morasco.

Brenna spoke. "Mr. Wright. We're looking for a former employee of yours by the name of Adam Meade."

He glanced at Brenna. If he remembered her at all as Candy Bissel from outside the golf course, he wasn't letting that be known. "I . . . I'm not sure I'm familiar with the name."

"He worked for Wright Industries from 1996 to 1999," said Morasco.

Wright stared Morasco in the eye for a long time, saying nothing. His gaze moved from the detective's face to Brenna's, as if he might find more help there, a more sympathetic set of features, perhaps even a different question. But she stared right back, silent as Morasco. Waiting.

"Adam," Wright said finally. "Was he the orderly from the Bronx VA?"

Her eyes widened. "Yes."

Wright exhaled hard. "I met Adam probably fifteen years ago. The Teasdale Foundation gives money to the hospital and I was there with my wife and mother-in-law, touring the facility. I spoke to Adam. He wasn't happy with his job. He said he was looking for something in security, and a few months later I wound up hiring him."

"Just like that?" Morasco said. "Someone you never heard of."

Wright aimed his eyes at him—sharp, defiant. "I'd heard of his father. A true hero. Born right here in Tarry Ridge."

"Why did you fire him?" Brenna said.

"I didn't."

She stared at him.

"The head of security did. He had his reasons, I'm sure." He gave her a flat smile. "Perhaps you can understand the fact that I don't become directly involved with every firing and/or layoff that takes place within my corporation. Now if you'll excuse me . . ."

Morasco said, "I'd like to show you a few photographs, Mr. Wright."

"I'm sorry—I really don't have time—"

"Golf, right? No worries, this won't take a minute." Morasco moved closer to him, and opened the folder he was carrying—a folder full of crime scene photos. Brenna watched him, the way he stared into the open folder, his jaw going slack, the color slipping from his face.

"Dear God," he breathed.

"This is what happened to Carol Wentz," Morasco said.

He showed him another picture, then another. "Here is what happened to Nelson Wentz, her husband."

"Please, I . . ."

"Graeme Klavel. Private investigator in Mount Temple."

"Why are you—"

"Timothy O'Malley. Some face, right? He's in critical condition. Hanging on by a thread." Morasco looked up from the folder and into Wright's face. "Ex-husband of Lydia Neff."

Wright's face went red. He backed away. "Why are you showing me these?"

Brenna said, "We believe Adam Meade is responsible for all of this."

"No," Wright said. "No, Carol Wentz was killed by her husband. He killed himself. I've been following the news."

"You can follow whatever you want, Mr. Wright," said Brenna. "That won't change the truth."

"Can you find Adam Meade?" Morasco said. "Can you tell us where he is right now?"

"I don't know where Adam Meade is."

Brenna stared at him, her jaw tightening, anger building.

She heard herself say, "Carol Wentz e-mailed you the night before she died."

"No she didn't."

"Before that e-mail, she'd spoken to Mr. Klavel and Mr. O'Malley." Brenna took a step closer to Wright, who appeared to be growing smaller by the minute. "So if you honestly don't know where Adam Meade is right now, I suggest you find out, as he seems to be doing quite a bit of damage on your behalf."

"I need to leave," Wright said quietly. "I have an appointment."

Morasco held out his business card. "If you think you might know where Mr. Meade is, give me a call." He smiled. "Sorry to interrupt your morning. Have a nice day."

Morasco and Brenna slipped back into the Impala with Wright staring after them, headed down the sprawling driveway without saying a word. Once they were back on the street, Brenna removed the microcassette recorder from her bag, played back the entire conversation while staring out the window at the lush scenery, mansions parading by . . .

After it was through, she asked Morasco, "What did you think?"

"He's definitely lying about getting the e-mail from Carol."

"That's a given."

"But unless he's either a great actor or incredibly self-deluded, I get the feeling he has no idea where Meade is, or what he's been doing." He pulled back onto Main Street and made a left, heading back toward the 287.

"I vote for self-deluded," Brenna said.

"Me too."

No matter what the truth was about his connection to Meade, Wright had clearly been lying when he said he hadn't received Carol's e-mail. When Brenna had mentioned it, she'd actually seen the discomfort, creeping up from his collar and into his face as if it was a solid thing.

It had been the same when Morasco had said the name out loud. *Lydia Neff.*

But what was it about that drawing?

After Morasco dropped her off at her apartment, Brenna opened the front door and climbed the stairs, her own daughter's art flashing through her mind like a slide show. Two smiling heads on stick legs—one with curly hair, one with no hair. "Mommy and Daddy," Maya had said, after handing Brenna the picture, drawn in day care, February 2, 1999. The picture of Brenna—the one in the mommy crown that she'd had reproduced for her key chain—April 12, 2000. A collage Maya had created on January 19, 2002; an imitation Picasso on March 3, 2005; a self-portrait—the teeth and forehead so much bigger than they were in real life, but still, as Maya's art teacher had said, "exhibiting real talent"— from November 4, 2008. Even the portrait of Miles, the one she'd completed last night . . . All of these works of art so different, but with one thing in common: a signature. First in spidery block letters, then in cursive, then simply in initials, Maya, like most every child, signed her artwork.

But there was no signature at the bottom of the flower drawing, and it was an aberration. Iris had signed the framed pictures that hung in her mother's house. She'd even signed the seat of her bicycle. But she hadn't put her name on this one piece of art, the one her mother had stashed away in a secret place, along with her other dark secret . . .

Brenna unlocked her apartment door. With Trent not in yet and Maya at Larissa's house, the place seemed emptier than usual—huge and still. She put down her bag and made for her computer, thinking, *What could that drawing mean?* Odds were, Lieberman had replied to her query about it—in the past, he'd always been quick with answers—and when she checked her e-mail, she saw he hadn't changed. She expected a long response. Lieberman had a tendency to over-explain, which was fine. In the case of this drawing, Brenna thought, the more explanation the better.

Brenna opened the e-mail, and started to read. But while Lieberman's response was indeed long, she couldn't get past the first sentence. She read it twice, then three, four, five times, as if repetition might change the meaning of the words—or at least, make them easier for her to grasp . . . If anything, though, the process only confused and upset her more:

This drawing was not done by a child.

Dr. Lieberman had gone on at great length about straightness of the lines in the drawing, the light touch of crayon to paper, and the way the stick figure had been drawn—with hair and a skirt but with no face, more of a symbol than an actual rendering and rare, if not unheard of, for a six-year-old girl. While the sun that shone out of the upper left corner of the page might be considered typical for a first or second grader, the squares that surrounded the flower were drawn with far too much precision for a child that age. What's more, the entire drawing had been created in an unusual amount of detail but in only one color —something he deemed "extremely atypical of a child" considering "the attention span required for such a work." Lieberman concluded by saying he would put the age of the artist at "young adulthood at the very least."

Brenna had to find Lydia Neff. With the possible exception of Meade and Wright, she was the only one who might be able to explain why this strange drawing—not done by a child—would elicit so much violence and death.

But how to find her?

Lydia Neff. The invisible woman. No credit card bills,

no car registration, and even her best friend Gayle Chandler hadn't spoken to her in two years . . . *But even invisible women have interests.*

She thought about what Lydia and Griffin liked to do together—*out at a diner maybe*, Morasco had said, *walking through the shopping center.* But that didn't give her much, seeing as the woman apparently hadn't spent a dime over the past two years. No, Lydia's interests were deeper than that . . .

Brenna could hear Gayle's voice in her mind. *Every morning, Lyddie goes there to meditate by the fountain. She's a very spiritual woman, you know . . .* Meditation . . . Not an easily trackable interest unless . . . Brenna recalled the meditation room in Lydia's house. The painted plaques . . . She went to Google and typed in the words: "Conquer the angry man by love. Conquer the ill-natured man by goodness. Conquer the miser with generosity. Conquer the liar with truth."

Several pages came up—some dedicated to famous quotations, others to Buddhist teachings. She typed in: "The greatest achievement is selflessness," and got the same pages. She opened the first one and learned: All the sayings on Lydia's wall were quotes from the Buddha.

Lydia was a Buddhist. She could have moved to Tibet, but that wasn't likely. Trent had found no airfare for her. Plus, leaving town was one thing, but it was difficult to imagine any mother moving that far away from the spot where her daughter had disappeared.

Brenna started to look up Buddhist temples and meditation centers in New York State, thinking all the while that this was a terrible waste of time. *Buddhists use credit cards like everybody else. But Lydia, on the other hand . . .*

And then, like an answer, she heard Trent's voice in her head. Trent, staring at his computer yesterday as if he were trying to hypnotize answers out of it, frustration tearing at the corners of that cool-dude lilt. *Maybe she joined a convent.*

"Trent is a genius," Brenna whispered.

She began researching Buddhist monasteries in the New York area. But as she looked, her state of mind went from hopeful to annoyed to overwhelmingly frustrated. There were dozens and dozens of Buddhist monasteries in New York State, spanning from Northern Westchester County, through the Catskills, and then all the way up to the Canadian border. Not one of them had a written list of members, though some did have pictures. Brenna began scanning photo albums. But looking through all those soft-focus photographs, all those orange robes and serene smiles and closed eyes, all in the hopes of seeing a set of features that remotely resembled Lydia Neff's . . . it wasn't long before Brenna thought, *I'm wasting my time.* It was draining. Her head throbbed and her knife wound ached and her eyes were tired from staring at the screen. Better to lie down and rest.

Okay, maybe just a few more.

Brenna called up the Lotus Monastery and the Weeping Tree Monastery and found nothing. But when she called up the next one on the search engine's list—the Mountaintop Monastery—her gaze rested on an image on the top of the screen and stuck there . . .

October 23, 1998. The sound of pumped water, the walk up the path, the cool air in Brenna's face, the wind through the young trees. Brenna approaches the path, the circle of five benches, the fountain in the middle. Brenna notices the black-haired woman sitting on the far bench. Lydia. *Brenna moves closer. She sees the woman's hands folded at her lap, pale against her black coat. On the right wrist, a tattoo: A dragonfly. Red body, blue and green wings.*

The exact same image was at the top of the screen, hovering over the M in Mountaintop. Lydia's tattoo was part of the monastery's logo.

Her heart pounding, Brenna went to the site's "about us" page and skimmed over its description: just a half hour north of Tarry Ridge, along the Hudson River. Zen fountains throughout the grounds. An emphasis on meditation.

Perfect. Brenna kept reading . . .

Hiking trails . . . hundred-year-old trees . . . breathtaking views of the Hudson River . . . extensive library . . .

"We encourage our members to give up worldly possessions—including words. After unburdening themselves of all guilt, all pain, our members take vows of silence and live a pure life, without the distractions of the material world."

Vows of silence.

Brenna flashed again on Lydia's tattoo. Even eleven years ago, Lydia Neff had been a follower of the Mountaintop sect. Even then she had a backup plan, knowing that if Iris was never found, she would one day leave all her worldly possessions behind. She would travel to Buffalo to see her ex-husband and unburden herself of her guilt. She would say good-bye to her friends, good-bye to the lover who no longer spoke to her. She would say good-bye to her pain and her good looks and her awful, crushing memories. She would say good-bye to the lack of her daughter. She would put her back to it all and drive away.

But she would stay very close.

Brenna grabbed her bag, hailed a cab to her parking garage. Half an hour later, she was headed up the West Side Highway while, in a rented Ford Focus parked two blocks away from her office/apartment, the alarmlike beep of a small tracking screen roused Adam Meade from sleep.

32

After dropping Brenna off at her office, Morasco headed straight for the station, questions crowding into his mind. When he'd initially come up with the idea of forcing Wright to look at what Meade had done, Morasco had figured on his being *shocked*—Wright wasn't the type to get his hands or mind sullied by reality. But the *surprise* on Wright's face—that was a completely different thing. Over the years, Morasco had questioned enough suspects to know true surprise when he saw it. And unless he was a sociopath, Wright had been unaware of what Meade had done on his behalf until this morning, when he'd seen for himself.

And even still, another question loomed: Meade had secured no known employment since getting laid off ten years ago. What was he doing when he *wasn't* killing off people who threatened to reveal Wright's darkest secret? Far as Morasco knew, Carol Wentz had been the first person to do that in a decade. Had this savvy business mogul—this great commercial mind who had made Tarry Ridge the recession-proof mecca it was today—had he honestly been paying off a killer all these years, simply because, should the situation arise, he'd be ready to take action? That didn't seem likely—which begged another question: What had Meade been doing the rest of the time?

Morasco pulled into his parking space and headed into the station. It was early—barely eight. Most of the other detectives usually showed up around nine, including Chief Hutchins, who was known to enjoy a leisurely breakfast après golf.

Golf with Wright. Hutchins was getting an earful this morning, that was for sure. Morasco didn't give a damn.

The squad room was empty, save for Baus and Fleiss, just back from the gym and wearing their sweats. "Hey, Nick," Baus said. "You want the paper? I'm through with it."

"Sure, thanks." Morasco took the copy of the *Tarry Ridge Times*, brought it to his desk. At the bottom of the front page, there was a story about Graeme Klavel, headlined "Switchblade Killer Strikes Again." A sad picture of Klavel stared out from under the headline, a coat-and-tie shot against a black background that looked as if it had been taken for some professional organization—maybe the Rotary Club or the Elks—the mouth downturned, the hair slicked lank against a broad expanse of forehead. Morasco remembered the corpse, the cruelty inflicted on it, *And for what?*

Morasco read: *"It is identical to the other switchblade murders," said Detective Cavanaugh, who will not reveal specific details of the killing due to the ongoing investigation* . . . And such awful details . . . the gut carved open, the neck so deeply slashed he had nearly been decapitated.

"Takes pride in his work, this bastard," Cavanaugh had said last night, eyes riveted to those wounds. And Morasco had nodded, stomach turning. "Quite the artiste."

Morasco finished reading the article, but he didn't turn the page, a thought working its way through his mind. He reread Cavanaugh's quote and his muscles tightened. The thought gained strength.

"How many others of these have there been?" Morasco had asked Cavanaugh last night.

"Over the past few years? Several. Three in the past six months. Two of 'em lived together. Brothers. Both killed together, this exact same way. This asshole's strong, that is, if there's just one of him."

Brothers in Mount Temple. Morasco thought back to a drug raid that had happened a few years back. Two Cuban immigrants operating out of a pastry shop on Main Street. The arrest had been a big deal—very few convicted drug dealers came out of Tarry Ridge. Hutchins had given one of his sappier press conferences about it, purple prose flying out of his mouth like a flock of doves. The Cubans, though— brothers, if Morasco wasn't mistaken—had gotten off on a technicality a few months later and moved to a neighboring town . . . Hutchins had been pissed off about it, to say the least.

Morasco went online. Looked up "brothers" and "switch-blade murders" and "Mount Temple." The name was in the first line of the first article that popped up on the screen: *Miguel and Luis Cabrero.* Same brothers. Stabbed to death in the "exact same manner" as the earlier switchblade victim, though "for the sake of the investigation," that manner wasn't revealed in this article, either.

"It has to be the same killer," Cavanaugh had said. "The style is identical to the others."

Identical. The earlier switchblade victim, Morasco learned from the article, had been named Carrie Reynolds. Morasco knew that name, too: Carrie had been a Tarry Ridge heiress—completely out of her tree. Refused her meds. Back when he was a uniform, Hutchins had taken her in at least three times for vagrancy and disturbing the peace and then Carrie would post bail. Before you knew it, she'd be back in the middle of Main Street, screaming at the top of her lungs that the CIA was poisoning her herbal tea . . .

"An embarrassment," Hutchins had called her.

Morasco thought about going online, looking up all the unprosecuted killings that had happened in the area over the past ten years, the brutal slayings of drug dealers and freaks and big mouths and gadflies . . . that handful of murders that went unsolved and, because of the victims, forgotten. But he didn't need to go online. *It was the same killer.* Meade hadn't been working for Wright all these years. He'd been working for Hutchins.

Morasco grabbed his cell phone and headed out of the station. On his way out, though, he noticed that Hutchins's door was closed. He stopped at Sally's desk. "Chief in already?"

She nodded. "He got stood up for golf," she said. "He's pissy this morning."

"Wait till later," Morasco said.

"Huh?"

"Nothing." Morasco headed out the door, to the shady trees by the fountain. He turned his back to the road, and called information and asked for the Westchester County DA's office. "Can you please put me through to Internal Affairs?" he said. But as soon as the receptionist had connected him with the investigator in charge of his precinct, a thought hit Morasco. *Meade's last job. Brenna.* And he hadn't been successful . . .

Morasco heard footsteps coming up the walk behind him and turned to see a man in coat and tie, striding—not walking, but *striding*—into the station at top speed. The man was Roger Wright. Morasco followed, just as fast.

The Mountaintop Monastery reminded Brenna, just a little, of the Cornell Medical Center. The grounds were nowhere near as expansive and there wasn't a golf course in sight, but it had that same collegiate look to it—a long gravel road, winding through rolling green grass dotted with Asian maples and pines and weeping willows. She passed some of the members of the order—that's what they were called, not monks—men and women, all in rust-orange robes, walking in twos along the path of a stream. "Here, we study the Buddha's eight-fold path in the sanctity of silence," the Web site had read.

She found her way to the parking lot and pulled into a space. She flipped open her cell to call Morasco—no service. Of course there was no service. The members of the order weren't even allowed to talk to each other, they didn't have much need for Skype and text messaging.

Guess I'm on my own.

Brenna headed out of the parking lot and made for the main building—a large wooden structure with big windows and a seventies-modern design. It looked more like a ski chalet than a Buddhist temple—nothing Eastern about it at all.

Once inside, she was greeted by a big empty space. There was a dragonfly mosaic on the floor—the same design as Lydia's tattoo—at the center of which stood a bubbling fountain. Brenna felt as if she'd been plucked out of this world and dropped into another—a landscape from one of those fantasy computer games Maya used to play, ancient and brand-new at the same time. Utterly unfamiliar . . .

Except for the sound of the fountain. Brenna listened to the pulsing of pumped water, and in her mind, she was back at the Waterside Condominiums eleven years ago, once again on her way to see Lydia Neff. She was walking out of the parking lot and heading up that path, that curving path, following it up to the circle of benches, the fountain in the middle, where Lydia Neff meditated every day. She could see it all before her—the fountain that stood atop a circular mound in the earth, five curved benches around it, *like the petals of a flower.* Out of the corner of her eye, she noticed the narrow paths to the right of each, then the clubhouse bounding off the area, the flicker of a swimming pool through the sheer fence, another wide path leading to it, *like rays of a sun* . . . Brenna pulled the drawing out of her bag and stared at it, and it all began to hit her, the same way a tunnel might fall in upon you if you pulled out one small rock—that one tiny rock that had been holding everything together, keeping you safe and in the dark for years.

Surreal, Morasco thought. That was really the only word to describe where he was right now, and what he had just done—which was to stand in Chief Hutchins's office and accuse him of hiring a killer off the books to destroy all his and Wright's enemies, Wright standing next to him all the while, nodding in agreement, backing him up. Hutchins sat at his desk looking up at them, that thick monkey jaw squared for battle, hatred dripping out of his eyes. "I don't know anyone named Adam Meade," he said.

"You know that isn't true," said Wright. "I introduced him to you myself."

Hutchins stared up at him, his jaw working. "Roger," he said quietly, "if I were to admit that I've met Adam Meade, I'd imagine there are a whole bunch of other things I'd have to admit."

Wright's face went pale. "That's irrelevant."

"Is it? Is the Teasdale fortune irrelevant? Because that's what you'd be losing, along with your wife, your children, your reputation . . . Your freedom. I'd like you to stand back, consider everything that might be gone from your very nice life if I were to start reminiscing out loud."

Morasco said, "Why would he lose his freedom?"

Hutchins trained his gaze on him. "If there's some vigilante out there, killing scum that should have been behind bars in the first place, then what's it to you, Detective Morasco?"

"Carol Wentz shouldn't have been behind bars."

"We both know Carol's husband killed her," he said. "He confessed in his suicide note."

Morasco's back stiffened. "I need to know, Chief Hutchins," he said, "if you have called Meade off of his most recent assignment."

Wright blurted, "OrangePineapple . . . I didn't know who that was. I didn't know it was Carol Wentz. I thought it was some stranger, some . . . extortionist."

"Careful," Hutchins said.

"I called you for help, Lane. I wanted you to find out who it was. I didn't want that person killed. I didn't want . . . God, Lydia's ex-husband . . . I didn't want any of that. I only wanted to protect my family."

Hutchins laughed—laughed hard with dead eyes, the laughter as forced and posed as everything else about him. He looked at Morasco. "He knew. He just didn't *want* to know."

"*Where is Meade?*"

"That little girl you spoke to, Nick," he said. "The one who saw the blue car. That was the best lead we had in Iris Neff's disappearance."

"Please don't," Wright said.

"Best fucking lead we had, but Griffin demotes you for it. He thought he was just covering up a love affair, but we know better, don't we, Roger?"

"My God, Lane."

"I'd like to make that up to you, Nick. Give you the promotion and the raise you deserve. I'd like to give you a position here, whereby the force could truly benefit from your expertise." He glared at Wright. "And your honesty."

Morasco stared at Hutchins, his muscles tightening. And then his hand slid under his coat. It went for his .33, as if that hand were some separate thing working for him, a machine built from his rage. The hand was pulling the .33 out of his shoulder holster. It was leading him around the desk and behind Hutchins, the other arm pressing against his neck as the hand, his machine, held the gun to the chief's temple, Wright wide-eyed across the desk, the chief gasping like a child. "No . . ."

"Call Meade now," Morasco said. "Tell him his assignment is over. Tell him to meet you here, at the station."

"I can't."

Morasco tightened his grip around the neck. "I swear to Christ I'll blow your fucking head off."

"Please . . ."

"Call him."

"I can't because—"

"Call him now."

"*I can't because the place he's gone to, it doesn't have cell phone service.*"

"Oh my God," Wright said, his eyes tearing up, his face moist and reddening, a vein popping out on his forehead, as if all the tears, blood, and sweat within him, everything that was human, was rushing to the surface, making itself known. "Oh my God, no, please. Please not Lydia."

Brenna moved through the great room as if she were navigating her way through thick water, her whole mind focused on the drawing in her hands. She found a smaller room off it, the walls lined with bookshelves. An older black man sat in a chair, reading, with a heavyset blonde woman sitting next to him, both wearing robes. "I need to see Lydia Neff," Brenna said. Her voice echoed.

They both gaped at her, saying nothing. *Goddamn vow of silence.* "If you can lead me to her," Brenna said. "Please. It's urgent. It concerns her daughter."

Finally, the man nodded. He stood up, and Brenna followed him out of the small room, past the fountain, around the building and up another winding path through a series of small cabins, bracing a good-sized woods with hiking trails snaking through them. He took Brenna to the one at the very back, the one closest to the woods. It was marked 323. He knocked softly on the door and left.

There was no answer at first. Brenna pounded on the door, more insistent than the man, and when there was still no answer, she shouted Lydia's name, her voice shattering the still air until finally, the door opened, and Brenna saw the face—the face from the life coaching Web site, only even duller now. Grayer, sadder, worn beyond its years. Brenna pulled the drawing out of her bag and unfolded it, her hands shaking. She showed it to Lydia. Her face went white. And that was all Brenna needed to confirm her thoughts.

"It's a map," Brenna said.

Lydia started to close the door, but Brenna was stronger. She leaned against it and then she was inside the cottage—a dark, sparsely furnished space—the door closing behind her. "The stick figure is Iris. Your daughter is buried in the Waterside Condominiums, where the fountain used to be. You weren't meditating by the fountain. You were visiting your daughter's grave."

Tears sprang into Lydia's eyes. She started shaking her head, again and again.

"Give up your vow of silence, Lydia. Being quiet about this isn't going to help you. It isn't going to change the truth."

Lydia kept shaking her head. It wasn't until she began backing away that Brenna realized how small the cottage really was, and that she and Lydia weren't alone. Adam Meade was sitting ten feet away from them, on Lydia's neatly made cot, holding his .45.

Meade had the drawing now. He'd folded it up and placed it in his pocket after holding the gun to Lydia's head and forcing her to tie Brenna's hands behind her back with duct tape. That completed, he set about tying Lydia's hands and marching them both out of the house, first Lydia, then Brenna directly behind her, the barrel of the gun firm at the base of Brenna's skull, aimed in such a way so that one shot would kill them both.

Brenna stared at Lydia as she walked—the broad back in the orange robe, the shoulders heaving. Sobbing, she knew, only without sound—something the mother of a dead child might do a lot of during a two-year vow of silence. They walked through the trees, most of them still thick and just turning, despite encroaching fall. "Roger isn't going to like this," Brenna said.

"Shut up," said Meade.

The air was cold, the barrel icy against her neck. "Roger loves her."

Lydia breathed in sharply, her whole body tensing with the breath.

Brenna said, "He will not forgive you, Adam."

They were reaching the end of the trail. Ahead of them, beyond the trees stretched a meadow, leading to the steep escarpment Brenna had seen on the Web page. A five-hundred-foot drop, the Hudson River below . . . *Breathtaking views . . .*

They came close to the edge. Scrubby plants clung to sharp rocks—a straight drop, nothing to hang on to, nothing to brace a fall. Brenna's knees weakened. She stared at the river below and that's what her blood felt like—cold, rushing water.

"Get on your knees," Meade said to Lydia. She obeyed. Her eyes were closed, tears trickling down her cheeks. She almost looked as if she was praying—*meditating*—save for the tightness of her mouth, the red of her skin. The terror. The robe billowed around her in the wind and Brenna wondered how Lydia could do it, with that much fear coursing through her. *How can you stay silent?*

Meade stared at Lydia. "You came here," he said to Brenna, "because you wanted to find out what happened to her daughter."

"Yes."

"Why?"

Brenna's throat was tight. "Because . . . I cared about Iris."

Meade paused for a moment. He seemed to consider. The barrel of the .45 moved from Brenna's head to between her shoulder blades. "Some fires happen for a reason," he said.

"What?"

With the other hand, he ripped the duct tape from Brenna's wrists. "Take her tape off," he said. Brenna complied, her mind whirring as she pulled the duct tape from Lydia's hands. She contemplated a sudden movement, maybe an elbow to his gut, but he was prepared for that. He grabbed her by the throat and yanked her to him and then the gun was back at the base of her ear. "Tell her," he said. He was speaking to Lydia.

Lydia stared up at Brenna, the black eyes bright with tears. She shook her head.

"Tell her what happened to your daughter."

Lydia's voice came then, for the first time in two years, the voice sneaking out of her, a croaking whisper. "She walked in on us."

"Iris."

"Yes. Iris." Lydia swallowed hard. Meade clicked and unclicked the safety—a warning. Lydia kept her eyes on Brenna's face.

"Talk," Meade said.

"Iris was supposed to be at the Koppelsons—an overnight playdate, but she came home and found Roger and me in bed. She screamed. I followed her, trying to explain. I told her Roger would be her new daddy. I told her Roger and I were in love."

Brenna's mouth went dry.

"She kept screaming. She kept yelling. Yelling about Santa. Santa hurting me. I . . . I took her by the arms. I just wanted to calm her."

"But she wouldn't shut up," Meade said.

"I was trying to . . . to make her quiet . . ."

"Talk."

"I was holding her and she was screaming and I . . . I said, 'Stop,' and I pushed her. I pushed too hard and she fell down the stairs." She looked at Brenna, tears spilling down her cheeks. "I wanted to confess, but I was too frightened. Roger said it would ruin him, ruin his family. He promised to protect me always. I was so scared . . ."

Brenna stared at her, the fear and pity inside her dissolving, replaced by a hollow feeling. *She killed her own child and hid*. She heard herself say, "Santa took Iris away in a blue car."

"Yes."

"Roger Wright carried Iris's body outside. He loaded it into his company car, the one he used specifically to see you. He drove your child's body to his construction site and buried it under that mound and then he had his men put a fountain there, same spot." That's what Maggie Schuler had seen out her window. Roger Wright, disposing of her friend's body. "Then he drew you a map."

Lydia looked at Meade, then back at Brenna, her eyes bigger now, imploring.

"She deserves to die," Meade said.

And Brenna thought, *Maybe she does*.

"Push her. Now," said Meade.

"You'll kill me, too," Brenna said. "Throw me over the

side. It will look like an accident. I tried to talk to her, chased her here. We both fell."

"Not necessarily," he said. "I have the drawing, after all. And if you do as I say . . . if you kill her . . . you'll have realized your true potential."

Brenna stared at the trembling woman. "Carol and Nelson Wentz are dead."

"No," Lydia whispered. "No . . . you're lying . . ."

"Your ex-husband, Timothy. Critical condition."

"Please, I don't—"

"Your friend, Chief Griffin."

"An . . . an accident."

"No it wasn't," said Meade.

Lydia shook her head, back and forth, back and forth like something mechanical. "No, no, no . . ."

"All of them dead because of you," Brenna said, feeling the rage building within her as the gun moved away from her back. "All of them . . . because you were *too scared to tell the truth*."

"No, no please . . ."

"Push her," Meade said.

Lydia closed her eyes and turned to face the river.

Brenna stepped forward, then spun around and socked Meade in the solar plexus. He stumbled back. He came at her, but she punched him again, this time in the stomach. He doubled over, then the gun went off. "Fuck!" he breathed, and Brenna knew why. He'd left ballistic evidence. He'd never wanted to leave it before—not one of his victims had died of a gunshot wound. For a few seconds, Brenna recalled Meade at Pelham Bay after the gun had discharged, his gaze darting all over the pavement, searching for a bullet . . . But now all bets were off, weren't they?

Brenna balled her hand into a fist, and lunged at him, panting. The knife wound tore at her abdomen. She cried out and her knees collapsed and her feet went out from under her, cool grass smacking into her face. She tasted dirt and blood, her forehead wet from dewy grass. She was dimly aware of Lydia on her feet and screaming, of voices in the woods . . . Brenna struggled up to her knees, and her mind played it out in slow motion, what she was seeing . . . Meade lifting the gun, aiming it at her head, grasping it with both hands, and the voice inside her, slow as well: *Close your eyes. Good-bye . . .*

And then Lydia, shrieking and charging . . . Lydia throwing herself on Meade, Meade stumbling back. Lydia throwing herself on the gun . . . The gun discharged, and still it all moved so slowly: Lydia's head falling back, Lydia's blood spreading like bright dye through her orange robe, Lydia dropping to the ground, toppling onto her back, and Meade staring at her, stock-still, something on his face that looked like shock . . .

And then time sped up and Meade was rushing at Brenna. She tried to stand but she couldn't. He was right at her now. She could see into the barrel of the gun, could see the black space within . . . Brenna closed her eyes. The shot was deafening.

Brenna opened her eyes to Meade rolling on the ground, clutching his leg, moaning. At the edge of the trees, she saw five or six uniforms, rushing toward Meade, with Morasco at the center, holding his gun. She pushed herself to her feet as they reached her, two of the uniforms cuffing Meade. Another radioing for medical attention. Morasco said, "Are you all right?"

"Yes," she breathed. "And . . . glad to see you."

Morasco smiled a little. He put a hand on her shoulder. "Thank God for my great sense of timing."

As the uniforms read Meade his rights and the paramedics arrived, Morasco spoke to Brenna in a calm voice, telling her about Hutchins and Meade, their decade-old connection, all that blood they'd shed for Tarry Ridge, for Wright. "Hutchins is under arrest."

"How did that happen?" Brenna asked.

"I had a little chat with him about it all. He more or less confessed."

"And Internal Affairs believed you?"

"It helped I had my cell phone in my pocket, with the DA's office on the line the entire time."

"What about Roger Wright?"

"Arrested, too," Morasco said. "He confessed to the killing of Iris Neff."

Brenna looked at him. "Wright confessed?"

He nodded. "I guess Iris walked in on him and Lydia. He says he tried to talk to her, but accidentally pushed her down the stairs."

"*He promised to protect me always . . .*" Brenna whispered.

"What?"

"Nothing."

"You know it's weird," he said. "After Wright confessed, he looked different. It could have just been my mind playing tricks, but I swear something happened to his face."

"How did he look?"

He turned to her. "Human," he said.

Brenna nodded. A newly arrived group of uniforms was moving toward Lydia's body. She stared at the face. The eyes were like panes of black glass, wide open and calm.

Epilogue

22 days later

A family vacation in Niagara Falls at the end of October in the middle of a cold snap wasn't the brightest idea Brenna had ever come up with—far from it, in fact. She blamed it on the mood she'd been in on the day she planned the trip—an unseasonably warm October 16, exactly one hour after telling an elated Sarah Stoller over the phone that she and Trent had found her mother, Elizabeth, alive and healthy, at Benedictine Hospital in Kingston, New York. *"How on earth did she get to Kingston?"* Sarah had said. *"Never mind. I'm wiring you a bonus. No, no. I mean it. I'm so happy, I feel like I'm ten years old again."*

Brenna had then received the call from Tim O'Malley, still recovering at Sisters of Charity Hospital in Buffalo, asking Brenna if it would be at all possible for her to come visit, and that had clinched it. Two hours and forty-five minutes and a few phone calls later, Brenna was picking up Maya at choir practice, telling her, "Guess what? We're going to Niagara Falls in two weeks!" To which Maya had rolled her eyes so far back into her head, Brenna feared they might actually stick like that. "We'll freeze to death," she had said.

And as the two of them huddled now in their hooded plastic ponchos on the *Maid of the Mist* on the very last day of its season (which probably should have ended a week earlier), the liquid ice that Niagara Falls had now become raining down on the boat like something out of *King Lear*, a chill wind biting their raw, red noses, making their ears feel as if they might snap off any minute, Brenna had to admit . . . the kid may have been right.

She tried, "The falls are a beautiful color, aren't they?"

"You know what?" Maya said. "Mars is a beautiful color, too. But that doesn't mean I want to be dropped on Mars with nothing to protect me but a plastic raincoat."

Brenna shook her head. She started to say something more, but the words faded, her mind reeling back to the previous afternoon, to sitting in Tim O'Malley's hospital room, the antiseptic smell pressing into her sinuses as she watched him—two sad eyes staring out from a mass of white cloth. He had just been through his first operation to heal the scars he'd incurred in the group home fire. He was head-to-toe wrapped in bandages ("Like my Halloween costume?" he had quipped) and yet still Tim O'Malley wanted to see Brenna. He wanted to see the woman who had "finally given Iris a proper burial." He wanted to talk to her. There were things he wanted to say.

Brenna had come to the hospital with such a long list of questions: What had Meade said to Tim at three on the night of September 29, when he'd stolen into his room, put a gun to his head, and forced him to set himself ablaze? How did Tim feel about Lydia now? Did he mourn her? Did he forgive her?

But as it turned out, Tim hadn't wanted to talk about any of that. "I heard you lost your sister," he had said, just as Brenna was sitting down.

"I'm still hoping to find her."

"Yes," he had replied. "That's the way I felt about Iris, right up until two years ago."

His words hang there. She starts to ask, "Is it easier or harder now, without all that hope filling your mind?" but then she notices the white envelope in his lap. He holds it out for Brenna to take. The envelope is sealed. Brenna looks at him. "Should I open it?"

He nods. The bandages rustle. "It's from Carol Wentz. Read the envelope."

Brenna does. It is postmarked September 25 and there is a note: Please give to Lydia.

"Millie kept it for me all this time. Never opened it herself . . . She's a real friend, you know? A real friend."

Brenna opens the letter, and reads.

Dear Lydia,

I am sure you never expected to hear from me, but I feel compelled to write. I have wondered for years what happened to Iris, and now I know. Tim told me. I have seen the pictures and the map. Rest assured, they are in a safe place. I will never tell.

While you may think I am writing to condemn you, I am not. I am writing to make a confession of my own.

I was angry with your daughter. I know that sounds strange—she was only a child and I barely knew her—but on the day of the Koppelsons' barbecue, I had a brief exchange with her that touched something within me, something ugly and mean. Later that day, I saw her and little Maggie Schuler across the street from my house. They had wandered off and were clearly lost. I saw them both, but I saved only Maggie. I scooped Maggie up in my arms, took her back to my home, and called her parents. I acted as if Iris hadn't been there at all—as if she was invisible. By the time I reconsidered and looked out of my window again, Iris was long gone.

I've seen her face a million times since then. She comes to me in dreams and she asks me why. I am never able to give her an answer. At first, I thought it was because of what happened between you and Nelson on those train rides. But that was never the reason. I'm afraid I simply didn't like the way she asked me for a juice box.

With deepest apologies,
Carol Wentz

Tim says, "Is there anything in that letter that I need to know?"

Brenna looks up at the bandaged face. She stares into the dark, lost eyes and she sees the eyes of his only daughter. "I don't think so," she says.

The boat was docking now, everyone stumbling to get off. Brenna watched them as they passed—a pair of elderly women with hunched shoulders and wet noses, holding each other's hands. A little boy, weeping against the side of his exhausted mother. A shell-shocked young girl, her mascara dripping, tapping at her lip, her boyfriend clutching her shoulder so tightly his fingertips were white . . . All of them with secrets, all of them with shame and regret and at least one mistake they wished with their whole hearts they'd never made—even if that mistake had simply been getting on this boat.

Brenna turned to her daughter. "You were right," she said.

"What?"

She pushed a lock of hair out of the huge blue eyes—not Clea's blue eyes but Maya's, Maya's wet yellow hair, Maya's confused little frown. "You were right about the Maid of the Mist. You were right about Niagara Falls," she said. "You are right about a lot of things."

Maya broke into a smile. "It's about time you figured that out."

Brenna smiled back. In this moment at least, she was glad for her memory.

Author's Note

Hyperthymestic Syndrome is real, but quite rare with only a handful of cases known to exist since its first introduction in medical journals in 2006.

The condition has been described as perfect autobiographical memory—the ability to call up any date of one's life and remember it, in full, with all five senses. Though some with hyperthymestic syndrome can compartmentalize these memories, keeping them tightly locked within a type of mental filing cabinet, others—like Brenna—find themselves plagued by frequent, random intrusions of the past. As one subject, interviewed by researchers at UC Irvine put it, "It is like a movie in my mind that never stops."

For me, that concept calls up so many questions: With the past so vivid in your mind, how can you fully experience the present? How can you move on from an event—whether tender or traumatic or even mundane—without the ability to let at least some of it go? How can you put things in perspective when they're all sharing equal space in your mind—your wedding day, the moment you heard that a loved one had died, the cornflakes you had for breakfast on June 12, 1995? How can you forgive and forget if you simply can't forget?

In creating Brenna, I tried to answer those questions as best I could, while keeping in mind that memory is also a blessing—our only way of truly holding on to those we care about.

Alison Gaylin

February 5, 2011

She's only a shadow, a silhouette stretching provocatively on a computer screen, revealing scandalous details of a life story that most likely isn't true. Yet when private investigator Brenna Spector is hired to find missing webcam phenomenon Lula Belle, her perfect memory tells her she's seen this mysterious young woman before, and at a time when she may have been in terrible danger. As Brenna comes closer to tracking down the real Lula Belle, she discovers shocking truths about her own past—and the disappearance of her sister Clea—that will change her life forever.

Don't miss the thrilling sequel to

And She Was

Coming Winter 2013

from HarperCollins Publishers!

She wants to die.

The thought flew at Brenna Spector like words on a passing billboard—there for just an instant but solid, real. Brenna was staring at the image on her assistant, Trent La Salle's, computer screen—their latest missing person, if you could call what they were looking at a person. She was more a shadow, standing behind a scrim, backlit into anonymity—all limbs and curves and fluffy hair, but no detail, no color. No face. It looked as though she was naked, but you couldn't even be sure of that. But then she tapped her lower lip, the shadow-woman on the screen. She tapped it one, two, three times . . . *and the thought flies at Brenna as she looks into the girl's watery eyes for an instant, just an instant, with the chill wind in their faces and the boat creaking beneath them, everything so icy-wet, so cold it burns . . .*

"She's so freakin' hot," Trent said.

Brenna came back from the memory, fixing her gaze on the screen once more. "Uh, Trent? She's a *silhouette.*"

"Hey, so are those chicks on truck mud flaps?"

Brenna rolled her eyes.

"You'll get it when you see more."

As if on cue, the shadow-woman began stretching her body into a series of suggestive yoga poses—a slow back-bend, followed by the sharp V of the Downward Facing Dog, a seamless shift to standing, after which she reached down, grasped her right ankle and pulled her leg straight out and then up, until her knee touched the side of her head.

"See?" Trent said.

With shocking ease, she yanked her leg, stole-like, around her shoulder. Her voice was a soft Southern accent, drifting out of the speakers like steam. "I'll bend any way you want me to."

Trent nearly fell off his chair.

"I get it, I get it." Brenna grabbed the mouse and hit pause. "Who is she?"

"Lula Belle." He said it the way a nun might say the name of a saint. "She's an artist."

Brenna looked at her assistant. He was wearing a black muscle tee with a deep V-neck, the Ed Hardy logo emblazoned on the front in glittery red letters. His hair was spiked and gelled to the point where it could probably scrape paint off the side of a bus, and, Brenna now noticed for the first time, he was sporting a new tattoo: a bright-red lipstick print, hovering just above the left pec. Trent's definition of an artist was, to say the least, dubious.

"A *performance* artist," he said, as if he'd been reading her mind. "She's on the web. You can download her, uh, performances."

"She's a webcam girl."

"No." Trent pointed to the screen. "Lula Belle isn't about porn. I mean, you can get off to her for sure, but . . ."

"But what?"

"Here—I'll show you." Trent moved the cursor, fast forwarding the screen image. Brenna watched the shadow twist and bend, watched her drop into splits and pivot, throw her pelvis over her head and somersault backward to standing, watched her pull up a stool and straddle it, legs spread wide as a Fosse dancer, watched her produce an old-fashioned Coke bottle from somewhere off camera, tilt her shadow-head back, touch her shadow-tongue to the tip, then take the bottle down her throat all the way to the base, all of this inside of twenty seconds.

Brenna said, "Well, I guess you could call that an art."

"No. Wait." When Trent hit play, Lula Belle was on the stool, legs crossed, fingers twisting in her hair. "Listen."

" '. . . You know that little soft part of your head, Lula Belle? Right next to your eyebrow? That's called your temple. Daddy took his gun, and he put the barrel of it right there at his temple, and he pulled the trigger, and his whole head exploded.' That's how my mama told me. I was just eight years old. 'Do you understand Lula Belle?' she asked me, and my heart felt like someone had taken a torch to it, melted it down to liquid right there in my chest. But I knew I couldn't cry. I wasn't allowed to cry. Mama didn't . . . she didn't take kindly to tears. . . ."

Trent hit pause and turned to Brenna. "You get it?"

"She bares her soul. Shares her secrets."

He nodded.

"And people pay for this."

"Big-time."

Brenna shook her head. "Weird."

"Well, the Coke bottle thing helps . . ."

"When did she go missing?"

"Six months ago."

"And the client?"

"It was a third party."

"Who was the third party?"

"A PI. Lula's manager hired him."

"And the PI's name is . . ."

"Brenna?"

"Yes?"

"Can I ask you something?"

"As long as you're not asking me in order to avoid my question."

"Seriously."

"Okay."

Trent cleared his throat. "When I first showed you Lula Belle . . . you . . . remembered something, didn't you?"

"Yeah." Strange how *remembered* could be such a loaded word, but in Brenna's world it was. Since she was eleven years old, she'd suffered from hyperthymestic syndrome, a rare disorder which allowed her to remember every minute of every day of her life, and with all five senses, whether she wanted to or not. It came, her first psychiatrist, Dr. Lieberman, had recently told her "from the perfect storm of a differently shaped brain and a traumatic experience"—*storm*, as it turned out, was a good metaphor, seeing as how the syndrome had descended on Brenna, battering her mind into something so different than it had been before. She had two types of memories now: the murky recollections of her childhood and the vivid, three-dimensional images of everything that had happened from August 22, 1981 to the present.

Brenna could recall, for instance, what she had for breakfast on June 25, 1998 to the point of tasting it (black coffee, a bowl of Special K with skim milk, blueberries that were disappointingly mealy and two donut holes—one chocolate, one glazed). But her father, who had left her family when she was just seven, had existed in her mind only as strong arms and the smell of Old Spice, a light kiss on the forehead, a story told by her mother, years after he'd gone. He wasn't whole in her head. She couldn't clearly picture his face. Same with her older sister Clea, who had gotten into a blue car on August 21, 1981 at the age of sixteen and vanished forever. Clea's disappearance had been the traumatic event that had sparked Brenna's perfect storm—yet ironically that event, like Clea herself, was stuck in her fallible pre-syndrome memory, fading every day into hazy fiction.

Brenna had known that would happen—even as a kid on August 21, 1982, the anniversary. . . . *Sitting at her bedroom window with her face pressed against the cool of the screen, glancing at the digital clock blinking 5:21 A.M. and chewing grape Bubble Yum to stay awake, her throat dry and stingy from it, trying with everything she had to remember the car, the license plate, the voice of the man behind the wheel . . .*

Brenna shut her eyes tight and recited the Pledge of Allegiance in her head—one of the many tricks she'd figured out over the years for willing memories away.

"So?" Trent said.

She opened her eyes and took a breath. "What was your question again?"

"What were you remembering when you looked at Lula Belle?"

"Not much—a gesture," Brenna said. "On October 23, Maya and I were in Niagara Falls on vacation, remember?"

He gave her a look. "I can remember four months ago."

"Well, we were on the *Maid of the Mist*, and there was a girl on the boat who tapped on her lip three times, just like Lula Belle did at the start of the tape."

"What did the girl on the boat look like?"

"Probably in her twenties. Red hair. She was leaving the boat with her boyfriend and she had mascara running down her face," Brenna said. "She looked like she wanted to die."

Trent's eyes widened.

"I know what you're thinking, but we *all* probably looked that way," Brenna said. "We were getting hailed on. It was freezing and windy and everybody was seasick and Maya was about ready to call Child Protective Services on me for taking her on that boat in the first place."

"Still," he said. "It could have been Lula Belle you saw. Two months after she went missing. On that boat with some jerk-off. Praying to be saved from him . . ."

"Hell of a coincidence."

"Happens all the time."

"Trent, it was just a gesture. Do we have any idea what Lula Belle looks like?"

"No."

"What about this third party? Do they?"

"Nope."

He shook his head. "Her own manager doesn't even know what she looks like. He lives in California. Never met her face-to-face. He maintained her site, made the checks out to cash, sent them to a P.O. Box . . ."

Brenna sighed. "In that case, *I* could be Lula Belle."

"Oh man, that would be so awesome."

Brenna's gaze shot back to the frozen image on the screen. "Do we at least have her full name?"

"Uh . . . no."

"What about her Social?"

He shook his head.

"So let me get this straight. All we have on this woman

is a fake name, a fake accent, a P.O. Box, and a very obvious skill-set."

"You think her accent's fake? Really?"

"Trent."

"Yeah?"

"Why did you accept this case?"

He picked at a fingernail.

"Trent."

"I'm a fan, okay?"

"Oh, for godsakes."

"I know, I know . . . I mean, I never heard of her before yesterday, but I can't get her out of my head. I can't stop watching her. I don't even care what her face looks like or how old she is . . . It's like Errol said—she gets under your skin and stays there."

"Errol?"

"Crap. I didn't mean to say that out loud."

"Errol Ludlow? He's the third party?"

Trent's face went pinkish. He bit his lower lip and stared at the floor like a shamed kid. "Yes," he said finally. "Errol Ludlow Investigations."

Brenna stared at him. "No."

"He said you were the best around at finding missing persons—that's why he wanted to hire you."

"No, Trent. Absolutely not."

"He wants to let bygones be bygones and—"

"No!"

Trent looked close to tears.

Brenna hadn't intended to say it that loudly, but she wasn't going to take it back either. In the three years that Errol Ludlow had been her boss, he'd put her in serious danger four times. Twice, she'd been rushed to the hospital.

Her ex-husband had made her promise to quit and then one time, three years after Maya was born, Brenna had made the breathtakingly stupid mistake of taking a freelance assignment from him; it had ended her marriage for good. Brenna couldn't let bygones be bygones. Trent should've known that. There were no such things as bygones in Brenna's life—especially when it came to a king-size jackass of a bad memory trigger like Errol Ludlow.

"No, Trent," she said again—quieter this time. "I'm sorry you've grown attached to this girl's silhouette, but we can't take this case."

Trent started to say something—until Ludacris's "Moneymaker" exploded out of his jeans pocket, interrupting him. His ringtone. He yanked his iPhone out of his pocket and looked at the screen. "My mom."

"Go ahead and take it," Brenna said.

Trent moved from the office space area of Brenna's 12th Street apartment, past the kitchen, and into the hallway that led to the living room. Brenna glanced at the shadow on-screen caught frozen, one delicate hand to her forehead—the swooning Southern Belle. "Sorry, Lula." Brenna wondered why Errol had accepted a missing person in the first place. From what she knew, he only handled cheating spouses. *Work must be tight.*

She clicked play. Lula Belle arched into a languorous stretch that seemed to involve every muscle in her body and sighed, her voice fragile as air. Brenna watched her, thinking about what Trent had said. *She gets under your skin and stays there . . .* Was Errol a fan, too?

"I miss my daddy," Lula Belle said. "He was the only person in the whole world could stop me from being scared of anything." She turned to the left and tilted her head up, as if she were noticing a star for the first time. "I used to be afraid of all kinds of stuff, too," she said. "The dark, ghosts, our neighbor Mrs. Greeley—I was sure she was a witch. Dogs, spiders, snakes . . . even cement mixers, if you can imagine that."

Brenna's eyes widened. She moved closer to the screen.

"I somehow got it in my head that those cement mixers were like . . . I don't know, giant vacuum cleaners or something. I thought they could suck me in through the back and mix me in with all that heavy, wet cement and I'd never be able to get out, wouldn't be able to breathe."

"Me too," Brenna whispered.

"But my daddy, he made everything better. He got me a nightlight. He protected me from mean old Mrs. Greeley. He told me those dogs and snakes were more scared of me than I was of them, and he was right. But the best thing my daddy did. Whenever we'd be driving and I'd see a cement mixer, he'd sing me this song . . ."

No . . . It can't be . . .

"I don't know whether he'd made it up or not, but it went a little like this . . . Cement mixer/Turn on a dime/Make my day 'cause it's cement time /Cement mixer, you're my pal/ Ain't gonna hurt me or my little gal . . ."

Brenna's breath caught. She knew the song—knew it well enough to sing along. She knew it like the blue leather backseat of the white Mustang her dad had called the Land Shark, knew it like the strong hands on the wheel, the smell of Old Spice, and the voice—the deep, laughing voice she loved, but couldn't hold on to. *"It's okay, Pumpkin, it won't hurt you, it's just a bus for building materials."* Dad. *"Just like the one that takes the big kids to school, only this one is for the stuff they make the playgrounds out of . . . Cement mixer/Turn on a dime . . ."*

"You know what my daddy called those cement mixers?" Lula whispered to the camera. "He called 'em school buses. For playground ingredients. Isn't that funny?"

"Man, I'm gonna miss her," said Trent, who was back in the room.

Brenna turned to him, fast. "We're taking the case," she said.